'Song of the Loon'

A Novel of Adventure & Romance
by
L. Frank Hadley

To Bill
From your
Friend Larry

[signature]

Aug 2000

'Song of the Loon'

A Novel of Adventure & Romance
by
L. Frank Hadley

L. FRANK HADLEY
PUBLISHING

Copyright 2000 L. Frank Hadley

All rights reserved. No part of this book may be reproduced or transmitted in any form or by any means, electronic or mechanical, including photocopying, recording or by any information storage and retrieval system — except by a reviewer who may quote brief passages in a review to be printed in a magazine or newspaper — without permission in writing from the Author/Publisher.

All names are fictitious and any resemblance to anyone living or dead is coincidental. *Song of the Loon* was written for entertainment purposes only.

Published by L. Frank Hadley Publishing

Photography and Cover Design
Jim Craig
Whitefish, Montana
U.S.A.

ISBN 0-9701221-0-1

Printed in Canada

Thinking back to those senseless days of war, I pray that we have learned something, if not, all was in vain. '*Song of the Loon*' is dedicated to those men and women who served and to the thousands who made the ultimate sacrifice.

'Song of the Loon' was written as a novel for entertainment purposes only.

Song of the Loon

L FRANK HADLEY

There are people who say each of us has a destiny which we must fulfill, that we cannot change our fate. How can this be true? Each step we take, whether to the right or left, changes what would have taken place had we chosen the other. I cannot comprehend the idea that every joy, hardship, sorrow and pleasure I have experienced in my life was a sequence of events set before me that I did not have a certain amount of control over. For these I stand ready to take both the praise and the blame.

My grandfather, a very wise man, once said, "The path you walk in life will be filled with adventures my son. However you must learn to recognize them for what they are, the bad as well as the good. I did not understand at the time that, what Grandfather meant by adventures was in reality, the essence of life.

To all who read my book, know that I have kept my promise, and my story happened just as I have written it.

Cole Morgan / LFH

Chapter 1

Sitting here holding pressure on Dodson's wound, I look at the tough son of a bitches that remain behind with me, and our fallen comrade. I've tried to get them to go on toward a PZ; (pickup zone) but they're a loyal bunch.

Again, I give the order to move out. "No hero's. Carter's in charge. I'll stay with Dodson; we'll be okay. Tell Dustoff (call sign for medevac helicopters) we'll be working toward the river. I can get us there by the time you can get to a PZ. Leave me three smokes." (Colored smoke canisters for signaling air traffic. Different colors denote enemy ground conditions.)

"No, fuck that! You said no hero's, remember? In for a penny, Sir," one of the grunts answers. "They'll send in a Jolly Green, (air rescue helicopter,) and air support for us. We're staying with you."

How do you distinguish between loyalty and duty? These men have a chance to survive if only they'd follow orders. That's what the Army is all about, following orders.

Looking at the grunts I realize what great men they are. History will not document them as anything more than cold faceless names. But someday, if I live through this fucking war, I'm going to write about the hearts and souls of these men. Looking at each of them now, I wonder what they did in civilian life. Hell, what are their names? Shit, they're willing to die here with me, and I don't even know some of their names. One is a black man, and looks like he could have been a football player. Odd what you notice about people. He has gentle eyes. I finally made out his name to be Johnson. He took a bullet in the left cheek of his ass. Not real bad, but it could stiffen him up by morning. I can't make out a couple of names because of the bandoleers they're carrying for the machine gunner. He didn't make it nor did the machine gun. Now they sit pulling the ammunition out of the belts, and throwing it into the brushes. They don't want the gooks to have it, and it's too damned heavy to carry.

Over to my left on lookout is a blond, wiry grunt. His nametag says Gordon or something like that. It's hard to figure how old he is, this fucking country puts years on you fast. He's had a cigar in his mouth since he boarded my helicopter. It's never been lit, but it's growing shorter with time. Just smelling that cigar is enough to make me sick, but he looks tough enough to eat it, and never blink. The kid squatting with his M-16 cradled on his knees looks about fifteen years old, although I'm sure he's eighteen, maybe nineteen. Give him three months and he'll look thirty. I wonder how many men he's killed. A great way to start your life, killing people. Carter I know. He's my copilot. He sits leaning against a tree, legs pulled up with his forearms resting on his knees, hands limp, staring at the ground in silence. Flies crawl across his face, and he doesn't even bother to brush them away. I wonder what he's thinking? Pilots are a strange bunch. I have to grin a little; hell he's probably thinking the same thing about me. How would he handle this situation? Can't let on I have doubts. How would I feel if my leader showed hesitation or doubt? Demoralized, to say the least.

We're in this fucking mess because of a lucky shot. It had caused the Huey to shudder violently, and damned near dumped some of the grunts into the water. At the same instant I lost tail rotor authority, and we were lucky to sit down in one piece. I was glad we weren't too far off the water, and had the sandbar to sit down on. The craft rocked wildly before settling back on her skids. How many times has this made for me?

It's hard to believe how life can change in such a short time, all because of one bullet in the right place. I check my watch, its been and hour an a half now. Shit it seems like a year.

I look down at Dodson. He can't be over nineteen or twenty. I guess I'm a lying son of a bitch for telling him I'd get him out of here. I don't know if any of us will get out. Fuck, I had to tell him something other than, "You're gut shot, and going to die here." He hasn't moved much in the last few minutes, and I'm afraid to look close. I promised to get him back to the base. A promise I knew I couldn't keep. There is no PZ in this foliage, and he can't be carried. He's been shot through the stomach, and his guts are trying to fall out of the exit in his back. We packed the hole as best as we could, but that hasn't stopped the bleeding, just slowed it. It's a matter of time and we'll have to leave the kid lying in this God-forsaken jungle to rot. I wonder if he knows he's dead?

Dodson takes a deep sobbing breath then moans. Damn, so young to die in a foreign country, fighting for what? What the fuck are any of us here for?

This was supposed to be a routine extraction. Not simple, but nothing I hadn't done dozens of times before. Skid on the river to the checkpoint, set down, load, and lift off for home. Simple enough. Open the throttle, pull some pitch, and climb out fast.

We had made the PZ and loaded in almost record time, when all hell broke out from across the river. The craft took a vital hit and started smoking, then the tail rotor took another. At the same time Dodson, my door-gunner, was hit in the stomach, and one of the grunts in the face. There was no doubt the grunt was dead, one look said it all. Dodson went down on his knees. He had been damned good for his short time behind the trigger. It's hard to believe looking down at such a young face that he could do this kind of work. How many lives had he taken in his short career? What was on his mind each time he squeezed the trigger? Killing gooks is like stepping on an anthill. The more you stomp them, the more crawl out to take their place.

When the craft had stabilized, I grabbed a grenade from the dead grunt, and pulling the pin, placed it under an ammo canister after we jumped from the crippled Slick, (UH-1 Huey helicopter armed only with door-guns).

The gooks would strip everything they could from our ship. The ammo boxes would be one of the first things they'd grab. When they lifted the canister of ammo it would be rock and roll time. That's what bought us some time now. We hadn't made it too far when the fireworks started, and within moments we heard all hell busting loose.

It's starting to grow dark now, I can tell because of the frogs and the fucking mosquitoes are getting worse, if that's possible. You can hardly hear yourself talk because of the constant whine. You breathe through your nose if you don't want a mouth full of the little bastards. It makes you realize that God knew what he was doing when he put hair in a man's nose. There are times when the numbers of mosquitoes make a face look blurry. Reaching for my mosquito dope I start to pour some into my palm, then take a second look at my hand. It's caked with Dodson's blood. It looks like a mixed blessing for the bugs, blood, and mosquito dope. I wonder if one will cancel out the other. Reaching down to the ground, I rub as much partially dried blood off of my palm as I can, then wipe my hand on my pant leg. With a shrug I squirt some repellent in my hand, and pat Dodson's face. A fly crawls out of his nose. I stare hard at the kid, then see his chest move a little. I don't know whether I'm relieved or not. If I had the balls I'd put my hand over his nose and mouth for a moment and end it. That would give us more precious time to put some distance between the gooks and us. He's dead whether now or in an hour, but I can't do it. I guess I'm a coward. I feel guilty for even thinking that way.

I brush flies off my face. Damned flies are probably laying eggs in Dodson's wound. Good or bad? Beats the hell out of me. I've seen bodies decompose in less than a week in these fucking jungles. Laughing one day; and just a pile of bones a few days later. I shake my head and feel the sweat drip off my nose and chin. The bandanna tied around my head is soaked, but I'm too tired to take it off and wring it out. I look down at Dodson, and think maybe he's the lucky one. He'll soon be out of here, but he'll never see home again. I wonder if I will?

In my mind's eye I can see home so vividly. I can even smell the air, and the pine trees of the Rocky Mountains. It's so brisk in the early mornings that the air slaps you awake when you step outside. Must be about five o'clock there. Annie is just waking up. I love the way her hair is mussed up and the soft dreamy look in her eyes when she first wakes up. She'll be getting dressed about now, probably blue jeans and a flannel shirt. Damn she's cute in jeans. They make her look like a tomboy, but she's every inch a woman. She has a figure that would make a beauty queen jealous. Her breasts are just right, not too big or too small. Her tiny waist accentuates nice hips, built for having our babies. Everyone says, with her fair complexion, light hair and blue eyes, we make a nice contrast. I took after my grandfather's side of the family I guess, brown eyes, dark hair, and olive complexion. The longing I feel to see, and touch my beautiful wife is almost more than I can stand. It feels like my heart is being squeezed right out of my chest. What I wouldn't give to be home with her right now.

She should be starting to cook breakfast, maybe hot cakes, and eggs with bacon sizzling on the grill. My mouth begins to water just thinking about it. Damn, what does home cured bacon taste like? I try to imagine the aroma, but all I smell is gut shot stench, blood, musty jungle, and death.

Swatting the flies away from Dodson's face is useless, his wound is drawing more insects than I can repel. Damn, I hate it here.

Chapter 2

As a boy growing up in the northwestern part of Montana, the Flathead Valley was my whole world. Everywhere else just existed in picture books and movies.

Our ranch is near Kalispell, which is just a few miles southwest of Glacier National Park. My family owned three hundred and sixty acres. Pop and Grandfather raise hay on eighty or so and run cattle on the rest.

Pop was a hard working man, not only did he work our ranch he also worked as a logger in the woods. He loved working in the outdoors. He wasn't a tall man, about five foot eleven inches, but built like a brick shit house, probably because of all the hard work he did. Pop was a fighter. He had been a boxer in the army and was middleweight champion of his division. I never saw him start a fight, but heaven help the man that crossed him, for there was none tougher or harder hitting. My mother was very striking with her red hair and fair complexion. Pop called her his little Irishman. She was the kindest most gentleperson I know. I never ever heard her say a bad word about anyone or saw her turn a bum away from our door without something to eat and usually a couple dollars to boot. I was an only child and ranch life can be lonely, and there was many times when Mom would stop what she was doing and play with me. I first met Annie and Freddy the summer I was eight years old. Up until that time no one with children my age lived close to us.

One day while I was eating lunch, Mom broke the tranquility of her kitchen. "I've got some good news for you, Cole. The Newell place was bought by a family that have children your age, two of them, I was told. You're going to have someone close by to play with."

I could tell Mom was very excited. As I listened I snuck a bite of food to my hound dog Jake, who was waiting patiently under the table.

"No girls though, okay?" I mumbled.

"I can't promise that, Cole."

"I don't want to play with no girls."

"You'll have children to play with, and I'll have someone near by to visit with." Mom said, ignoring my complaining. "I think they have a boy and a girl. I bumped into Mrs. Jackson in town, and she told me all about the new family. Maybe we'll go over tomorrow and introduce ourselves."

That evening Mom baked a cake, and the next day we drove up the road a quarter mile to the old Newell place.

As we pulled into the driveway, I spotted a little girl holding a stuffed animal, a bear, or at least that's what it looked like to me. There was a lady washing windows outside, and upon seeing us, she put down her cloth and waved. She was tall with light brown hair. A very pretty lady, the kind you would see in a catalog or a movie.

"Hi! Welcome," she said as she walked toward our car. The girl, clutching her stuffed animal walked over to her mother's side and leaned against her.

Getting out of the car, Mom spoke, "Hi, I'm Betty Morgan. We're your neighbors from the next ranch down the road. We thought we'd come over and introduce ourselves. I hope we're not interrupting anything."

"Goodness no, not at all. I'm Helen Gray, and this is my daughter, Annie," she said, coming forward and shaking Mom's hand.

"This is my son, Cole," Mom said, pointing to me still sitting in the car. She opened my door, and taking me by the hand, made me get out.

"I thought you said they had a boy," I said, looking around hopefully.

"Cole, this is Annie," Mrs. Gray said. "We also have a son but he went into town with his father to pick up some supplies. They'll be home this afternoon. You'll like Freddy, Cole, he must be about your age, I think. How old are you?"

"Eight," I said, looking at Annie. I guess she would have to do until the boy got home, but I was disappointed.

"Annie will be seven in December, and Freddy is eight. Sounds like you children are going to hit it off just right." She turned to my mother, "Won't you come in and have a cup of coffee, Mrs. Morgan, and we can get acquainted."

"Please call me Betty," Mom said as they walked toward the house, leaving the two of us kids staring at each other.

After what seemed like an hour, Annie timidly broke the silence. "Would you like to see my swing?" Without waiting for a reply, she turned and walked toward the backyard. Uncertain, I stood for a moment before deciding to follow her.

She swung for a minute, then got up and actually gave me her swing. Boy, she had a lot to learn. I had learned from experience that you never give up a swing until you were totally through with it. Annie sat down on the ground still holding her old stuffed animal and began talking to me in a soft, low voice.

"Momma says I should share my swing with people. I hope you're having fun, because then I'm being polite," she said, looking up at me with big blue eyes.

"You want your swing back?" I asked. I couldn't believe it; I was giving up the swing to a girl.

"I want you to swing and have fun," she answered.

"Well, I think I'm through," I said, feeling awkward. I jumped off the swing, and ran into the house.

"I see you and Annie are hitting it off, Cole. I'm so glad. Would you like a piece of cake?" Mrs. Gray asked, smiling warmly.

Never being one to turn down cake, cookies, or pie, the answer was obvious. Annie came in a couple of minutes later, and her mother asked her if she would like a piece of cake.

"Yes please," Annie answered, then sat down at the table and waited for her mom to serve her. Mrs. Gray cut her a piece so small it would insult someone of my caliber. To top it off, Annie never even finished it. She was really disgusting. Not only had she willingly shared her swing with me, but she acted like a lady. Mom had told me how girls were ladies and should be treated that way. I was supposed to hold the door for them and let them go first, and if there weren't enough chairs, I was supposed to give them my seat. Treating girls like that could cause a lot of damage to a guy's life. I had learned that from the movies I occasionally saw when I went to the theatre in Kalispell. It seemed when a guy started getting around girls, he stopped shooting and fighting and started thinking about kissing instead. That's where they could end the picture as far as I was concerned. Girls really were an unnecessary part of life, and it was a mystery to me why God made them.

The next day, Mrs. Gray came over to have tea with Mom. Freddy followed her car on his bike. This was my type of guy; he came prepared. Guess who else showed up to ruin everything? Yup, Annie with her old stuffed bear named Jaju.

Freddy and I hit it off right away. After a brief introduction we were off and running, the perfect match. He liked all the things I did. Playing soldier, cap guns, fishing, hunting with slingshots, climbing trees, riding bikes and camping, as long as it was daylight. Life took on a whole new meaning when the Grays moved into the old Newell place.

Our barn had a clean out door with a concrete ramp. Grandfather hadn't cleaned the barn after milking this morning, and the area was a little green in spots. Freddy and I, daredevils that we were, each on our own bike would race down a little incline toward the barn. Hitting a board we had placed on the pile of fresh manure we'd become airborne, attempting to land on the concrete ramp and stop close to the door. With each run our bike wheels spread the manure around as we skidded to a stop. It wasn't long before our death defying rides got a little boring, until Freddy with a mischievous grin suggested we have some fun with his sister, kind of an initiation, so to speak. We asked Annie to stand where we were going to stop our bikes. She was supposed to judge who stopped the closest to a line we drew.

"You got to watch real close, Annie," Freddy instructed.

"Okay," came the little voice as she made her way to the line, being careful not to step in any cow manure. She was anxious to be included in our game, and to be the judge was a real honor. Annie beamed as she bent forward to see who would win as Freddy and I came speeding down the hill, side by side. We made our jump, skidded sideways to a stop and sprayed Annie with fresh cow manure. I don't think we could have done a better job if we had been using shovels. With a screech that could be heard all the way back to the house, Annie, still clinging to Jaju, stood frozen for several seconds, not believing what had just happened. Seeing her look of disgust mixed with hurt, made my hair stand on end. No words could possibly convey the horror in her eyes. The look I saw that day is still branded in my memory. I have never forgotten her expression, nor did Annie ever forgive either of us.

"I'm going to tell Momma," she yelled at us, tears streaming down her face as she tried to wipe some of the manure off her dress.

"Go ahead," Freddy said, "and I'll hide Jaju from you, tattletale."

Annie started for the house, and I figured I was going to get a licking when Pop found out what we had done. But Annie never did tell on us. When Mrs. Gray asked her what happened, she said she fell down. I had to grudgingly admit to myself, although I would never say it out loud, Annie earned a small amount of my respect that day.

Mom lent her some of my clothes to wear home so she wouldn't get cow manure all over the Grays car. That was certainly punishment enough for me. I didn't want any girl wearing my clothes. I didn't say anything though. I figured if I did, Annie might tell the truth.

Chapter 3

Freddy and I became fast friends, and it wasn't long before we were roaming the hills together with Jake.

Grandfather had given me Jake, a hound pup, on my fourth birthday. He was my constant companion and best friend. Mom always said if she could see Jake or hear him bawling she knew where I was, and as long as he was with me I was okay.

As soon as our chores were done, Jake and I would meet Freddy up at the springs, and we'd be off on a hunting excursion in the fields or anywhere there might be something to hunt. If there were any critters around, Jake would sniff them out. He usually treed pine squirrels or an occasional mink. However he didn't have a preference and all animals were treated with equal respect, and took to the trees if they knew what was good for them. Sometimes it wasn't what we wanted, and if it was a skunk, we'd all end up stinking, because Jake would rub against us during the course of the day. If the wind was right, you could usually smell us long before we came into view.

House cats were our specialty. If we could get close enough to catch one, we'd put it in a burlap feed sack. Then one of us would hold Jake while the other drug the bag along the ground to leave a scent trail before turning the cat loose. At last when the magic moment was at hand, we'd release Jake and he'd be on the trail of that old cat and have it treed in record time, howling up a storm. We were never very far behind.

"Yahoo, listen to that mountain music!" I'd yell as Freddy and I ran to catch up. I had heard Grandfather call the baying of the hounds mountain music. When we got to where Jake had treed the cat, we'd hold him back and push the cat off his perch. That old cat would hit the ground running, and the chase would start all over again.

After awhile it got pretty hard to get close to any cats. If we approached one, it would act as if a vicious dog were attacking, streaking off. This always astounded Mrs. Gray, but Mom knew the truth. She was just too embarrassed to say anything until she got me alone.

"You've been at it again, haven't you? What would Helen and John think about you two playing together if she knew what you were doing? You're teaching Freddy a lot of bad habits, and I am sure his mother would not appreciate your influence on him. What am I going to do with you? Wait until I tell your father. I think I know what he'll do. He'll probably make you get rid of Jake."

I would keep quiet and let her talk. I didn't dare tell her that training Jake to hunt cats was Pop and Grandfather's idea. Although I think mountain lion was more what they had in mind. Grandfather was a lion hunter and raised hounds for hunting. Every once in awhile he would let us take some of his pups out to hunt with Jake. He said Jake was an enthusiastic hunter and it was catching. He'd inspire the pups. Grandfather would lend me his old cow horn bugle to take with us. Letting me use the horn was a badge of honor even though Freddy and I couldn't blow it at our age. However, the pups heard our attempts and responded with yelps of pure appreciation.

Grandfather often warned us not to let the woman folk know that we used house-cats.
"They won't take kindly to you boys treating the cats that way, even though it doesn't hurt them any. If Annie ever finds you using her old yellow tom and tells me, I'll take a belt to the both of you. You leave her cat alone. Savvy?"

"Yes sir!" Freddy and I would say in unison. Nobody crossed Grandfather, his word was law, and we didn't break his laws, nor did we have any desire to. Next to God's, his word was supreme. He thought a lot of Annie and treated her like the granddaughter he never had. She was our real problem, always threatening to tattle on us. I know there wasn't a day that went by when Freddy wouldn't have gladly traded Annie for Jake. After all, Jake was the envy of any boy who valued true wealth.

"You're lucky you don't have a sister," Freddy said as we walked the ditch line along the road. "I wish I could trade her for a good dog like Jake."

"I sure wouldn't want to trade for anything like that. I don't like your sister," I said, reaching down to select a rock for my slingshot.

"Freddy, Grandfather told me not to say anything about what Jake did yesterday, so you can't tell anybody, okay?"

Freddy nodded.

"Yesterday, Jake killed the old yella tom. He really chewed him up. He was deader than a steer's nuts."

"Annie's old yella tom?" Freddy ask.

"Yeah, you could even see some guts sticking out his side. Grandfather said it would break Annie's heart if she was to find out. I don't think we should tell her. Besides, Grandfather would get mad at us if we did. I don't want him mad at me."

"Me neither. Wish I coulda got to see it though. What did you do with it?"

"Grandfather buried it out behind the barn. If you want to see, we can dig him up, long as we don't get caught. Maybe we can wait until they go to town or something."

"Yeah, maybe if he ain't started stinking yet," Freddy said.

"Grandfather says they don't turn into a skeleton for almost a year. If we don't wait too long, we can dig him up."

Jake started bawling over in the bushes, which meant he was on the trail of something, so Freddy and I took off at a dead run in hot pursuit.

A few days later while Grandfather and Pop were out cutting hay and Mom had gone to town for groceries, Freddy and I dug up the old yellow tom. It was quite an experience, what we saw met all our gruesome expectations.

Annie looked for that old tomcat for a long time. We never told her what happened to it. Mr. Gray said a car probably hit it or maybe a coyote got it. I felt bad for Annie, but I wasn't about to tell on Jake.

At the ranch, Pop and Grandfather kept the old wood-truck on a slope at the timberline. It was parked with the front end pointed down hill toward the apple orchard and barn. The truck was on the hill for a purpose. It was a hard starter when cold. Parking it with the front pointed downhill allowed Pop or Grandfather to coast it fast enough to pop the clutch and start the engine. I had watched Dad or Grandfather start it many times, and could have done it myself, if they'd just let me try. I knew all the moves.

Where the truck was parked stood a big boulder, perhaps five or six feet tall and eight feet wide. This was Annie's favorite place to sit and watch the reckless, daring but imaginary drives, Freddy and I made, as we took turns behind the steering wheel. Jake sat between us, tongue hanging out, looking as happy as an egg sucker in a chicken house.

When Annie and Freddy weren't visiting, it was just old Jake and me driving the roads of my mind, careening around corners at a hundred miles an hour, all the time making the noise of a powerful engine and tires squealing on the corners.

Every once in a while we would get into a terrible wreck. Jumping out of the truck as if hurled and hitting the grassy slope. We tumbled over and over, finally coming to rest in the awkward position of a body mangled by a high speed crash. Old Jake would lie beside me, deader than a doornail. That is, all except his tail. He had a bad habit of dying with his tail thumping the dirt. But his tongue lolling on the ground made up for it. We were supposed to have our tongues hanging out when we were dead. I know because I had died so many times that I was an expert. Then, by some miraculous stroke of luck, we'd come back to life and jump up to repeat the tragedy all over again.

Mom was watching Freddy and Annie while the Grays went to Missoula, a town about a hundred miles south, to buy some equipment for the ranch. After breakfast, we boys headed for the old truck, and Annie tagged along as usual. It was a hot, still day in August, the kind where the air never moves. As we climbed into the cab, I announced I was going to take it down the hill and drive around the pasture. Not only that, I was going to give everyone a ride. Annie immediately climbed out of the back of the truck where she had been sitting and up onto her boulder with Jaju. Freddy climbed out and came around to the driver's side, looking skeptically at me.

"You're going to get in trouble, Cole."

"No, I ain't. I know how to drive." Seeing he wasn't for the idea and feeling determined, I asked him to knock the blocks out from in front of the wheels. With a look of skepticism, he obeyed, then climbed up and sat on the rock with Annie. It didn't matter to me, because I had Jake sitting beside me and after they saw my driving, I knew they'd beg for a ride. I might even drive up to the front of the house and give my mother a ride. She would be proud. She was always proud of my achievements.

"Anyone want to go with me? You can ride in the back. Jake wants to ride in the front," I said as a last chance offer.

"I want to watch from up here," Freddy said, then added, "I get the second ride, okay?"

Taking the brake off, I took the truck out of gear, and slowly it began to roll. I was actually moving. The truck gained speed fast as it rolled toward the shed and apple orchard. Halfway down, I learned I had a problem. I was still a little too short to be driving. I couldn't reach the pedals like Pop and Grandfather. The steering was harder than it had been before. When I tried turning the wheel, Jake and I could feel the centrifugal force pull us toward the open door and the ground that was flying by faster and faster.

Because there were no doors on the old truck, I had a good view of the ground. It was a blur. Jake sensed something was wrong and started whining. His whines were the finishing touch to my fast growing panic. I could see the apple trees coming up fast and didn't know what to do. I couldn't go into them; I'd never make it through the orchard. The gap between the trees and the tool shed was my only hope, that is if I could keep from hitting the shed. The steering wasn't doing what I thought it was supposed to, so I gave a hard jerk to the right and decided to abandon the truck. The truck lurched sideways. I jumped for my life, hitting the ground so hard I was momentarily stunned as I tumbled and bounced down the hill. Jake did likewise, jumping from his side, yelping as he hit the ground.

The truck kept picking up speed, then bouncing off an apple tree it cleared the shed and rolled into the field, coming to a stop just short of the fence.

I sat in the road, blood running down my face from a cut on my head. I could hear Annie and Freddy calling to me as they raced down the hill. Glancing back up the road, I saw Jake lying motionless where he had stopped rolling. This time there was no wagging tail, waiting for me to tell him he was doing good. Scrambling to my feet, I ran up the hill to where Jake lay. Dropping to my knees, I lifted his head and called to him over and over. Jake was beyond hearing. He wouldn't be riding with me anymore. I knew I had killed my best friend. I sat in the dirt and hugged Jake's head to my chest, rocking back and forth, praying he would wake up and lick my face like he had so many times in the past.

Freddy and Annie had reached Jake and me by that time, both dropping to their knees beside my dog. With tears running down my cheeks, I looked at Annie. The sorrow in her eyes said it all. She put her hand on my arm, tears welling up in her eyes. "Oh Cole," was all she said. As we sat there in the dirt mourning the loss of a friend, I realized that Annie and Freddy loved Jake almost as much as I did.

I never played in the old truck after that. I had lost all interest in practicing my skills as a driver. Pop and Grandfather buried Jake up by the big rock. Annie picked flowers and put them on his grave when she was over to play, for a long time after.

School started the first week in September, which helped occupy my time. But each time I walked through our gate and Jake wasn't there to meet me, grief surrounded me and I knew my life would never be the same. For the first time I felt the emptiness and hurt that the death of a loved one brings.

Winter was a long time passing. A lot of my evenings were spent listening to stories Grandfather told as he sat at the foot of my bed. I guess having lost Grandmother years ago gave him a special understanding of my feelings and the emptiness I felt.

One day led to another, and as I was walking to school one March morning, I felt a warm breeze. A Chinook. Winter's back was broken, and spring wouldn't be too far away. Somehow I knew on that day everything was going to be all right.

Chapter 4

My grandfather was an old hunter and woodsman. He was born on the Northern Cheyenne Indian Reservation in 1874, the grandson of a medicine man. His mother was a full-blooded Cheyenne and his father a Scotsman. Grandfather was a natural born philosopher with a Ph.D. in mountain lore. He was my role model and mentor. Rumor had it he had mystic powers, something I took for granted when I was young. Folks said he had the ability to see into the future and often sought his advice in tight spots. A man of few words, he listened without interruption, never speaking without having something of value to say. When he spoke they listened, for his wisdom was highly respected by all.

Sitting around the wood heater or a campfire, I would listen to Grandfather talk about the things that mattered, the philosophy of life mainly. That was the beginning of my education, as best I can remember.

In the summertime, Grandfather would take us up to his cabin on Whisper Lake for camp-outs. He always made these outings interesting by teaching us the signs of nature. He taught us how to track animals and recognize dens where they lived. Grandfather told stories about his life on the reservation, and showed us which wild plants we could eat if we were to get lost or sick. I learned you can make a tea of the inner bark or the leaves of Aspen tree to help stop pain, and you can survive on Kinnikinnick berries but they are bitter and taste awful. Chokecherry berries are edible, although they are very sour. Indians used the bark of the Chokecherry to make cold medicine and treat sore throats. We worshipped Grandfather, and as far as we were concerned his every word was gospel, or as he would say, "It is so."

On one particular camping trip at the lake, we were each given a totem according to Indian tradition.

Sitting around the campfire after roasting hot dogs, we waited, hoping Grandfather would tell us stories about the ancient ones as he often did when we were out camping. He began by explaining how the moon came into existence and how the sun was always warming those it loved as a hen warms its chicks. He said that man was created from the dust of the earth, and as we are a part of it we must always respect and care for it. The ancients thought of the earth as their mother, and the bounty of the earth was given by the Great Spirit for all to share. These stories had been passed down through the generations to the children of the Cheyenne.

Grandfather said his totem was the mountain raven. His grandfather had told him the mountain raven would guide and protect him throughout his life. "The mighty raven is very brave, and other animals of bravery such as the cougar and bear will share its food with the raven, and he will warn them when danger approaches. He tells the hunter where to search for game, and what to beware of. When the hunter makes a kill, he shares part of it with the raven. The raven is also a trickster, because he cleans the ground where the dead animal was, so no one can know what happened. The white men do not know the voice of the raven, they think it is only the sound of a bird. The Indian knows better, for he listens to the animals. The mountain raven is a powerful totem. He is not like the common raven that you see. To this day the mountain raven talks only to those who listen. It is so," he said, as he laid his hand on his chest.

"Grandfather, does everyone have a totem?" Annie asked.

"Yes, little one, everyone has a totem. Most people don't know they have a totem, they do not believe."

"What does a totem do, Grandfather?" Freddy wanted to know.

"A totem is a spirit guide, the shadow people," Grandfather said, "The shadow people help us when we need guidance, and watch over us as we travel this world. You can see them sometimes from the side of your vision, but you will only see them as animals when they are in front of you. They move silently in our lives. At times we have to call upon our spirit guide to give us strength when we are weak or confused, to help us chose the right path, although sometimes we ignore their help anyway and do as we want. Many people do not believe animals have a spirit, so they do not want animal totems. The white people believe they have a guardian angel that watches over them and helps them when they need direction. The People believed all living things the Great Spirit created were given a spirit so that they might talk with the creator. Our animal totem is a reflection of ourselves in many ways; he knows our hearts and can help us in times of need if we listen with our hearts. That is why it is wrong to destroy anything without purpose. We might kill our animal totem and destroy our spirit guide. All living things are sacred. If an animal is hunted and not killed clean but is still living when a hunter comes upon it, he must ask its forgiveness, then kill it clean. This releases the spirit."

"What is my totem, Grandfather?" Annie asked, looking at him eagerly.

"You, Annie," Grandfather said, "are like the loon who dives into the water without fear. Grace and beauty are your plumage. You are quick and intelligent and will not be easily caught by your enemies. You, Little One, are one with the loon. Accept the loon as your totem now and forever. You will hear the song of the loon and share the wisdom with all who will listen with their hearts."

Annie seemed to brighten at the thought of her totem being the loon.

"What am I, Grandfather?" asked Freddy.

"You, my son, like to play. You are like the otter that appreciates the joys of life, preferring to romp and frolic. You see life as a game. Yet you are courageous and valiant, unwavering to the people you love, a powerful and vicious fighter when you need to be." Drawing his hand near his chest as he made a fist. "You are at home on land or in water, as is the otter. The river otter shall be your totem, my son."

"And me, Grandfather? What is mine?" I asked eagerly.

Grandfather drew a puff of smoke from his pipe as he looked at me intently for a moment. "You are always listening to the sound of the coyote, the smart little dog of the mountains and prairie. He is cunning and quick, brave and a good hunter. He is loyal to his family and will give his life to protect his home. He is shrewd and listens to the voice of reason inside himself." Grandfather placed his hand over his heart, palm first, "Not always trusting what he sees with his eyes, but often relying on what he feels in his heart. You and the coyote are as one, my son. Listen to his voice. He will not lead you astray."

That evening, sitting around the campfire, Freddy, Annie and I waited patiently, hoping Grandfather would tell us a story about some hunting or outdoors experience that had happened in his youth.

I could tell when a story was coming or perhaps a bit of wisdom. A kind of sadness or a smile would come over his face as he stared into the flames, poking the burning wood with a stick. Sometimes we would be disappointed, as his face would show that he was looking into a place that held no room for any other than him. These times were sacred, and a certain sense came over us to let him alone. However, there were other more frequent times when our waiting would be rewarded.

As we sat staring into the fire, watching the sparks jump into the night sky, Annie broke the silence.

"I saw a bird," she proclaimed, pointing into the dark.

"You saw a bat," Freddy corrected her.

"No it wasn't. It was a big bird."

"Perhaps it was," Grandfather broke his silence. "Was it a large dark bird, Annie?"

"Yes, Grandfather. I think it was black."

"It could have been a night traveler with a dream to deliver."

I knew as soon as Grandfather started speaking that tonight's story would contain a bit of wisdom.

"Everything has purpose, but we must search for the meaning. As Jesus said in the Bible, "You have ears, but do not hear, you have eyes, but do not see." This is true. We are blind and deaf. Look at the animals. They know many things that we do not. They grow their hair when it is going to be cold and lose it when it is hot. Their young, when they are born, know where to find their food. Look at the calf or colt when it is still wet and can just stand. It knows where to get the milk it needs. That is because they listen with their hearts to the Great Spirit, which speaks to them, no matter how small and insignificant they are. He promises this to all his children. Man is the only one that does not listen. To man the Great Spirit gave a brain, capable of thinking on his own, and man shows his contempt by not listening and seeing with his heart and mind. Man goes to his church and pretends to do as he is supposed to. This is for only one day a week. The other six days he does good only when it's convenient. This is wrong. Always do as your mind and heart tell you. This is what the Great Spirit and his son, Jesus, want us to do. Women are different than men; they are gentler and listen to the voice of God, following their hearts. It is said by The People, always listen to the counsel of women, for they have a third eye."

Grandfather continued to stare into the flames. "The night people have a job to do. The bird you saw just now, Annie. It could be a messenger, and this was your sign that you will receive an important dream tonight."

Grandfather got up to pour another cup of coffee. As he returned to his seat, Annie, always one to spoil the mood asked, "Grandfather can you tell me what I will be when I grow up. Who will I marry? Can you tell me, Grandfather?"

"No Annie, I cannot tell you that, nor would I if I could. The path you choose to walk in life will be your choice only and filled with wonder and adventure. If we knew how life was going to turn out, perhaps we would not want to walk the path. Some would sit and wait for the end of life, others would be arrogant. Always do your very best with what you have."

"What about if you have to go to war and kill people. Is that wrong, Grandfather?" Freddy asked.

"Killing is wrong, my son, but sometimes it is necessary. Taking life for anything other than protection or food is not good."

I have always remembered these words of wisdom my grandfather spoke. The outside world would put me to the test and I would, in my eyes, fail miserably to live up to the standards my grandfather had given me.

Chapter 5

Looking down at Dodson I can see that his breathing has become irregular and ragged. It won't be long now. Feeling a hand on my shoulder, I turn and look at the grunt with the cigar.

"I know what you're going through, sir. It's hard to leave someone behind. We've all had to do it from time to time." He stands waiting for what he's said to sink in.

He's right. Dodson's not the first nor will he be the last. Placing my finger on his jugular vein I feel a slight heartbeat. Reaching into his pocket, I remove his wallet and thumb through the pictures. There's one of his parents standing in front of a nice house, and a couple pictures of young kids, that look like school pictures of his brother and sister. Then there's one of the whole family taken in the yard while they were building a snowman. Taking the pictures from the wallet, I place them inside his shirt. At least he'll have his family with him. His ID I put in my pocket, then give the wallet a pitch into the underbrush. No sense letting the gooks have it.

"Southeast of here is the base. With teamwork we'll get back in one piece." I say to no one in particular. "Hell, maybe it'll snow tonight and cover our tracks," I say, bringing a chuckle.

I always hated shoveling snow when I was a kid, but right now I would give my left nut to be home shoveling a path out to the barn. Montana is famous for its snow. I've seen it so deep the cows could step over the fence.

The winter I was in the sixth grade was so miserably cold that you could hear the popping and breaking of trees freezing in the woods if you listened closely. Equipment refused to start, so horses were hitched to a sled to haul hay for the cattle. We spent a lot of time indoors playing cards and other games our mothers found to save their sanity.

Finally February rolled around and so did calving season, which kept everyone busy. Pop and Grandfather spent several weeks taking turns going out to the calving area day and night to make sure none of the cows were having difficulty. Occasionally a first time cow had trouble calving and died or just rejected her new calf, not allowing it to nurse. Consequently, there were always orphans, and it was my job to bottle-feed them until they were old enough to be out with the rest of the cattle.

I was glad to see summer come. The cattle were moved to the upper range and school was out. It was called freedom and meant swimming, fishing and camping. To add to this, my cousin Sparky, from Spokane, would be coming to stay with us for the summer. He was a lot of fun to be around. We had nicknamed him Sparky because he peed on an electric fence once while he and my aunt and uncle were visiting. Old Spark never repeated that mistake.

About a week before Sparky was supposed to arrive, Freddy and I were exploring the back fields when we happened to find a large bull snake. Making a swift grab, Freddy caught the slithering, withering two footer, admiring the beauty of the coiling, wiggling creature.

"Damn Freddy, snakes give me the willies," I said. I had hated snakes for as long as I could remember.

"I'm keeping him. I can put it in a box under my bed," Freddy said, ignoring me, "Mom won't find out." Then he brightened, " I gotta a better idea. Come on."

"What?" I asked, as we jogged back toward his house.

"You'll see." When we got close to the house, Freddy stuck the snake down the neck of his shirt. I cringed at the thought of that cold slimy body withering next to his skin. It was more than I could stand. I walked on ahead so I wouldn't have to watch the withering bulge around his waist. Shit, how could he stand to have that thing touching him? A shudder ran down my spine.

We walked into the kitchen where Annie and Mrs. Gray were working, grabbed a cookie then headed toward Freddy's room. The right side of the hall had three doors, the first was Annie's bedroom, next was the bathroom, then Freddy's.

As we got to Annie's door, Freddy looked back to see if all was clear. With a mischievous grin on his face, he turned and entered with me following. Going over to Annie's dresser, Freddy pulled open the second drawer. He removed the snake from his shirt and slipped it under some clothes. "That oughta get her," he said.

It was a week before he was allowed out of the house or could have any company. But I got filled in on what happened, and I have to admit, it was worth it. Freddy said that the next morning the race was on to see who would get to use the bathroom first, he or Annie. This wasn't anything unusual; she was always trying to beat him.

Annie was rushing around getting her clean clothes laid out. In the process she opened the drawer and wrapped her hand right around the coiled snake. She grabbed a slip and pulled it out, lifting the snake out before she realized what she had hold of. Annie let out a scream that almost shattered the windows. Mrs. Gray came running. It turned out that she was scared to death of snakes, and when Annie had dropped the snake, it had slithered over toward the door. Upon entering Annie's room, Mrs. Gray stepped right in the middle of the snake with her house slippers on. Being a large snake, it hadn't been hurt, but immediately coiled. Mrs. Gray let out a blood-curdling scream that even scared Freddy. He said that's when he knew he was in what he called, "deep shit!"

According to Freddy, women were running all over the house yelling like crazy. I sure wish I could have been there.

Freddy confessed that it had been worth it once the dust settled. It was so great that I couldn't have topped it with anything. It left me jealous of him for quite awhile, but darn proud to be his best friend.

Sparky showed up from Spokane a few days after the snake incident and really cracked up when he heard what Freddy had pulled. But being the politician that he was, he showed sympathy toward Mrs. Gray and Annie when they told him in their words of the atrocity.

Chapter 6

Grandfather had planned a special camping trip for us kids while Sparky was visiting. We were going to spend a couple days at Whisper Lake, then visit some interesting places in the mountains that were considered sacred. Grandfather always included Annie on these outings, even though us boys didn't much like the idea of a girl tagging along.

After we stowed our gear in the cabin and built a fire, we sat around roasting hot dogs and marshmallows for lunch. Grandfather was in a story mood, and began to tell of his people.

"In the days of old, when the young men reached your age, they would go alone into the wilderness in search of a spirit guide. Some were arrogant and felt they didn't need guidance or anything but food and shelter. They were never destined to accomplish much. Others were touched. The People believed when a person was touched, it meant he was special to the Great Spirit so they treated him kindly, fed him and gave him shelter. But some of the young men were driven to become more. The Great Spirit would give these young men wisdom in all things, as they were ready. Still there were those that wouldn't listen to the messengers of the Great Spirit and they got lost, perhaps never to be found and guided back to the right path. Youth is a difficult journey we all must travel to reach our destination. Sometimes the paths are short and so the end of life would also be short. At other times the path would be long and hard to follow. Some young men would see the trail they had chosen was not good and would return to their home and listen to the advice of the elders, then go again to walk the good trail with their spirit guide to help them. There were elk and deer for food and clothing on life's journey and long ago, the buffalo, until the white man saw fit to destroy the mighty herds of the plains, and the trail became bad for the Indian. The People's time was over only because the Great Spirit had spoken."

He hung his head for a moment as if remembering, then looked up and far away. "When I feel sick in my heart, I come to the mountains for peace. I build a fire for company and lay out under the stars with my bedroll. The friends of the mountains keep me company until I feel better. They talk to my heart and I feel peace within. This is good medicine. The white man's medicine is good, but the mountains also have medicine that is good for the spirit. Man's medicine is bad if you take too much at one time. The mountains cannot give you too much. You only grow stronger."

"Grandfather," asked Annie, "why do you come to this lake so often?"

"This lake, Annie, is special for me because this is where my lady sleeps. She waits for me up on the hill overlooking the far end of the lake."

""Where?" she asked.

"Come, I'll show you," he said, taking up his walking stick and rising from his seat next to the fire.

We immediately stood and followed him as he walked along the lakeshore toward the west. Following the path, we hiked up a little hill overlooking the end of the lake. It wasn't much of a climb before we came upon a place that was covered with wildflowers and a small stone. On the stone was the name of my grandmother, the year she was born and the date of her death. She was only twenty-eight when she died.

"Grandfather, tell us about your wife," Annie asked, "What was she like?"

"This lake holds many memories of her. She was a gift from the Great Spirit our Father."

As Grandfather spoke of my grandmother I could see sorrow as he remembered the woman he loved and the loneliness of her loss.

"She was beautiful both on the inside and out, and her kindness and generosity were known throughout the valley," he said. "Her path was not long upon this earth, because the Great Spirit missed his beautiful daughter and called her to return and be with him. I named this lake Whisper Lake because she used to say it was so quiet here that you could hear a whisper from one end of the lake to the other. She had to leave many years ago when we were young. These flowers we call bluebells," he pointed to the ground. "They were one of her favorites. She would pick a bouquet and put them on the table, then she would put out our meal around them. The food would taste better with the flowers, she claimed, and it was so." Grandfather stood quietly, his old Stetson in his hand.

Just above the little grave stood two old apple trees. "My wife planted those trees many years ago. She loved plants and trees," he said,

"I have taken good care of them every year since. This will be yours someday, Cole. Then, my son, it will be up to you to take care of it. Your father knows that I want to be buried here with my lady. One day I'll be with her again," he pointed at a place beside the stone with his hat. "Together we'll race the winds."

I felt saddened by this proclamation. But there was no sadness in Grandfather. On the contrary, he sounded like he was looking forward to the event. He would be reunited with his wife. He had spoken of her often. Many a night I had watched him as he stared into a fire with sad eyes, and I knew he was thinking of his beloved. Looking at this old man standing by the grave of his wife, you would never have guessed him to be the tough rugged person he was.

"Grandfather?" Annie whispered after a few moments of silence.

"Yes, Annie."

"Tomorrow, I will pick some bluebells and put them on the table, if that's okay with you?"

"That would make this old man very happy. Flowers are a nice way to greet the day," he looked at her affectionately, "Annie, you are the flower, picking a shadow of yourself."

That evening we sat before the campfire feeling the heat, letting it soak into our bodies and souls. No one spoke for quite some time, lost in our own thoughts and dreams. Grandfather said that unless you have sat and looked into a fire as night settles in, you cannot be at true peace with yourself. There is a feeling of well being that comes over you, knowing that you are one with the Great Spirit, a part of earth and sky. As our Father holds this earth spinning upon the tip of his finger, so he holds our destiny in his heart and in the palm of his hand, but the final choice is in our own hearts to choose.

"Grandfather, how did the Indians marry?" Annie asked breaking the silence.

"The people had different ways and customs, Annie."

"What if they didn't have anyone to marry them, Grandfather?"

Grandfather looked out on the lake where the loons had started their evening serenade and after a moment of silence, pointed to a rock, which sat out a few feet from shore.

"Do you see that rock?" he asked. "That is a wedding rock. In the old days, before the white man, when a young man and maiden wanted to unite as one and no one was willing to marry them, they would go to a marrying place, such as that rock, in the late afternoon. The sun would shine on them as they stood on the rock facing the sunset. The young warrior would take a piece of leather that the young maiden had softened by herself, and he would bind their wrists that were joined by holding hands, along with his knife which he held in his bound hand. The softened leather was a symbol of her pledge to provide for her husband and their children to be. His knife was his promise of food and protection for his family. They stood together until sundown not speaking with their lips, only with their hearts, to the Great Spirit. At last light, the Great Spirit would send his answer to them with the song of the loon. The first song after the sun had completely gone behind the mountain would signal the wedding was complete, and no man had the right to question their marriage."

"What if they changed their minds?" Freddy asked.

"There was no changing of the minds like there is today, son. The song of the loon was forever."

"What happened if they didn't hear the loon?" Annie asked.

"Then the Great Spirit did not approve of the wedding, and the marriage was never to be. The young people would have to respect the wisdom of the Great Spirit, just as everyone had to respect their marriage."

"What about the father of the girl who got married? Didn't he have to be given something special for her? I mean, he got gypped," Sparky said.

"No, he in turn had the right to take whatever the young man possessed, all but his weapons and bride," Grandfather said.

"Maybe it wasn't such a bad deal after all," Freddy said and grinned.

We boys laughed, but Grandfather and Annie just looked at us, which caused the three of us to feel a little sheepish at our witticisms.

"Can white people marry that way?" Annie asked.

"If the white man believes in the Great Spirit, who is the Creator of the world, then yes. But you have to understand that if he says no, then it is no forever. You cannot believe in only half of the Great Spirits words. I am a Christian, but I have my Indian beliefs also and they are sacred. I do not take them lightly."

"Grandfather? Do you have an Indian name?" Annie asked.

"I was called Wind Racer because they said I liked to race the wind when I was young."

"Grandfather, you lived when General Custer was killed, back in the old days, didn't you?" I asked, hoping for a story.

"Yes, Son. But I was only a baby then. The People called Custer Yellow Hair. My uncle, Brave Wolf, came close to him in battle."

"Did the Indians dress and look like they do in the movies?" Sparky asked.

"No, not really. The young warriors had war hats to wear when they went to do battle. Some had little animal spirits that were tied into their hair. These were a talisman, said to give the young warrior mystical powers. Brave Wolf had a stuffed hawk that was tied into the back of his hair. When he rode against Yellow Hair, it is said by many that the hawk came alive and flew over his head when he blew four times on a whistle made of bird bone, and no enemy could touch him because of his spirit guide."

"Were The People afraid of Custer?" Freddy asked, growing excited.

"They did not know it was Yellow Hair. But no, they were not afraid. The Cheyenne and Sioux were very courageous people," Grandfather paused for a moment to reflect. "There were many young men among The People who were willing to sacrifice themselves for the safety of others. The white man called them suicide warriors. There would be a great celebration the night before a battle and these suicide warriors would be honored. They went into battle knowing they would not live beyond the one attack, for to survive the battle was a dishonor. The suicide warriors attacked first to run off the soldier's horses, then fought hand to hand to the death. Their only purpose was to give the other warriors time to get set for the battle".

"Why are there wars, Grandfather? Why do people want to hurt each other?" Annie asked.

I gave her a scowl, "Girls don't know anything about fighting and going to war," I said with disgust. "Men have to fight or the enemy would take us over. Men fight to protect their homes. Isn't that right, Grandfather?"

"Some of what you say is true, Cole. People do fight to protect their home, but not always. There are times when they fight because they feel they must make others believe as they do. Why, I do not know. We are all brothers.

"But they are brave men and they die with great honor and some come back heroes," Freddy said.

I could see the excitement in him as he thought about being a hero.

Grandfather looked at him sadly. "Many great men die in battle, my son. They die with great honor, fighting for what they believe is right, but they are still dead. Always remember, there is no honor in war, only great loss."

This last statement left us boys silent and in deep thought.

The next morning we left the cabin, and Grandfather took us into a rocky canyon in the mountains. There he showed us pictures, which had been drawn long ago on a cliff. Then to a cave which was out of sight to the casual observer. The cave had handprints on the walls. Alongside the handprints were drawings of strange animals. Looking down on the floor of the cave, I found a stone knife in almost perfect shape. Grandfather said it was probably used to sharpen the charcoal for drawing the pictures. He said The People used different colors of earth and charcoal mixed with animal blood, berry juice and bear fat.

"Grandfather, why is there four pictures of many things?" I asked, flashing my light around the walls.

"Four is a magical number for The People. Look at the entrance, see the four black birds? They watch the cave. All who visit here and leave it undisturbed are welcomed. The knife you found must not be taken from the cave. It is the property of the ancients," he said in a low reverent voice and pointed to the four black birds. "Leaving things as they are, you will be repaid someday, my son."

Looking at the four figures, I could see their fiery eyes staring at me. As I stared I heard far away drums and chanting. Through a haze I saw images of warriors long since gone, and battles fought many years ago. I stood spellbound, then all was quiet, and the images were gone. I quickly looked around at the others, but they seemed not to notice anything strange. The vision must have lasted only moments. I replaced the knife carefully, and heard a grunt of approval from Grandfather. Looking at the birds again, I noticed there were no eyes, only the shapes of four black birds. I realized then that the blood of my Indian ancestors flowed strongly through my veins. Grandfather must have seen the same glowing eyes I had. A knowing look crossed his face, but neither of us spoke.

Chapter 7

Life was getting a little more complicated by my mid-teens. It seemed like all Freddy and I talked about anymore were women. How they looked, what they said and what we'd like to say to them, or better yet, what we'd like to do with them. We had a stack of girlie magazines hid and we spent a lot of time pouring over the pictures, discussing the attributes of each woman.

Corky, one of our gang, had gone to Oregon to spend a couple of weeks with his grandparents. While he was there, he had gone to the county dump with some friends to see what they could find. Always the lucky one, he hit gold. When he came back he showed us his treasure. A pack of playing cards. Not just any old playing cards mind you. There were thirty-seven very unique cards that had naked women on one side of them, each posing differently. One even had her tit caught in the wringer of a washing machine. It didn't look like it was hurting a lot, but she was making a "Oooh" looking sound with her lips.

Now this was trading material, and it wasn't long before I was minus a pocketknife and Freddy had lost a stack of comic books. Old Sparky, the cheapskate, didn't trade for any. He claimed to have better pictures at home, hidden in the basement, and knowing my cousin, he probably did.

We'd all meet in the schoolyard down the road from our ranch and bring our trading materials, hoping someone would like what we had. Pictures of naked women were in big demand. The neat thing about the cards was, they were almost indestructible. Pictures out of a girlie magazine would wear out where you folded them.

One day in July, while riding our bikes, we pulled into the schoolyard. There was Sparky, Corky, Don, Russ, Tom and myself.

Freddy, late as usual, skidded sideways to a stop and breathlessly burst into the conversation with an important announcement.

"Guess what. You'll guys are never gunna believe it. I overheard them saying they're going skinny-dipping. All of them," Freddy looked around to see what our reaction was.

"Who's going skinny-dipping?" Russ asked.

"Annie and her girlfriends! I overheard them say they were going down to Miller's bend. They ain't taking bathing suits neither. Just swimming naked."

He definitely had our undivided attention now. I had never seen real live naked girls before, except little babies and they didn't count. Annie and her friends were almost grown; they had the bumps and curves in all the right places. It sure would be better than looking at pictures. Two of the girls, Pam and Rhonda, had big tits. Boy, this was going to make my day. No, it would make my life! Pam was in the tenth grade and the oldest. Annie's birthday fell in December. In school that had put her a year behind Judy and Rhonda, who were ninth graders.

I had tried to look down their blouses every time I got a chance. Sometimes I felt they knew what I was up to because they would move. But I never got tired of trying. Once in a while it paid off. Standing behind them pretending to read over their shoulders worked the best, until they caught on. Then they'd spoil it by moving or holding the neck of their blouses shut. Sometimes I got to see all of the front of their bras. It wasn't as good as seeing tits, but almost because my imagination took over.

"You sure?" Sparky asked. "How they going?"

"Pam's driving her folk's car. I heard Annie talking on the phone. They're gonna meet at our house this afternoon around two. I'm pretty sure they said about two. Anyway, Annie was talking to Pam. She'll be wearing her big knockers and nothing else. I don't know how many are coming, but we'll get a good look at a lot of tits."

"If you're lying, we're going to throw you in the river," Sparky threatened.

"Honest, I ain't lying, honest, no shit!" Freddy said, holding up his hand. "I heard her talking and she didn't know I was listening. Honest!"

"How'd you like to run down there and rub your face in all those tits?" Corky said and grinned.

"Sounds good to me, especially Pam's. She looks like she'd put out if you did," Tom said.

Tom was the oldest and most experienced in the field of girls. No doubt he knew more than all of us put together. He probably had even seen a naked girl up close.

"Okay, let's keep a cool tool," I said, trying to sound like a leader, "You're sure they said today?"

"That's five miles down to the bridge. It'd better be true, ten miles round trip," Corky said, "I don't want to pedal my ass off to find out it ain't true."

"If Annie says they're going, they're going!" I said defending her, but not sure why.

"We gotta stay out of sight until they pass us. If they think we're on to them, they'll call it off," Corky said.

"We could head down there right now, then hide for awhile in the woods and wait for them to pass." I said. "That way we'll be closer instead of killing ourselves peddling our asses off. We could go hide in the water ditch. If we laid our bikes over they'd go right by."

"That's okay with me. We can take our slingshots and hunt for a while, maybe get a rabbit or something," Russ said.

"You couldn't hit your ass with a slingshot," Tom said.

Russ flipped him the finger.

The rest of us laughed, relieving the tension. I still couldn't believe our good luck. What was it going to be like? These were real live women, flesh and blood girls. This had to be a dream. The adrenaline was running in my veins, and my heart pounded so loud I was afraid the others could hear it.

Listening to the guys I realized how much they sounded like idiots. I was afraid to open my mouth for fear I would sound worse than they did.

"I wish we could take pictures or something," Russ said.

"I gotta camera. It ain't got any film though," Tom said.

"You idiot, they won't develop it anyway. We'd probably go to jail or something," I said. Everyone nodded in agreement.

"My sister has a camera," Freddy said.

Sparky piped up, "Taking nudie pictures of a girl with her own camera. That's really funny."

"We better not. She wouldn't like it," Freddy laughed.

"No shit! Here's your camera back. I hope you didn't mind us using it to take pictures of you naked while you were skinny-dipping," I said, holding out an imaginary camera.

We howled with laughter. Finally regaining our composure, we decided we'd best be off. We didn't want to be caught anywhere near Miller's bend. It would blow the whole thing, and we didn't want anything going wrong even if we had to lay in wait all day.

As we rode, we jabbered back and forth about everything under the sun. The faster we peddled the louder and faster we talked. Reaching a place to turn off to the old water ditch, we dismounted and drug our bikes under the barbed wire fence. This was the perfect place to wait. At first, we sat on the ditch bank and swapped lies about hunting and fishing, and of course, women. Growing restless, we decided to leave one guy as lookout while the rest of us went into the woods to hunt squirrels and rabbits. However, no one volunteered to be lookout so that idea was cast aside.

"Hey, Cole. You can write about this, you know, for a girlie magazine or something. You could make lots of money," Freddy said.

I was a fledgling writer and had almost got a story published in an outdoor magazine, almost. My story had been a hunting tale, about a hunter that got his bull elk, grizzly and a huge mule deer buck all before noon on opening morning. To me it sounded like a pretty good story, but they didn't buy it. I guess they were publishing for ordinary hunters at the time. The magazine sent me a letter of appreciation though, saying I should keep up my writing and when I got older they would like to see some more of my stories. My mom framed the letter and hung it in my room.

"I think Mr. Gray would have my ass if I wrote this for a magazine," I said. That brought a moment of silence from all of us.

"What would happen if one of the girl's parents found out about this?" Corky asked.

"Shut up, Cork," Tom said.

The afternoon drug on, but every time we thought about what we were going to see, it seemed worth it. We would have waited all day in hundred-degree heat for an opportunity like this. Finally around two we began to get a little bored.

"Maybe they changed their minds or maybe they were just bullshitting," Russ said.

"Naw, girls don't bullshit each other," Tom said.

"They coulda changed their minds and done something else," I said with the dreadful thought that I could be right.

"Maybe they couldn't get a car," Freddy said.

We all turned to look at him.

"I think they'll get a car though. They're pretty lucky," Freddy added, looking around at our disappointed faces. He had no more than shut his mouth when he looked up the road. "Hey look, I think that's them. Everyone get down, get down!"

We hit the dirt, our hearts pounding with excitement. Carefully we looked through the grass that grew on the ditch bank and spotted the car with the girls laughing and singing. The big moment had finally come as the car passed without them ever suspecting we were laying in wait. We stayed hidden a little longer making sure everything was okay. No one wanted to have the rest of us down on him for messing up the greatest adventure any boy could ever hope for.

Finally we ventured a look and found the way clear. Dusting ourselves off, we picked up our bikes and rolled them to the road. Mounting, we began the second to the last leg of our great adventure. Within minutes we caught sight of the bridge. Dismounting, we pushed our bikes along the side of the road. Then just before we reached the turnout where the girls had parked, we stashed our bikes in the bushes, making sure not to make any noise.

Stealthily we began our stalk up the trail to Miller's bend. Our breathing sounding more like we were climbing straight up a cliff rather than a level river path.

"You want us to stop so you can play with your pud, Cork?" Spark joked.

"Screw you, Spark," Corky said.

"Shut up!" I said in a low, threatening voice. With that we continued without further insults. We were caught up in our own thoughts about what was ahead, keeping alert for anything out of the ordinary. Freddy was in the lead when he suddenly held up his hand. We all froze. We could hear laughter and giggling up ahead. But standing right in the middle of the trail was a problem, the Gray's dog. Damn, the girls had brought the dog. Rocket would bark at anything. He was their lookout. They had planned well. One bark from Rocket would spell the end of our well-laid plans.

Just as Rocket looked our way, Freddy reached down and pretended to pick up a stick and throw it. Instead of barking, Rocket ran after the stick that wasn't there. He looked for a couple of minutes, then came over and sat down in front of Freddy. Good old stupid Rocket. He wasn't interested in barking a warning being that we weren't new now. We could continue our quest.

Miller's bend is a giant elbow in the river. The swimming area is about fifty feet wide and a hundred feet long. On the inside of the bend is a sandy beach. At the upper end of the bend is a giant rock that sticks out of the water a couple of feet and makes a great diving platform. The other side of the river has a cliff with some large pine trees. The sun hits Miller's bend early in the morning and lingers late into the evening, making it an ideal place to swim all day. Just behind the beach, the trail comes to a small rise covered with tall grass overlooking the bend. A person can sit on this little hill and survey the whole area.

As we approached the bend, we got down on our stomachs and crawled ever so slowly the last fifty feet to the crest of the mound. Not daring even to breathe, we slowly lifted our heads and peered over the top.

Annie was the first girl I spotted. She had her back to us and wore nothing but a suntan. She was looking at the edge of the water for something. Sitting on the beach were Judy, Pam and Rhonda, without a stitch on. I couldn't believe my eyes. So this was what girls looked like naked.

Stunned, we laid there and stared. Judy sat with her back to us and Rhonda sat sideways with her hands clasped together around her knees. Pam sat facing us at a quarter angle, giving us the best view we could've wanted. If I'd had gum in my mouth, I would have choked for sure. She had the biggest breasts I'd ever hoped to see.

Annie turned toward us; suddenly I was hit with what I can best describe as a thousand volts of electricity, all concentrated in my stomach and heart. She was so beautiful. The way the sun glistened on her skin and hair took my breath away. I couldn't breath but I didn't care. I was bewitched. I was looking at the most beautiful girl in the entire world. She turned back to the water and began wading out then sliding gracefully into the water, and with even smooth strokes swam toward the diving rock. Her grace was as attractive in the water as it was out.

The girls on the beach had been sitting on towels when Judy got to her feet and turned to straighten her towel. For a moment she stood still as she faced us, sensing something was out of place. I held my breath, finally Judy seemed satisfied that all was okay and sat down again. She lay on her back, and we really got a look at her.

"How'd you like to run down there and bury a boner?" Russ whispered.

At that, some of the guys cracked up.

"Shut up, you dumb shits," Tom said in a stern whisper.

I was too caught up in all this to make any noise. From very early childhood, I had hunted with my grandfather, and he had instilled in me the value of silence while stalking prey. I just wished I were here alone. This was like hunting with clowns.

Annie finally reached the rock and without hesitation, climbed gracefully out of the water. As she stood for a moment before diving, my breath caught in my throat, and I felt like my chest was going to explode. She was magnificent.

I'd been raised around Annie, but up until now, had only given her a bad time at best. Now here she was, the most beautiful girl in the county, looking like a goddess standing on that rock. I realized at that moment that I was in love with this girl and had been all my life. The worst part was she didn't even know I existed, except as her brother's friend.

"Look at all those tits. I wish I had a camera," Tom whispered. "Just run down through there and snap some close-ups. My dad's movie camera is what we need."

"Nobody would develop the pictures. Not nudies," said Corky.

This was the first and only word we had heard out of him. He was engrossed and words were a waste. Twice he removed his glasses and quickly wiped them as if he couldn't believe what he was seeing.

The guys were growing restless and started talking low rather than whispering. I knew it was just a matter of time before we were discovered. I wanted to slam their heads together.

Finally Spark broke the spell by yelling out, "Who needs a rape job?" The rest of the guys began laughing hysterically and rolling around on the ground. At the same time, there was screaming on the beach and a mad scramble for towels. Annie didn't lose control like the others. Instead she covered herself as best she could and with a dignity befitting nobility, walked over and picked up a towel.

"They're going to catch us. We'd better get out of here," Tom said, "If they do, we'll get in trouble. Come on!" Then they were up and running.

I couldn't pull myself away from Annie even though she had covered up and was looking to see who had been watching. Freddy ran back and began tugging on me. With great effort, I managed to get to my feet, then found I wanted to run for all I was worth. I felt the same urgency the others were obviously feeling to get some distance between the girls and us. Racing for our bikes, the guys began shouting at each other, laughing and hooting loudly.

As for me, I just didn't want to get caught by Annie. Then there was Grandfather to be reckoned with. I knew what he would think, and I didn't want Grandfather to think less of me.

Reaching our bikes, we stopped to catch our breath, then realized the girls would be getting dressed and heading for the car. There was a quick calculation as to how long it would be before their car would overtake us. We had to find a place where we could hide until they passed, knowing we'd be in deep trouble if they could prove it was us who had spied on them. Catching us would be all the proof they needed. Going down the road a few hundred yards we found some brush and hid.

Summer lost its excitement after that, except when I was around Annie. Freddy must have known. He was like a brother to me, and Sparky also knew something was wrong. I had lost interest in the cards with the naked women on them. Not totally, but they no longer held any mystery. I had seen the real thing, and my heart belonged to Annie.

Grandfather noticed the change in me, and I felt his eyes studying me many times. He didn't ask questions or press me for answers I couldn't give. Then one day in mid-August, while Grandfather and I were out by ourselves working on the tractor, he started in with a curious conversation.

"How you and Annie getting along?" he said as he wiped some grease from his hands.

Caught off guard, I just blurted out the truth. "I think I've blown my chances of ever getting her to like me, Grandfather."

"What makes you think that?"

"I've treated her like a pest all my life. Freddy and I have both treated her that way," I said.

"You haven't blown anything, son. You were kids then. You're young adults now. You take it from me, Annie thinks a lot of you, and it isn't like you are her brother either. You kids were made for each other. Just be patient and time will take care of everything else. A young tree does not bear fruit."

With that, he walked into the shop and the conversation was over as fast as it had begun.

That weekend we took Sparky to catch the bus in Kalispell. His going marked the end of another summer. Annie and Freddy came along to see him off. As Mom and the four of us stood around waiting for the bus, Annie slipped her arm through mine for a moment, then Sparky had to mouth off and ruin everything.

"Hey, look at that. I think she likes you," he said with an exaggerated look of surprise.

With that, Annie pulled her arm out of mine, and smiling, made a half hearted swing at Sparky's shoulder.

All too soon our time with Sparky was over for another year. As we heard his bus being announced Mom gave him a hug, "Have a good trip home, dear."

"You're right. She's better than the playing cards," Spark said, then turning, got on the bus.

"What did he mean?" Annie asked, frowning as she looked first at me then at Freddy.

"Nothing," I said. Looking up at a window, I saw him grinning from ear to ear. Good old Sparky. I shielded my hand with my jacket so nobody but him could see, then flipped him the finger and grinned.

Chapter 8

In high school, Annie was a hit with everyone, especially the boys. I felt a pain in my heart whenever I saw the jocks talking to her, which was every chance they got. I must admit, I tried forgetting her by looking at other girls, hoping to find someone I could like as much as I did Annie. So far I'd failed miserably.

There was a new girl, who caught my eye. Her name was Kathy, and she was a beauty. She had just moved from Libby, a town ninety miles west of Kalispell. All the guys were talking about how cute she was. Between classes she couldn't walk down the hall without half a dozen guys following in her wake. It took a while but I finally worked up enough nerve to ask her if she would go to the Halloween dance with me. To my surprise she said yes.

Freddy and I were going to triple date with Annie. He had been going steady with Judy for about six weeks and claimed to be madly in love. That was Freddy. I think he was born in love.

Annie was dating Bob Peterson. Like Freddy and me, he was a senior, and unlike Freddy and me, he was the star quarterback on the football team. A good-looking guy, or so all the girls thought. They always seemed to be flocked around him. To me he was a piece of shit! Every time I saw Annie with him I got a knot in my gut and had a hard time trying to control my jealousy. Being that Annie was just a sophomore, I thought he was too old for her and vowed that if he ever hurt her I would make hamburger out of his face. My dislike for Peterson grew daily. Peterson was on my shit list and the time would come when my tolerance would wear thin. Secretly I looked forward to it.

After the dance we all met at the drive-in for sodas as usual. I sat next to Kathy on one side of the booth, with Annie and Peterson across from us. Freddy and Judy sat in a booth across the isle. Peterson, Freddy and I were talking about hunting when Kathy surprised us by saying she had taken a whitetail buck her first year out and had killed a two-point last year. Us guys sat transfixed as she described in detail how she had taken them with a 30-06 Winchester. Kathy seemed at home with the conversation as much as we guys were. Annie and Judy sat in silence watching us as we listened spellbound to Kathy.

"I'm going out in the morning with my dad. We hunt together every year. I think I'll go for a nice whitetail," she said, looking at me. "We're hunting around the Thompson River. You ever hunt the Thompson, Cole?"

"Several times with my dad and grandfather. We're going to hunt the Cooper's ridge area in the morning. Right Freddy?"

"Yep, we have a date with a big buck or maybe an elk if we're lucky," Freddy said.

"Dad says there're grizzlies up there," Kathy said, concern in her voice.

"They don't worry me. I'm packing a 30-06 that my grandfather gave me," I said, looking around for the approval of the guys.

"I tried my dad's 300 magnum once," Kathy said. "It hurt." Then she reached up and almost put her hand on her right breast. I noticed Annie roll her eyes and look at Judy.

The next morning shortly before six, I headed for Freddy's place. As I pulled into the Gray's driveway, I noticed two people standing in the kitchen, Freddy and Annie. She was in her bathrobe and slippers. I went in without knocking.

"Hi, you ready to roll?" I asked Freddy.

"Yeah, but we got a real twist. Annie wants to come. She says she wants to see how it's done, but she doesn't want to watch while we shoot," Freddy said, raising his eyebrows in a mock surprised look.

"You want to go hunting with us? You?"

"She's been acting weird this morning." Freddy said in a low voice.

"You really serious? You want to hunt the ridge with us?"

"I want to see if deer hunting is as fun as you say. I don't have to watch you shoot it, just be on the hunt. After it's shot and just a corpse ..."

"Hold it," I interrupted, "deer are not corpses. They're animals we shoot for food. Corpses are dead people. We're deer and elk hunting, not people hunting," I said defensively. She was getting under my skin like old times. Corpses! That was city people's mentality. I had grown up with the country way of supplying the table with what you hunted, and it graveled me to hear talk of animals having the first bid on the woods. It was hunter and prey ever since creation and was no more wrong for me to hunt than it was for the lion or wolf. Grandfather had taught me that we are all brothers with other predators, killing only for protection or food. That was the unwritten code of the mountains. I poured a cup of coffee while Freddy went about fixing something for his breakfast.

"Well?" Annie asked, looking at Freddy then me. "Can I?"

"Can you what?" I said, I wanted her to beg. "You always bitch at us for hunting. Now you want to go?"

I turned to Freddy. "Dazy Crockett wants to kill a deer?"

"I said I wanted to come along. I didn't say I wanted to kill anything. Good grief, I just want to go hunting for once. If you don't want me to go, I'll stay home," she said as she turned, and started out of the kitchen.

"You really want to go? You have to help if we get something down," I said, really pushing it.

Annie turned, and looking excited spoke, "I can be ready in fifteen minutes."

"Bullshit. You better be ready in five or we're leaving without you," I said, feeling the power come over me.

"Why'd you tell her she could come with us? I ain't hunting with her. She goes with you. You ever hear her in the woods? She sounds like a cow," Freddy said.

"You liar!" Annie called out as she went to her bedroom to get dressed. She sounded in high spirits, and in a few minutes she was ready and back in the kitchen.

"What are we having for lunch?" Annie asked. opening the refrigerator.

"Lunch?" I said, looking to Freddy. "I got a candy bar."

"Candy? You can't hike on just a candy bar," Annie said. "Give me five minutes and I can fix something to take. Okay?"

Freddy looked at me, raising his eyebrows a couple of times, approving of the idea of a real lunch.

"Maybe she's worth it after all," I said. Annie smiled and went to work making us a lunch.

Mr. Gray walked into the kitchen. "What's going on?" he asked, pouring a cup of coffee.

"Annie wants to go with us this morning. She says she wants to try hunting. Can you believe it?" Freddy said.

"Annie?" Mr. Gray asked in a surprised voice.

"I thought I'd go along and see if I liked it. Mom suggested it last night," she said.

"Is that what you and your mother were talking about so late last night?" Mr. Gray asked. "You got to learn to sleep. You girls are regular hoot owls."

"That's the only time we get to talk without you being around," she said.

"Bull pies," Mr. Gray said, sipping his coffee, then turned and gave us guys a wink. "They just don't have enough work to tire them out."

"Wait till I tell Momma what you said," Annie said and grinned devilishly at her dad. She finished making the sandwiches and then put a piece of cake in for us guys. Now this was living.

"I'll carry the lunches," Annie announced. "That way you won't lose me in the woods. No Annie, no lunch, got it?"

This is great, I thought. Not only do we get a lunch instead of a candy bar, but I get to spend some time with Annie.

"You kids had best get going. It's getting close to daylight," Mr. Gray said.

Annie rode in the middle, holding onto the barrel of my rifle as we bounced along in the pickup. She seemed in high spirits and admittedly I was too. After all, I could feel her thigh against mine, which was exciting.

"You think Kathy really likes to hunt? Or does she just want to impress the boys?" she asked, sounding a little too casual.

"Yeah, she likes it. She's a good hunter. You have to be to get deer like that," Freddy said. "I just wish I could find a girl that liked to hunt. If I wasn't laying her, I could be hunting with her," he grinned.

"Freddy is that all you ever think about, going to bed with every girl you meet. No wonder you can't keep a girlfriend," Annie said, still looking down the road.

"Look, there's a rabbit!" Freddy shouted, "Did we bring a 22?"

"Nope," I said, "we're deer hunting. If it ain't got horns, it don't get shot."

"Shit," he said.

"Why do you have to be such a potty mouth?" Annie asked.

"Cram it," said Freddy.

"See. That's what I mean."

"Hey guys. Let's enjoy ourselves and the hunt. Take me, I can't wait to gut shoot a Bambi," I said and grinned.

Annie gave me a playful jab with her elbow and made a disgusted look. Everything was back on the level again.

"She really shoot a 30 thing?" Anne asked.

"Who?" I pretended not to know whom Annie meant.

"It's a 30-06," corrected Freddy.

"Whatever," Annie said, glaring at her brother.

"Yeah, I think she knows her guns. That's a 30-06 you're holding. Grandfather gave it to me," I said. "It'll take care of anything in these mountains."

"Even grizzlies?" Annie asked.

"Yeah, it'll kick hell out of anything," I said, sounding a little boastful. I was proud of the old gun.

"Can I shoot it?" Annie asked.

"If you want to get knocked on your butt," Freddy said and grinned.

"She can shoot it if she wants too," I told Freddy. "It isn't as bad as they say. All you do is take off the safety and put the cross-hairs of the scope on what you want to hit."

I couldn't help but feel the tension in the truck. Maybe this was the way it was with girls when you took them hunting. I wasn't sure whether I was going to enjoy this outing or not.

"I'd like to shoot a rifle that's big enough to hunt with. Bobby said he wants to take me out with him and his dad next week," she said looking straight at me.

'Way to go, Annie,' I thought. You can kiss my ass if you want me to teach you something about hunting for that prick. She had made me instantly mad at the thought that she wanted me to teach her how to please Peterson.

I was so upset at what she said that I missed our turnoff and had to turn around and backtrack about a quarter mile.

Freddy and Annie both knew she had said the wrong thing and kept quiet. I parked the pickup at the end of the side road and we got out.

"I think you ought to teach your sister how to hunt," I said. "That's what brothers are for. I'm going to take the north ridge. I'll meet you two at the springs up in the basin around two or so." I shouldered my rifle and got ready to go.

"You going up the north ridge? That's straight up. Only thing up there is grizzlies and mountain sheep. Why you want to do that?" Freddy asked.

"I just want to," I said, shrugging my shoulders. Turning I started out for the north ridge and solitude. Freddy sensed that I needed my seclusion and Annie knew why.

"I ought to kick the hell out of Bobby baby in front of her and half the school," I said, talking to myself in a low voice. "That ought to show her who the best man is." I didn't just hike up the north ridge. I attacked it. It wasn't long until I felt better. I found that my animosity toward Annie had quieted, even though I still thought about scattering Bob Peterson's teeth all over the ground. When I got done with him, he would look like he'd tried to mate a grizzly. With that thought, I smiled and felt better. Let's see how she liked kissing a face that looked like it had been stuck in a meat grinder."

I climbed the ridge trail deep in thought. Most of the foliage was scrub pine and fir. Trees of any size either had a good root system or lay on the ground from high winds that hit the ridges. I started getting thirsty and looked forward to the springs at the basin.

I was still absorbed in thought and not watching what was up ahead, when I came around a couple scrub pines that were growing on the spine of the ridge. I was doing everything exactly opposite of what I had been taught to do in grizzly country. First I had my rifle slung on my shoulder, and second, I wasn't paying attention. I was daydreaming. There, not over thirty yards up the trail was the most feared animal in the mountains, a grizzly. As the trail dropped to the right and went around the trees, a grizzly sow and her two cubs stood in the path. I froze, hoping she hadn't heard me stumbling along. Standing motionless, I thought about how fast the sow could cover the thirty or so yards and be in the middle of me. Many a mountain man had met his fate because of a careless moment. I was not exempt from that destiny. I'd be the hamburger instead of Bob Peterson. What should I do? Drop down and roll up in a ball, like Grandfather had told me? Or should I try removing the rifle from my shoulder and go for the kill shot. I knew running was foolish. A grizzly could outrun a horse running at thirty-five miles an hour for at least a couple hundred yards. I wouldn't stand a chance.

It was morning and the winds would be starting to blow uphill with the warming air. I only had moments before she would wind me. Now was decision time. I decided I'd fight. I couldn't let her maul me up here where it would be difficult at best to try to get out on my own, if I survived. At least Freddy would hear my shot, and he'd find whatever was left of me. It would have to be all or nothing. As she turned her back toward me, I slowly edged my hand up toward the top of my rifle sling. Her hearing was acute. Grizzlies, especially females with cubs, would wheel and attack without even looking to see what the threat was. It was the mothering instinct. When she did wheel, it would be at top speed. She would come at me fast and furious, tooth and claw.

I also knew there was probably a ninety-five percent chance one of us was going to die in the next few moments, and I didn't want to die. As my adrenaline peaked, my fingers settled on my sling. I began slowly sliding my hand up toward my shoulder so I could pull my rifle off and bring it into firing position in one smooth motion. I had practiced this maneuver many times. Now it was going to have to be right the first time, no replays if it hung up on my clothing. My mind raced. Do I wait for her to make the first move? Do I make the first move and hope it's the right one? If I made the first move, it would give me the edge, not much, but better than nothing. If anything went wrong, I would be the one to pay for the screw up. I took a deep breath and braced myself for whatever was to come. The shot would have to be exact if it were to kill her in her tracks. That meant a brain or spine shot. Nothing else was going to stop her before she had me, and nothing would be worse than a wounded bear tearing into me.

With a jolt my mind raced to another question: Had I left the bullet out of the chamber in my anger and haste to leave Annie and Freddy? Damn, I couldn't remember. That was something I always did under normal conditions, but today hadn't been normal. I had been really ticked off at Annie. That took the normal out of the equation.

Grandfather had taught me always to be prepared for the worst, but I had allowed my emotions to let me get sloppy. Now it was time to pay the piper. At this range I would be stupid to pull a rifle that didn't have a live round in the barrel, and I probably would also be dead within moments of my stupidity. "Strike two, three strikes and I'm out!" I thought and took a deep breath, starting my final countdown. Then a shot rang out down in the lower area where Freddy and Annie had gone.

The grizzly jerked her head up at the sound and let out a low bellow. Wheeling, she shuffled off over the north rim of the ridge with her cubs trailing. Sliding the rifle off my shoulder, I checked the chamber and found that I had slid a shell into the barrel. I wasn't sure how I felt about everything. There was relief and disgust, accompanied by a sick feeling in my gut. I had been stupid and had lived to think about it. I swore to myself and to Grandfather never to let it happen again.

Waiting with rifle ready for her to return, I stood for what seemed like fifteen minutes, but probably wasn't more than a couple. Sweating profusely, I could feel the tension in my muscles. My back started jerking. Slowly I eased up and looked over the edge with the rifle ready. To my relief, she was gone.

I pondered what Grandfather would say about my encounter with the grizzly. I suspect he would do the worst. He would say nothing, leaving me to punish myself. That was the way he handled things. Never again would I be caught off guard, I vowed.

I turned and continued my climb up the north ridge, this time carrying my rifle as if I were hunting instead of blundering up the mountain like a greenhorn.

I continued up the trail and within a short time came to the basin with the springs. The greenery in the little basin was, as Annie would say, breathtaking. The foliage grew along the gravel trail the animals had cut into the mountainside over thousands of years. Looking up the basin, I could see places where the trees had been kept cleared by snow avalanches over the centuries. The country was beautiful but deadly if a person didn't know the rules.

Lying on my stomach, I drank my fill of cold spring water as it tumbled over the rocks and moss, splashing my face. The smell of the fresh cold water helped clear my mind, and I felt so refreshed and at peace that I was even willing to let old Bob live with all his teeth, at least for the time. I leaned against a rock and took a well-earned nap.

I was wakened by the sound of a rock on the trail below, probably kicked by Annie. I figured it wasn't Freddy, because he was careful where he put his feet when hunting. Easing to a sitting position, I waited for them to top the last small hill, still not able see them. Annie was making a lot of racket as they climbed the incline, and I knew it would be only moments until they were in sight. Then feeling mischievous, I jumped to my feet and ran over to where I could look down on them, ready to offer a hand to her. I was over my feelings of hostility; now I just wanted to poke a little fun at her noisy feet.

As I came to the edge of the slope and looked down, I was startled by the biggest six-point bull elk I had ever seen. Actually we surprised each other. I stood there just staring at the bull with my gun still leaning up against the rock thirty feet back up the trail. The bull stared at me for several seconds, allowing me plenty of time to have taken good aim and made a clean shot, if I'd had the forethought to bring my rifle.

I felt stupid. Twice I had forgotten my woodsman-ship, and I was starting to feel pretty humble.

"A smart person learns by his mistakes, just hope they aren't your last lessons," Grandfather had said.

"I'm learning a lot this morning, Grandfather," I whispered and slowly backed away, making sure not to make eye contact with the bull.

When I was out of sight, I turned and immediately tripped over a rock in my haste to retrieve my gun. The noise was deafening. I laid there in total disbelief at all the stupidity I had uncovered in such a short time. Then there was the report of a rifle. Jumping up I walked over to the edge of the rise and looked down at my worst nightmare. Annie was standing in the trail with one hand covering her mouth and a look of shock on her face. Her other hand held a rifle. The bull lay dead fifty yards beyond. Freddy was running to catch up with Annie. Turning, I retrieved my rifle and walked with as much dignity as I could manage, down the trail. Standing just above the magnificent six-point bull elk I waited for them to finish their climb up.

"What happened?" I asked as casually as possible.

"I had to go to the toilet. I told Annie to take my rifle and go on ahead. That's all I know," Freddy said as he gulped air. "Nice shot, Cole. Where'd you hit him?"

"I didn't," I stammered and nodded towards Annie.

"You gotta be bullshitting me," he said, looking first at Annie then me. He thought about it for a second and shook his head. "Naw, let's see your gun."

Freddy looked in the chamber of my rifle, then smelled the barrel for the smell of fresh gunpowder. Looking puzzled, he reached over and took the rifle from Annie. Opening the bolt he extracted the freshly spent case, then looked back at me with a sick look on his face. He looked at the elk puzzled, shrugged his shoulders and for a rare moment was speechless. I wasn't sure how he felt about the whole thing. Hell, I wasn't sure how I felt. This was going to call for some thinking. Neither of us had ever killed an elk. I turned to look at Annie standing back about twenty feet or so. She was crying silently and staring at the magnificent bull she had just dropped with a single shot from Freddy's rifle. I looked at Freddy for an explanation.

"We could kill her right here and swear it was an accident. No one would ever have to know," he said, grinning sickly.

He again shrugged his shoulders and shook his head in a beats-the-hell-out-of-me movement. We were silent for a moment.

"Congratulations, Annie. You're going to feed us a lot of great meals," I said. "You've done something us guys haven't got to do yet. You've taken a big bull elk. You'll be added to the great hunters at school."

"Even as good as Kathy?" she asked, smiling like a child.

"Greater than two of her," I said.

With that she brightened, but still hung back from her kill.

"You guys do what you have to do with it. I'll just watch, okay?" She turned and started up the trail, walking way around the bull. She turned her head, avoiding looking at the elk as she asked, "Where is the spring?"

After telling Annie where the spring was, Freddy and I drew out knives. We had our work cut out for us and it would take the rest of the day. After cleaning the kill, we broke for lunch. Walking up, I noticed Annie had picked some wild flowers and arranged them on a large rock. She had placed the flowers in the middle with some moss to hold them upright. Freddy and I walked over to the trickling spring and washed our hands, making sure we washed all the blood off before going anywhere near Annie. Pulling our caps off, we dropped down on our bellies and took a well-earned deep drink of the cold water.

Walking back over to where Annie was setting out lunch, I thought about all the decisions that had been made and carried out that morning. Annie was again bright eyed as she set our lunches before us. This was what heaven was all about.

"How's your shoulder?" I asked.

"It hurts a little," she said, reaching up and rubbing it.

"That's a lot of recoil for a girl." I said, "But you really laid that bullet where it counted. I don't think Freddy or I could have done better."

She glowed with pride. "Need any lessons?"

Freddy and I exchanged grins. "Only in gutting and carrying out the meat," I said.

"Sorry, that's the man's job. I'm good at packing guns. Come to think of it, that's how this all got started," she said, laughing.

After lunch, we checked the time and determined that we had just enough daylight to get the meat out of the basin before dark, not wanting to lose any of it to other predators. While Annie cleaned up our lunch leftovers, Freddy and I went back to work quartering up the bull. Finishing the job, we looked around to make sure we weren't leaving any of our equipment. Then cut some brush and laid it over the meat we couldn't carry. We were going to have to make a second trip. This would keep the birds from the meat for a while. The animals would clean up anything we left in the mountains before twenty-four hours were up. By then we'd have our meat safely out of the woods.

Walking back up to where Annie was waiting on a rock beside the spring, we washed our hands again, and after taking a good cold drink, told her we were ready. With reluctance, she got up and walking hesitantly behind us, followed down the hill to where we had been working on her elk. I glanced at her while we finished lashing the meat to our backpacks. She was holding up well, and I felt a certain pride in her. She held back, but wasn't about to back down from her responsibility, doing everything she was asked. It was decided that she would pack the rifles, one on each shoulder and the antlers, which we had cut from the head. I made sure to cover the skull part so she wouldn't be offended. I think she noticed my special effort because of the look she gave me. After explaining to her that there would be at least two trips up and down the mountain and possibly a third, Freddy and I each hoisted up our backpacks of meat and set off for the pickup. The trail was mostly downhill and the going was good at first, but then our knees and feet began to tire. The extra weight of approximately a 125 pounds to the quarter was pushing from behind, causing us to brace our legs with each step. The steeper the trail, the harder it got.

Upon reaching the pickup, we took a short break, then before getting stiff, headed back for what we hoped was the last load. The only thing that might make us go back for the third trip was the hide, heart and liver and that sounded less and less important all the time.

As we started up the trail, I turned and told Annie we'd try to be back before dark.

"Wait a minute. I'm in for the whole ride. What do I look like? Just a girl? I'm Annie the elk hunter." With that she reached over and took my rifle off my shoulder, then settling it across hers, marched ahead of us with an exaggerated stride. How I wished that she was interested in me instead of Peterson. Shrugging my shoulders, I tried to get my mind off Annie.

We left Freddy's rifle at the pickup because of the added weight and took only mine in case a grizzly had found our kill. Grandfather always said that if I ever encountered a grizzly trying to steal my animal, it would be best to let the grizzly have the meat. But this was Annie's first, and very likely last, elk. No bear was going to take it if I could help it.

As we got close to the kill site, I took the rifle from Annie and assumed the lead. A couple of whiskey jacks were all we saw. The birds showed little fear, just hopping out of our way, waiting to share the meat scraps with us. I watched as Annie talked gently to the birds.

Noticing the time, we decided to bone out the ribs and leave the heart and liver to the woods creatures. They'd make short work of them. With the last of the meat loaded on our backpacks, we set out. Annie carried my rifle again, although she made sure she was close enough to hand it to me on a moment's notice. She had been unusually quiet, but I figured the two trips up and back had tired her out. Just at last light, we came upon the pickup and saying nothing deposited our loads in the bed of the truck, knowing we had put in a full day's work. Freddy decided to take a short walk down the road to take a leak before we left. Annie walked around the truck to where I was unloading my rifle.

"Cole, can I talk to you?"

"Sure." I looked up at her. She was standing with her arms folded across her chest, looking down the road. She took a deep breath and with a look of determination turned to me. "Cole, what do you think of me?"

"What do you mean? You're Annie the elk hunter," I said.

"I'm serious, Cole."

"What do you mean?" I asked wondering what the heck was going on now. "As a girl? You're a good looking girl," I stammered, feeling foolish. "Peterson is very lucky."

"I'm not talking about Bob. What do you think of me?"

"On the level? Go for broke answer?"

"Yes."

"I envy Peterson," I said sadly. "Why Annie?" I ask beginning to get upset. What was she trying to do, make me look stupid? "Why are you asking me this right now?"

"I love you, Cole," she said, softly looking me in the eyes. "I've always loved you."

I was stunned. I think I must have stood there for a full minute with my mouth hanging open.

Freddy walked up before I could get my thinking straightened out. He looked at Annie then back to me. "You know what, I think I'll walk out to the main road and wait until you two are through." He turned and started down the road.

"Okay Freddy," I said. "We'll be along in a few minutes."

"Annie?" I realized she was crying.

"No, Cole, please listen to me. I know you think I'm just Freddy's kid sister and you like Kathy, but I had to tell you the way I feel. Cole, I'll say it again, I love you. I have always loved you." Then she added, "but don't worry, I wont get in the way of you and Kathy."

Annie was sobbing. I couldn't believe what she had just said. Reaching over I put my hands on her shoulders and turned her face to me.

"Annie. Oh, Annie," I said pulling her toward me. I put my arms around her and held her tightly. "Annie," my voice broke, "do you know how long I have loved you? How long I've watched other guys with envy when they took you out? Why didn't you say something before?"

"I was afraid, Cole. So afraid you would laugh at me. I couldn't stand that."

I took her upturned face in my hands and kissed her. "I love you Annie. Lord, girl, how I love you."

Annie gave a little sigh as she laid her head on my chest. I don't know how long we stood holding each other. I knew all I wanted was to hold her like that for the rest of my life.

"Cole, do you realize if I hadn't said I love you, we could have gone on like that for the rest of our lives?"

"No Annie, I don't think so. You see Grandfather told me a long time ago that things would work out. I guess I should have believed him," I said, hugging her to me again.

Finally I broke the spell. "We'd better go, your brother will probably be home by now."

Laughing she reached up and kissed me once more then got into the pickup. It was with immense happiness that the old truck bounced out of the side road and onto the main route home. There on a rock beside the road, sat Freddy, hands folded waiting patiently.

That winter we had a lot of good elk steaks and all because of one girl wanting to prove she was as good as another. Annie was and always would be head and shoulders above any girl. And best of all, she was mine forever.

That season Freddy and I did our best to bag an elk to save face at school but the hunting season ended in December with both of us just taking deer. Annie never bragged about her bull elk. She didn't have to. I did enough bragging for her.

Chapter 9

The first weekend in December our families got together to go for Christmas trees. Freddy and I helped Grandfather hitch the draft horses to a large sled we used for hauling hay to the cattle in the winter. While the women packed a picnic lunch, Dad and Mr. Gray made sure the axes and saws were sharp and necessities were loaded. When all was ready, we climbed aboard.

Grandfather took the reins then making a clucking sound, the sled gave a lurch and we were off. The adults were in the front while Freddy, Annie and I sat in the back, dangling our feet and legs off the end as we had done for so many years.

The horses climbed up the road that Pop and Grandfather had built while logging Skinner's meadow. With the exception of a few tall, thin lodgepole pines heavy with snow, bending over in the road, it was clear sledding. Grandfather would stop the horses long enough for us boys to run up front and knock the snow off the bent-over trees, so the horses and the grown-ups wouldn't get wet from snow falling on them as the trees sprang back upright.

Mom and Mrs. Gray started singing Christmas carols, and it didn't take long before we joined in. Every once in awhile Freddy and I would sing off key and Annie would look at us and roll her eyes. She had a beautiful voice, and many times we'd all sing a little quieter just to hear her. We sang every song we could think of, even though some weren't Christmas songs. But no one seemed to mind: we were having fun.

At last we came to Skinner's meadows, and while the women looked for that special tree, the guys got a fire going for the picnic. We unhitched the horses, and after hobbling them, turned them out in the meadow to paw up the grass that was under six inches of snow. For the horses this was no problem. Raised in the northwest Montana, snow was a normal part of their lives.

After a huge picnic of fried chicken, potato salad and fresh bread, with home made butter and strawberry jam, I topped off lunch with a piece of Annie's pie, then settled down to take a nap. Lying in the front of the sled with my eyes closed, I was brought back to the land of the living by a bunch of snow dropped into my face. I instantly sat up to find Annie laughing, her blue eyes sparkling with mischief as she quickly backed away.

It was not to be forgiven. I bounded over the side of the sled, catching her by surprise. With a scream, she tore away from my light grasp and bolted for the protection of the other women, who separated with squeals of laughter. Picking Annie up, I carried her out into the meadow with all eyes watching and laughter resounding from one end to the other. Laying her down in the snow, I picked up a hand-full of the fluffy white stuff and held it above her head.

"No! Mercy!" Annie screamed as she laughed uncontrollably. "I'll be good. I promise."

I let her up and turning to the crowd, said, "This is the way we gentlemen act," and bowed gallantly.

"And this is the way we repay you," Annie said as she dumped another handful of snow down my back.

Everyone roared with laughter as I screamed. Annie took off, laughing hysterically.

"Daddy! Protect me, I'm your little girl!" she screamed as she held onto his arm, hiding behind him and giggling with glee.

"You're safe for now, but you have to leave your daddy sooner or later," I said, grinning as I shook my finger at her.

The day turned warm around one o'clock and we took off our coats to enjoy the sunshine. This time of the year can be beautiful, but this afternoon was exceptional.

I asked Annie if she would like to go for a walk with me and check on the horses. She grabbed her coat and we told our folks we'd be back in a little while. Freddy gave me a funny look but didn't offer to come along, I was glad; I wanted to be alone with Annie. She put her arm in mine, and we walked the meadow from one end to the other, with her stopping to look around every few minutes. She looked radiant and I couldn't take my eyes off her.

"It's so beautiful. I'd love to have a home here some day." Annie said. "Maybe when you're a famous writer we'll build one. What do you think?"

"I'd love to build a home here for you Annie." Stopping I turned her toward me. "I have something I what to give you." I took my class ring off and held it out to her. When she saw the ring, she grabbed me and began to cry.

"I love you, Morgan," she said, wiping her eyes with the back of her hand, "Thank you!" she held the ring up admiring it as if it were a large diamond instead of a class ring. "I've always loved you. When we first met and I gave you my swing, I loved you even then. She drew me close, and we kissed long and passionately. I could feel her heart beating rapidly, and with each moment mine promised to come out of my chest. Time seemed to be suspended as we held each other. I hated to let her go.

She pulled back and looked into my eyes. "Cole, tell me we're forever, I want to hear you say it."

"Annie, our love is forever. I'm speaking from my heart when I say that. I'll love you forever. When you're out of school, we'll get married and we'll never be apart again. We'd better get back before someone comes looking for us. I took her hand and we walked back to the picnic.

The rest of the afternoon seemed to fly. As the day drew to a close, we cut down our Christmas trees, then bundled them in ropes to keep from damaging the limbs. As we got ready to reload everything, I finally saw an opportunity to get even with Annie. She was busy helping pack the picnic supplies and wasn't watching me as I helped hitch up the horses. I caught Freddy's eye and winked. He knew something was up and watched intently as I worked my way over toward the women.

Annie had on an attractive sweater with an open neckline, perfect for a handful of snow. Grabbing a handful of snow. I was upon her and dropped it down her neck. Annie shrieked and grabbed the front of her sweater. Everyone laughed as she tried to shed the snow without exposing herself. I on the other hand had a bird's eye view, and I must admit my heart skipped a beat or two.

On the way home Annie lay her head on my shoulder. I could smell the freshness of her hair and skin. She had hold of my right arm with both her hands and every once in awhile she lovingly stroked my arm with her fingers. If ever there was peace and contentment on this earth, I was feeling it now. "Thank you, Lord, for this wonderful day."

The next morning I woke up about four thirty and went into the kitchen where Grandfather was. He looked up from a book.

"Good morning, Grandfather," I said, trying not to show much expression. "I couldn't sleep, so I thought I'd see if you were up."

"Get some coffee and we'll talk," he said. Grandfather waited, puffing on his pipe slowly.

"I had a strange dream," I said, as I sat down.

He waited, smoke from his pipe curling toward the ceiling.

"I dreamed I was flying on the back of a dragonfly that was shooting dark colored arrows at an ant hill. I had reins and was making the dragonfly hover over the ants."

"How did you feel about this?" Grandfather asked.

"I don't know. I don't think I liked it. A look of sadness touched his face for a moment. He was silent as he waited for me to go on.
I took a sip of coffee, then, setting it down carefully, continued. "One of the ants shot an arrow back, and the dragonfly fell from the sky. I wasn't hurt or anything, but I didn't like it. I woke up and couldn't go back to sleep."

"You're too young to worry about dreams, Cole. Best go back to bed and get some rest, my son. We have work ahead of us in the morning.

I went to bed but couldn't get to sleep. The dream kept going over and over in my mind. Grandfather had told me that I was too young to worry about dreams, but that same day he made me a medicine bag, and told me never to be without it.

"Do I have to keep it around my neck?" I asked.

"That's why the white man has pockets," he had said, his eyes twinkling, "Nothing can defeat you with your medicine close by. But remember, even though you cannot be defeated, you can be killed."

That morning at the breakfast table, Grandfather looked at me. "Cows are getting out onto Forest Service land. We best look for a hole in the fence, Son."

After breakfast we grabbed gloves and a saw in case a tree had fallen across the fence. Taking the jeep, we drove the fence line watching for a break in the wire.

It was a perfect time to talk to grandfather, and he seemed to be waiting for me to start the conversation. That was one thing that made it so easy to talk with this wise old man. He was patient beyond all understanding.

"Grandfather?" I started, as we neared the upper fence line.

"Yes, Cole," he answered quietly, without looking at me.

"You know how Annie and I feel about each other," I said, not knowing quite how to start.

"I think I do," he said without looking at me.

"You think we're too young to get married?"

"According to the white man's customs or the Indian's customs? I don't know which half you're asking." He looked at me and smiled.

"I'm asking your heart, Grandfather," I said.

His smile disappeared, and he looked at me for a long moment. "How do you and Annie feel?"

"I love her very much. She loves me the same way. We don't like being apart," I said, holding his eye as I spoke. This, he always respected.

"I'm pleased at this," he finally said. "Since you two were little, perhaps even before time, you have belonged together."

"In a couple months I'm through with high school, but Annie has two more years. I want to marry her right now, but we're too young according to law."

"Yes, according to the law, you can't marry until you're of age."

"Grandfather, you are the grandson of a chief, aren't you?" I blurted out.

"No, a medicine man," he said, his face impassive.

"You have the rights of a tribal elder?"

"To some."

"Just supposing you could marry us, would you do it? What would we have to do? I mean, just supposing?"

"Unless you wanted a renegade wedding, you would both have to get your families' approval. If I were to marry you two under any other than the right circumstances, I would have to move out of the house and into the mountains. I'm pretty old for that," he said solemnly.

So much for that, I thought.

"Son, even though you love Annie, and I do believe you two are meant to be together, there is more to marriage than just a ceremony. How would you support her? Where would you live?"

"I know what you're saying Grandfather. It's just that I love her so much and I want to be with her forever," I said.

"Sometimes Cole, we have to put aside our wants and wait until the circumstances are right. You need to start life together under the right conditions, otherwise you may not be happy."

"I know you're right, Grandfather. It's just that sometimes waiting is really hard to do."

"There's the problem," he said as he pointed at a tree that had blown across the fence. Within minutes we had it cut and the fence wire stapled back to the post.

"Your time will come, Son. Just be patient," he said as we drove back down the mountain and into the ranch.

Chapter 10

After graduation I knuckled down and went to work for Dad in the logging business. That August Annie and her mother went to Oregon to visit Mrs. Gray's mother, who hadn't been well lately.

Freddy and I had been cutting firewood out behind the barn. Between the two of us we had cut almost enough to heat both houses through the winter. Another half a day would do it. I checked my watch, then spoke to Freddy. "What do you say to taking a break? Mom made a pie, maybe we can talk her out of a chunk."

I pulled off my gloves as we walked toward the house, passing behind the barn where we'd set up straw bales with a target for archery practice.

"For a quarter," Freddy said, drawing his hunting knife.

"You're on," I said, reaching for mine.

Freddy and I were always competing, betting on who could out-shoot or out-throw the other with knives, hatchets, bows and guns.

"After you," I said. "You thought of it; you throw first." The distance was about twenty-five feet.

"Piece of cake," he said and threw. The knife flew true, sticking about seven inches below the center of the bull's-eye. "Beat that!"

Flipping my knife up in the air and catching it by the blade, I drew back and with all my concentration, threw. It was a well-balanced knife and flew straight as an arrow. It stuck a half an inch below the bull's-eye.

"Lucky throw," Freddy said.

"You owe me a buck," I said, looking at our knives.

"A quarter, you lying bastard," he said as he walked over and pulled his knife from the target, "Damn, you cheat."

I grinned at him as I pulled my knife out. "You're a bad influence on me. Come on, I'll give you a chance to get even later." We sheathed our knives and walked on to the house.

As we entered the kitchen, Mom looked up from her work. "I'm getting a little worried about your grandfather, Cole. He should have been back from the cabin by now."

"Why is that?" I asked.

"He said he was only going to stay a couple of days. He was due in last night. You know him; he's always on time."

"Maybe he had car trouble," Freddy said.

"Maybe, I don't know. But if he isn't back by noon, I'd appreciate you boys driving up to the lake to check on him. He's getting old. A tree might have blown down across the road or something," Mom said.

I checked my watch; it was ten-thirty.

"We can take old Blue," Freddy said.

Old Blue was Freddy's pickup. We'd rebuilt the engine in it, and she could flat move.

"You boys don't go driving fast. I don't need more worries," Mom added noticing my grin. She poured Freddy and me some coffee and cut each of us a healthy piece of coconut cream pie.

By eleven we were ready to go back to work. As Freddy and I walked back toward the barn, a large raven flew up and sat on a fence post, looking at us. We walked toward it, seeing how close we could get. When we were about ten feet from the raven, I stopped.

"Something's wrong here," I said. "He should have flown by now."

The raven stared at us for a moment, then with a raspy voice the mountain raven called to us. After a pause of perhaps ten seconds the bird jumped into the air and flew north, calling to us once more with its raspy deep throated, "Caw."

I turned to Freddy, panic welling inside me. "Let's go."

"You got it," he answered, and we started back for the house.

"Let's not worry Mom," I said, opening the door. As we came into the kitchen she looked up from her work.

"Don't tell me you boys are still hungry," she said.

"Naw, not for at least another hour. Actually, we thought we'd go on up to the lake and check on Grandfather, Mom. We're bored."

"I think that's a good idea, just drive careful," she said.

We drove the same route that Grandfather always took in hopes of meeting him driving home. Turning off the main highway, we started the last leg of the trip to Whisper Lake.

"Hey, Cole, where you at?" Freddy broke the silence.

"Huh? Sorry, I don't know. I feel something. I don't understand what," I said.

Freddy looked over at me as he drove. "What?"

"I can't explain it. It's almost like Grandfather's thinking about me. Like he's talking to me. I don't know what it is, but something is different or …" my voice trailed off.

"Hope he's okay," Freddy said in a low voice.

"Yeah, me too," I was really starting to get worried

We turned onto the side road that leads to where we had to park; the last quarter of a mile to the cabin would be on foot. We stopped the pickup beside Grandfather's old Jeep. As we started up the trail Freddy grabbed my shoulder. "Cole?"

"I see him," I answered as we both stared at a raven sitting in the trail not more than twenty yards away.

"I don't like the looks of this," Freddy whispered.

"Nor I, my friend," I said as my stomach tightened. "Come on."

The raven took to the air and flew up the trail leading to the lake. Following him, we finally rounded the last bend and spotted the cabin. As I approached the steps of the porch, I was full of dread. I called out, "Grandfather!" and opened the door. I could see at a glance, it was empty. It had been cleaned and the bed was made, which was my grandfather's way.

Freddy and I exchanged silent looks as we went back outside. We took a different direction and searched around the cabin.

"See anything?" I asked.

"Nothing."

"Let's check the other side of the lake. He has to be around here somewhere," I said, then I cupped my hands to my mouth and called out, "Grandfather!"

A large raven flew from the top of a tree where he had been perched. I could only assume it was the same one we had followed on the trail. The black form flew toward the west end of the lake, cawing loudly. I stared at it for a moment, then turned to Freddy.

"Grab a couple paddles out of the cabin," I called to him, turning and running to where we stored the canoe up against the side of the cabin. As I drug the canoe toward the lake, Freddy returned with the paddles and dropped them in the craft, then helped me pull the canoe to the water.

He climbed into the front. Placing one foot in the canoe, I shoved us off. The vessel drifted quietly out into the lake. Taking a seat, we began paddling toward the far end, watching for anything on the trail.

My heart sank as we neared the other end. I could see Grandfather sitting on the ground, leaned back against a ring of wood we had cut and rolled down to the apple trees near my grandmother's grave. Grandfather had sat under those trees many times while visiting with his lady.

As we headed for shore, Grandfather turned his head and smiled the smile that had soothed our souls so many times in our childhood.

Freddy hopped out of the canoe and drug it onto the shore. We approached with apprehension, keeping our eyes on Grandfather. There was a strange and powerful feeling in the area around him. Freddy and I both sensed it.

"Grandfather, we were getting worried," I said in a quiet voice.

He smiled at us. "I sent a messenger to you, my son. Did you not see my messenger?"

"We saw a raven on the fence post. Is that what you mean?" Freddy asked in a whisper.

"It was my messenger that you saw."

I bent down to help him up. "Grandfather, let us help you home. Mom is worried."

His hand came up in a sign to hold still and listen. "It's my time. I have heard the voices of our ancestors and have spoken to the Great Spirit and my lady. She waits for me. His eyes closed and he took an irregular breath. "This will be hard for your mother, Cole. I'm glad Annie isn't here." He gasped, then signed for me to come close. "Listen, I'm going to leave you soon. Son, you'll find life's path hard at times. I wish ..." his breathing labored, he struggled trying to speak. " I could say it'll always be a good path, but it won't. Cole, always get back to your feet, no matter what happens." He spoke in a whisper then squeezed my arm weakly as if to emphasize what he was saying, "Always get back up, son. Life can't defeat you. You are strong. You have the blood of many wise and great people." He took another ragged breath, then looked at me. "Your destiny is before you. Fulfill it. There will be times ..." he paused struggling, "you will doubt yourself. You are stronger than you know." He closed his eyes as a grimace crossed his face. "They can kill you, my son, but they can never defeat you. Only you can defeat yourself."

"Grandfather don't talk. We'll get you home," I said, knowing in my heart it was too late.

"I am home. Cole, hear me," he said with urgency, as a ragged breath escaped his lips. "A time will come ... sorrow will be your companion. You must ... defeat it. Steel is forged in the fire," a light flashed in his eyes of many battles fought and won, then they dulled again.

"My son," Grandfather said, turning his slowly fading eyes to Freddy, "you and Cole ... brothers ... need each other. Remember. Paths ... separate, but will meet again." His eyes closed as if resting, then again he looked at Freddy, "always walk with God."

Looking back at me slowly, Grandfather spoke once more. I had to place my ear to his mouth. "Cole, remember ... teachings of our people. They will come, as you need them. Be strong, always, my son."

Grandfather's look became very far away and a tear formed in the corner of his eye, something I had never seen before. Then a faint smile crossed his lips, he held his hand out in front of him as if to take someone's hand. "The wind is calling," he whispered hoarsely to no one. At that moment there was a high wind that rustled the trees tops and his hand went limp. My grandfather died to this world we live in. Wind Racer, the name his people called him in his youth, once again was free to run with the wind.

From the woods two ravens flew toward each other, circling, calling excitedly. The large black birds rose freely on the air currents. Their wings touched as they turned toward the mountains. Freddy and I looked at them, then back at this once mighty man. Grandfather looked at peace; he had finally joined his lady. He had waited fifty years for this moment, and it had at last come to pass. The last of the giants was gone.

"Sleep well, Grandfather," I whispered, tears running down my cheeks. "You will forever be in my heart."

Slowly I looked at Freddy and saw tears flowing freely. Turning, I walked to the edge of the lake. A hundred yards to the northeast was a point where the bank jutted out. I had fished there many times with my grandfather while we leaned back against the old pine tree. It stood, even though it was now dead. In my mind's eye I could see an old man and a boy lounging against that tree. The boy knew nothing of life's endings, only its foreverness. He laughed at something that was said and the old man reached out a hand, rumpling the boy's hair and smiled.

A deep pang of sorrow gripped my chest as I realized a special part of my life had just ended. I had taken him so much for granted. Life is supposed to be eternal when we're young. This day I had been forced to realize my mortality and face life as a man.

Freddy walked up from behind and took my shoulders in his grasp, squeezing them gently. "I'm sorry, Cole. You've lost your grandfather, and we have all lost a great man. He was a grandfather to me and Annie also, Brother." He added after a moment of silence, "I'll cut some poles and we can make a litter."

I nodded my head. "I'll be okay, it's just going to take some time. Come on, I'll give you a hand."

We lifted Grandfather onto the litter and with heavy hearts we placed him in the canoe.

Silently, we paddled back to the cabin. As we started out to the truck with the litter, we stopped to check the cabin before closing it. Grandfather knew his time had come and had deliberately walked around the lake to my grandmother's grave and sat waiting for the wind to visit him. He had said the wind gave you breath and the wind took it back. It was hard to believe we would never again listen to his stories or hear his wisdom.

After a silent walk out to the parking area, we tenderly placed him in the back of the truck, and I placed my folded coat under his head. We heard the wind howl through the trees, and knew grandfather was racing the wind once more, for was he not Wind Racer?

The rest of the trip out was done without a stop, without a word. Both of us were lost in our own thoughts and memories.

Annie and Mrs. Gray were not present for the funeral. I was a relieved. Having to deal with Mom's grief was more than I thought I could bear.

We buried Grandfather beside his beloved wife, at Whisper Lake. I stayed for a week by myself at the cabin to sort out life and its true meaning, if there is such.

I returned home to find life had taken on a certain quietness. Grandfather's absence was overwhelming.

Chapter 11

That summer brought many changes into our lives. One day while fixing a gate behind the barn, I glanced up and saw Freddy's pickup pull up. He had a piece of paper in his hand as he got out of the truck.

"Love letter?" I ask playfully.

"Yeah, they want my body," he said and handed it to me.

"Shit," I said, looking at the draft notice, "I'll be getting one anytime too, I suppose."

"Let's go get a beer. Army boy's buying."

"You got it," I said, putting the tools in the back of my truck. "Didn't want to fix this damned gate anyway. Your folks know yet?" I asked as we drove toward town.

"No, I just checked the mail. You're the first person I've told. Can't you see me marching along looking for girls?" he said and grinned, "I hear chicks dig uniforms."

"Yeah, that's what I hear," I said without much enthusiasm.

We sat at a table in the back of Al's Bar. We were both feeling pretty low. I couldn't imagine going hunting this fall without Freddy.

"Set us up again, Al," Freddy called to the owner.

Raising a hand to show he had heard, Al opened another two bottles of beer.

"Think they'll have this over there?" Freddy asked, holding up his fresh brew.

"Demand it or don't go. Hell, a couple more of these and I might go in with you."

"You mean it?"

"Yep, I mean it, pal," I said, starting to feel the beer.

"What about Annie?"

"Better to get it over with than get married and have to leave her," I said, not sure I meant it. But as I thought about it, enlisting made perfect sense.

We drained our bottles and started feeling a lot better about everything. It's amazing what a few beers do to one's spirits.

"Another beer?" I asked Freddy.

"Yeah, I'm thirsty. Hey, Al, two more and some of those pepper sticks," he called out.

Freddy reached for his money but I put my hand on his arm. "My turn," I said, then added, "I wonder where the recruiting office is now. Someone said they moved it."

"Hey, Al, where's the recruiting office now?" Freddy asked as Al brought our beers and pepper sticks.

"Two blocks over, by the Post Office, I think. You guy's aren't thinking about enlisting are you? You nuts? Cole, you better take Fred home before you guys end up doing something you'll both regret. Let me buy you fellows a hamburger or something. Maybe you might think different with something beside beer on your stomach."

"We're fine, Al. Freddy got his draft notice in the mail today, and I'll probably get one too."

I held out a five for the beer and pepper sticks but Al pushed my hand away.

"On the house," he said, looking unhappy and walked slowly back to the bar.

Finishing our beers, we waved to Al and turned toward the door.

"Good luck, fellas," he called.

Later on that afternoon we drove back toward home, singing all the Army songs heard in old war movies. They didn't make any sense to us, but after the beers they sounded pretty good. Freddy and I had enlisted together. We were supposed to report in seven weeks. In step with our nature, we had signed up for helicopter flight school. The only hitch was, we had to sign up for four years. But what the hell, we were going to fly. No infantry for us! Army Aviators, that's what we were going to be called according to the recruiter as he pushed the papers toward us for our signatures.

"You excited?" Freddy asked, as he attempted to open a bottle of beer while driving.

"About your driving? You bet," I said and took hold of the steering wheel just in time to save the pickup from taking out a few small aspen trees growing in the ditch.

"No, about what we did?" Freddy said, taking control again.

"I think as the Army would say, we shit in our mess kits, personally," I said, then grinned. "Annie won't be too happy with me. You got to promise me you won't leave me alone with her when I tell her what we did. Promise?" My stomach tightened at the thought of what she was going to say. My parents were going to be bad enough, but Annie was going to hit the ceiling.

The beer had begun to leave my system and along with it all the brilliant ideas that I was known to have at times. The latest, being joining the Army with Freddy.

"I'll stick with you. Besides, you're the man; you're the boss. Of course, it's Annie we're talking about. That puts a whole different spin on the ball," he trailed off.

"I'm so glad we had this talk, Fred. I feel so much worse." I was getting ready to meet my death by the tongue of the woman I loved.

"I'm in deep shit, Fred. I need another beer. No, I need another case of beer," I said and reached down to the floorboard, grabbing another brew.

Why hadn't I thought more about how Annie would feel before I had signed on the dotted line. Oh, I hadn't sworn an oath yet, but going this far, I knew the Army would have my name even if I backed out. I was screwed. As we approached our ranch I told Freddy to drive on by and head for his place. I might as well start at the top and get the worst over with first. The rest would be easy compared to what was waiting behind door number one.

We pulled into the Gray's driveway and sat in the truck for about five minutes working up the nerve to go in and face the firing squad. Finally I reached for the door handle and opened it. "Let's do it."

"She's going to have your nuts," Freddy said, giving me his famous grin. "Just think, I won't be able to call you my nutty buddy."

"Always a smart-ass in every crowd."

As we came into the house, we saw Annie and her folks sitting in the living room. Mr. Gray was reading his paper. Annie and her mother were working on a quilt.

"You're not supposed to see this yet," Annie said, smiling at me. "It's supposed to be a surprise."

She got up and gave me a kiss. Then gave me a serious look. "Good beer?" she asked, smelling my breath then looking at Freddy. "How many?"

"Lots," Freddy said, reaching into his pocket and taking out the now tattered draft notice, which he immediately handed to his dad.

"Damn." Mr. Gray exclaimed. "Damn it all anyway."

Mrs. Gray got up and came over to where he was sitting. Taking the notice, she looked and immediately put her hand up to her mouth to stifle a cry. Her eyes became tearful. "Dear God, no!" she said, slowly shaking her head.

"What is it?" Annie asked. Taking the notice out of her mother's hand, Annie read it out loud at first, but her voice became fainter as she read on, until at last she read to herself.

"Oh, Freddy." she said. "Oh, Freddy," she repeated as she walked over and put her arms around his neck.

"Hey it isn't all bad. We got the jump on them."

"What do you mean by we?" Annie said, her eyes growing bigger.

Freddy turned to me so I could tell my part about how we got the best of the Army. How many times down through the years had we played this game when we were in trouble.

Thanks, Freddy, I thought. "Yeah," I stammered, "We went to the Army recruiter's office and enlisted as aviators. Helicopter flight school."

"You what?" Annie said, "You did what?"

"Now Sis, it's the best way to go. Cole was next on the list."

"You did what, Cole?" she said, ignoring Freddy. "Tell me you're joking, please say you're joking."

Tears formed then ran down her cheeks, her lower lip trembled. Mrs. Gray held Annie and helped her sit down on the couch.

Annie wilted. "No!" she said between sobs, shaking her head. "No, I don't believe this! Cole, how could you?"

Mrs. Gray took Annie in her arms and began rocking with her, all the time murmuring as if to a child.

"I'd better be getting on home," I said, feeling helpless, "My folks will want to know."

As I turned toward the door, Annie came to me.

"I'll go with you, Cole. We'll be back later," she announced to her family, tears still flowing down her cheeks as fast as she wiped them away. She turned and walked out in front of me.

"She'll need a lot of love and understanding, Cole," Mrs. Gray said to me as I started out the door. "She loves you more than life itself."

Mr. Gray said nothing but had gotten up and walked to the door with Mrs. Gray.

"You want me to go with you, Cole?" Freddy asked.

"No, I'll be okay. Thanks for offering though," I said, "I'll see you tomorrow."

As I got into the car, Annie sat behind the wheel looking straight ahead. "I still can't believe you did this, Cole," she said, wiping her eyes with the back of her hand. "You and Freddy not being here. You not being here. What am I going to do? You know where they'll send you, don't you? They'll send you to Vietnam. They'll be shooting at you." She broke down again, only this time she leaned over and put her head on my chest, sobbing her heart out. "It's not too late, Cole. Let's run away. We can go to Canada. They'll let us live up there. We could get married, and I'll finish school there. Please, Cole, before it's too late."

What a fool I had been. In a moment of stupidity I had hurt the person I loved most. "Annie, I can't cut and run even if I wanted to, you know that. Believe me, down deep I do want to for your sake, but I would be going against everything I stand for. I can't break my word, besides I would be a deserter," I said feeling a conflict between my love for Annie and my honor. "Annie I love you with all my heart, but some things a man has to do when he says he will. You wouldn't want me any other way, would you?" I put my hand under her chin, lifting her head until her eyes met mine.

More sobs wracked her. "If something happens to you, I'll ..." her voice trailed off as she cried as if her heart were broken.

"Nothing is going to happen, I promise. You know I wouldn't lie to you, Annie. I promise that I'll always come back to you. You have my word. Look at me. It's my word of honor. I'll come back to you. You've got to believe that, okay? Now let's go. I've got to tell my folks," I said with as much determination as I could muster. "You're in no condition to drive. Why don't you let me."

"Okay."

As we pulled into our driveway Annie sat in the passenger's side crying quietly. "Wait, give me a minute, okay? I don't want them to see me crying."

"Okay, take your time." I watched as her chin came up in the determined way she had. As she wiped her eyes, I knew she was in control.

As we walked though the door, Mom and Pop looked up. They could see Annie had been crying. Pop got up and came toward us, "What's wrong, Annie?"

Mom came over and put her arm around Annie's shoulders. "Come over and sit with me, Dear," Mom said, leading Annie over to the couch.

"What's going on, Son?" Pop asked.

"Freddy got his draft notice today and instead of waiting, we joined up together," I blurted out.

"What? You did what?" Mom said as if she hadn't heard right.

Pop gave me one of his looks.

"You did this to Annie and your family?" Mom asked, looking like she was going to cry. I knew that if she started we'd have both women crying at once.

Pop's expression went to total confusion. I could see he was trying to think of something he could say without starting the women off on a weeping spree. Finally he shook his head, realizing it would be a losing battle. "Want a cup of coffee?" he asked, rising from his easy chair.

"Yeah," I was glad to get away from the women for awhile. Listening to women cry was not something I could tolerate well, especially knowing I'd caused it.

I explained to Pop that Freddy and I had the opportunity to go to helicopter flight school. "It's kind of a long shot, but it sure beats the hell out of where they'd stick us if we waited to be drafted. Besides, you know how we both like to fly."

Pop chuckled. "Yeah, you boys have tried several times to kill yourselves with flying contraptions." He shook his head, a far away look in his eyes. "You'll do fine, Son. We're going to miss you two like hell around here. Your Grandfather is gone and now you'll be leaving. Damn!" He said, shaking his head in amazement. "I guess that's the way things go when you start growing old. What about Annie?"

"I'm going to ask Mr. Gray if we can get married. Nothing fancy, just get married."

"What do you think he'll say?" Pop asked.

I shrugged. "I don't see anything wrong. We're kind of young, but considering the circumstances …" I trailed off. "What do you think he'll say?"

"I don't know, Son. You know him as well as I do."

"Just talk to him man to man. What's the worst thing he can say … no? Things will work themselves out. You got to trust your own judgment, Cole. Go to John and tell him how you feel. Talk to him when you two are alone. It's hard to talk about these things when there are women around. Besides, you don't want to back him into a corner."

"Okay. I'll talk to him. Maybe help him when he goes to do the chores tonight."

Pop gave a nod.

That evening I walked out of the Gray's house with John and Freddy. As we headed for the barn, Freddy gave me a look that said he understood something was in the wind. I jerked my head back toward the house, indicating to him that I wanted him to leave his dad and me alone.

"I forgot my gloves," Freddy said. "Back in a flash."

Good old Freddy. He always seemed to know when to do the wrong thing and occasionally the right thing, like now.

"Mr. Gray, I want to ask you something," I blurted, unsure of how to approach the subject. "Me and Freddy are going into the service in a few weeks." Shit, that was a far gone conclusion. Already I sounded stupid. "Well, I was wondering how you'd feel about Annie and me getting married?" There, I had said it.

Mr. Gray stood with his back up against the old John Deere tractor wheel. He put his heel on the rim of the tire as he looked at me with a steady gaze.

"I have nothing against you and my daughter getting married, Cole. I think of you like one of my own. But I will not have Annie getting married until she is out of school. Besides, she's to young … you both are."

"But I'll be in the service; I can take care of her."

"It's not a matter of you being able to take care of her, Cole. I know what's probably in store for you and Freddy. The war in Asia is full tilt. You boys will complete your training and end up over there. I don't want my little girl winding up a widow. It would be bad enough to lose one of you boys, but to compound it with my little girl becoming a widow is something I won't let happen. I know how you kids feel about each other, but you should have thought this thing out before you enlisted. You're the one to blame, Cole. You made a choice without thinking of the consequences. Now you'll have to wait until you come back from the service."

With that, Mr. Gray turned and started for the barn.

"But I love Annie and she loves me."

Mr. Gray turned and looked at me. I could see he was getting angry. " Cole, I won't banter with you about this, damn it. That's my decision and I'm not going to change my mind. Damn it to hell, Cole, I will not have Annie ending up a widow, maybe with a child on the way. What kind of a father would I be if I let that happen? You should have thought boy. Now this conversation is ended."

I knew there was no sense in arguing. Mr. Gray was like Pop, once he had said his peace, neither hell nor high water would change his mind. My heart sank as I saw Freddy approaching. He knew from my look that things had not gone well.

Chapter 12

"I want to go to the cabin, Cole," Annie said one day. "Let's go for a week. You can teach me to fish."

"You already know how to fish."

"Daddy's going to Billings for a livestock auction and to look over some breeding stock at a couple of ranches. He'll be gone at least ten days, and Mom's going to go with him. Cole, we could get married while they're gone."

"I already thought about us getting married without his permission. What would happen if they found out. Your dad would probably make a steer out of me. One last act as a whole man. The Army sounds better all the time," I said, looking at her. "Besides, we're not old enough."

"Freddy and I were talking. He knows how Daddy feels about us getting married. When I brought up Grandfather and what he said about how young Indian couples got married without permission, Freddy said we should do that. What do you think? We could go up to the lake and have a whole week together. I've thought about it a lot, Cole. I think it would be a great way to get married. It would be like when Grandfather and your grandmother got married there. Don't you see? It would be better than any other kind of ceremony. Think how romantic it would be? We could go right after Mom and Daddy leave. We'd have a whole week together!"

By the time she finished her speech, I was excited too. I saw those big beautiful blue eyes welling up with tears of happiness. She knew I was going to say yes. How could I have said anything else? Annie was all I lived for.

Quietly making arrangements for the trip to Whisper Lake, we packed. The next day Annie's parents left for Billings, which is clear over on the eastern side of Montana, hundreds of miles away. As soon as the dust settled, we met at Annie's house and loaded her things into the back of my pickup. Then with a hug from both of us, Freddy gave the thumbs up sign as I pulled out of the driveway.

We drove north, two very excited young people. My heart beat wildly with a mixture of fear and excitement. Annie ran over all our plans, making sure we had what we needed to get married. My grandfather's people had certain protocol and we couldn't overlook anything if we were going to do this right. I was glad she remembered all the procedures. She didn't realize she was in charge. If she had sounded retreat, I'd never have said a word, just turned the truck around and headed home.

"You wouldn't consider continuing on to Canada, would you?" she asked as we reached the road leading up the North Fork.

"Now don't start that again."

She was quiet for several miles.

My mind turned to what I was facing, and I wondered if I had done the right thing by joining the Army. Freddy was my best friend, next to Annie. I couldn't let him go without me. Best friends don't desert when the going gets tough. All for one. We believed in it, even if it was bullshit to others. Annie, Freddy and I were the Three Musketeers. We were in this world together to the end. I reached over and took hold of Annie's hand.

"I love you, Cole,"

"I love you, too," I whispered back. "Annie, do you understand why I did what I did? We stand or fall together. Freddy needs to know that he's never alone. You will be watched over by our families. I'm going to watch over my brother, and he'll watch out for me. We're going to be fine, Annie. This I promise you. Nobody is going to get the best of us Montana boys.

Around noon we came to the end of the road that led to Whisper Lake. We parked and got our backpacks out of the back of the truck.

"Someday I'm going to hide a wheelbarrow in the brush. It sure would beat packing everything on our backs," I said, shouldering the heavier things we'd brought.

Taking our time, we started up the trail. We were in no hurry as the sun was shining through the tree, making shadow figures on the trail. A grouse flew up from its cover in the bushes, and blue jays scolded us from above. As always, we were enraptured with the beauty of the mountains. Before long we arrived at the lake. The water gleamed with the reflections of the sun through the trees and bushes that surrounded the shore. There was a peaceful feeling here that pulled and kneaded at the very foundation of your soul until all unhappy thoughts vanished.

Pulling off her shoes, Annie waded into the lake. "You want to go swimming, Cole?"

"Not right now, I have work to do before dark. Don't stray too far, I'm going to need some help."

"Gee, Daddy, can't I go play?" she mocked.

I shook my head and grinned at her. We had the cabin set up in no time and Annie busied herself setting a lunch out on the picnic table. "Isn't it beautiful here, Cole?"

"Yup, it's nice," I answered, looking out on the lake. "Wonder if the fish are biting?"

"Fish? You came up here to fish? I'm wondering what to wear for our wedding."

I cuddled her to my chest, letting my eyes roam around the area. Over to the south side of the cabin was the old canoe. It lay upside down, propped against the wall. Pine needles covered the bottom of the canoe as it silently waited for someone to drag it down to the lake, as we had done so many times in the years past.

Giving Annie a squeeze, I released her. Walking into the cabin I found the paddles and taking them went outside and pulled the canoe down to the lake, pushing one end into the water. Now we were in business. All that was lacking were the fishing poles and tackle box. The poles hung on a wall in the cabin to the left of the door. I paused. Grandfather's pole hung just above Pop's and mine on the third set of nail pegs. One day my children's poles would hang there too.

Taking a couple of poles and the tackle box down, I walked over to the table to examine the fishing tackle, getting it ready for the evening.

Annie was in the kitchen. "Honey, would you get me some more firewood. I'm fixing you a surprise. You're really going to like this, big guy," she said smiling broadly.

I went out and chopped an armload of wood and stacked it in the box beside the stove.

Annie put another piece of wood in the cookstove.

I sat straddling a chair with my hands resting on its back, watching her. A strand of hair keeps falling in her face, and she brushes it back with the back of her wrist. Annie chews on her lower lip when she is concentrating. Her movements are supple and sexy. My eyes are drawn to her breast and the slight cleavage just above the button on her blouse. My mind and body were beginning to join forces, thinking about tonight after we are married.

"What happens if the loon doesn't call?" she asked, looking concerned.

"I honestly don't know, Annie." I said feeling a sudden jolt. "We just have to trust in God." As far as I was concerned nothing would ever separate us but death and that wasn't going to happen for many, many years.

Getting married by the white man's law was out of the question, so I had made up my mind, with Mr. Gray's help of course, to wait until I returned to the states before marrying his daughter. That is until Annie talked me into doing this.

Getting married the old way would satisfy our need for a ceremony. I loved her deeply and she would be mine even if it was by the tradition of my grandfather's people. Grandfather had done his work well on me. I believed in the old Indian traditions and was proud of my heritage. At times I felt I was born a full blood, instead of just an eighth.

"Are you excited?" Annie asked eagerly.

"About what?" I answered, toying with her.

She punched me in the stomach. "Let's go right now." Annie said, her eyes shinning with excitement. "What do I wear?"

"You look great just the way you are, but the mosquitoes will probably think so too. Better change out of your cutoffs and put on a long sleeved shirt. Oh, don't forget a jacket. It gets cold up here after sundown. Grab one for me too will you." I opened the door and stepped onto the porch.

Turning, I called out to Annie, "You got everything we'll need?" "Yes I think so," she said holding out my hunting knife and a homemade scarf for me to see.

A raven flew onto a treetop and began cawing loudly as Annie handed me a jacket. She looked up and then back at me.

"Cole?" Annie said, squinting up as the raven flew into the sun. It landed in another tree as if waiting for us to follow.

"I don't know, Annie. Maybe," I said, shaking my head slowly. The raven called again then took flight up the canyon in the direction we were walking.

Several times Annie and I stopped to marvel at the beauty of our country. I almost regretted that we hadn't taken the canoe.

The end of the lake finally came into view. To the right, a meadow rolled out gently for a couple hundred feet before being swallowed by the trees. At the edge of the forest were the two old apple trees that marked the spot where my grandparents rested.

"Cole, it's so beautiful. I wish we could live up here."

"One day maybe we will, Annie," I said as I gathered some dry sticks to build a fire so we could roast a hot dog. I had looked forward to a picnic and I was getting hungry.

"What are you doing?"

"I'm hungry. We can have a hot dog, I brought some for supper." I said, looking around to see if I could find a couple of hot dog sticks.

"How can you think of food at a time like this, Cole?"

"I'm hungry. We can't get married until almost sunset," I said sheepishly.

"You're thinking of your stomach at a time like this?" Annie asked. Then a dreamy look came over her face, like a child remembering. "We're getting married in the most sacred way we can. Grandfather said the white man's way is on paper with words spoken by people. The Indian way is to speak with our hearts to each other and to God. That's the way I want to be married. Someday we can be married in a church with a minister and all the trimmings, but today is our day and the day of your grandfather's people. I wish he were here with us right now. It's strange, in a way, I can almost feel him," she said, searching my eyes.

I forgot all about the hot dog and hugged her. As I was holding Annie, a loon called from across the lake and a raven flew up into the dead pine tree that stood on the lakeshore.

I checked the position of the sun and figured it was about three-thirty. The afternoon passed slowly. A couple of times I forgot myself and tried to get overly friendly with Annie, but she gracefully escaped my attempts.

"Not until we're married, my love. You can wait; you're a big boy."

That's when time began to stand still, and every five minutes I checked the sun. Finally as the shadows began to grow long, I turned to Annie.

"It's almost time."

We walked to the lake and after looking over the rock, walked up to where Grandmother and Grandfather were.

"Cole, do you suppose Grandfather knew this was going to happen? I mean, he was so careful to tell us everything in exact detail and the raven, it's his totem. You think that could have been him? He seemed to know so much."

"I don't know, Annie. Perhaps. When I was with him I've seen strange things in my short time." I thought of my grandfather's people and what we were about to do.

Turning, I spoke to my grandparent's resting place, feeling they could hear me.

"Grandfather, you married Grandmother on the wedding rock. Now I wish to marry Annie the same way. You married Grandmother first in a church; I don't have that option right now. I have agreed to marry Annie in a church after I return. Grandfather, I ask your blessing and a blessing from you, Grandmother. Even though you have been gone since before my time, I am sure you would approve of both Annie and me. I know Grandfather has told you about us and that you love us as we love you. Grandfather has always talked about you, and we know you were a great woman. Thank you for listening. Be now our witnesses."

I looked at Annie. Tears ran down her cheeks. She folded her arms, and sobbing quietly, turned and walked to the shoreline.

I walked down and stood silently beside her. Annie put one arm around my waist and drew me toward her. She was looking intently out at the rock.

"Look," Annie pointed her finger at the lake. "There're two loons," she said, wiping her eyes.

"Grandfather is kind of stacking the deck," I said smiling at her.

"Whatever it takes," she said, nodding her head in wonderment.

"Come on," I said, and taking Annie by the hand we waded out the few feet to the wedding rock.

I don't think either of us felt the cold water as we climbed onto the rock. Annie turned to me then reaching up with both hands, cupped my face. Then drawing me down, she kissed me passionately.

Taking her into my arms, I crushed that lovely body against me, feeling the breath go out of her.

Laughing, with tears of joy running down her cheeks, she spoke. "I want you to remember this desire for me tonight, Cole. All night," she whispered.

"All my life, my love, until the last breath has gone and then beyond. This I swear."

"And I, to you."

As we stood on the sacred rock, Annie bound our wrists together with the scarf and placed the knife in my hand, which was bound to hers.

Who would've thought the old knife that had been passed down to me by my father and my father's father, would play such an important part in my life? The knife now symbolized my part as protector and provider. We turned to face the setting sun, and holding hands, we listened for the loon to speak on behalf of the Great Spirit.

As the sun slipped behind the mountaintops, we stood with hearts pounding. All was silent as we faced the long shadows of sundown. The lake had taken on a stillness that was unusual for this time of the evening. It seemed as if the whole valley were listening for heaven to open.

Suddenly the cry of the loons shattered the silence, not just once, but more than I had ever heard before or probably ever will again. There was no question in our minds that God had spoken. Grandfather was right; this was mightier than all of the white man's words and paper.

Annie sobbed and turned to me, her cheeks wet with tears of happiness as she kissed me with all the passion she had.

"You're mine at last, my husband," she said looking up at me, "All mine. No church could have given me this. I wish our parents could have witnessed our marriage, Cole. It was an unbelievably beautiful experience. Darling, let's go home," Annie whispered.

I always hated the mushy talk women used, that is until this moment. This was one of the few times I didn't mind being call "darling." Rather I felt that it was the talk of a woman expressing her love. I was deeply moved.

"You are mine now and forever, Annie," I declared. "And forever is a long time."

I don't know how long we stood on the rock, but I eventually stepped down and turning, took my wife by the waist. I lifted her gently from the rock and carried her to the shore, which was but a few feet away. Gently I set her down on the grass.

Annie's eyes never for a second left mine as I lowered her to the ground, nor did she stop the tears of joy. I knew she couldn't have been happier if we had been wed in the biggest chapel in Montana. When I thought about it, I guess we had been.

"Forever," she whispered, as her eyes turned to the heavens. "Dear God, I promise, forever. Thank you, Lord Jesus."

We returned to our cabin an hour after dark. I built a campfire down by the lake while Annie fixed our evening meal.

"Annie?"

"Yes, dear."

"Dear?" Yeah, I like that, I thought. "You want to have dinner out here on the picnic table?"

"Too many bugs. I set the table in here," she said through the screen door.

"I think you'll like the sounds out here better than in the cabin," I called back.

"Why?"

"Come here and listen, Annie." I said quietly.

As she stepped from the cabin to listen, a symphony of loons continued their evening serenade.

"They sound so lonely." She was quiet for a moment. "I'll bring our supper out here." She turned and went into the cabin, reappearing with our meal.

"This is our first meal married, Cole. Would you say the blessing? We have so much to be thankful for."

We bowed our heads and with a grateful heart, I thanked God for this wonderful woman whom I had wed in the ways of my grandfather's people. I was ever so grateful for this gift.

We listened to the sounds of the night, and I felt at peace with the world as we set at the picnic table. The campfire crackled and popped, with sparks jumping into the night air like moving stars. An occasional wisp of smoke drifted our way as the night air shifted directions.

We sat and talked about our future. I would go through the service. When I returned, we would have a church wedding to satisfy everyone. Then we'd go on to the University at Bozeman in central Montana, where I would become a writer.

"You will keep up your writing in the Army, won't you? I don't want you to stop, Cole."

"I don't think I'll have time for much other than writing to you and the folks."

We sat silently, staring at the flames, each occupied with our own thoughts. I put my arm around her while we listened to the sounds of the night. Coyotes had joined the loons in a moonlight serenade. The wild dogs were all tuned up, and the young ones were trying to out-do each other.

"That's your totem we're listening to, Cole. Every time I hear the coyotes I think of Grandfather giving us our totems," Annie said as she stared into the fire, smiling faintly.

Around eleven that night Annie got up from where we had been sitting and headed for the cabin. "Give me a minute or two, then come in," she said, sounding a little nervous.

I watched her step into the cabin, ready that instant to follow. After what seemed like hours, I heard her call softly to me. With heart pounding, I reached for the screen door. As I stepped inside, the last sound I heard was the loons. Annie sat on the bed in her nightgown. She anxiously searched my face for approval.

My eyes traveled down her form ever so slowly until they came to her breasts. I swallowed, unable to move, my breathing becoming labored. The candlelight silhouetted her, whether intended or not, I never knew. Looking at her shape with the light like it was, I could see her breasts under the pale translucent gown she wore. My eyes continued down the lovely body before me, to a waist that was emphasized by well-shaped hips. Annie sat with her legs curled beneath her on the bed. She didn't move other than the rise and fall of her breasts each time she took a breath.

I moved toward the bed. Mesmerized by her beauty, I couldn't take my eyes off her. As I advanced, Annie followed me with her eyes, a faint smile on her lips. She was the most exotic creature I had ever laid eyes on.

I felt awkward for the first time around Annie. Not knowing what was expected of me or what I was supposed to do. I could tell she was feeling the same as I looked down at her.

"What do I do?" I whispered.

"Blow out all the candles but one. At least that's a good start," she said in a low soft voice.

I started blowing them out one at a time until I came to the last. I left it burning.

Undressing slowly, I could feel Annie's eyes on me. When I got to my shorts, I stopped and sat on the bed, leaving them on, my nerve gone.

"Are you scared?" I whispered.

"Yes ... no, I don't know. I feel awkward. I've never done anything like this. I've never been a bride before."

I lay down on the bed and reaching up, gently drew her to me. I had held Annie many times as we had kissed and made out, but this was a thrill beyond any of my expectations. The feel of her body, covered only in the sheer fabric of her nightgown, was more exciting than anything I had imagined in my short life.

There was no sleep that night, but who needed anything more than what we had, with the sounds of the night serenading us.

The last thing I remember was the sun just starting to peek over the mountains when I finally fell asleep. The next thing I knew I awoke to what felt like a light rain. Instantly my eyes came open and there stood Annie in her wet bathing suit, wrapping a towel around her head.

"Time to wake up, lazy bones," she said, smiling.

"What time is it?" I had put my watch in the kitchen's window ledge when we first came to the cabin. There was no use for it here.

"It's almost eleven," Anne replied after looking at her watch. "I'll fix you something to eat as soon as I change into some dry clothes. I went for a swim. The lake is warm in the cool of the morning. If you want, I'll go back in with you."

"You're nuts. You could have a heart attack like that. I'll bath with warm water, thank you." I said, grinning at her.

"Men are big babies when it comes to swimming in cold water," Annie said, as she laid out her underwear, shorts and blouse on a chair by the cook stove.

"Turn your head so I can change," She said, making a circular motion with her index finger pointed down.

Grinning, I turned my back to her. After a few moments, I peeked over my shoulder. She had her back to me. I eased out of bed quietly while she talked. Tip-toeing up behind her, I grabbed my wife by the waist. Annie screamed, then began to laugh, trying half heartedly to escape my grasp. Her body was cold, but felt great as I drew her against me. I picked her up and carried her to our bed, laying her down in the middle of it. Annie immediately tried to roll over to the other side and escape me, but I was too quick for her and lunged at the fleeing form.

With a squeal Annie tried to ward off my attack, laughing uncontrollably. Then she grabbed me around the neck and I was her prisoner.

"Now I've got you," Annie whispered in a husky voice. "I'm not letting go until you make love to me."

I looked down at her lying beneath me. "You're the most beautiful creature God ever put on this earth, Annie," I said, as my hands began slowly searching her body.

Each part of her was even more sensuous to me, though I had been over her last night, time and again. As my hands found her nipples, she closed her eyes and began breathing heavily, a small moan escaping her lips. I kissed her under the ear, then ever so slowly began kissing down her neck. As my lips advanced closer to her breasts, she arched her back and her legs began encircling my hips.

Her hands shot up from where she had been holding my back and grabbed my hair. As my mouth came within an inch of her nipple, she pulled my lips onto it. Putting her head back against the pillow, Annie moaned. My hands hadn't been idle, as I slid my left one between her legs and touched her gently.

"Cole," Annie whispered in a frantic voice. "Love me, now!"

Then our bodies melted into one as Annie moaned loudly. She held onto me as if she would fall off the end of the world if she loosened her hold around my back.

There was no tomorrow, no yesterday, only the moment. Our bodies rose and fell on a riptide of passion. I felt her body shudder and she crushed her hips hard against mine, the desire swelled until I could no longer contain the urge to climax. The ecstasy of release was so intense nothing else existed. Our bodies welded into one as we clung desperately to the moment. At last we relaxed our grip on each other. Annie laid her head on my chest, and stroked my face and neck as we lay in each other's arms.

"Let's go swimming," I said finally.

"You serious? You'll go in with me?" Annie asked, excited at the prospect of me freezing to death.

"Yeah, I think so. Besides, I can't wait to see you skinny dip," I said, grinning mischievously at her.

"You can forget that. What would happen if someone walked up on us?"

"Chicken," I said as I got up and went outside bare naked. "There's no one within twenty miles of here."

"Honest?" Annie asked.

I could detect a little bit of adventure in her voice. "Honest," I answered. Running onto the little dock, I dove into the lake and surfaced, looking up in time to see Annie streaking down the path, squealing with glee. She ran out on the dock and dove gracefully into the lake.

As she surfaced beside me, I turned toward the shore and called. "Hi. You'll have to excuse us for swimming in the nude."

Annie let out a scream as she followed my gaze to shore. Then seeing that I was joking, playfully slapped at me for scaring her. "You're a rat, Morgan. A dirty rat," she said, making a grab for my neck.

We sank down under the water before she released me. As I made a grab for her Annie struck off for the middle of the lake at a speed I couldn't begin to match. Her body cut through the water like a loon as she laughed at my awkward attempt to keep up. She was in her element and loving every moment of it.

As each day at the lake went by, Annie and I drained every moment of time from the passing hours, making love and enjoying each other's company.

She had been here several times in the past, but had always been more interested in picking flowers or watching birds and animals. Now she took more of an interest in the things I had to show her. The old raft sunk in the lake that Pop had built when he was a boy. The stump where Freddy and I hid our cigarettes when we were kids. A cave where bear had hibernated in the winter.

I don't think there was a rock or a tree that I hadn't touched at one time or another. If I missed any, I'm sure Pop made up for it when he was a boy. The area held a lot of family history and good memories, but the best memory was being made right now with Annie.

The cabin took on a whole new appearance. For the moment it was ours, and seemed almost eternal. Grandfather had built it, Pop owned it now and it was to be mine by birthright. God willing, it would be my descendants'. Annie and I would share many nights here, confiding in one another our innermost thoughts and feelings.

One afternoon we took the canoe out and began paddling slowly around the lake. I had started teaching Annie how to fly fish and enjoyed watching the fever grow. Grandfather had taught her to fish streams and creeks, but this was a new challenge. It was still too early in the day for any serious fishing. Annie seemed very interested and sat quietly in the canoe, listening to every word, nodding occasionally that she understood. As we paddled at a leisurely pace, the glass blue-green waters showed every rock and sunken log in the little lake.

Annie began to get the fishing fever. "Look, there's a good place. I want to try that log tonight," she said, excitedly pointing at a place she thought a big trout might be lurking.

"In the evenings a slight breeze blows down the canyon and across the water, causing the canoe to drift back toward the cabin. That way we can fish and drift at the same time," I told her.

"That's a lazy way to fish."

"Hey, that's what being up here is all about, conservation of everything, including energy. The only thing you should spend energy on is making love to your woman."

"Looking at it in that light, I can't argue. Ever make love in a canoe?" Annie asked, wrinkling her nose.

"Now you're talking naughty," I said and gave her a fatherly look. "Besides, I tried making it with Kathy in her dad's canoe and we almost drowned."

"You what?" Anne sat up almost dumping us as she turned to face me. "You did what?"

"Up at Roger's Lake last summer. She made a pass at me. I couldn't help it. I screamed for help, but she kept pulling me on top of her. It was horrible," I said, making a terrified face.

Annie began to laugh.

"Go ahead and laugh. All you women ever want is our bodies. Is that all women think about? Sex, sex, sex! It's disgusting the way you are," I said, pretending to hold back tears.

"I'm sorry, I won't mention sex anymore. We'll keep this strictly ..."

"Hold it," I interrupted, "don't say anything that I'll regret. I've changed a lot since I was a puritan."

I suddenly stood up and put a foot on each side of the canoe. It rocked wildly and Annie screamed. I pretended not to understand what she was screaming about and searched all around as if looking for a bear, all the time making the canoe rock. Our ripples rushed toward shore and lapped at the bank.

"Cole, you dummy, you're going to dump us," Annie yelled.

"No, don't say we're going to fall in. This is where the Whisper Lake monster lurks." I shouted in my corny melodramatic voice and threw my hand palm out, across my eyes. At the same time, I lifted my left foot from the side of the canoe and over it went.

Annie screamed and hit the water, and I managed a very graceful belly flop. We surfaced together laughing.

"Damn it Morgan, you're insane, you know that? Daddy says you and Freddy are about half a bubble off plumb. I think he's right."

She had dunked her head backward in the water, and with her hair slicked back, darkened by the wetness she was gorgeous. Here was a face that could launch a thousand ships. I almost started to sink and drown; I was so entranced with her loveliness.

"It was an accident, I swear. I guess I just panicked. I'm so ashamed," I said, looking meek, then gave her a big grin.

The wooden canoe floated on its side. The paddles were within twenty feet.

"Now we have to go back to the cabin and change," Annie said.

"Are you thinking naughty again?" I said. "See? That's what I mean. All you women think of is taking advantage of us helpless men. We're just sex objects, play things," I wailed. A couple of fake sobs escaped my lips as I began a slow swim toward the paddles.

We pulled the canoe to the shore and righted it. After I promised not to dunk her again, she got back into the craft and we headed for the cabin to change clothes. Annie was paddling from the front of the canoe and as the craft's prow beached she jumped out and gave the canoe a push back out into the lake.

"Hey," I shouted, knowing she'd bested me.

Annie ran for the cabin, laughing as she made it to the door.

"It's almost time for fishing, and I want to go to my spot. You can change after I finish. It's your fault we're all wet," she said, turning around to face me.

I poured power to the paddle, and the canoe shot back toward the shore faster than Annie had anticipated. Leaping out as it touched the beach, I sprinted for the cabin.

Annie saw me closing fast and let out a squeal, then wheeled and grabbing the door latch jumped into the cabin, slamming the door behind her. I heard the lock trip.

"Let me in, my little pussycat," I said with a French accent.

"Who are you, sir?" came a shy voice.

"I am the notorious lover from up the canyon," I answered, still trying to sound French.

"My husband will find out if I let you enter, sir. He's very mean, he threw me in the lake but a moment ago," she said behind the door. I heard her giggle.

"I will be gentle and loving. Perhaps even take you on a luxury cruise on the lake if you let me enter. Being near you is all I want and desire."

The door came opened a little and a rather shy looking damsel peered through the small opening.

"I am strictly honorable I assure you. Please let me enter and prove myself," I pleaded.

"Enter, sir," she said and opening the door did a curtsy, keeping her eyes lowered. This innocent gesture, even though it had been done in fun, melted my heart. Annie's lowered eyes would have torn the heart from any man. I wanted to throw myself at her feet. Instead, I reached out and lifting her chin kissed her tenderly.

You are truly a princess, I thought. How can anyone look at the likes of you and say there is no God.

Our lips met once again, hungering and full of passion for one another.

We didn't get much fishing in that evening. Lying in each other's arms, we talked of the past, yesterdays we remembered together.

"We've had good times, Cole. I can't wait for us to start our lives together after you finish with the service. What made you and Freddy want to fly helicopters? Why not planes? You guys were always building some kind of contraption to kill yourselves with."

"I don't know, I guess the choppers were something we could hover in without coming down. Most of our flying experience was our bodies hurling through space, after the damned contraptions we'd built came apart and left us stranded in the air. It was all Freddy's fault, you know."

"Um hum. I know you were just a victim of his wild imagination, you being such a wallflower," she jabbed me in the ribs with her elbow, "Poor Freddy could have been killed with some of your schemes."

I chuckled.

"What are you laughing at?" Annie asked, raising her head.

"Oh, just some of the crap Freddy and I've pulled."

"Like what?" she asked, turning to look me in the eye. That mischievous little smile on her face.

"What haven't we tried?"

"It's a wonder you both lived long enough to grow up, at least chronologically." She said, snuggling back onto my shoulder.

"Listen," Annie said holding her breath. "Are those wolves howling?"

"No, Coyotes."

"How close are they?"

"Don't know. Probably a couple hundred yards down the canyon."

"Do you like to hear them that close?"

"Hell, I'd like to hear them in the yard. That's mountain music," I said and gave her a squeeze.

She snuggled again, "I guess I like to hear them too then."

"They shouldn't scare you. It's man that you have to watch. You should have heard the coyotes the week I stayed up here after Grandfather died. I've never heard them make that much noise before." Memories of Grandfather saddened my heart and cast a shadow on the moment. There were times I could almost feel his presence in the cabin.

"Hey, where you at, Morgan?" Annie raised up and patted my chest, her lower breast touching my ribs.

"Oh, just thinking about fishing. We need to try the point early in the morning,"

I don't know how long we lay talking, before we finally drifted off to sleep.

Early the next morning Annie was up building a fire in the cookstove before daylight.

"Cole?"

I was lying in bed pretending to be asleep. When the coffee was made, I planned to jump up and enjoy the good life.

"Cole?"

"Hum?"

"What's that sound?" Annie asked.

I listened for a moment, not hearing anything. Then the racket started again, coming from the lake.

"Canadian honkers," I said, "They're out on the lake. Sounds like the far end."

"I hope they're still there when it gets daylight. I want to see them. Maybe I'll be able to get some pictures."

"I wouldn't hold my breath on that one, Annie. The honkers are early feeders, they'll probably take to the air before full light."

She never got to take the pictures, the geese took off for parts unknown shortly before sunrise.

Our last night at the lake was one of sorrow, because we knew we would soon be parting for a while. I took the situation better than Annie did. She would cry, then wiping her eyes, she would want to snuggle.

"Just hold me, Cole," she murmured.

That night we went to bed around nine and made love for what seemed like hours. I'd finally started to drift off to sleep, when Annie started talking to me.

"Cole? You awake?"

"Hum?"

"Talk to me, you can sleep anytime."

"You have any idea what time it is?" I asked without opening my eyes.

Annie raised on her elbow and reaching over, lifted my eyelid.

"You're nuts, you know that? Here it is after midnight and you're talking and pulling a guy's eyelids open. You're crazy, woman," I said, grinning at that mischievous looking little face that was above me.

"Tomorrow we have to go home. This is our last night together for a long, long time. Talk to me, darn it." She emphasized her feelings by lightly beating her fist on my chest.

"You're a pain in the ass, you know that?" I said and reached up and drew her lips toward mine.

"Yeah, but you love me, right?" Annie said, jerking her head up before I could kiss her.

"You're okay," I said and kissed her.

"Cole? Would you do me a favor?"

"What now?"

"I have to go out to the outhouse. I don't want to go out there with coyotes lurking around. Would you go with me?" she said, sounding like a little child.

After looking at her face, I knew I was on my way outside. The air at this time of night is crisp to say the least. I stood in my shorts and wondered how the Indians ever made it. When we came back in, it was a toss up as to whether or not I loved her enough to let her put her cold feet on me, but once again, she won.

We laid in bed and talked for hours, until I drifted off once more.

Never have I heard such noise in the cabin as Annie making a fire in the cookstove. After that, she made the noisiest pot of coffee I'd ever heard. Annie had her back to me, mixing pancake batter.

I lay in bed, pretending to sleep, until finally I could take no more. "Hey!" I shouted as I sprang out of bed.

With a shriek, the bowl went flying, scattering flour all over the counter and floor.

I began laughing at her as she turned with the still terrified look on her face. "Morgan, that wasn't funny," she said, looking around at the mess I had caused. Then Annie laughed and I gave her a hand cleaning up.

"You gotta be the noisiest woman in the mornings that I've ever slept with."

"It worked. You finally woke up. Wait a minute, how many women have you slept with?"

"Seven in the morning?" I said, ignoring her question. "Come on, it's too late to fish and too early for lunch. How about going back to bed and fooling around?"

"Morgan, you're incorrigible."

I patted her backside then walked over to the closet and got dressed.

After breakfast, I went outside and dragged the canoe up beside the cabin.

As I hung the poles on their pegs, I looked up at Grandfather's pole. I reached up, and with fondness, removed it from its resting place. Someday I'd take it out and use it to catch a fish. Someday, I thought as I replaced it.

The time had come for us to pack up and return to civilization.

"Before we go," Annie said, "can we go back up to the apple trees? I want to see them one more time."

"Sure, I'd like that, too."

We walked around the lake quietly, cherishing our last moments alone, knowing that soon we would have to be apart. It was going to be hard having to go back to our parents' homes after being together as husband and wife. Annie picked two bluebells, and wading out, she placed them on our rock.

"We have to go," I said in a low voice, hating to spoil Annie's reverence.

"Will we return, Cole?" she asked without looking at me.

"Sure we will. This is home, Annie."

"Will you promise me?" she asked, looking into my eyes. "Promise me we'll come back here."

"This is your lake, Annie. That's your rock."

"Our lake and our rock," she tearfully whispered.

We turned and reluctantly started back toward the other end of the lake.

We were silent as we drove home, each occupied by our own thoughts as Annie snuggled up against my shoulder.

We pulled into her yard and started unloading her things. We had beaten her folks home.

Chapter 13

The days passed all too quickly, and soon it was time for Freddy and I to leave for boot camp. Over the last two weeks Annie became quieter and clung to me.

Freddy seemed excited when the day arrived for us to depart, while Annie looked like she was going to a hanging. Our parents were not too happy either.

While we waited for our departure we sat having coffee. The men kept giving us tips on the do's and the don'ts of basic training. They had both been in the Army, so Freddy and I paid close attention.

"Don't show them what you've got at first. If you do, they'll want more out of you. If you just keep a low profile and do what you're told, you'll do fine," Pop said.

"You come from good stock. Show them what your made of," Mr. Gray said. "When you get back from overseas, we'll have one hell of a wedding," he added looking at Annie.

Annie gave my arm a tight squeeze.

"I take it we have your approval then," I said and smiled at him.

"Son, you've always had my approval. The timing just hasn't been right."

"I have to go to the ladies room," Annie said. "Cole, would you walk me?"

"Sure." I said, and we walked toward the other end of the building.

"Cole," Annie said.

"Yeah?"

"I have to tell you something. It's something I'm not very proud of. I mean, it's something you should have been aware of," she said.

"Okay, you're going to be dating Peterson while I'm gone, right?" I said.

"No Silly, now be serious, we don't have much time."

She looked like she was on the verge of crying.

"I haven't been taking any birth control." she blurted out and the tears ran down her cheeks.

A shock ran through my body as it dawned on me what she was saying "What? Why?" I asked, pushing her to arm's length. "You can't be serious? You could be pregnant, considering all the times that we've made love."

This wasn't like her. She was too intelligent to let this just happen. Then it dawned on me. She wanted to be pregnant. I couldn't believe it.

"Annie, what in the hell were you thinking of anyway?"

"Cole. What happens if you never come home? I just couldn't stand the thought of you not being here. With a baby, a part of you is always here with me. I know it sounds crazy, but you can't leave me completely if part of you is still here. Don't you see? Do you understand what I'm saying?"

I held her tight. "Damn, woman, I love you," I said in a low voice. "I'll always love you."

"Hold me, Cole."

I finally pushed her away from me far enough to look her in the eyes.

"Annie, are you pregnant?"

"I don't know," she said, wiping her eyes. "I hope so."

"Your dad is going to kill me, if you are."

"You better join the Army," she said.

"Good idea," I wasn't sure what I wanted. It would be good to have a child with Annie. It would be nice to know that we would go on forever even if something happened to me. If! I didn't like thinking about that.

"Annie, I have something for you which Grandfather said was to be yours one day. It's a little late. I put off giving it to you until now." I said and reached into my pocket. "Annie, this was my grandmother's wedding ring." It was just a simple gold band. I took her left hand in mine, and slipped it on her finger.

Annie threw her arms around me and I could feel tears wetting my neck.

"Thank you, Grandfather," she whispered "Thank you, Cole."

"No, thank you for loving and marrying me," I whispered. "Now when you get lonely you'll have part of me with you."

"Cole, how long will you be gone?"

"I'm not sure, basic training, then flight school, close to a year to complete, I guess. From there I'm not sure. That is if I can make it through flight training. I hear it's a pretty tough school. Their helicopters are harder to fly than the contraptions Freddy and I built."

"You'll make it. I know you, Cole. You'll be the best they have ever had," she said.

"I wish I had that kind of faith, I'd pass up the flight school and just go straight into flying."

"They'll send you and Freddy to Vietnam. I know they will."

"Maybe, but flying a chopper will be the safest job there," I lied.

"Really?"

"Yep."

"You're not fibbing to me, are you?"

"Honest injun," I said, holding up my right hand. "They said I'd just be running the mail from the ships to the coast. There won't be any enemy within 500 miles. My job is the envy of all the Army," I said, really winging it as I went. I didn't even know how the mail came, but the story seemed to satisfy her and I felt better seeing Annie's face light up with the bullshit story I was giving her.

"How long will they send you to Vietnam for?"

"A tour of duty in Vietnam is for only one year, then I will be stationed state side for the rest of my enlistment. It'll go fast. Besides, I'll have Freddy to watch after me."

"Oh, that makes me feel so much better, the blind leading the blind," Annie said rolling her eyes.

As we stood holding each other, I felt like it was the first time. My heart pounded with the excitement of being so close. What I wouldn't have given for another evening with this lovely creature I had married.

Annie returned my look. I was certain she was feeling the same way. Her eyes searched mine.

"We had better get back to the others," I finally said, breaking the spell.

"I don't want to share you," Annie said, pulling me down to her lips. After a long kiss, she released me and quietly said, "Come on."

We walked hand in hand back to where the others were waiting for us.

Annie put on a bright smile. To a stranger it may have looked convincing, but everyone here knew her and knew she was putting on a front for their sakes.

"They say when we go to flight school it will be in Texas," Freddy said, "Wonder if our flying all those contraptions we've built made them decide they needed our experience."

The men chuckled at this and I grinned myself.

"It was the bike plane that did it. They were impressed with the way we set it down," I said. "Helicopters are expensive, setting them down on manure is preferred to rocks."

Once again there was the laughter from the men and weak smiles from the women. Annie wasn't enjoying any of the conversation about wrecking either the bikes or helicopters.

Pop looked at her and changed the subject to the weather. All too soon the loud speaker came on and announced our bus. Reluctantly we stood up.

Annie looked panicked and for a moment or two I thought she was going to become hysterical as she clung to me.

"Cole? It isn't too late. We can pack and be in Canada in a couple of hours. You love the mountains. We could buy a little ranch up there."

She was trying to keep from breaking down by talking. Annie knew me better than that. Picking up our coats and bags, Freddy and I started out the door toward the waiting bus. Our parents followed close behind, and Annie stuck to me as if she was going to get on the bus with us.

"I hear we get some time off for good behavior when we finish flight school. We won't get to come home after basic, our flight slot starts within three days after basic. That's only a few months off though, then we'll have a couple of weeks off to just have fun. How does that sound?" I asked Annie.

"I'll be waiting, Morgan. Count on it," Annie said, spunky like the Annie I knew. Annie and our mothers smothered us with kisses. The men shook our hands. With that, Freddy and I started to step on board the bus.

"Hey, son." Pop said, as he stepped forward and threw his arms around me, "make us proud. Remember what I told you."

I looked in his eyes and could see a tear. I gave him a wink. I was starting to get a little wet-eyed, too.

Looking at my Annie, I tried desperately to hold back my tears, but we were soul mates and she knew what I was feeling. Annie threw herself into my arms.

"I love you, Morgan! I love you!"

I crushed her to me. The bus driver walked out of the station and announced once more, "All aboard, please."

Freddy and I sat on the side of the bus closest to the station. As the bus pulled out, I watched my beautiful Annie, tears streaming down her cheeks. "I love you, girl," I mouthed silently as I looked at her through the window. Slowly the bus moved out into the night.

Chapter 14

The first week of basic was the worst, with haircuts, new uniforms and shots. Freddy took cutting his hair off pretty hard. Me, I didn't give a damn. I wasn't looking for a women, I had the best woman I could ever hope for and then some. My hair would grow back. The shots weren't my cup of tea, and I kind of wished I'd taken Annie up on Canada before I was through. It seemed the DIs (drill instructors) were at our throats more than they were the rest of the platoon.

At first Freddy and I were ready to take on the whole damned bunch of DIs, then we got to talking about what Pop said. He had been a pilot in the Army. "They're going to give you so much hell you'll be tempted to take a swing. That's what they're trying to get you to do," he said. "They'll want to know if they can break you. They know you're going to be aviator candidates. It cost the Army a lot of money to put you through the school. It's a lot cheaper to wash you out before you start. They'll push, shove and scream insults at you. You'll think you have enlisted in hell. They want to know how much you can take, make you blow up if they can. Always keep that in mind." Pop was a wise man, like Grandfather.

The only thing that made it all bearable was mail call. Annie wrote every day. In the middle of the third week, she broke the bad news that we weren't going to be parents after all. I had started believing I was going to be a father, and now I felt the let down. She had taken it hard and I could feel her tears in the letter. Sitting down that night, I wrote her a long letter, telling her how much I loved her and missed holding her. Then I stood by the mailbox for several minutes trying to decide whether to mail a mushy letter like that. Would it make her feel better or worse? I slipped the letter inside.

Training became tedious as the weeks slowly rolled by. Sometimes it was hard to keep my temper with the DIs, not being used to taking abuse. Back home someone would be lying on the ground, taking inventory of his teeth for a lot less.

Then one day Freddy snapped at an instructor, and the proverbial shit hit the fan. Until then we thought we were pretty tough, coming from Montana. We were in for a real lesson. The instructor seemed to enjoy the invitation for a brawl, and Freddy was all for it. He had been primed for a fight since we'd gotten here.

We gathered around as the instructor took off his cap and reassured Freddy and the rest of us that this would be off the record. I think it was the DI's way of inviting any of the rest of us to get in line, that might want to try his hand at whipping up on the Army. I have to admit I was tempted to sign his dance book. I had a lot of pent-up frustration inside me too. After watching what happened to old Fearless Freddy, I'm glad I didn't.

Freddy delivered the first punch, unfortunately it was his last. The instructor seemed to play with him, making sure not to put him down too soon. Although with all due respect, Freddy was giving him his money's worth. I think the drill instructor was beginning to tire a little because the intensity of the fight increased in tempo. Freddy kept coming at him and taking the whipping like a man. If the instructor didn't finish him before long, he might live to regret it, as Freddy could take a lot of punishment. He knew after he threw the first punch that he was out-gunned, but that was right up his alley; he was never a quitter. When the whipping was over, the instructor helped Freddy to his feet, then knocked him down again before walking away. Freddy laid there for a moment. With a grin on his bloody face, he gingerly helped himself up after refusing a helping hand with an I'm all right, gesture.

"You're a dumb shit, Freddy. Someday someone's going to kill you," I said.

"You got room to talk, you bastard," he said, half grinning through bloody teeth and a fast developing fat lip. "Someday I'm going to learn to fight like that, then come back and kick his ass."

We finally got our chance at learning to fight. Freddy went on to advanced hand-to-hand combat training and I had to go along to keep him on the straight and narrow. We both hobbled around for the first few days, then toughened up.

As far as the rest of basic went, we marched until our butts fell off, then marched some more. We made beds the military way, cleaned toilets, and were given the occupational opportunity of a lifetime, cleaning garbage cans.

Finally after what seemed like several years of taking crap off of someone you'd rather have killed, graduation from basic training rolled around. No more marching, we were through with the bullshit. Now we were going to be pilot candidates, respected and dignified, then with time be appointed to warrant officers.

We shipped out to Fort Rucker, Alabama, the Army's primary helicopter schools. They didn't waste any time popping our bubbles. Basic training, as we had known it, was a joke. The first thing was an ass chewing from a sergeant as we reported for duty.

I thought the harassment was over but soon found that candidates were below basic training recruits. We double-timed everywhere, and when we weren't double-timing, we were braced by senior candidates, while they screamed at us. If ever I wanted to bury my fist in someone's face, it was now. I wanted to grab the sons of bitches by the throat and pound them to a pulp. I'd go to bed at night and dream of going down through the list of names, one by one, beating the hell out of them. I couldn't wait to be an upperclassman. My anger had reached an all time high because of the hazing. We couldn't even go to chow without sitting at attention and squaring the angles with our forks as we ate.

And last but not least, there was the elimination board, everyone's private hell. We were continually reminded by our instructors of how easy it was to be pulled out of the running.

"We have too fucking many asshole candidates, Morgan, and I've thought about kicking your ass out. We don't need your kind around here. You're a Montana cocksucker. You like me, Morgan?" The sergeant would scream as he stood three inches from my face.

"No, sergeant!"

"Why not, you pansy-assed prick? You'd like to take a swing at me, wouldn't you?"

"Not until I graduate, sergeant." I stared a hole through his head.

At the end of our first four weeks, they posted a list of candidates for review by the elimination board. By some miracle, my name wasn't on it. Freddy and I had made it so far. The instructor kept swearing we would be on the next list. "Little bastards like you don't belong here, Morgan," he would snarl, standing inches from my face, "You belong back in Montana, screwing sheep. This is for men, Morgan. You're a pussy."

A pussy? Let me get him somewhere private and I would do my best to change his mind. As he yelled at me, I could feel my veins stand out on my neck. He seemed to know this and pushed with all he had. Each day was a struggle, but I managed to keep my temper in check.

Eventually we became the upperclassmen and the tables turned. We were ready to make someone else squirm. Freddy made a great senior classman and I might add, I didn't do too bad myself. We were like junkyard dogs, maybe even meaner. We screamed at the lower classmen, watching the sweat break out on their faces. They were probably thinking how great it would be to have a list of the names of the son of a bitching Senior classmen like us, then going down the list beating the shit out of each one of us.

Then came the day we were issued our flight equipment, flight suits, gloves, helmets, flight sunglasses, etc. Even though we were treated as candidates everywhere else, we were respected as potential pilots at the heliport. There were a few things that kept our feet on the ground though; we had to wear our hats backward to show we hadn't soloed yet. That was okay. At least we were close to real helicopters.

The IP's (instructor pilots), were as tough as the rest, perhaps even worse. They didn't yell and scream as a rule. They didn't have to. They just watched us like hawks, and that was enough. The least bit of a scowl totally demoralized me.

We started our practice flights with the H-23. This helicopter constantly reminds a pilot to say his prayers every night. Each time we went up, I wasn't sure I'd live to see chow time again. If I could master this craft, I was going to be ready for anything.

Every night I went to sleep concentrating on the cyclic control stick, collective pitch control lever, the directional control pedals and how to handle all three at once. I was poor company for anyone who didn't want to discuss flying. I ate and slept helicopters. With each practice I improved, even though it was ever so slight. I learned to put the craft in impossible places and then how to get it back out of the same hopeless places without killing myself and the IP. I think I might have made Christians out of a couple IPs. Several times as I tried getting us out of a tight spot, I'd hear them utter the Lord's name. I would wake up many mornings depressed from dreaming I had washed out.

We learned translational lifts. This would allow us to take off when the weight of the craft exceeded the rules of lift that were dictated by the conditions of altitude, humidity and temperature. This condition we were later to find was very prevalent in Vietnam. Cool air is ideal. But if we were going to survive, we would have to learn to fly in the worst of conditions, hot, humid and overloaded.

We studied maintenance, weather and aerodynamics. Hours were spent in bleachers watching classmates do maneuvers, and I couldn't help wondering how I would escape if one of the students goofed and flew at us.

We learned VFR (visual flight rules), and IFR (instrument flight rules.) Finally the day came. We soloed and no longer had to wear our hats backwards. We were pilots, real honest to goodness helicopter pilots and we had finally earned our wings.

While stationed at Fort Rucker, we flew the H-19 Sikorsky, cross-country and tactical. The H-19 had a hydraulic, rather than a direct mechanical linkage and was a slug as far as I was concerned. I wanted something racier, and then finally the dream of all new pilots was realized. We were introduced to the Bell UH-1 Iroquois, more commonly known as the Huey. The Huey was powered with the T53-L-11 gas-turbine engine, which gave the craft 1,100 horsepower. The newer Hueys had more horsepower, but we settled for the older models to start with. I had finally made the big time and fell in love for the second time. The Huey had a forty-eight foot rotor system with a twenty-one inch chord (width of the rotor blade) and an eight foot tail rotor, it weighed 5000 pounds and was all business. This was what the big boys were flying.

After eight months of rigorous training, our big day finally came, graduation. It had been months of hard work, but Freddy and I were to realize a dream we'd had from childhood. We were pilots. We had both made it. With graduation came a well-earned leave. I would see Annie again at last.

Our orders had been cut, but we decided not to tell Annie or our parents, not wanting to dampen the reunion with our families. We were scheduled for overseas and we were pretty certain it was Vietnam.

Our plane flew into Glacier Airport, and my heart skipped a beat. I hadn't realized how much I'd missed this country. As we disembarked, Annie come racing through the gate and threw herself into my arms. My parents gave us a moment together then as Annie and I walked through the gate, they met us. Mom couldn't seem to stop kissing and hugging me. Pop held back waiting for her to have her chance, then stepped forward and gave me a hug. "Good to have you home, Son. Say, let me look at what's on your chest." He reached out and touched the silver wings. Pop looked proud as his eyes met mine again.

Annie and I spent our days together, and some nights we didn't come home until early in the morning. It wasn't that we didn't intend to, but we got carried away. Our families seemed to understand. The one I feared was Mr. Gray, but he seemed to appreciate our feelings. At least he didn't make me a steer. He treated me like we were in-laws already. But he stuck to his guns about us getting married until I came back and Annie had finished school.

On our last night to ourselves, Annie and I were coming out of the theater in Kalispell when she suggested we get a motel room for a couple of hours. As we entered our room, Annie said she had to talk to me.

"Cole, I'm still trying to get us pregnant."

I loved the way she put it, "us." I had never tried to get pregnant before. I had to grin.

"Stop grinning. I'm serious, Cole."

I straightened up my act.

"Cole? You're not upset with me wanting a baby, are you?"

"No, I wanted you to be pregnant while I was in training. I have to admit it was a scary thought, but I was excited about it at the same time. If I thought it would do any good, I'd tell your dad that it would be better to get married. At least if things did go bad, you'd have a pension to live on. But I know your dad; he wouldn't go for it. Once he makes up his mind, he's hard headed."

"Kind of like someone else I know," she said. "You two are so much alike. I don't like you to say things like 'things going bad,' Cole. I can't think like that. You might be able to, but I can't." Tears began to roll down her cheeks.

We lay in each other's arms for a good part of the night, not just making love, but holding on for all we were worth. There was no telling how long it would be before we'd get this opportunity again. I didn't want the night to end.

At five in the morning, we decided we had best get along home. Our parents were early risers.

The ride home was a silent one; each of us lost in our own thoughts. I was wondering how it was going to go this afternoon when Freddy and I caught our flight out and was reasonably sure that was on Annie's mind also.

We sat in the car in her driveway until sunrise. With great reluctance we finally went into the kitchen to have coffee with her parents.

"Hey, look who's here," Freddy said. "Quite a long movie huh?"

"Shut up, Freddy," Annie said. "Cole's going to Canada with me," she smiled at the thought. "You with me, big guy?"

"I'd go, but I'd be missing all the big money Uncle Sam is paying me," I said, winking at her.

"They're going to Vietnam," Annie said, the tears starting again.

Freddy looked at me.

"I didn't say that. She's guessing," I told him.

"You boys are going, aren't you?" Mrs. Gray asked as her hand came up to her mouth.

"It looks like we might stop over," Freddy said, avoiding his mother's eyes. He poured himself another cup of coffee.

"You don't have to lie to me, Freddy. You boys are going to Vietnam, aren't you?" Mrs. Gray persisted.

"Hell, Mom, everybody goes to Vietnam. It's a big country. We're going to the south. All the fighting is in the northern part."

"Pop, did that Angus bull ever turn out to be any good?" Freddy asked in an attempt to change the subject.

"He's done his job," Mr. Gray said, taking the hint. "I'm thinking about swapping him to Brown for his bull. Don't want any inbreeding."

"When?" Mrs. Gray asked, not caring about the bull or the attempt to change the subject. It had been a feeble attempt at best.

"Soon, I'm not sure what day," Freddy replied. "Look, Mom, it's no big secret that helicopter pilots are as much in the Army as anyone else. We have good jobs and it beats the sh …" Freddy caught himself, "the dickens out of the infantry. It isn't like we'll be stuck out in the muck and grime like a lot of guys. We get to return to a base and sleep on a bunk bed. Sounds pretty good, doesn't it?" He was doing a pretty good job of selling the helicopter program, even though he was feeding everyone a line of bull.

"I've got to get home and see my folks." I said. "I'll see you guys in a little while."

I started for the door.

"I'm going with you," Annie said.

"Okay."

We drove to my house with Annie sitting so close I could almost feel her heartbeat. I drove slowly, wanting to keep her at my side. I hated myself at that moment for having to leave. This was the way life was supposed to be. She and I, side by side through everything. Babies to love and be played with. Babies to watch nurse in Annie's arms. Knowing that we would be together forever and have a ranch of our own. Annie was my mate and I hoped she was pregnant! What in the hell had gone wrong? Why couldn't things be the way they should be? I had screwed it up, that's why. I had done this to the woman I loved so deeply. How could I have been so stupid?

We turned off the road into my driveway, and I stopped the car. "Annie," I said, turning a little to look at her.

"What?" She answered quietly.

"You don't realize how sorry I am for what I've done to you. I'm so sorry, Annie. I love you more than life. You've got to know that." I reached over and cupped her head in my hand.

She closed her eyes and leaned into my hand.

"I'm coming back to you. You have to believe me. I will be coming back," I whispered. "Always believe that, okay?"

"Okay," she whispered.

I drove on up and parked in front of the house. Mom and Dad were in the kitchen having coffee as we came in the living room door.

"In here son," Pop called out.

Annie and I walked into the kitchen and pulled out two chairs as Mom got up to get us some coffee. She looked tired.

"How are you doing, sweetheart?" Mom asked Annie.

"I'm fine," Annie said. "A little tired, we haven't had any sleep."

"I didn't think you had. You look pretty anyway," Mom said and laid her hand on the back of Annie's head in that, motherly way.

"How are you, Cole?" Mom asked, looking at me like I was a child again.

"I'm okay, Mom. Just a little tired, but I'll have time for a nap on the plane."

"You're going to write your mother once in awhile. I know you'll be writing Annie quite a bit, but I want a letter at least once a week. It'll give Annie and me something to talk about," Mom said, then looked at Annie for support. Annie nodded.

"Of course, I'll be writing every other day or so," I said defensively.

Chapter 15

All too soon the time came for us to depart. We got both families together for lunch at Sykes, an old downtown restaurant where a lot of the ranch people meet for coffee and the best home-cooked food in the town. The noise was so loud with the old-timers talking and laughing that we almost had to shout in order to hear each other. The hubbub was great and gave our spirits a lift. Freddy and I knew it would be a long time before we would enjoy another get-together like this.

I sat, looking at the familiar faces of the old-time cowboys sitting around the tables shooting the bull about their stock dogs, horses, the elk they had taken or were going to take. The usual bullshit stories.

Would we return? We were indestructible; we couldn't die. That was for people we didn't know, faceless and nameless. I hated the thought of not living to return here. The realization of what we were going into had started to hit me hard. Could one of us die? What would it be like sitting in a bar drinking a beer without Freddy? What would it be like sitting here in this old restaurant looking at an empty seat across the table? I had to get off this. We were forever.

"What are you thinking about?" Annie asked.

"Nothing," I said. The others were talking, and Freddy was holding up my end of the conversation with his usual bullshit.

"We have two hours left and you're thinking about nothing?" she said. "I've been watching you, Morgan. You're a thousand miles away. Where are you?"

"I'm just wondering how many of these old-timers will be alive when we come back," I said, half truthfully.

We talked about nothing of importance, just listened to each other, absorbing all the tones of one another's voices. It was like music to our already lonesome ears and hearts. I could see stress building up in Annie. She had a strained look on her face that was evident to everyone present. Pop, Mr. Gray and Freddy noticed but didn't bring it up. I could see the love and concern for Annie in Freddy's face, although he was trying not to let on. Annie and Freddy were very close even though they fought like cats and dogs when they were kids.

We had all come in one car. It had been crowded with four in the back seat, but Annie and I didn't mind. She snuggled up so close, that I could feel her right breast pressed against my side. I liked that; it made me aware of her, not that I really needed a reminder.

As we approached the parking lot, Annie began to unconsciously squeeze my leg. The tension in her body was building and she was desperately trying to keep it under control.

Pop parked, and it became very quiet in the car. Everyone knew it was just a matter of time now before we would be parting for a long time, perhaps forever. This could be the last time for any one of us. The thought hit me like a sledgehammer. I hoped I wasn't showing it.

The women were holding up better than I expected as we walked to the terminal, but then again, these were strong women. When they cried, it was because they were hurting.

Annie stopped and looked at me as if she were seeing a ghost. "Cole," her voice was on the verge of panic.

"What?"

"Cole," Annie repeated, "I need to talk to you." She grabbed my arm and tried to lead me away.

"You guys go ahead and get us some seats. We'll be right there," I said.

"Cole," Annie repeated for a third time, "do you remember asking Grandfather about a dream you had a long time ago?" Annie asked, looking into my eyes and frowning.

"I've had a lot of dreams, and I'm sure I have asked him about a lot of them," I said. "What dream are you talking about?"

"That time you dreamed about riding on the back of a dragonfly?"

My mind went back to the dream. It had stuck with me because of its vividness. I had told Annie about the dream that same day after talking to Grandfather. I was amazed that she would remember it.

I hadn't thought of the dream for a long time, and yet it came back as clear as if it had been yesterday. Automatically my hand went to my pocket and the medicine bag I still carried.

"Cole?" Annie said, tugging my arm, "you okay?"

I started at the sound of Annie's voice, "Sorry, I was just thinking."

"Of the dream?" Annie asked.

"No, that was a dumb kid's dream," I lied. I still didn't like thinking about it, even after all these years.

"Cole, I thought of what the dream might mean. I'm scared. Remember you said the dragonfly was hovering over ants?" She was looking at me and I could see she was frightened.

"Could that be a helicopter? The ants, they could be people. Think about it? Cole, I'm getting scared," Annie said, on the verge of crying.

"Annie, you're going to have to get used to the fact that I'm in the Army now and will be for another three years. I fly helicopters just like a thousand other guys," I said. I held her shoulders and looked her in the eyes. "I'm a pilot. Flying is what I do for a living now, and I'm damned good at it. I don't believe in getting into trouble, and I'm damned sure not going to get my men into any, okay? Hell, I don't want to get hurt any more than you want me to. But Annie, I have a job to do and I have to do it regardless of bullshit dreams. Now come on, snap out of it. Let's make these next few minutes good ones. All right?"

I had been grasping her shoulders while I talked to her and now realized how hard I had been holding her. Annie reached up and massaged where my fingers had dug in.

"I'm sorry, Annie."

She shook her head. "It's okay. It didn't hurt much."

My heart was heavy. I hadn't meant to let myself go like that, and now I had inadvertently hurt the person who meant more to me than anyone else in the world. I held her close, and we kissed long and passionately.

I was in uniform, and people knew we were parting. So kissing her here like this was acceptable, I figured. If it wasn't, they could kiss my ass.

We walked back to the others.

Our plane came in and taxied up to the terminal. I felt a sinking feeling in the pit of my stomach as Annie clung to me.

"Cole," she said in a weak voice, "I don't want you to go. Please don't go."

Everyone looked at her, then our mothers began to cry. This was the moment I'd dreaded the most, the tears of three women I loved dearly. I looked over at Freddy and knew he was feeling the same way.

Pop and Mr. Gray were holding their wives and trying to comfort them.

Pop looked at me and winked, wearing that famous grin of his. "You boys will do fine, just keep your wits about you. Sometimes that's the only thing that will keep you al——." He backed up and rephrased his sentence, "keep you on your feet."

It was too late; Annie had caught what he was going to say. Pop dropped his eyes, something I'd never seen him do before.

Annie stared at him, then looked at me. There was a look of alarm, but she didn't say anything. Her look was a speech in itself. She grabbed onto me like she was never going to turn lose.

"Come on, Annie. Remember our talk and my promise? Stop worrying. We're going to South Vietnam. That's the good-duty area. They don't move us around like they do the troops. We stay on an air base out of the war zone. If you're going to feel sorry for anyone, feel sorry for the men that have to go out there and fight."

I was winging it like Freddy, but it sounded convincing. Pop gave me a look that said, "Bullshit," but kept quiet.

Freddy walked by me a couple of minutes later and mumbled, "You ever think about selling used cars, Cole?"

I grinned.

"What are you smiling about?" Annie asked.

"Nothing, Freddy was just making a comment."

"Something from his dirty little mind?" She asked.

"You know Freddy," I said and smiled.

"Who doesn't, especially the women," Annie said and looked at her brother, shaking her head. "I'm going to miss you, big brother," she softened as she threw her arms around him, giving Freddy a big hug. "Think of all the hearts you're breaking by going overseas."

Six foot and almost 200 pounds of solid muscle, Freddy was the envy of a lot of guys and the idol of all the girls, with his sandy hair, blue eyes, handsome face and winning smile. His smile melted many a girl's heart. He was a towering giant compared to Annie's five foot six inches of curves.

Boarding instructions were called out for a second time and we all stood up with reluctance. Freddy and I started for the gate. Hearts sank as we exchanged hugs from our dads and hugs and kisses from our mothers. Then it was our moment. Annie was fighting a losing battle with tears. Her beautiful eyes looked as if they were bursting with pain.

My heart ached at the thought of leaving Annie. Everyone stood back to give us room to say our good-byes. With a loud sob, she threw her arms around me and began to cry uncontrollably.

I pried her from me after a few moments, taking her head between my palms. I kissed her for the last time, then walked through the gate and out into the night. Freddy followed, putting his hand on my shoulder.

We sat on the left side of the plane, and I sat next to the window. Staring hard to see Annie. I finally found her as the plane taxied.

"I love you, Annie," I mouthed as we pulled away. I know she was saying the same thing.

After the usual instrument check, the plane raced down the runway and at last we were on our way to the unknown.

I wondered if either of us would ever see Montana again or would they just return our bodies, if we were lucky enough to be found. We had heard stories of how bodies were lost in the elephant grass, to lay there for eternity, not that it would really matter.

My main concern was for Annie. I knew then that no matter where my body went in this world, my heart would always stay in this valley with my lady.

Freddy fell asleep within the hour. I couldn't sleep. My mind was a jumble of thoughts, and I was glad for the time alone. Within days now, we'd be in Vietnam.

I lay awake, thinking about the training films they had shown us in flight school. What we were headed for was hell on earth.

Chapter 16

We loaded and left out of Mobile, Alabama, for our luxury cruise to the sunny beaches of Vietnam. Our helicopters had been loaded on the same ship for the long voyage across the ocean.

"We should have booked first-class passage," I told Freddy. "Next time listen to me, okay?"

"Where are the women? I hope they don't expect us to have sex with ourselves," he said and grinned.

"Too much pulling it will cause you to go blind, I've heard," I told him. Several pilots chuckled.

"Who laughed?" Freddy said, squinting and pretending to look blindly around. There was another round of laughter.

"Seaman. There's been a mistake. I have a private room with a view," Freddy said to a sailor helping settle us into our cramped quarters.

"Yes sir," he smiled back as he helped us through the passageway with our duffel bags. "The maids are still cleaning it, sir."

"I guess this will have to do for now then," Freddy said, looking around, "Where's the bar?" Without waiting for a reply, he continued on by the sailor looking for his bunk.

"It isn't exactly the Hilton, is it?" I had been under the naive assumption that being pilots we were going to get special treatment, two men to a compartment with a large porthole for a view. That's the way they had shown it in old war movies. What the hell, we hadn't been spoiled yet, why start now? I could wait until we landed. Then we'd get better living quarters, more to our liking. After all, the Army took care of their pilots. We were the ones that made sure the Army got where they wanted to go and back safely. We flew soldiers around the bullets.

I spent a lot of my off-duty time writing Annie, and Mom and Pop every once in awhile. It would seem that on a ship I'd run out of things to say, but somehow I never did.

The trip went considerably faster than I expected. The first day was the longest, with nothing to do but try to figure out what the hell we were supposed to be doing. We studied our manuals and refreshed ourselves on notes taken in flight school. We went over formations and their variances. Heavy left and right, diamond, echelon left and right, staggered trail left and right. I felt like I was playing football. We went over maps, overlays, photos and proper identifications. Classes never seemed to end. Even though I hated the paper work, it helped to pass the time.

We arrived in Lang Mai Bay south of Qui Nhon in South Vietnam early in the morning. On deck, the navy was busy. Helicopters were being readied for take off. The excitement produced a feeling anxiety. I walked around, trying to let my breakfast settle. Other pilots were doing the same thing, probably for the same reason. We knew we had to fly the Hueys off the carrier. I don't know about the others, but I was feeling like I was in over my head for the first time since flight school. In desperation I mentally reviewed everything I had to do, and was blessed with total confusion. I doubted if I could even remember how to crank up.

The Hueys were turbine powered and prone to overheating on start up. After sitting on deck for weeks without being cranked the danger of overheat was even greater, they said. Hell, they overheated every time we cranked up, what was the big worry? However the navy took a dim view of burning up one of their ships. They had fireman standing by with large fire extinguishers. That was great for morale.

I won't say I was scared of flying off the carrier deck. Let's just say I needed to pee more than usual as the time drew nearer for us to saddle up. However, I wasn't alone. Everyone was apprehensive, which didn't really help. We had always relied on our adventurous spirit to bolster each other. If one of us was willing to jump off a cliff, the others wanted to go first. In this case none of us wanted to be first or last. We tried not to show it, but our common bond as aviators gave us an ability to sense each other's feelings.

Two officers from shore had flown in to give us a short briefing on what to expect in Vietnam. As we gathered and took our seats in the briefing room one of the officers looked us over.

"Gentlemen, so far you've been put through flying conditions that have been as rigorous as the United States Army could make them. Vietnam is the curve ball we've been trying to ready you for. You'll not only have the heat, but humidity as well. You're going to feel like your craft is already loaded. Get used to it as quickly as possible. Questions?"

"Yes sir, load capacity variances?" A pilot across the room asked.

"There'll be times you'll feel you can't lift capacity and you'll be correct. There will also be times you can compensate with half fuel or in emergencies use translational. Each day you'll be given your ACL (allowable cargo loads,) according to the weather conditions for the day. Do not exceed this. No heroes gentlemen, remember your training."

Then came a short ground lesson. If it was to give our emotions a break, they failed miserably.

"There are thirty-three different species of snakes in Vietnam, thity-one of them are poisonous, so watch yourselves and don't play with the crawlies. Some are hemo-toxic and will cause internal bleeding. Some are neuro-toxic and will shut down the nervous system, heart, lungs, etc," he paused. "We don't want to send you home in a body-bag and have to explain to your families that you were fucking with snakes."

This information really helped my morale. Not to mention my breakfast, now setting in my stomach trying to figure the quickest way out. Damn I hated snakes. This was just great; I'd be jumping at every rope left laying on the ground. Then came the bug warnings. Scorpions and spiders topped the list. We were told to check folded clothing, bedding and boots before putting them on.

During the briefing we went over the entire country from one end to the other. Vietnam is long and narrow, extending about a 1000 kilometers, running north and south. A chain of mountains called the Annamite Range, runs through the western part of South Vietnam. It's forested, and as it is sparsely populated, mainly by the Montagnards (mountain people), and is not an overly developed area. By the time we were through, I knew Vietnam as well as home, or so I thought.

"Gentlemen, you have been given the best training money can buy and the United States Army can give. You're the best of the new pilots and have been chosen for your high scoring grade points and flying abilities. Now I don't want to blow smoke up your asses. We're going to be weeding some of you out. The Army is after the best of the best for some special schooling. For you that make it, if you think you've had it hard in flight school, you're in for a surprise."

Freddy and I gave each other the here we go again look.

"North of here is Da Nang, and that is where the Marble Mountain Air Facility is located. The Army has a special training program there. We're going to send some of you up there for extra schooling. Those of you, which were chosen for that training will be briefed later. Now gentlemen, if you have your notebooks handy, enter these names and numbers. Our company's call name is Blackbird. Copy these numbers down. These are your radio frequency numbers for the flight in. You'll be given new ones later. You will have a further briefing on shore at 1300 hours."

We were given our numbers and frequencies, followed by the lift-off sequence.

We wrote the radio frequencies in our notebooks, double checking to make sure they were correct.

"Any questions?" His eyes roamed around the room. "Good luck and good flying, gentlemen."

Freddy grinned as we left the briefing room. "You ready for this shit?" he asked in a low voice.

"Yeah, about as much as I'm ready to stick my dick in a beehive," I said, "The next time your sister says, 'Let's go to Canada,' I'm packing."

My crew chief was Sp-5 Raymond Peterson. He liked Pete and Pete it was. Pete knew every nut and bolt in and on the Huey. I felt lucky to have him.

Climbing into the Huey, I ran through the cockpit check, my eyes running over the instrument panels. I started with the center console, checking the switches, and circuit breakers, making sure of their positions.

Pete pretended to be mildly interested, but I knew he was watching every move. As I checked my shoulder and lap belts, he gave me a wink and a thumb up. I would learn to look forward to this when I was around Pete. This was the wink that made everything seem okay even in the deepest shit.

As time neared for lift off, my muscles became taut with anticipation, and the sweat trickled down my back, causing my flight suit to feel slightly wet and sticky. Checking the instruments for the third time, I looked at Pete.

"Let's do it, Sir." He said, and winked.

My left hand sweated on the collective pitch control lever. I flipped the master switch on the radio. With all systems a go, I squeezed my starter ignition trigger switch, and the starter motor whined into action as the rotors began their clockwise rotations above me.

Hitting the igniter, the turbine kicked in. I watched the EGT (exhaust-gas temperature) gauge carefully as the rotors became a blur, and the gauge went into the red. Then the EGT moved back into the green, and I relaxed. Within moments the turbine engine had reached 330 rpm.

I gave the watching Navy fireman the thumbs-up. We were past the hot start point. The fireman returned our thumbs-up, then turned with his extinguisher to the next helicopter.

Sweat ran down my face and neck as we sat in the craft waiting for the signal to lift off. I started thinking about some of the mistakes I'd made in my life. There wasn't time however to complete the walk down memory lane. With the signal the lead helicopter lifted, followed by number two a minute later.

I had tapped the gauges so many times to see if everything was functioning properly that my knuckles were sore. Worried that I might be overlooking something, anything. Opening the throttle a little I checked the cyclic, moving it around, making sure it felt right. Pulling the collective up slowly, the nose of the Huey became light, coming up a little. Then the skids got light as the ship leaned back. She was ready even if I wasn't.

I was number three. As we lifted off, I could sense this was a whole new ball game. The craft felt heavier than I had remembered, like it was telling me not to take it off the deck. I would have shut down right then and there, and rowed a dingy for home if they would have let me. The dinghy would've been crowded though, I found out later.

Hovering a few feet above the deck for a couple of seconds to make sure everything was a go, I pushed the cyclic ever so slightly forward. The craft moved over the ship's deck and the view through the chin bubble suddenly showing nothing but water. I flew off the carrier, and began to follow the flight pattern to our destination, the base just outside Qui Nhon. This was no practice run; it was the real thing. My stomach felt like grasshoppers were doing a square dance in it. Within moments we were over land.

"Any chicks on the beach?" I tried to sound calm and collected as we flew over the first stretch of sand.

"I'm looking," Pete said. He knew I was nervous.

Sitting in my webbed seat I began to feel alien not only to where I was, but also to the helicopter. I felt alone for the first time since I'd left Montana. Oh, I knew I wasn't alone. I had Freddy, and he was probably feeling the same way. I suppose all the new pilots were. I wished they'd put Freddy and me in the same helicopter. Boy, that would have been a real catastrophe, Heckle and Jeckle or Abbott and Costello. Vietnam would have been in for a real treat.

Following the directions of a ground man, we were guided into a landing slot then he drew his hand across his throat indicating shut down.

"This is home, Pete?" I asked looking around.

"Looks like the place, " he said, nodding his head. "I hear this is one of the better locations."

"You gotta be shitting me," I said. We grabbed our duffel bags and followed the other pilots.

The heat in Qui Nhon even this early in the morning was like being in an oven and the humidity made it worse.

"Welcome to paradise, gentlemen," came a greeting from a pilot standing next to a large tent.

Freddy caught up with me, "Where's the beer and chicks?" he asked, with a hungry look in his eyes.

"Women that way," replied the pilot jerking a thumb toward town, "beer over there." He pointed the other direction. "Warm and wet."

"That's the way we like our women. What about the beer? Is it warm and wet too?" Freddy asked. He looked like he was going to drop his duffel bag and head for town.

"Come on, you dumbshit," I said. "Let's find out what we're supposed to do."

"Yeah, you're right," he shouldered his duffel bag again.

"Mail call at 1100. Better move your asses," one of the other pilots said as he passed through the bunch of us standing around. "The Hilton's right over there."

We threw our duffels on empty bunks in our quarters. None of us wanted to miss mail call. I was anxious to hear from Annie.

Roll call was made, and everybody checked in. I thought we were never going to get our mail, but at last it came. I had four letters from Mom and sixteen from Annie. Sixteen, I couldn't believe it. Mom's had three full pages in each letter. Annie's had six and seven pages. At first I tore them open and later regretted being so harsh on the envelopes. The last one I savored. Shamefully, I read Mom's letters second from the last, because I wanted Annie's letter to be last.

The rest of the first day went by with a briefing and introduction to Vietnam.

The briefing officer explained the dos and don'ts. "Don't shave with hot water, use cold. It'll keep infections down. Don't forget aftershave lotion or alcohol. Report any sores. Watch for snakes." They had to mention the damn snake thing again. "Don't soap up in the rain to shower, or if you ever have to, do little areas of importance first. Real showers are on occasion, but don't expect them every night. Report anything suspicious. Watch your feet and take care of them at all cost."

I lay awake that night unable to sleep, going over all that had happened today, wondering what tomorrow would bring. I wasn't alone.

"Hey, Cole, you awake?" Freddy whispered.

"Yeah." I was lying on my back staring up at the ceiling.

"You ever think about why we're here? I mean why we're really here."

"Yeah, I've thought about it."

An old pilot we had met that afternoon told us that this work was best done without conscience and that we should pack up our morals and send them home. This bothered both Freddy and me a lot.

"You boys are going to see things that no one should ever have to see," he said. "In order to live with it, you have to be numb. Without feelings. That's why you have to forget they're people and instead, think of them as the enemy. If you don't, you'll die here. Maybe not physically but you're going to die in a worse way," he said, frowning at some memory and shaking his head slowly as if trying to forget."

"You guys are going north to Da Nang I hear. Some kind of special schooling, I hear. You'll see a lot of Marines there. It's a Marine base. Good men, you'll like them. Da Nang's a beautiful city. Sure beats here."

Now in the darkness we lay replaying the day's activities.

"I've been thinking about what that pilot said," Freddy said in a low voice, "It really bothers the shit out of me."

"Me too, Freddy," I whispered, "me too. I was just thinking about that."

"You reckon we'll ever have to kill anyone? I mean just us alone?" he asked.

"I don't know." I turned my head toward his bunk. "I hope we don't. Damn, I sure hope not."

"Me too."

A voice in the dark spoke out softly. "I'm with you guys, I joined to fly helicopters, not kill people. I mean I know we gotta haul grunts back and forth from the kill zones, but I don't want to shoot anyone."

All was quiet for a moment or two as we laid there thinking about what it would be like to actually have to shoot someone. Someone's father or husband or son or brother.

"We might get our asses in a sling if they hear us talking like this. Not that I'd mind being sent back home. I doubt if they'd do us that favor though," I said. "Besides, I don't think it's unusual for green pilots to wonder about these things, it's probably normal."

A pilot by the name of George Pride had evidently been listening to our conversation. "Anybody have an extra broad they want to loan me? This pulling it, is giving me a blister on my hand," he drawled.

Everyone must have been awake. I could hear them chuckling.

We had seven pilots in our sleeping quarters. It turned out Pride was from Georgia and was 21 years old. He was good-natured and always ready for a laugh. Pride was left-handed, and that made him a good guy from my perspective. We were both left-handed. He was a gambler; we'd learned that from playing poker with him on the ship.

Dan Farrel was from New Jersey. He was 22 years old and he talked funny. He was good-natured, single, and also liked to gamble.

William Jackson, or BJ as he was called, was 22 years old and from Chicago. He seemed to be very street wise, single and an excellent pilot.

Frank Bilare, from California, was the oldest, at 28. A career man, he was married and had two kids. Bilare was the smart one of the bunch and read everything he could lay his hands on. He had transferred here from Korea.

John (Killer) Campber was from New Mexico and was 21 years old. We hung the name Killer on him because he was always rolling up a perfectly good magazine and swatting everything that flew or crawled, and everything here did.

Freddy and I rounded out the team. We were all part of a group that had been picked for special training in contour flying. They called the pilots who went through this school, skidders. We had been given one week to make up our minds while we participated in the program to see if we could cut it. If we decided against it, we would be transferred to a different Air Cav. Unit, no questions asked. The Army had laid it on the line with their no frills famous speech, "Some of you may not live through the training and we'll have to ship the pieces back to the states. You want out, now is the time. To the rest, welcome to hell."

We arrived at the Marble Mountain Air Facility in Da Nang the next morning, where our training was to take place. After being given our quarters, the Army wasted no time getting down to business. We spent the next two days sitting in a briefing room listening to what to expect. That first week went by all too quickly, and soon our low-level training began. We were taken out with IPs (instructor pilots) flying Hueys at levels that were by far too low for air safety regulations. The trees along the different routes showed the punishment a Huey could dish out and still fly, at least we hoped they would still fly until we could get our asses out of them. At the end of each flight we'd do a little glad to be living jig, to show how glad we were that we survived the training session.

At the ends of the forty-eight foot rotors are ballast weights, allowing Heuy rotors more centrifugal force than other types of helicopters, thus better and stronger rotation. The Huey was the only craft that once on the ground with the engine shut down, still had the force to pick itself up and turn completely around in the air by just the centrifugal force of its rotors.

In this training class there was no such thing as bad grades; you lived or you died. Our IP's were rough on us. By the end of the third week, two of our pilots washed out. Both alive however, but their nerves were shot and they lost their flight status. That made the rest of us go over everything we were uncertain of, and review our notes with each other. Why I didn't want to wash out of a program that was so dangerous was a mystery to me. Considering the events that followed, I should have done just that. But youth had a certain pride, or was it stupidity?

On training missions, we flew hugging the ground, following trails. The Vietcong guerrillas had little or no time to shoot at us. On the contrary, we scared the hell out of them. Flying so low they had to hang onto their hats and jump for the bushes or our skids would have taken off their heads. It was hard for them to shoot at us, when they were having to scramble in order to save their asses from the devil flyers, as they began calling us.

The NVA (North Vietnamese Army) adjusted quickly to our helicopter deployments. They adapted to tunneling miles of underground paths, built to handle large numbers of troops. The tunnels also ran at different levels to deal with the concussion of explosives and had doors to block gas. I shuddered at the thoughts of our men going down in them.

They were booby trapped with everything the NVA could think of, trip wires, poisoned punji sticks and poisonous snakes tied in various places to strike an enemy on the head. The entrances were concealed in some of the most unexpected places, sometimes even in village living quarters, hidden under mats. Usually they were just outside the villages, perhaps under a pile of straw or in a pigpen.

When a tunnel was discovered, the family hiding it was assumed to be VC and were likely to be shot right on the spot or at the least they could depend on their hooch's (homes) being destroyed. When an entrance was discovered close to a village, it was a black mark for the whole area and hell would erupt. Either way the villagers lost, some were shot by our side for being VC. Others were killed by the Vietcong.

The loss of these tunnels and villages was crippling the VC and NVA. It made it harder to hide from our troops and helicopters. Our men destroyed their supply lines, munitions and rice that was stored in the tunnels, which meant they were going to go hungry for a while. The problem with destroying their food supplies meant peasants starved too, because they confiscated their food.

I believe a lot of the hill tribes weren't even aware of why the fighting was taking place all around them. They didn't care who ruled their country. They were a peaceful people intent on farming and feeding their families. They were taken advantage of by the NVA and the VC, not to mention the good old US of A. However, if they didn't like you, they could be vicious enemies.

Chapter 17

Time passed quickly and our flying improved with every day. We were now capable of flying below the treetops, contouring the canyons, roads and trails at speeds far in excess of all flight safety rules. We all felt like Superman, not realizing at the time that we were dead men just waiting for a good place to prove it. Being young and invincible, we weren't afraid, and perhaps that gave us the edge that we needed for quick reaction time.

Forty-one men had started in the skidder-training program. By the end of the first month, the number had dropped to thirty-five. Several of the pilots had lived long enough to be transferred out; a few weren't that lucky.

While in the air I never had time to worry about whether I was going to live or die. I just concentrated on what was ahead for the next few seconds. Anything more would have been suicide.

Contour flying left enemy soldiers in a constant state of turmoil because they couldn't hear us at such low altitudes. The foliage absorbed the turbine engine and rotor noise until we were so close there wasn't time for them to react.

The door gunner had to act swiftly as we passed over the VC, although sometimes I wondered if they weren't just peasants trying to get the hell out of the way. I chose not to dwell on that too much. I chose not to dwell on a lot of things.

Toward the end of the training program, we began to fly actual combat missions. The first time I flew into a hot LZ, transporting fresh troops into hell and dead and wounded out, I got my first real taste of war and all its glory. As grunts loaded the dead and wounded onto my craft, I couldn't help feeling the impact, this was real. It had been different shooting at people as we passed over their heads. I had to concentrate on what was up ahead and didn't have time to think about what was happening on the ground. Now as I looked at the stark reality of death, I realized that war had no glory. I had seen death before, when grandfather died and again when I had attended the funeral of old Mr. Bigsby. But neither of those deaths had prepared me for the violence and inhumanity man can inflict on man.

I hadn't realized the tenacity of the human spirit or the endurance of the human body, until I saw a grunt barely recognizable as a human loaded onto the Huey. He was crying while drowning in his own blood. With what little was left of his neck and chest, he should have been dead. Yet he fought on. At that time I saw the true face of combat. It was depraved and full of ugliness, without honor or glory. I felt physically sick. Lifting out of the LZ with my cargo of mutilated flesh, I wondered how mankind could possibility benefit from all this pain and death?

People from two different parts of the world coming together to do battle, neither understanding why they must kill and be killed. What right had I to come to this country and kill? The physical and mental stress began to build. At first, no matter how hard I fought the emotion, the knowledge that I was doing something hazardous produced an adrenaline high. Every time we sat down and loaded up, adrenaline surged through my body. Helicopters and their pilots were the main targets of the gooks. The feeling of living with danger, playing sky Russian roulette was like a drug, and I was becoming addicted. I think subconsciously I looked forward to flying and dreaded it at the same time. I believe most of the other pilots felt the same. Training while under combat began to do things to my system. I couldn't put my finger on anything in particular, but something was happening inside my head. I guess it was the fact that I was cheating death on a regular basis.

As our training progressed, so did our mood. Tempers shortened and fights broke out over small differences of opinion: what baseball or football team was best or who would win the pennant. It was time to take a weekend leave.

We headed for Da Nang and the excitement of the nightlife. First thing on my agenda was a steak and seafood. There were several good restaurants in Da Nang, but one in particular I had heard of from several of the older pilots. The restaurant was owned by a beautiful French woman, I was told. She made an appearance nightly and was a feast all by herself. If you were lucky, she would stop and visit with you for a moment or two.

I was faithful to Annie in body and mind, but I longed for female companionship and would welcome talking to a woman who spoke English. As far as my physical needs, they would have to wait until I returned home to the lady I loved.

I had looked forward to this weekend for several days, because I had been depressed over the loss of John Campber (Killer.) He had flown into a cable stretched across a canyon. Killer hadn't even had time to blink before his Huey struck the cable. The only good thing we could think of to say about his death was it had been quick. That wasn't much consolation however for his family.

Our first drink was to Killer. We all stood as I gave a toast to him. "To our friend and brother pilot, Killer. May we learn from his misfortune and thank him in the beyond. May all our deaths be as quick," I said, lifting my drink.

"To Killer," the other pilots said, as all saluted the farewell. Other pilots that had died before him were just names and faces we saw around base. But killer had bunked in our quarters and looking at his area, empty now except for a rolled up magazine that lay under his bunk, was a constant reminder that a friend and fellow pilot had died.

After a couple of drinks we were feeling better and the women began looking even sexier, if that was possible. Vietnamese women are attractive and little. Being small in stature doesn't mean they didn't have curves in all the right places, on the contrary. Some of the best figures are to be found in this part of the world. I became cautious of getting too friendly with any of them for fear I'd weaken and wrong Annie. I didn't want that to start. I had heard of guys letting this happen, and then they figured what the hell and had thrown their morality to the wind. One had been a chaplain, or so the story went.

"Hey, guys, I'm starving. I think I'm going to go grab a steak. Who's with me?" I asked.

One by one the guys finished their beers and stood up.

"Let's go to that fancy place, the one with the good looking gal," Farrel said as he stood. We left a pile of Dong on the table for our drinks and headed out.

Entering the restaurant was an adventure in itself. Lush plants grew everywhere, and exotic birds were caged in one corner with colored lights on them. The place was plush but comfortable. The dining area had a dark decor, which was elegant with a candle glowing in the middle of a small floral arrangement set in the center of each table. Looking around, we saw nothing but GIs.

As we were being seated, the most gorgeous woman I had seen in Da Nang walked by within twenty feet of our table. I felt my stomach do a flip-flop. I hadn't felt this way since leaving home and hoped this was the exception rather then the rule, otherwise I was in for a long tour of duty.

There were four women sitting across the room. Freddy swung into action, and tipping a cocktail waitress, found out they were Army medics.

Had I been without a woman that long? Or were they as attractive as I thought? I tapped Freddy on the shoulder.

"Hey, Captain Horny, is my imagination running wild or are those women as good looking as I think they are? I mean, I'm just curious."

"They sure as hell are, where did the Army get so many good looking women. Hollywood you think? That blonde sitting next to the window, that's the one I'm going to ask to marry me," Freddy answered without taking his eyes off her. "First though, I want her to have one of my children."

"Freddy, you horny bastard, you want all good looking women to have your children. I think you could re-populate a country all by yourself."

"I'd be willing to try, starting with her."

The beautiful lady returned to the dining area and our eyes locked for a moment.

"Hey, you see that? She was giving you the look," Freddy said leaning over the table towards me.

BJ grinned. "Maybe you're going to score the big one, Morgan."

Farrel joined the fun. "When you get done maybe you'll end up owning the business, too."

My stomach still had butterflies. There was something in her look. Nothing I could put my finger on. It was just there.

Our steaks came with some kind of green salad and a strange kind of potato with a sauce on it. It was all right, but I preferred the kind we raised in Montana. But what the hell, I was hungry.

"Hey bird-men, guess what. We're worth a lot of bucks to Charlie," Farrel said.

"How's that?" I asked.

"I heard from one of the old timers that the NVA are offering the gooks fifteen hundred bucks for each chopper they shoot down. American dollars, not this Dong shit. Just think, we're worth something after all," he said, then continued. "You're not going to believe this shit though, the medevacs are worth more than we are. We're going to have to show them that we're worth just as much as they are."

We chuckled. Although, I doubt any of us found any humor in it. We were beginning to laugh at some pretty bizarre things. What was happening to us?

We finished our meal and were having drinks when we had a visit from our hostess.

"How are you gentlemen enjoying your evening?" the hostess asked.

We all stared at her tongue-tied. She was a knockout. I'm sure it was only for a moment, but I felt like a kid seeing his first naked woman. It was hard to control the impulse to scan her from top to bottom, but I had perfect peripheral vision. She wore a simple light blue oriental dress with a slight split up the thigh. The silky garment clung to her figure as if it had been made by magic, although I'm sure she's the one that made the magic.

She was not Vietnamese, although she seemed to have some oriental blood. Her eyes were an exotic blue, and her lips full and youthful. Her whole demeanor fascinated me.

She broke the trance when she spoke. "My name is LeeAnn, I'm your hostess. You're Army officers? I see you're wearing wings," she said in perfect English. "You're pilots?"

"Yeah, just four lonesome pilots looking to enjoy an evening out," Farrel said, looking hungrily at her.

"I'm sure there are some young ladies that can distract you for an evening," she said looking him in the eye.

"Who are those ladies over at that table by the window?" Freddy asked. He already knew who they were, but wanted in on the conversation.

"They're from the military hospital. Three are nurses; the one next to the window is a doctor. They come in a couple times a week. I'm sure you'd like them. Would you like for me to introduce you?"

"Yeah, I would," Freddy said and stood up. Farrel and BJ followed.

"You coming, Cole?" Farrel asked.

"No, you go on ahead. I'm going to sit this one out."

LeeAnn gave me a questioning look, then motioned a waiter to bring me another drink. She waited until I had it in my hand before escorting the others over to the women's table.

A bus boy busied himself clearing our dishes. I tipped him and he bowed his thanks, his eyes never leaving mine.

Probably a VC, I thought, sipping my drink. Everyone was suspect, and we were right in most cases. Wait tables for you during the night and shoot at you through the day. It was a hell of a world.

I stared at the floral arrangement, deep in thought.

"Have you been in Da Nang long?" came a woman's voice.

I looked up. Our hostess stood looking down at me. Damn, she was beautiful.

"Not long. Would you care to join me?" I asked, motioning to a seat.

"Yes, thank you."

I stood as she sat down. She had extraordinary poise. "You speak English very well," I said, not knowing what else to say.

"I'm LeeAnn Marcotte. I was educated in the United States. Boston to be precise. My father has relatives there. He's French; my mother is French and Vietnamese. I have one brother. He's a mining engineer and lives in Africa, and I have a sister in Qui Nhon. Am I missing anything?" She rolled her eyes up and to the right. "No, I don't think so." She smiled.

Her eyes laughed like Annie's. I liked this lady instantly.

"You're different from your companions," she said, looking at me. "I can feel it. So, what about you? Your name and a little background."

"Me? Cole Morgan. Not much to tell. I fly helicopters for the Army. I've been in this country for almost two months. I have a beautiful wife back home in the states, Kalispell, Montana, to be more precise. Have I missed anything? Nope," I said.

We both laughed.

"I like a man who is uncompromising and has a sense of humor. I can tell you love your wife. It shows. I like that," LeeAnn said, putting her chin on the palm of her hand and resting her elbow on the table.

Her hair was just a little short of touching her shoulders, dark but not quite black, with a slight curl under. She was about the same height as Annie and I had to reluctantly admit that her figure appeared to be almost as good. I felt like a traitor thinking that way, but I was always honest about my opinions even if I didn't voice them.

"You own this restaurant?" I asked, knowing she did.

"Um hum, I bought it three years ago. I'm from Qui Nhon, which is south of here. My family still lives there. They're in the tea business. What does your family do for a living?" LeeAnn asked, showing sincere interest as she stared into my eyes.

"I'm from the northwestern part of Montana. We raise cattle and my father logs to supplement our income. Not very interesting," I said.

"I think it's very interesting. A real cowboy sitting at my table. I feel honored. Most of these soldiers are just out for a good time."

"Hey, I'm as dangerous as the rest," I said, grinning.

"I don't think so," LeeAnn said, laughing.

We looked at each other for a minute, then I dropped my eyes, feeling a little uncomfortable. Glancing back up at LeeAnn, I noticed she hadn't taken her eyes off me. I picked up my drink and drained it. She immediately signaled for a waiter.

"No, I've had enough. Thanks," I said smiling at her.

"Have you toured our fair city?"

"I can't say I saw very much with that bunch of guys," I said, grinning at the memory of our outings. Strip joints mainly. "They're more interested in girls than the sights."

"Uh huh. That's soldiers the world over. Will you be in town tomorrow?"

"Yeah, we're staying at the hotel up the street. At least I am," I said.

"If you'd like to get together for breakfast in the morning, I'll give you a tour of my beautiful city."

"Tomorrow would be great. What time and where should we meet?" I asked.

"I'm a morning person. How about eight? The side door of the restaurant, I'll take you to a great place for breakfast," she said as she stood up. "Right now I should be getting back to work." Her eyes danced with merriment as she looked at me.

My heart pounded at the thought of seeing her again. I also felt a little guilty. I brushed it off. I was being foolish. I had no intentions of anything more than companionship. Annie would approve. At least I hoped she would.

I walked back downtown and after looking in a couple of bars, finally found Farrel, BJ and Freddy with their dates. They were making so much noise, I probably could have found them blindfolded. As I entered the bar the guys jumped to their feet and began shouting for me to join them. Grinning, I shook my head at all the noise and walked over to their table.

"Hey, bring on the beer!" BJ shouted at the waiter.

"Where's the goddess?" Freddy said.

"LeeAnn had to get back to work," I said, sitting down. "We're going to get together in the morning and see the sights."

"Man, she is the sights." Farrel said, making his hands go in and out as if drawing her figure. "Don't get much better than that."

"She's a cutie," added his date.

"Yeah, I have to admit, she's attractive," I said, wanting to change the subject.

BJ got up and pushed another table over to the already crowded one we were at. The waiter showed up with the beer and waited for one of us to pay him with the money that was lying on the table. No one knew whose money it was. They had just piled the Dong in a heap. When it ran out, they'd do it again. There wasn't much else to do around here in the evenings except drink or go to the show and most of the shows were in Vietnamese. Cowboy shows were popular. I couldn't help chuckling when John Wayne spoke in a dubbed singsong drawl.

I returned to the room early that evening, leaving romance to my buddy's. I couldn't sleep right away but lay there on the cot they called a bed and sweated. I stared at the ceiling thinking about what Annie was doing. Probably she would be asleep considering what time it was back home. "Damn, I miss you," I whispered to the darkness. Then I felt better as I saw her in my mind smiling. I closed my eyes with her image and drifted off to sleep.

The next morning I woke to the snoring of three very drunken pilots. Freddy lay on his back in just his shorts. There was lipstick on his right hip and a half smile on his face. Good old Freddy, he's always the same.

I went out in the street and was pleasantly surprised that the traffic at this early hour was almost nonexistent. Probably the whole town is VC, and they're all out hunting us, I thought, and chuckled at my early morning wit.

I walked to LeeAnn's restaurant. Going to the side door as she had instructed, I rang the bell. An older Vietnamese woman answered. Peeking through a small window first, then after she was satisfied, she opened the door. She motioned me to enter. She was very polite and offered me a seat, then left me to wait.

In a few minutes LeeAnn came in. "I hope I didn't keep you waiting Cole?" She said pleasantly, holding her hand out for me.

"Not at all," I said as I shook her hand. It seemed good to be with her. There wasn't that uncomfortable feeling I had encountered with so many women, just an easy feeling of belonging. I realized that LeeAnn had class and that was something else I'd missed since being away from Annie.

"First that breakfast I promised you last night," she said as we headed for the door. Here was someone that was going to be a lot of fun, a real live wire. I could tell, not only was she extremely attractive this morning, she was full of energy and raring to go. I liked that.

As we walked along the sidewalk, she pointed out landmarks. "After we eat I want to show you some of the old ruins, but first things first ... food," she said and smiled that gorgeous smile again. If there's one thing I find attractive in a women it's a nice smile and a willingness to use it often.

We sat at an outdoor table near the marketplace, where everyone greeted LeeAnn on sight.

"These are good people, Cole. They fear Americans, but they aren't unfriendly," she said in their defense when they bowed but showed uneasiness for my uniform. "First stop is the museum, then I'll show you the treasures of Da Nang."

Breakfast was leisurely and elegant. We drank tea and talked about our worlds. LeeAnn was curious about Montana. She wanted to know if we still fought with the Indians? Did we ride horses into town? Did we have electricity and running water? I was amazed at how little the people here knew about our part of the world.

If you were from California, you lived with movie stars, or perhaps were one. Montanans were still fighting Indian wars. Chicago was still a place to be machine-gunned by mobsters.

LeeAnn at least knew a little more than the average person did because she had gone to college in New England, but she was still ignorant of my part of the country. Too many movies, I guess.

Arriving at the museum, she sounded like a tour guide. LeeAnn had tremendous knowledge of the surroundings and culture of the area.

"This museum was built in 1915. It houses many sculptures dating back to the 7th and 15th centuries. Chinese art and architecture obviously had a strong influence on Vietnamese culture. Cole, what are you looking at?" she asked, half-amused and half-curious.

"Sorry, I was just looking at you and thinking how much you remind me of someone else."

"I don't know whether to thank you or be disappointed that I caused you to think of someone else. For right now, thank you, I think," she said, looking serious. Then that great smile reappeared.

After the museum tour, we stepped back out into the sunshine.

"Now we will see some of the countryside," she said.

We took a pedal cab to the country, making sure we stayed on well-beaten roads. I knew better than to get too far out of the city. Being a round-eye, I'd be a sitting duck for some VC, and there wasn't any shortage of them.

After the ride, we walked along the beach, and I turned more than once to admire my hostess, trying not to be obvious.

All too soon the day came to an end and with great reluctance LeeAnn and I returned to town.

"Will I see you again, Cole?" she asked.

"I hope so, LeeAnn. I might be able get away next weekend. We could maybe get together if you like."

"I'd like that very much. I am planning an afternoon cocktail party for some people next Saturday, I would love to have you and your friends come. They could bring their dates."

"That would be nice LeeAnn, I would love to come and I'm sure the others would to."

Until next Saturday then?" she held her soft, delicate hand out for me to take.

"Until next Saturday," I said as we shook hands.

Returning to the bar where I was supposed to meet my buddies, I found the most hungover three guys in Da Nang.

Slapping my hands together loudly, I yelled a greeting. "Well! Aren't we a cheery looking bunch."

Freddy held the side of his head, "Fuck you, Morgan."

"Double from me," BJ said.

Farrel just gave me the finger.

"That smoky, bouncy, smelly old bus should be here anytime now. I feel great. Nothing like a lung full of good old smoky, stale air," I said and smiled. Breathing in real deep, I beat on my chest with the palms of my hands.

The three of them looked at me with disgust. I began dancing around to show them the difference in being sober and hung over. As I finished my little jig, I bowed to them and held my hands up for applause.

Three middle fingers went up simultaneously.

"Let me reiterate my feelings, asshole," Freddy said standing. "Go stick your dick in a tail rotor. I hope you die a virgin!" Then he shuddered at the thought. "A virgin," he whispered as if it were a curse and grimaced.

The bus showed up and we piled in. Each of the three sat next to a screened window, looking like death warmed over. Me, I whistled and had a great ride back to the airfield.

"Hey, look at that," I'd say with excitement in my voice, trying to find things to point out that I thought interesting. My acting should have got me an Academy Award. The middle finger was displayed more times that trip than I'd seen in a month.

"Hey, guys!" Merger called to us as we walked toward our quarters, "they posted the duty roster on the board in the operations tent this morning. We've been assigned to different air Cav. units. Information and dates are listed. We're going big time."

At this news the three drunks seemed to recover some composure. We gathered around the operations tent.

"I can't fucking believe it," Freddy said, as we stood looking at the roster, "The bastards are sending me south. An Khe. What the hell is there in An Khe? Hey, your name isn't on the roster, Cole."

"You ship out a week from this Thursday." I said, "That means we'll all be able go to LeeAnn's party. She invited me and told me to bring you clowns.

"We wouldn't want to intrude." Freddy said, raising his eyebrows a couple of times.

"Don't look at me like that, you dumb shit. She's just a friend. Annie would approve."

Freddy grinned at me. "Sure Cole, I know how it is. LeeAnn probably pulled some strings to keep you in Da Nang. She carries a lot of weight in town."

I gave him the finger.

Chapter 18

That week I had to fly a couple of brass up the coast to Hue from Da Nang, for a day of meetings. This was the kind of duty all pilots dream about. The only thing that would have been better would be to be assigned as a C and C (Command and Control) pilot. C and C helicopters flew battalion commanders to oversee a battlefield and stayed at least 1500 feet above it all. It sure beat getting punched full of holes all the time.

Upon landing I had time to kill. As I wandered around trying to entertain myself I watched the Vietnamese people closely, trying to see how much difference we had made in their lives. It was amazing how we had damaged what should have been a peaceful way of life. The people were of a gentle, easy going nature, yet were fearful and even sometimes hateful of our military. They had good reason and I felt like hell knowing I was a part of it. When I look back at what we helped do to a beautiful country with lush tree covered mountains and rich in cultural heritage, it grieves me deeply.

By Thursday we were on our way back to Da Nang. At the air facility things hadn't changed much. We had some replacement pilots or FNGs (fucking new guys.) They regarded me as an old timer, and by now, I couldn't dispute them. At times I felt fifty years old and sometimes found myself calling younger pilots 'son'. The worst part was they listened to me like I was fifty years old. Looking in the mirror, I began noticing my mouth turning down at the corners and lips growing thin from setting my mouth. They say that when your mouth turns down and your lips grow thin, they'll never change back. Too much death had begun making it's mark on me.

When I looked at the new pilots, I realized that was the way I had been just a couple of months ago. I had come here big eyed, believing that we were keeping a people free to chose their way of life and eventually live in peace. Instead I found a country that had been torn by war for centuries. The people didn't care that we were dying for them. To most Vietnamese, we were the invaders, not the NVA. They said the United States had no right to bring soldiers into their country. Some thought we were still the French soldiers who had occupied this country before us. I felt sorry for the innocent people that were being torn from their homes, and a way of life that had been theirs for many generations. But at the same time, my hatred for the VC and NVA was building by the day because of what they were doing to our soldiers.

The words of the old pilot came back to me more and more often: "Send your conscience home. If you don't, you will lose yourself here." I knew now exactly what he was talking about.

That evening Freddy and I sat in the officer's club having a few drinks and listening to a fellow helicopter pilot by the name of Flagger, who was from the 5th Air Cav. He talked about getting shot down around Dak To, which is north of Pleiku, in South Vietnam. Flagger sat at our table getting loaded. To say that he was well on his way to accomplishing that goal would be a gross understatement. He was a lifer, someone who's in for twenty years or better. That translated into being insane as far as we were concerned. As he sat with us, he told of how they were transporting grunts when the NVA hit them hard with their fifties. His crippled craft went down a couple of miles from the LZ. Fortunately no one was seriously hurt. They say any landing that you can walk away from is a good one. This one had been good.

Chewing on the stub of his cigar, Flagger spoke about the ship's sides looking like they had been hit with Claymores. (Claymores are antipersonnel mines that when exploded, throws seven hundred steel balls with a kill radius of fifty meters.)

He spoke of endless jungles they had trudged through. Not knowing where they were, their only objective was just to stay alive. The NVA had been on their asses from the moment they hit dirt. There wasn't even time to destroy the guns or radios, just jump and run.

Flagger was pretty hot under the collar, and the more he drank the hotter he got. Looking at the large size of his frame and deadly looking eyes, I'd hate to have him pissed at me.

He scowled. "The sons a bitches in politics don't know whether their asses are punched or bored. They have no idea what we're doing over here or what the hell they're asking us to die for. It's all bullshit. These fuckers have cards they're not showing. They sure as fuck don't have any of their relatives over here so we could ask them their opinions. We die taking ground, then give it back. What the fuck do they want from us?"

He was snockered, and his speech was slurred, but what he was saying interested us, so we bought another round of drinks. Flagger sat and stared at his drink for a long time. We could tell he was thinking, so Freddy and I kept quiet, and waited.

"You know," he said, "when we were walking out, we came across a couple of graves in the trees. Just two. They had crosses stuck in the ground. Our guys. I know why they buried them there; there wasn't any place close to sit a ship down for a pickup, too many trees. Dead men start rotting after a few hours in this heat, but that was sure as hell a fucking lonely area to spend eternity. A lousy way to treat someone who came over to the other side of this fucking world to give his life for some mother-fuckers that just want to make money. Fucking politicians are just as guilty. They could say no. But they're more worried about their jobs. They're the ones responsible for all the bodies that are going to be left here. Somewhere out there all nice and cozy, is a handful of motherfuckers that rule the world and everything in it. Mark my words, they're out there quietly raking it in. Fucking blood money is what it is. I hope they all rot in hell!"

He chewed on the stub of his cigar, obviously deep in thought. "Shit, it's like they're playing chess, and we're the pawns. We're fucking expendable by their rules. They just reach in the box, and get some more replacements. Sons a bitches make the rules up as they go."

He sat for a moment weighing his next words, then lifting his drink to his lips, drained it. "It seems we catch all the fucking sky bullets, then when we sit down, all the damned ground fire." He shook his head slowly, staring at nothing. "We should be flying gunships (attack helicopters) instead. Charlie keeps his fucking head down when they fly over."

"This damned country is tailor-made for ambushes," Freddy said to no one in particular.

I'd been on quite a few missions by now, and I could vouch for that. I'd often thought of what it'd be like to go down in some of the areas we flew. If we were lucky enough to walk out, we could look forward to wading through bogs up to our ass, pounds of mosquitoes, and snakes galore, not to mention the gooks. Damn, I hated bugs almost as much as snakes, almost.

"You know what the average number of rounds fired for each kill is?" he asked, as he ordered another drink. "You ready for this one? A fucking four hundred thousand rounds or more. That's a fact. Four hundred thousand fucking rounds per gook!"

Freddy and I looked at each other.

"You mean four thousand, don't you?" Freddy asked, looking over his beer.

Flagger shook his head, "Fuck no, four hundred thousand rounds per kill!" Leaning forward he tapped the table with his finger as he repeated the figures. "Spray the bullets in the general direction. I overheard the brass in Saigon talking about the stats. You know how they want us to keep track of our kills, even if we have to dig them back up after the gooks bury them. And you know how the assholes keep track of our munitions. If they say four hundred thousand rounds per kill, it's probably more than double that. We got a lot of fucking liars leading us, and taking the bows. If they can stretch the truth a little, it's a feather in their cap. We'd better damn well straighten up our act or we're going to lose this fucking war. You ever hear of the military industrial complex?"

Freddy and I both shook our heads.

"Well, I have," he said, after looking at each of us. "'Beware of the military industrial complex'. Eisenhower warned us about it. Made fucking sense then, and it really makes sense now. They start wars to use up all the ordinances. Tanks, planes, helicopters, and so on, then they manufacture more for us to use. In the meantime, you young fellows give your lives for them. Not for your country like you think, but for the mother-fuckers producing the armaments. Show me just one person back home that's in danger from these gooks. Big business and the military, that's what it is, bedfellows. And the politicians are puppets just like we are. If they want to get re-elected that is, or buck them, and get killed. Kennedy for example," he added, and seemed to sober a little.

We all took a drink, and I thought about the assassination of JFK. Flagger sounded like he knew what he was talking about. Why the hell was he sticking it out in the Army? He had to be at least thirty-five years old, maybe older. Perhaps there was no place else to go. At least no place that needed an old helicopter pilot.

"Who you boys defending? America? The world against the Vietnamese farmer?" Flagger shook his head slowly as he looked at his drink. "Fuck, we're giving our lives for the one thing that's the enemy of the whole world. Wealth, greed for the almighty dollar. Ain't any of us in love with these fucking gooks, but I'd just as soon go fishing as kill them. But that wouldn't make any bucks for the fuckers supporting this great cause."

I bought the next round. The woman waiting on us was Vietnamese, and was very attractive. She wore an open necked dress, and when she served our drinks she bent over the table. She didn't wear a bra, and looking at her breasts made my stomach feel like a bunch of butterflies were having a barn dance. I loved it when she bent over from the other side of the table, and sometimes I think she did it on purpose, because she would look me in the eye and smile. I wanted to reach over, and take a handful of her tits.

The waitresses were all good looking, but Joy, which was her American name, had them all beat with a body that would make a dying man get a hard on.

American women are great, but there's something about Vietnamese women that's unique. I think it's the fact that they're more condensed. Your eye doesn't have to travel very far to see everything. American women are different sizes and shapes. Vietnamese women are all built the same. The longer we were here, the more appealing they became.

All Vietnamese employees had to be off duty and off the base by 2200 hours. I hated to see that time come. After they left we had to get our own drinks, going up to the bar where some ugly son of a bitch would wait on us. What a let down it was having a man bartender after Joy. It was 2130 hours, and it would only be a short time before she was off duty. As Joy leaned over to put my beer on the table, her eyes caught mine.

"Morgan, you like to come over to my place, and listen to records? I've got new ones from United States. I fix you food. Okay?" Joy asked, looking me in the eye.

Freddy was listening, a half smile on his face.

"Good medicine, Cole," he said raising the beer to his lips. "It'll cure what's wrong."

"Nothing's wrong with me," I said, and turned my attention to Joy again. She was still bent over the table showing me her chest.

"Not tonight, Joy. I've got things I've got to do. Thank you anyway," I said, smiling, forcing my eyes to come up to her eye level.

She smiled that she understood, and patted my hand. "Maybe sometime soon?"

"Maybe," I said as I watched her cute little butt sway back to the bar.

Flagger ignored the goings on, and continued, "You know what you should do? You should shoot yourself in the toes."

"What?" I asked, not believing what I was hearing..

"Shoot yourself in the fucking toes. You get to go home if you have a bone injury. Flesh wounds heal, then you're back out there being a flying target again," he said taking another drink.

The gooks took every opportunity to shoot our choppers out of the skies. The helicopters were a real thorn in their sides, making it possible to go almost anywhere without roads, and bridges.

I finished my drink, and stood up, not liking the way the conversation was going. Shoot myself in the foot, my aching ass. We had enough trouble keeping the gooks from shooting us. Why help them?

"Got to hit the sack."

"Me too," Freddy said, and joined me.

"Think about what I said, okay?" Flagger raised his drink in a farewell salute.

Walking back to our quarters, Freddy asked me what I thought about our conversation with Flagger.

"I think he's pretty smart. Probably thinks a little clearer when he sobers up though."

"You think there's anything to what he said about that military industrial thing?" Freddy asked.

"Makes sense if you're even a little paranoid, and I think I'm getting there."

"Yeah, me too," he said, then added, "You should take Joy up on listening to her record collection. I wish she'd invite me over. She'd be picking out baby clothes in nine months."

I grinned at Freddy's way of thinking with his dick. Someday it was going to get him into trouble his mouth wouldn't be able to get him out of.

I thought about when we were kids. We'd gotten a job one summer at Danny's dad's service station. We were sixteen, and full of piss and vinegar.

Our big treat was when a certain good-looking rich woman came in for gas. She always wore her dress hiked up to where we could see her panties if we looked straight on from in front of the windshield. Sometimes she even forgot to button her blouse all the way up, and we could see a little tit. Old Freddy and I always fought over who washed her windows. Most of the time Freddy beat me to it. I never saw a windshield so clean. I grinned, remembering how once when she was really showing her crotch. I had gotten to the windshield first. Freddy was supposed to be on the gas pump, and under the hood, but seeing my extra attention, came over and was pretending to inspect her wiper blades. She had lit a cigarette, and was smiling at us as she sat there. She wore lacy black panties that day, and we could see through them if we looked really hard. We both were. Thinking about it now, I still get butterflies in my stomach. That had been a fine looking woman, and very horny, we figured out in our later years. She could have taken us both on, and probably would have if we'd had sense enough to push it. A piece of ass from her, and a cold drink of water probably would have killed us both.

Our last weekend together in Da Nang came around all to soon. As we readied ourselves for LeeAnn's party and our last big fling on the town before Freddy shipped out for An Khe, he turned to me.

"Cole, you got plans for LeeAnn's virginity?" he asked.

"Stop worrying about my sex life. It'll take care of itself. It's yours that you should be concerned about. Your pecker is going to fall off," I said, as we headed for town.

"Yeah, from overuse."

We had a great time at LeeAnn's party. She was a wonderful hostess. The food was out of this world. Her chef from the restaurant had prepared the menu.

Freddy kept trying to get LeeAnn off to himself, but she had a way of turning his advances aside until finally he decided his attempts at flirting weren't getting him anywhere, and gave up.

After dinner and drinks, we took a couple of cabs to downtown Da Nang, and before the night ended I think we hit every bar in the area. There would be some hangovers in the morning. At around 0300 the night finally came to an end, and we headed for the base to sleep for a whole three hours.

Chapter 19

After Freddy left for An Khe I felt lost. I was on standby status until the weekend when I was scheduled to fly some brass to Hue. Early that morning I was called into operations and told I had been rescheduled to pick up a crew that had gone down in a red zone near Khe boi, northwest of Da Nang.

They had been hit and gone down on auto-rotation, radioing in their position before deserting their chopper and taking cover in the jungle. I was ordered to take a search team, get in and get them out before the VC had a chance to home in on them. Two gunships would go in with us and take care of any problems we might run into.

As I touched down lightly, I let the search team out, then sat waiting while they inspected the downed Huey. There was no sign of anyone near the craft so they spread out with their radios and began to search the area.

I monitored the radio while keeping the helicopter light on the skids for immediate lift off. It wasn't five minutes until one of the search team found the missing men.

"We found them, Sir. They're dead, looks real bad. We're at three o-clock, about a hundred meters. Looks clear, Sir. A gunship has us in sight."

At the sound of alarm, I told Bently to take it.

"Got it," he replied, taking over the controls.

Drawing my pistol I jumped out and ran to where the men were, figuring they could use all the help they could get. As I approached the hanging gore, I stopped like I had been hit with a baseball bat. I had seen men, women and children blown in half and with great difficulty had adjusted to it. But seeing this made me physically sick.

Five bodies hung by their feet. All had been stripped naked and tortured to death in various ways. Two had been gutted while alive, judging by the openings of their stomachs. Their guts hung over their heads. Another was cut from his pelvis to his throat with what appeared to be a machete or meat cleaver. His insides lay in a pile on the ground just below his very bloody head. The intestines had been completely severed from his body. A butcher couldn't have done a more thorough job. The gooks had probably done them one at a time while making the others watch. After stripping the men they were hoisted up and hung by the feet, then with one man on each arm, they were held while a knife was inserted into the stomach wall at the pelvic bone. Making sure not to cut any vitals, they swiftly drew the knife to the breast bone, spilling everything down into the faces of the men. My hatred peaked.

Black flies covered the carnage. As they cut the men down, one by one they dropped into the gut piles with a thud, like a sack of flour. These men had been alive less than an hour and a half ago. Now they were reduced to lifeless pieces of meat.

One of the medics had gone back to the ship and got the body bags. The one who had been completely gutted was put in without his insides. I looked at the pile, seeing his lungs, heart and liver along with his stomach and intestines laying on the ground, covered by flies.

"What about these?" I asked a medic. "They go?"

"He don't need them anymore, Sir," came the soft but resolute answer.

We picked up the bags, one man on each end, and ran where possible, not wanting a repeat of this.

"We're getting a call from Roundup. They got the gooks that did this. At least they think it's the same ones, VC. They're two klicks west of here. Let's take a look," Bentley said.

I had reservations about going, but with a little nudging from everyone, we flew over to view the captives. Setting down near the smoke, I left the craft idling, and we walked over to where they held eight VC, their hands tied behind their backs. The sergeant turned to me. "Caught these mother-fuckers carrying their plunder, Sir. They didn't even clean the blood off their machetes. We waited for you to get here. Thought you'd appreciate the way we handle these things."

"I can't haul them back with the weight I have already, Sergeant, my ACL (allowable cargo load) is maxed." I said, looking at the little fuckers sitting on their knees.

"Not a problem, Sir. Intelligence won't have any need for these bastards anyway."

Drawing his pistol, the sergeant walked over to the VC. He glared at them and pointed his pistol at each one, watching their reactions.

The first gook glared with pure hatred at all of us. He was about twenty-five years old and looked like the leader.

"Bring that gook over here," the sergeant told one of the grunts, indicating a spot in front of the others that were still kneeling.

The other prisoners showed some fear of the sergeant. One began asking questions in Vietnamese. The first man continued to glare at him as they roughly lifted him to his feet and hurled him to the spot the sergeant had indicated.

The sergeant drew his knife and grasping the gook by the hair, roughly jerked his head back and forth a couple of times. Then before anyone knew what they were watching, the knife was inserted into the brain at the base of the gook's skull, and with a twist of the blade the execution was finished. As the body fell forward, the sergeant pulled the knife out and using the VC's shirt he wiped off the blade. Blood continued to pour from the wound at the base of the head for what seemed like an eternity as the nerves made the body twitch.

The questioning went on with little or no results. Drawing his pistol the sergeant stepped to the next, and as I watched in fascination, the executions continued. Methodically the VC were each shot in the head. At first I started to object, then the thoughts of what I had in the helicopter stopped me. I felt nothing as I looked at the gooks on the ground, and I later wondered if the sergeant had asked me to execute some, would I have done so? Regretfully, I would have. I knew I had at last sent my conscience home.

During the time I was stationed at Marble Mountain Air Facility I spent most of my time off in Da Nang. What I really looked forward to were my visits with LeeAnn. She was an exciting, intelligent woman and her ability to make me feel at home in this hostile land was something I needed. We went for walks, out to dinner and visited historical sights. There were many evenings we spent at her home, drinking hot chocolate, while playing cards and discussing the differences in our cultures.

Our friendship deepened with the passing of time. I was glad she understood the special circumstances of our relationship. My fondness for this woman grew with each encounter and I looked forward to her companionship. The feelings were mutual, I was sure.

The last of January, I was surprised when I received new orders. I was being transferred to An Khe. We had been suffering heavy losses of helicopters and pilots in that area. (An Khe was nicknamed the Golf Course.)

Damn, it would be good to see old Freddy again. I had a weekend pass and had planned on spending it at LeeAnn's, now my pass had been canceled. Orders were to ship out at 0600 the next morning. I called LeeAnn to explain.

"I'm sorry, I have to cancel our plans LeeAnn. But you know how the life of a soldier is. Don't worry, I'll be just fine. I'll be flying with Freddy again." I explained.

"I know, Cole, but I will miss you very much. We have become such good friends. Why do they do this now? I worry for you."

"I'll miss you too, LeeAnn, more than you will ever know. You don't know how much I have come to count on our friendship. First leave I get I'll come back to Da Nang for a visit."

"Promise?" LeeAnn asked. "And you will write me, Cole?"

"Yes, LeeAnn, I promise," I laughed. "I have to go now. You take care of yourself, and I'll be back to see you when I can."

"Oh, Cole, be ever so careful. I have only one friend like you. Please be careful."

"You don't have to worry. I'll be very careful. I have to go now. I'll see you first leave I get, okay? Take care."

"I will, Cole, au revoir."

I started to hang up the phone when I thought I heard her say, "I love you, Cole." I put the phone back to my ear. "What did you say?" I asked. But the line was dead.

Chapter 20

The next day I was on my way to An Khe. At a briefing before taking off, we were warned again about the presence of VC in all the villages. My flight orders were to hold at three thousand feet, and stay out over the water as much as possible between Da Nang and Qui Nhon, where I was to pick up some documents to be delivered to HQ. I didn't like the idea of dodging fifties, so that was all right with me.

Qui Nhon is a strategic port city. An Khe, also called the 'Golf Course', lays due west, marking the half-way point between Qui Nhon and Pleiku which lays further west, two thirds the way to the Cambodian border. This part of Vietnam is a combination of valleys, rice paddies, heavy jungle foliage, tall trees, and elephant grass. Red dirt covers all of the country and quickly coverts to red gumbo when wet. For each leaf or blade of grass, there's a mosquito.

When it rains, everything rots, including uniforms, gloves and boots. Mine were no exception. The .45 automatic pistol I wore in a shoulder holster had signs of rust even though I kept it cleaned and well oiled. Most of the pilots were using .38 revolvers, but I wanted to be able to put a lot of flak in the air fast, and had requested keeping the .45 automatic, affectionately known as the "thumb buster." Like many other pilots, I had bought a .22 magnum Derringer for a hideout gun, but it was cheaply made and started rusting internally. I ended up trading it for a boot knife and a couple of bottles of rotgut whiskey.

I often thought of Pop and Grandfather. They'd go nuts over all the logging quality trees here. Some of the trees grew over two hundred feet tall, making it impossible to penetrate from above by helicopter. The fortunate thing is there are rivers and trails that are thousands of years old, both can be flown at some risk.

The peaceful look of this part of the country is deceiving. It crawls with VC and NVA. The VC might be anybody from small children to old men or a pregnant woman with a baby on her back. All Vietnamese were suspect. Any one of them could be carrying a grenade and were capable of using it regardless of the risks to themselves. This forced me to re-evaluate what I would and wouldn't do and the reality was overwhelming. I got drunk when I could.

While stationed at An Khe, we transported paratroopers to hot LZs. Jumping had proved to be fruitless in most of the area due to the foliage. At the PZs I studied their hardened faces as they loaded. The war was changing rapidly with the NVA and VC going to tunneling. Between that and the tall trees and jungles swallowing up the enemy, the paratroopers had been forced to change their tactics. They became more reliant on air-mobile tactics. That's where we came in with helicopter combat techniques. Our job was to get them into the hard-to-reach areas and the wounded and dead out. LZs were sometimes hard to come by, most being hot to get in and out of. Going into a hot LZ was always risky. We found our chances of survival were cut in half after 15 seconds on the ground. So we tried to off load and reload in as short a time as possible. Many times we took direct fire as we came in and loaded. With the noise of the helicopter, we couldn't hear the shooting unless it was hitting us, then we heard only the ticking of the bullets passing through the ship's hull. I figured if I could hear the ticking I was okay, it would be the silent one that mattered.

In the air there is no mistaking when we were the target because tracers would fly by us like bright balls of fire. If we flew lower at dusk or flew in the dark, we could see the muzzle flashes of the small arms as well. Those, the door gunners tried to take care of as best they could. Oftentimes a large percentage of the slicks were shot down.

There were other times when we had to drop chain saws to cut trees and other vegetation out of the way so we could get in for a extraction. It looked strange to see trees falling from above as we waited for enough clearing to get on the ground. Sometimes we did a little chopping ourselves with the rotors, making a tree-prune landing as we called them. The forty-eight foot rotors with the ballast sent branches flying in all directions as we settled in. Often we would put the tail boom in between two trees in order to have room to sit down. As we lifted, everyone held their breath as the tail-rotor missed the trees by inches. But God was with us, and we somehow made it.

My first week in An Khe I met other pilots who had been selected from different aviation support groups to join up with our special task force. As Freddy and I sat across from each other sipping a beer, we made note of the different pilots. We had been in Vietnam long enough to know green pilots from the old salts.

"See that guy sitting over there?" I said to Freddy.

"Yeah. The guy with the mustache?"

"Yeah. His name is Striker. Nice guy, kind of like we are," I grinned. "Anyway, we were talking over at the canopy today. He was telling me he knows of a golden Buddha statue. It's supposed to be about eighteen inches tall and he says it's made out of solid gold. How many pounds would that be?" I asked.

"Beats the shit out of me. Probably about the same as lead, I guess. I'd hate to try to run with it. Did he say where it's supposed to be?" Freddy asked.

"Somewhere in the mountains north of here, some old temple that's been deserted. He says he flew a couple of guys out last month who'd found the statue and then buried it. One was dead before he got to him; the other guy lived for about half an hour. His guts were shot out. The guy knew he was dead and told Striker where they had buried it. Says we can find it without too much trouble. Only thing is getting in and out. It would have to be fast. That's where we come in," I said, trying to read Freddy's expression.

"You're nuts, Cole. We could be court marshaled. If they did that, we'd get shipped back stateside." A grin crept across his face. "We'll have to plan this very carefully if we want to stay in paradise."

"I figure if we look over all the possibilities and plan our escape route in case things go awry, it'd be a snap."

Striker looked over at Freddy and me, then lifted his beer in a salute. We held ours up, and all three of us drank to something. We didn't care what, as long as the beer kept coming.

Striker got up and came over to our table. "This your buddy from Montana?" he asked, standing at our table.

"Yep. This be the man. Sit down and get acquainted," I said. Reaching my foot under the table, I pushed the leg of an empty chair out toward him.

At first glance Striker seemed taller than his actual five foot eight or nine inches. He weighed a solid 165 pounds. He had flown both gunships and slicks.

Freddy immediately liked him, and the easy way he handled himself.

"You tell him about the Buddha?" Striker asked as he reached for his cigarettes.

"Yeah, I mentioned it, but I figured you would be better at the details," I said and took a sip of beer.

Freddy waited. That's the way Grandfather had taught us, patience. It always paid to be patient.

"You guys are trained in skidding, right? I've heard of your abilities. Not too good of odds for you going home in one piece though," he said, as he drew in a puff of smoke.

"We'll get by," Freddy said. "Better stories to tell our grandchildren."

Striker shook his head slowly, smoke curling from his cigarette.

"I hear there's only twenty-six of you guys left. How many did you start with?" Then added, "Don't really matter I guess. When our time's up, it's up."

"I don't believe that way. I think we can stretch our time on earth out if we're careful," I said.

It was the age old argument of fate. How many fatalistic people down through time had made that statement then turned around and had to eat their words.

Striker must have sensed my feelings. "I take it you're not a fatalist?"

"You better fucking believe I'm not. That old crap about 'when your time is up, it's up', is a lot of bullshit," I said. "They don't take this kid without a fight, and they'd better bring an army and a lunch."

Striker stared at me for a long time, then grinned. "I like your spirit, kid."

"I've got some paper work to do. I'll catch you guys later," I said and finishing my beer stood up to go.

"Tell Annie I love her," Freddy said.

"Okay, I'll do that. Take care Striker." Then slapping Freddy on the shoulder, I left the table.

Before turning in I sat down and wrote Annie my usual one-page letter. I always felt guilty that I could never think of anything interesting to say to the most important person in my life. I refused to drag her down or make her worry about what went on over here. What was I going to tell her?

"Dear Annie, today I saw a little child blown in half, not to mention an old farmer and his wife, holding each other in terror as bullets ripped through them. Not to worry though, they were old and thought be VC. Oh and I don't want to forget, I also saw a village that had been destroyed. There wasn't one thing left alive that I could see. We'd killed the villagers and all their pigs and chickens. I know we've improved the world's security with the annihilation of that village.

Annie, tell me, what are we trying to prove? That we can kill people that are defending their own land? That we can destroy a way of life that is not being lived according to our way of thinking? That we can destroy a way of life, and force people to accept a government, whether they want it or not? I feel sorry for the Vietnamese people, Annie, and yet there is a growing hatred in me toward all Asians.

Today a fellow pilot took a walk. They found him with one bullet used out of his 45. He didn't have to desert and shame his family. They will write that he was killed in action.

Instead, I just wrote:

Dear Annie,

I just have a few minutes to write and tell you how much you mean to me. I think about you all the time, and as you know, your picture is with me everywhere I fly. I look forward to your letters because they are the only thing that makes having to be away from you bearable.

Life here is pretty boring. I fly mail everyday with you. You didn't realize I was a mailman, did you? I have your picture on the console of my helicopter. Damn girl, you sure have a beautiful smile.

It's hot here, but I guess I've mentioned that a couple dozen times already. Took a shower outside in the rain the other day. The Lord decided to turn the shower off while I was all soaped up. The water wagons were empty so I walked over to the mess hall and the cook poured his used rinse water over me. I think I prefer the soap to getting rinsed with that soup. Mosquitoes prefer to pick their meals and they don't really like me. The other night I heard one of them say the same thing we say at the mess hall, "Not this shit again!" Ha-ha.

Going to go over to Qui Nhon next week and comb the beach for bottles with messages. Last week I found one while I was waiting to pick up the mail. It had a message in it that told of several ways to get a discharge. But when it got to how to do it, it said, refer to the second bottle. I've been looking for the second bottle very diligently.

Must close for now and get some sleep. It seems strange that when I go to sleep, you're just getting up. Weird huh?

Love you lots,
Cole

PS. Has the buckskin mare had her colt yet?

Chapter 21

The next day at a special briefing, Freddy and I were asked to stay behind. After everyone had left, the briefing officer informed us that we had lost two supply helicopters just south of the border junction of Laos and Cambodia, which is on the western border of Vietnam, north and west of where we were stationed.

"We need replacements. We've lost several helicopters over the last few months. They're wanting to send in special task force flyers. You're part of it," he said. "We need pilots with your abilities to get in and out fast. I want two replacement helicopters by the weekend. Any idea who the other helicopter team should be?"

I didn't hesitate, "I think Elm and Bently are good men."

"I've read over the records; you and Gray are well qualified. I'll give Elm and Bently some serious thought," he said. "Now down to business."

We listened as he went on with his briefing.

"We've got a lot of real estate out there that we're trying to keep an eye on. The highlands are close to impossible to penetrate with any effectiveness. As you know, the Ho Chi Minh Trail goes right under our noses there. We have Special Forces camps along the borders manned by Green Berets. If enemy forces are located, they call in the B-52's to handle them. I can't tell you how important all this is to us. The Special Forces camps are entirely dependent on our helicopters for supplies, and we can't seem to keep our supply lines open. We've given it a lot of thought. We're going to use Skidders. This isn't going to be a picnic by any stretch of the imagination. You will not only re-supply, but bring in reinforcements if the camps are attacked. That's where it might get hot on you. They get overrun often times before we can get the RFs in to help them. (Reaction Forces are special standby forces to assist with hot spots.) That means you'll be in more hell than anyone should ever have to be subjected to. Charlie will do anything to stop you and the RFs from getting in. I don't like this any more than you do. But without helicopter support, the Berets and their mountain tribesmen are in deep shit. If we can't stop the buildup here, the NVA will cut Vietnam in half. We can't let that happen."

He waited for our comments.

"It sounds like it's time for us to earn our keep." I said.

Freddy looked over at me, knowing I wasn't sold on this anymore than he was.

"Good. Here are some charts and maps of the area I want you to concentrate on. You can use the office across the hall. Study them and report back here at 0600 tomorrow. That's all, gentlemen." he said.

"Yes sir," we said and left.

The 1st Brigade, 101st Airborne Division had been sent into the central highlands to counter the enemy threat. They were a kick-ass bunch and I felt better knowing they were there.

The NVA, however, were no slouches when it came to jungle warfare. They were well equipped and had the best of training for this kind of fighting. This was their turf and they knew how to use it. The infantry found that out on more than one occasion. This war was far from being the turkey shoot the media wrote about back home. We were constantly amazed by what we read. The only thing that came to mind was bullshit!

Most of the time the NVA was the aggressor, and initiated nearly all of the contacts. When it got too hot, they'd melt into the jungle like ghosts or cross over into Cambodia or Laos, which were their sanctuaries. We weren't allowed to follow according to our rules, which were laid down by ignorant asshole politicians who pulled the strings. During the mean time, the NVA played by their rules. We were starting however; to play by some new rules we made up, but so far had kept from the media and the fucking politicians.

The LRRPs (long-range reconnaissance patrols) were working the highlands, calling in air strikes, and heavy artillery whenever they encountered enemy operations. The A1-Es dropped their payloads of bombs and napalm until the smell of smoke and burnt flesh seemed to hang in some areas for days, only to be replaced by the stench of rotting flesh.

One of our biggest concerns at the air bases was mortar attacks. The infantry instituted a series of SD operations (search-and-destroy). An all out effort was put into force to keep the NVA and VC beyond mortar distance of all installations. Defoliants were spread with helicopters to clear large areas around the bases. These were mostly odorless, and they were spread oftentimes without enough gas masks to go around. The rotor wash would pick some of the defoliant up and pull it back into the helicopters. I wondered how it would eventually affect the men having to spray it or what it would do to the rest of the men, with the defoliants airborne, and drifting back over the compounds. Only time would tell.

I spent the rest of the day and part of the night studying the charts. The contour maps were fairly accurate. I knew the marks locating the LZs were close to camps where we would be delivering supplies. Looking at them brought a hard knot to the pit of my stomach. This wasn't going to be easy. No wonder they were losing helicopters. It didn't take a mental giant to figure where we had to set down. They probably would be waiting for us.

Striker's conversation came back to me. "You boys don't live long, do you?" he had said.

For the first time in quite awhile I felt apprehensive. I wasn't afraid of death; it was the thoughts of never seeing Annie again. Death had to come to all of us sooner or later, of this I was reminded every day. But I had plans for the next fifty years with my lady.

We were in the briefing room again at 0600, only this time there were two more familiar faces, Bentley and Elms. Both were top-grade pilots with plenty of experience. Elms and Bently had gone through contour schooling, and I felt confident in the choice of men.

After our briefing on the objectives and the question and answer session, we broke for coffee. Elms got assigned to Freddy's ship, and Bentley was to fly with me.

Sitting around the briefing room drinking coffee, we exchanged tidbits about combat encounters. Bentley was a great kidder, and I thought he was joking when he said he'd had his chin bubble shot out three times. The chin bubble is a rounded Plexiglas window located just in front of the cockpit and down by the feet, allowing direct forward ground visibility. We laughed at his joke.

"No shit. Three times, honest," he said. "The other pilots started grabbing extra chest protectors and laying them over the chin bubbles."

"Shit, I don't know whether I'm flying with a jinx or the luckiest bastard in Vietnam," I said.

At that, laughter broke out again. I joined in, but couldn't put my whole heart into it. Freddy must have sensed my apprehension.

"Bently, you sound like a fun guy to have around. Let's trade, you can fly with me," Freddy said. "Morgan has to live long enough to make me an uncle."

Again laughter broke the tension.

"No, not as long as he has good news about his flying partners," I said sipping my coffee.

"They don't want to fly with me anymore," he said and grinned. "They say I'm a bullet magnet."

"As long as they're still saying that, that means they're living, right?" Elms asked, chuckling.

"Yeah, but they had to change their shorts each time we got back. Their asses bit a hole in them."

We all roared at that.

We flew to Pleiku, which was directly west of the Golf Course. This base put us within reach of the western Highlands. There we were quartered. After settling in we grabbed a bite then went to briefing.

The next morning at 0600 we were in the air, flying supplies and ammunition to Hill 869. The helicopters were loaded so heavy, we were forced to make translational takeoffs. Translational lift was accomplished by skimming along the ground until we picked up enough speed for our rotors to reach undisturbed air. At around twenty miles an hour we'd get lift. We were glad for an airfield that meant no stumps to catch the skids on and flat ground. At times when we came into an LZ to extract wounded and were over our ACL and didn't have enough room in a straight line to make a translational takeoff, we had to do the merry-go-round, hoping we had enough room to make lift. As the ship's speed picked up, the circling would become wider. There were more than a few times that we escaped when we should have piled it up, according to the rules. On translational take-off the Huey has to reach twenty miles per hour to reach undisturbed air, which is essential for lift. Because of these strokes of luck, we became known as cowboys, and our reputations grew much bigger than we felt comfortable with. We did things because we had too, not because we were hotshots. We just wanted to stay alive and get all our asses back safely.

That day, as we approached to within minutes of the LZ, we flew above low clouds that hung in the valley.

"Shit! We're taking some fire," the door gunner yelled.

"They can't see us," I said. "They're just guessing."

About that time we flew out of the cloud cover and the guessing was over. The door gunner opened up with the M60 and the excitement started. As usual, I felt like my head was in a metal milk bucket and someone was beating on it with a hammer. Damn, those guns were loud when you sat only a few feet from them. I got to where there was a constant ringing in my ears.

"I think we smoked the little mother-fuckers. They stopped when I opened up," the gunner said excitedly.

Truth was, we had out distanced them, but I didn't say anything. He was new and had a lot to learn.

I hugged the treetops as the clouds cleared. We were in a jagged part of the mountains, and as we approached our coordinates, I asked Bently for one last check.

"Shit. That's the mother over there on the right. It's on a fucking cliff. No fucking wonder they keep losing helicopters, there's no place to touch dirt."

Over the radio a voice came in, "Red four, red four, this is Zebra, repeat, this is Zebra, We have visual. Do you copy?"

"We copy, Zebra. Where the hell is the LZ?" I asked.

"Red four, we rolled out the carpet just north of you. Kind of tight ain't she?" The radio crackled.

I saw the short burn of the locator smoke smoldering. "Keep clear Zebra, I'm going to chop a little," I said, and gave some pedal to turn us for the approach.

The LZ was barely big enough to set the front two thirds of our skids down with the tail boom hanging out in space. We had enough room for the rotors to keep from hitting the side of the mountain if we didn't crowd any more than we had to, a foot to close and we'd smash them into the rock. The rotors were doing a great job of trimming the brush and vegetation, sending branches in all directions.

One man was shielding his face with his arm as he tried to get close without getting hit with flying debris. I was glad for the height of the rotors or this could have been a real disaster.

They off loaded the supplies as quickly as they could, then two slightly wounded grunts hopped on board. They both had arm wounds and didn't need any attention, which was a good thing, because we didn't carry a medic. I was glad; I hated hauling grunts that had their guts hanging out, especially if they were still alive. I always worried about getting them back in time.

I could see one of the men asking the crew chief something. The chief grinned and asked me if I could fly this "piece of shit."

I grinned and gave a shrug. These fuckers had just made a tactical error. Then the man on the ground gave us the wave off. I had only one way out of the LZ. As I powered the Huey, and began to slip backwards, the two soldiers yelled out in alarm. They both began cussing as they hung onto their seats with white knuckles, according to the chief's play by play account of their ride. He had told them to buckle in. They had, now they were checking to make double sure they were snapped.

The Huey leaned back, and began to fall away and down the steep canyon. Admittedly, it was kind of a questionable takeoff, but I had no real choice because we had a steep mountain in front of us and trees on both sides. I have to admit I could have made their flight a little easier, but they looked like they could use some excitement, and after all, they weren't sold on my flying ability. I hated to disappoint them about whether or not I could fly this "piece of shit."

Dropping the tail boom is natural for the Huey when taking off in this direction, and the tail rotor with its high-pitched buzz threw more vegetation as the front of the ship rose in the air. As we backed out, clearing the foliage on the mountainside, I pushed on the left pedal, and the tail boom and nose of the Huey swapped ends. At the same time it dove down the canyon, and the white knuckled men gave another loud curse.

Feeling the tension and the excitement, I chuckled, glancing over at Bently, who was getting used to me. He was grinning ear to ear. "You smell anything? Kind of like shit?" he asked as he glanced back at the two men.

The crew chief should have been nominated for an Oscar. He had a scared look on his face as the grunts watched him in horror.

Bently gave me a wink. "Our passengers are wondering if you're qualified to fly one of these. They keep shouting questions at the chief."

I headed toward the bottom of the canyon at a pretty fast clip, then at the last moment flared the craft. The force was enough to finish off the grunts. They completely forgot their wounds and thought about toilet paper.

There were three clicks on the mic. "Yeah chief?" I answered.

"They're apologizing for giving you shit, Sir," the chief said over his microphone. "They didn't say so in so many words, but they nodded their heads when I asked them. I think they were too busy chewing their lunch to answer."

We returned to base that afternoon, and we were met with orders to take some troops down to LZ X-Ray, in the Ia Drang valley.

"We're due for some down time," Bently objected. "We've logged eight hours today and almost fourteen yesterday."

"Sorry, we can't spare anyone. It's hotter than hell out there right now. They need fresh troops. Refuel and move out." The major walked away, holding one hand up at elbow height in a half salute.

"Shit, can you believe this crap? They trying to get us killed? I'm going to get us some peppers (amphetamines). You fuel us," I told Bently.

We were only supposed to fly four hours a day, according to the flight safety rules, because the constant vibrations and racket had a tendency to dull the reflexes, and reflexes were what kept us alive. After a four-to six-hour stint, our reflexes were shot. I headed toward the medics.

We got coffee, and after popping three pills each, then chasing them with the hot liquid, we went over and picked up our troops along with the other ships. It was a large gaggle (group of helicopters).

The LZ was big and would take several ships at a time, which put some of them a little too close to the foliage for my liking. Coupled with the fact that we were keyed to bring back wounded, meant landing close together. Charlie couldn't miss a gaggle like that if we sat down in large sets, and that was the only way to get these men in and out fast.

As we approached the LZ, the pathfinder called from the hill for Red and Orange to come in. We held our hover, waiting our turn. As they touched down, the grunts hit the ground running, and the stretchers were hurriedly slid in. Orange and Red were in the air in seconds and it was our turn.

"Heavy fire, heavy fire! Abort landing, abort, abort!" came the call over the headphones.

"Shit," I said, and we circled away from the area while a couple of A1-Es were called in for a strike, followed up by the gunships.

The all clear was given, and we returned to the LZ. Before our skids had hit the ground, the grunts were off. I could feel the lightness for just a moment, then they began sliding the stretchers onto the deck. The whole time, we kept the choppers as light as possible on the skids, ready at a moment's notice to lift off.

I watched the grunts from the other helicopters hitting the ground running, and at the same time scanning the underbrush for any enemy activity.

I remembered why they were called grunts. Each soldier was required to carry so much weight he grunted trying to shoulder his gear and when they off loaded. Figuring each man carried a dozen fragmentation grenades, a thousand rounds of M16 ammunition and a couple of belts of M-60 ammunition for the squad's machine gunner, you grunted for them as you watched them jump to the ground. Some also carried other armament ammunition such as a round or two for the company's mortars. Then there was gear of the more personal nature, which included C rations. I had been told the loads averaged over a hundred pounds per man.

"Go! Go!" came the shout in my earphones, and we lifted along with the other ships.

Returning to base, I was all jived up with the pills we had taken before we left. I drank a half a fifth of Jack Daniel's before drifting off to sleep.

I was awakened at 2200 hours. "Morgan, the old man wants to see you before first light, something about a rescue."

"Okay," I muttered as I tried opening my eyes to see who was talking to me, "got it." I drifted off once more into an unsound sleep. Flashes of orange lights burst around me as my craft rocked violently. "We're hit; she's going to blow!" I was too high to sit down in time. I could hear voices calling.

"Morgan. Hey, Morgan." Someone was banging on my foot. My eyes shot open. Caldwell stood at the end of my cot shaking my foot. "You got to report to briefing, remember?"

I reported as ordered. Little did I realize that today would be one of the worst days I would endure in this fucking war. In later years, at night in the twilight between wake and sleep, when my thoughts were unguarded, the memory of it would come stealing back.

"We've got a helicopter down somewhere in here. It went down last night," the briefing officer said, indicating on an air chart. "It's hotter than hell in there. Get in, get our men, and get out, gentlemen. We'll give you as much cover as we can. If you can't locate them immediately, get out. We'll send in troops."

We were airborne within minutes after the briefing with a five man recovery team. Three were medics. On the site we found the gunner dead, he had bought it on the way down they figured. Fifty feet away we found the crew chief in a sitting position with his hands tied to a tree behind him. He had been stripped, then while he watched, his belly had been cut open, and looked as if he had witnessed his own guts spill out. We found the two pilots naked bodies about seventy-five or a hundred feet further. Neither had eyes; Charlie had scooped them out. One had been castrated, and his cock crammed down his throat. He had probably choked to death. As one of the men reached for a body bag, I grasped his arm. I had been standing at the foot of one of the pilots, looking at the carnage. Flies covered his crotch in a black mass. The movement of one of the medics had disturbed them for a moment, and I could see a wire had been run through the inner thigh of his leg.

"Wire, Corporal," I said, as I stared at the black mass that had recovered the area. I waved my hand, and the fly's scattered again. "There," I pointed.

"Dickson," he called, and a grunt came over. "We got a wire," he said and pointed at the crotch.

"Dickson is our wire man. He'll take care of it. Better move back, Sir."

Bile rose up in my throat, and I had to keep swallowing to avoid throwing up as we walked back toward my craft. I couldn't allow my mind to think about how these men had suffered. At that instant pure hatred was born and I wanted to kill. There was not an Asian man nor woman safe from the blinding rage I felt at that moment. On that day a little more of my humanity was whittled away and a part of me died with those men.

Chapter 22

My mind snaps back to the present. It looks like Dodson has finally stopped breathing. I stare at his pale form for several moments. Reaching down I feel the jugular for any sign of a pulse; there is none. Dodson is gone. Raising, I stare at what was once one of my crewmen. Taking his dog tags, I attach one to him and pocket the other. I'm both relieved and saddened. "Sorry kid," I whisper.

It's up to me, as senior officer, to make the decisions. I know the VC can't be far behind us. Looking at my charts, I figure we've been hit at least a couple day's hump from home base, and I don't like the looks of what's ahead of us. The VC are more active around the roads and rivers, and we have both to maneuver. A pick up would be almost impossible for a Jolly Green in this triple canopy stretch of jungle, even with air support from a gunship. I know if we go by the river route, it won't take long for the gooks to pick up our trail and have our asses for sure.

"Gather around lads. We're here, our objective is there," I pointed at my map. "We have to stay clear of here and here," pointing at likely places for Charlie to be. "I don't want any heroes, team work, you hear? We've got to keep our cool and stick together." I looked around at the men, "Any questions or ideas?"

They all shook their heads.

"Okay," I said, looking at each of them, "Let's get the fuck out of here, I want us all to have a beer together by this time day after tomorrow."

It began to rain hard that afternoon and we stood under a canopy of trees, waiting for it to let up. Why, I've wondered several times, being that we were already soaked to the bone. After what seemed like an eternity the rains slacked a little and we headed out again. The smell of wet, rotting vegetation was strong in our nostrils. Several times we were forced to lay low at the sight of VC moving by. The second time we should have been spotted. We were breaking out of a canopy of trees with very little cover when a patrol of VC broke into an opening not a hundred feet from where we had crouched. Gordon had taken point and was just ahead of me. His fist came up to his shoulder and we froze. The VC had us dead, and we were going to start our defense when I noticed a strange thing. On a low branch about twenty feet in front of us were four large black birds. They sat facing the gooks. The VC had been headed toward us when they must have seen the birds. They stood for a moment talking excitedly, pointing our direction with faces averted, then they turned and started walking away from us.

"What the fuck!" I heard Spence whisper just behind my back.

They had to have seen us. Why had they just walked away? That night we held up rather than risk a mine or trip wire. Either would have spelled our doom.

As we sat huddled in a small group, eating our C rations, I was sure everyone was wondering the same thing I was.

"What happened back there, Sir?" Gordon broke the silence. "Those gooks had to have seen us. We were dead meat."

"Didn't you see those birds?" I asked. "The Vietnamese are very superstitious about black birds. They believe looking at one is bad luck"

"What black birds?" Spence asked. "I was too busy counting gooks."

I took first watch with the evening fog silently hugging the ground and foliage as it crept first into all the low places. Soon it would offer a blanket of cover to searching eyes.

As the hours passed, I kept my mind busy thinking about home. Who would have thought fifteen months ago that I would be sitting here in the middle of Vietnam, wetter than hell wondering what tomorrow would bring? As for the birds, just in case, "Thank you Grandfather."

I started thinking about the person that mattered most in my life; Annie. It would be daylight at home, and I was sure she would be helping her mother with chores around the house. My mind drifted back to the good old days.

I remembered a time when I was around fifteen. I had gone over to see Freddy, and walked up on Annie hanging out washing on the clothesline in the backyard. She was wearing a light blue dress, and with the sun behind her, I could see through the material. How beautiful she was, a slight breeze gently blowing her hair across her face. Silhouetted as she was, I could see the curve of her hip and thigh, the way her legs met each other and the way her breasts jutted out when she turned sideways. I don't know, maybe it was my imagination but for a moment I thought I could even see her nipples as she reached up to hang a piece of clothing. She looked at me and smiled that beautiful smile of hers.

Seeing her like that had taken my breath away. For a moment I couldn't move, and I felt my pulse hammering from my head to my toes. Thinking about it now still makes my stomach quiver. That picture of Annie is burned into my memory forever. "I miss you, Annie," I whispered.

As the hours slowly ground by, my thoughts of Annie sustained me. I thought about the times we had made love. How soft and smooth her skin was, how she felt to me as I lay over her body listening to her softly moan, digging her fingernails into me as she climaxed. My heart began racing wildly and I had to shake the thoughts out of my head. Instead of being beside her now, I was stuck over here in this hell-hole of a place, with the wet molding earth as my companion.

I gave a start. While sitting on the ground with my back to a small tree, I had put my left hand on the ground. A shock ran through me as I felt something slowly slithering over my little finger and then the back of my hand. Almost panicking, my first impulse was to jerk my hand away, then I regained control. I immediately thought of all the snakes the Army had warned us about.

I never realized how slow a snake moves. It took forever for that slithering bastard to crawl across my hand. I thought about God and swore off everything I could think of on short notice, and that was a lot. Talk about slower than molasses in January, they should have named this son of a bitch a Molasses in January snake. This one had to be at least two to three feet long and cold to the touch. My mind raced with the different possible kind of snakes, while the sweat poured as I thought about what would happen if the bastard decided to coil up in my lap.

"Vietnam has thirty-three snakes and thirty-one are poisonous," came the voice of the briefing officer again as I sat sweating. "Some can kill you before you take two steps. That fast, gentlemen. Don't play with them and watch where you squat, we don't want to send you home in a body bag."

Moments seemed like an eternity as sweat ran down my face and back. I would rather face a grizzly bear with a skinning knife. At last it moved slowly and silently off into the jungle, and I breathed a sigh of relief, but sat motionless. Finally I grasped my flashlight, then hesitated, no sense trying to see what kind it was. It was headed off away from the men.

I remembered the stunt Freddy had pulled on Annie back when we were kids. Now I know how she must have felt. Another shudder ran down my back. I came to my feet and checked the time. My watch was up. Going over to Stevens, I kicked him lightly on the foot. He opened his eyes, and I told him it was his watch. Without saying a word, he got to his feet and assumed the watch while I took his place on the ground. I don't remember much the rest of the night as I stretched out, falling asleep before my head hit the ground.

Waking before daylight, I laid on the wet ground making plans for the day, hating to get up even though I was soaking wet. I felt better about our position, knowing we had to be close to a PZ. Perhaps eight or ten miles at most. Breaking through VC parameters would be touchy. I just hoped my wounded hadn't stiffened up through the night, especially Johnson, the man with the shot up butt. It was going to be tough sledding as it was and to have to carry a man would be a disaster in the making.

Just before dawn I spoke in a quiet tone to the sleeping men, "Up and at um, lads, She's daylight in the swamps." Damn, I used to hate it when my dad would open my bedroom door and call that out to me. Now it was appropriate. I thought about it and wished I was back home hearing that from Pop now.

They rolled out without saying a word. Two stood with their backs to one another peeing.

"Hey, man. You shake that thing more than twice and you're playing with it," Johnson said, showing his good nature, his white teeth gleaming against his black face.

I knew this man was going to go the distance even with his butt shot. His toughness was a boost to everyone's moral.

"How you feeling, Johnson?" I asked.

"I'm a little stiff, sir. Maybe I'll loosen up. I think I'd trade all this for a good hospital bed and a hot breakfast though. I might drag my leg a little, kinda like that Frankenstein fella."

"Hang in there," I said.

We opened some C rations and gulped down what little bit we could stomach, then buried the container and left overs.

"Five minutes and we move out. If you want a smoke, now is the time. When we get going there'll be no smoking or talking. Any questions?" I asked as I checked my watch.

In five minutes I gave the order, "Let's move out."

They came to their feet slowly. The day was all we expected it to be, bugs, vines, and several snakes, not to mention all of the slithering bastards that went unnoticed. One of the snakes, a bamboo viper, slowly slithered away into some tree roots, reminding me of the night before, a cold chill went down my back just thinking about it. "Fucking snakes," I mumbled. Slapping a mosquito off my neck I added, "Fucking bugs. If I ever get home …," I corrected myself, "when I get home, I'm going to go up to the swamp above the ranch and dump a quart of oil in the water, then sit and gloat at the mosquito larva that I'll be killing." Damn, I hated the little bastards.

Toward mid-morning, we took turns helping Johnson as he began to falter. I was amazed that he was even able to start on his own and then to see the way he forced his body won my undying admiration. He had lost a lot of blood and the mosquitoes were taking the rest.

We held up for a short break and ate more C rations around noon. By now they tasted like steak and lobster to me.

"Sir, can we light up?" one of the soldiers asked as he waited for the rest to finish eating.

I had said not to smoke because I didn't want to give the gooks any hints of our presence. I could smell smoke from a cigarette at a hundred yards when I was out in the woods, and I figured some of the VC could too.

Looking at the faces of the men as they waited for my reply, I couldn't say no. They were entitled to some enjoyment, be it ever so small, and it was for damned sure they earned it. "Fuck the gooks. Light 'em up, just don't exhale," I said and was immediately rewarded with chuckles as the grunts reached for smokes.

That afternoon found us closer to home than I had anticipated. Checking our coordinates I saw a large rice paddy off to the right that I'd remembered flying over a dozen times. I knew this area well. I couldn't remember any others in the area that had been bombed and charred like this village.

Slowly we made our way to the village. As we came up to the first burned hooch, I could still smell the char in the hot air. It would take a long time to rid the region of that smell. The bomb craters would be around long after we were dead and gone. Some of them had been filled in as mass graves for the Vietnamese who had died because of them. If nobody bothered to bury the dead it didn't take long in this heat and with these blowflies for the bodies to become just a pile of bones. I would find skeletons with blowfly larva that hadn't had time to hatch before the flesh was gone. They looked like pounds of brown rice mixed with bones.

Often someone would pick up a skull and stick it on a stake. Some of the helicopters had them attached to the toe of their skids. I didn't allow skulls on my ship, and I made that plain.

Looking around carefully, we made sure the perimeter was secure, then I used the hand radio to send our coordinates and code, Red Horse. I checked the time, it was 1328 hours. We waited.

At a little past 1400 hours a Jolly Green spotted us, with a gunship watching over the pick-up. The VC, if they were around, didn't try anything.

The popping of the helicopter was music to my ears and before the ship set down, we loaded. The pilot powered the helicopter and the blades whipped up a red dust storm as we lifted.

"Welcome aboard," a medic mouthed over the racket of the noisy ship.

By 1430 hours we were back at our base in Pleiku and heading toward the debriefing.

Chapter 23

I got to sleep in on the next day, but by mid-morning it was too hot to rest. I rolled out and went to a canopy with my writing material. Canopies were canvas covered areas that provided shade. As I sat sipping a warm pop and looking through my letters to find the latest one from Annie, a pilot named Barker stopped to chat.

"Letters from home?" he asked.

I glanced up. "Yeah, too fucking hot to sleep. Wish I could see some snow."

"Snow? What's that?" he said. "I think I read about snow one time in a fairytale book. You're from Wyoming or somewhere out West, aren't you?"

"Montana," I corrected, "Northwestern part, up by Glacier Park."

"Beautiful country, Glacier Park. I've seen pictures of it. Always pictured Montana as being sagebrush country."

"The eastside of the Rockies are prairie. I live on the west side of them, all mountains and valleys. Totally different country. My folks have a ranch near Kalispell. I can't wait to get back home. This shithole is for the birds," I said.

"Yeah, I feel the same way. You bust your nuts learning to fly, then when you do, you get stuck in this hell-hole. I can just see me getting a job in the states flying helicopter for some civilian tour company. They go to get in and I say, 'Fasten your fucking seat belts.' Can't you see their expressions?" Barker said.

"I see your point. That's the way it'd probably be with me, too. I'm amazed at how bad my fucking language is."

We both laughed.

"I don't think I want to see another helicopter as long as I live," I said. "I thought I wanted to fly when I got back home. Bullshit! I think every time I'd climb in one, I'd be thinking I had to fly like hell, and that would scare the shit out of all my passengers. I can see some old broad wanting me to let her out on the top of some mountain. She'd probably say something like, 'just let me out right here. I'm going to report you to the authorities!' And I'd probably pull my .45 and say, 'Old broad, I am the authority.'"

We laughed again, but we both knew I was telling the truth. We were survival pilots, and to survive we had to have complete control of everything. One mistake and you were dead.

"I gotta get going, take her easy, Morgan," he said and giving me the thumbs-up, walked away.

I turned back to my cherished letters from Annie. They meant more to me than anything else I owned. I found the last two letters and re-opened them with excitement. I had read them probably ten times and knew them by heart, but that wasn't like seeing and feeling them. Annie had touched them, wrote them and had probably kissed each page before she mailed them. My heart raced with the thought of that.

As I read her words, I couldn't help reaching up when no one was around and nonchalantly wiping the mist out of my eyes.

"Damn it, girl, I love and miss you so much," I whispered. I would gladly have cut off a finger to just reach out and hold her for a moment. I sat for several minutes thinking about Annie, then got out my paper and wrote her a letter.

I knew she would be feeling bad enough that I was over here, so I gave her the old bull-shit pitch I gave her each time I wrote.

"Having a great time. Not as great as if I were with you, but close. The girls over here are gorgeous, but with a little work and imagination you probably would beat them in a beauty contest. The sand on the beach is nice and white. However the weather is hot, and we have to lie under large palm trees to keep from getting too much of a tan. War is hell since my magazine subscriptions are running out."

These kind of letters beat hell out of the tear jerkers some of the guys wrote home. No sense making someone you love feel bad. I made sure Mom got the same kind of letters. Pop would read through them differently, but would approve. I smiled as I imagined his look and his famous all-knowing wink of approval.

Somewhere I could hear Roy Orbison singing the blues, and it made me feel lonesome and home sick. I finished my now hot pop and gathering up my writing material, and walked back to my quarters.

I was ready for sky duty again. At least it kept my mind off home and it was cooler up there. Besides, flying was the one way I could get my thinking straight. Some of the guys said the only way to forget the war was to drink and screw. The drinking wasn't too bad, but I was true to Annie. Not that I blamed anyone for wanting and finding a woman.

I had come close several times. I have to admit that the girls were getting prettier and more sexy by the week. Lilly, one of the barmaids, was always trying to get me to come to her place. She was a good looking woman and a lot of men were interested in her. Most of the guys thought I was nuts for constantly turning down her invitations. She on the other hand, kept trying harder to get me to come over to her hooch.

That evening Freddy and I sat drinking a beer, and as usual, he started giving me the same old shit.

"You're out of your fucking mind to turn her down. I'd give my left nut to stick that," Freddy said. "Hell, Cole, I haven't heard you whistle for months. When we were at home you whistled all the time. You weren't messing with my sister, were you?"

"Me? Get real, besides, she's my lady. I can whistle just thinking about her. Listen," I faked a faltering whistle.

"See!" he said, "See! You were messing with my sister, you bastard. I knew you were taking unfair advantage of her."

We both laughed. Damn it felt good to laugh with Freddy. We had very little to laugh about anymore. Slapping me on the back, he got up. "Have to take care of laundry. See you later."

I sat thinking about our life over here. Death had become our constant companion in the months since we had landed in Vietnam. Seeing a dead man was like looking at a flat tire. I didn't like the indifference I felt most of the time. I have to admit that some had shaken me up a little, but I wasn't alone. Even the medics had their moments.

I shook my head as I remembered one medic sitting in the back of a medevac helicopter eating some C rations with three dead men lying at his feet. There hadn't been any body bags, and one grunt had his head blown off. As I sat in my craft readying for lift-off I stared at him eating with bloody fingers and wondered what kind of person he was going to be when he returned to the states. Hell, I wondered what kind of person I was going to be. Would I ever again feel compassion? Strange how the thought of death changes as you get used to seeing and living around it. Living with death on a daily basis had hardened and numbed me. Some men go nuts, others just change their values. I had changed mine, not permanently I hoped, because I sure as hell didn't like the way I felt.

One of the hottest areas in Vietnam was the highlands, running the length of the western border, dividing Vietnam from Cambodia in our area. If you wanted your ass shot off, you flew the highlands. Point at hand, there was a village last week that had been shot up and burned.

The VC had been present when the infantry came across it. The old people, women and children had suffered the consequences.

That afternoon, being short on medevacs, we were keyed to pick up the wounded and dead GIs. While they were loading my craft I looked around at the bodies of the villagers. I saw a little girl about five or six years old lying as if she were looking at the sun, her little face looking sad and dead. I couldn't stand looking at her, yet I couldn't keep my eyes off the little body either. I scanned the area and saw the remains of what might have been her mother laying five or six feet away. A grunt stepped over the child without even seeing her, as if she had been a stick.

I couldn't wait to get loaded and get to hell out of there. I keyed my microphone, "Chief, tell them to get a move on. Let's get the fuck in the air." My eyes were drawn back to the child like a magnet, sweat running down my face.

"They're calling for you, Sir," a corporal said, snapping me out of my deep thoughts as the sweat poured off me.

"Huh?"

"You're wanted at operations, sir," the Corporal repeated.

"Thank you, Corporal."

"Yes sir. You're welcome," he said, flashing me a smile. He was probably nineteen, maybe twenty. I looked at him, shaking my head as I thought about all the young men I had seen shot up or dead. The fresh smiling faces, showing up expecting just a newer version of war games, only a couple years ago were playing with play guns. The fresh good natured look would be replaced with a very old, haggard expression in just days or weeks. That is, the ones that lived that long. I know, I had been young and fresh just a few months back. Now I felt 50 and fatherly.

I walked into operations. The operation officer Major Hodges looked up from his desk. "Mr. Morgan? Have a seat." He studied me for a moment. "I got a job for you. How well do you know the highlands?"

"Fairly well," I answered, getting that old sinking feeling. "I've flown them for a couple months now, Sir."

"You ever run over the border?"

"Not that I know of. I wondered if I did once," I lied.

"You've seen the charts though, right?"

"Yes Sir, I've looked them over. We were assigned as a special task force for awhile in some of the western Highland areas."

"We have to get a couple of men in and out of a hard to reach region. It's imperative to be invisible and fast. That's where you come in. It's going to take everything you've got to get in without detection.

If you had the job, any ideas on who you want to go in with you?" he asked.

"Yes Sir. Gray and Hanson. They're both good men."

"Gray's a good man. The records show you go back a long way together. Hanson would make a good chief. I think you're on top of it."

"Thank you, sir," I said, feeling pleased with the compliment.

"Get your crew together and meet me back here at 20 hundred hours. Don't make plans for the next couple days. If everything goes well, the three of you can have some time off," he said as he stood up, "Oh, by the way, Morgan, this is classified."

I stood. "Yes sir." Saluting, I turned and left the office.

The only thing I could imagine being better than time off would be getting to see Annie. I walked back to my quarters to see if Freddy was still around. Probably over at the officer's club having a beer, I thought. Hanson would be reading, knowing him.

"You seen Gray?" I asked Jenkins, another Slick pilot, as we met at the door.

"Yeah, about an hour ago he was over at the canopy. Might still be there."

I turned toward the canopy. It was a favorite hangout for anyone wanting to stay out of the stale hot enclosures. It had picnic tables, butt cans and a pop cooler at one end that did a poor imitation of keeping the pop cold. About all this one did was keep them from popping their caps. Freddy had taken up smoking since coming to Vietnam and the canopy was his favorite hangout when he wasn't at the club. Two pilots sat at one of the tables. "Anyone seen Gray?" I asked to no one in particular.

They both shook their heads. Nobody was very talkative during the heat of the day. That left the one place I should have checked first. The obvious. I walked over to the club.

There he sat with a can of beer and a cigarette dangling from his lips, staring off in a daydream. As I came through the door, he looked my direction, then gave a whoop that told me the beer had done its job. "Hey, Cole, over here!"

Good old Freddy wasn't feeling any pain. I didn't blame him though; anything we could do to get away from our job for a while was worth it. He had the day off and deserved every minute of it.

"Come on over and let me buy you a drink, Morgan," Freddy yelled out.

"What's the occasion, Gray? You're usually a tightwad about this time of the month. You rob a bank?"

"I'm flying a fixed wing to Da Nang to bring back a new ship. It'll take about two days they say, but I can stall it into three. There are a lot of questionable things that will have to be looked into. Anything you want me to tell LeeAnn?"

He sat there looking so smug that I didn't know how I was going to break the news about the change in his plans. I decided to tell him the truth.

"Freddy, I don't know how to tell you this, my friend. But the Major picked you and me for a job starting tomorrow. I tried to talk him out of your going, but you know how brass are." I gave him my best innocent look.

"You son of a bitch! You're a lying dog, Morgan. I know that benevolent fucking look of yours. You cocksucker. Did you volunteer me for something?" he sat looking at me.

I continued to look hurt. "You know, usually I would be guilty of something like this, Freddy, but you really hurt me this time. I had nothing to do with this, I swear."

"You ain't lying this time?" His expression changed, then he softened. "Sorry, Cole. I didn't mean it. I was just funning you, you know that. Sit down and I'll buy you a beer. I'm really sorry. Okay?"

"It's all right. I guess I had that coming for all the shit I've gotten us into. I'll have a pickled egg with the beer if you're buying? I left my money back at quarters." I figured one more prevarication wouldn't hurt. After all, I'd be in shit up to my nose when he found out the truth.

"Sure, I'll buy you all the beer in the joint to make up for what I said. I just thought this was another attempt to screw things up in my life. I keep forgetting we're grown up."

I had Freddy by the balls, and I figured if I could hold up my sad face, it would be good for several beers.

"So what's our big mission anyway?"

"Can't say, I don't know, just that we report in at 20 hundred hours tonight."

"Shit. The bastards are going to spring something big on us," he said draining his beer. "They never ask for us at that time of the night unless it's big."

"Yeah, probably fly someone to Cambodia or something," I said and laughed.

Freddy laughed with me. "I hope not, we go down in there, and they'll leave us to rot. Besides, that's a thousand to one shot. We'd better not get too tanked up on this horse piss." He shoved his last beer over to me, "Here. This proves how sorry I am about awhile ago."

"You shouldn't," I said, and I meant it. He really shouldn't. I never could outrun him when I had too many beers, and he was going to kill me for sure when he found out I had something to do with messing up his plans.

"I still can't get over my bad luck. I mean, I had everything lined up. Then this crap. I don't fucking believe it," he said, shaking his head slowly.

"Let's grab some chow. Might be the last hot meal for a while," I said.

That evening as we entered the operations headquarters the corporal looked up.

"Just a moment, Sir," he said. "I'll tell the major you're here."

A few seconds later found us in the major's office.

"Morgan said you were the right man for the job, Gray. I think he made a good choice. Sit down, gentlemen," he indicated the two chairs drawn up in front of his desk.

Freddy gave me that old look of his that said I was in deep shit. I wondered if I could still outrun him. Of course, there was always the possibility that maybe he had outgrown the urge to kill me at times, but then again, maybe not.

"Gentlemen, what I'm about to propose must never go beyond these walls. This is a covert assignment, TS-30 (Top Secret, thirty years silence) project. If you have any reservations or doubts about a TS-30 assignment, say so now."

A TS-30 assignment is not for the weak of heart. In our business they were quite often fatal. We had been told in contour school that at times we might be asked to carry out high-risk jobs. That's why the additional training, to help make us as invisible as possible. He shuffled some papers on his desk and waited, giving us time to think it over.

What the hell, we were young and cocky. Maybe if we were really good, we could cut the odds, and put them in our favor. Give Freddy and me capes, and we'd leap tall buildings in a single bound, at least that was the way we thought.

Major Hodges finally looked up, not trying to put any pressure on us, but to see if we had made up our minds yet.

Freddy spoke up, "Sir, what's in it for us?" Good old Freddy, always looking for the best deals.

"When this mission is over, three weeks R & R, and a silent thanks from all the men whose lives you will have helped save," he said.

Freddy looked at me.

I returned his look without saying anything. I didn't have to. We were usually on the same mind track. That's why he had smelled a rat when I'd told him about this to begin with.

"Got anything planned for the next couple of days?" I asked Freddy.

"Nothing exciting yet," he gave me the old, I'll get even, look.

"I'm in, Sir," I said turning back toward the major.

"Me too, Sir."

"You're in top security quarantine as of now, gentlemen. I'll take your dog tags and all identification," he said and reached his hand out for them.

Freddy and I exchanged looks as we removed our tags and handed them over.

"What about pictures, sir?" I asked.

"Anything that can be identified by names or addresses written on them or showing anything military will have to be turned in. If it's just first names, you can keep them."

I was thinking of Annie's pictures I flew with. None were identifiable. I kept them.

"You're relieved of all duties as of now."

Something big was brewing. Operation Sam Houston had just gotten over. All pilots including special task force pilots were to be assigned to the 335 AHC (Assault Helicopter Company), which meant we were to transport troops of Alpha and Charlie Company, 1st Bn, 173rd Airborne Brigade for operation Francis Marion, just a few days away. I didn't know whether to be glad or not about being relieved of duty.

"Now, down to business. Forty klicks across the Cambodian border is a strategic NVA command center. There's a man in the command center who makes all the decisions as to who moves where and does what. He's a chess player, gentlemen. A good chess player, I might add. He makes all the right moves, not only for the NVA, but almost all the insurgent activities in South and Central Vietnam. Allied forces are suffering tremendous losses because of this man. We have to stop him. That's where you come in. I need to get two men into and out of Cambodia as quickly and quietly as possible. Both men are specialists in handling these problems. We'll only get one chance. If we miss, they'll move the target, and we may never get the opportunity again. We can't afford any slip-ups. The helicopter you'll be flying looks like a derelict. Don't let it fool you. This machine has been modified to produce better than anything you've flown so far. There isn't any way to trace it. It's been stripped clean, making it lighter and faster. I don't think you'll be too dissatisfied with the way it handles. There's a detonation tripper built into the machine that'll make the Fourth of July look like a Girl Scout campfire, if you have to blow it. You've got a two-minute delay after activation. You'll be briefed on that.

You'll meet the other part of your team later on today during that briefing. In the mean time, here are charts and maps of the area and your objective, all updated and verified. The helicopter is in the hanger at the far end of the field. We don't want it on the apron until you lift out just before dawn in the morning. For what it's worth, you won't be required to turn in flight records or mission reports upon your return, if that's any consolation." He half smiled for the first time. "No dash-twelve, just a debriefing."

I hated paper work and so did Freddy. We were not lazy by any means, but we'd rather take a punch than have to do the dash-twelve, which was always plaguing our line of work.

Walking down to the hanger, we looked over the ship.

"Shit. I want out of this mess. Look at that bastard. We made better looking death traps than this when we were kids. Cole, you son of a bitch, you got me into this, get me out!"

"Come on, Freddy. Look at it this way. What happens if this piece of shit actually flies? I mean, it could!" I looked at it again. "Naw. This is worse than shit. Think they'd let us build our own death trap?"

We climbed into the cockpit and looked around. All seemed in place as I felt the collective pitch control lever, my other hand on the cyclic control stick, fingers resting on the microphone trigger in the front of the control stick. Everything felt right, but the looks of this derelict made me wonder how long we'd be in the air before it came apart, that is if we got it in the air. On the collective at my left side was the search light on off. I flicked it on, then began trying the others; which included the stow switch, landing light on-off switch, the landing light extend-retract switch, search light extend-retract control switch, engine idle release switch, collective pitch control adjuster, the power control throttle, power control friction adjuster, the governor rpm increase-decrease switch and last, the one thing that I hoped didn't work, the starter ignition trigger switch.

Automatically my hands toyed with the different switches on the console without thinking about them. "Everything feels right," I said to Freddy. "We need to get the chief to look this thing over though. I don't want to fly this contraption without a thorough pre-flight."

"I'm with you. By the way, you bastard, I had it made until you did this. Now I gotta go get killed instead of getting laid. You're a prick."

"Freddy, I'm going to get killed on this mission and I wanted you, my best buddy, with me. I knew how bad you'd feel with me dying and your not being there when it happened. I didn't want to leave you behind without anyone to worry about you. Who would get you in and out of these messes? See what I'm talking about?"

"You son of a bitch. Okay, I'll go this one time, but if we make it through this in one piece, I'm going to kill your ass all by myself. Do you remember the bull elk you missed up on Sheep Creek? I fucked with your scope," Freddy said, looking smugly at me.

"I knew it! I knew something was wrong with that rifle! I should have hit that bull," I said, feeling my hackles raising. "You bastard. You know who took the rubbers out of your glove box? Me! I hope when we get back she's got a kid and you have to marry her. What kind of asshole trick is that to pull on your best friend? Screwing with my riflescope over a lousy ten-dollar bet. I can't believe you'd do something that low. You're an asshole, Freddy."

Freddy watched me getting madder by the minute and enjoying every moment of it. We had bet ten bucks on who'd make the first kill. I'd missed and lost the bet.

He climbed on to the top deck of the Huey. "Hey, they thought of everything, even a rotor," he yelled back down.

"We ought to crank this sucker up. If it's going to blow, I'd rather it be right here on the ground. I hope the major was right and it flies better than it looks," I said.

Hanson walked in. "I thought I'd find you here. Let me take a look at this doll."

I was glad the chief was here. He could either confirm that this was truly a piece of shit or that it would actually fly.

"Glad you're here, chief. What do you think of her looks? I hope it doesn't reflect on performance," I said.

Freddy came up on us. "Hi, chief. Want to see our dream machine?"

"I'll look it over, but don't let looks fool you. Sometimes the ugliest woman is the best fuck."

He went over to the engine cowling at the rear of the ship. Soon we heard him whistling as he went about checking the helicopter from the tail rotor gear box to the turbine engine and transmission. Climbing on the top deck, Hanson began checking the upper units from the swashplate assembly to the end of the rotors.

Coming back down from the upper deck, he climbed into the cockpit, and without missing any notes in the tune he was whistling, began checking the cyclic and collective for play, pushing on the left and right pedals. Satisfied, he hit the starter button on the collective and listened to the whine of the starter motor. The rotors spun without the turbine engine kicking in. I was glad it didn't. We were inside the hanger and the rotor wash would have blown hell out of things. Hanson shut it down and with the rotors still turning from the centrifugal force, climbed out, seemingly satisfied. Finishing his inspection he walked over to Freddy and me.

"Fine machine, sir," he said, waiting for us to comment.

"You mean this thing will actually fly?" Freddy asked.

"Yes sir, I think it will. She's a mechanical beauty. Not much for looks I have to admit, but if she flies like she looks mechanically, she should kick some ass."

I felt better after hearing that. Hanson was a crew chief who knew his stuff, and a good crew chief took second place to no mortal.

That evening we met our counterparts. The larger man looked hardened beyond his years. He was the trigger I figured, and the other had to be the spotter. His eyes took in everything around him as we waited.

Taking the initiative, I introduced Freddy, Hanson and myself, to the two men. They in turn introduced themselves as sergeants Hamlin and Macron. They were pleasant men, and I would never have guessed their occupational skills.

As we talked about our jobs and equipment, we learned that Hamlin used a Winchester model 70, 30-06 with a scope. Both Freddy and I lit up at the mention of hunting rifles.

"Glad to hear someone talk who knows good guns. You guys being from Montana, I suppose you've tried them all," Hamlin said.

"Maybe not all, but a good lot. My favorite is a 30-06 my grandfather gave me. It's an old Springfield, but I can drive nails with it," I said.

"You use a scope?" Hamlin asked.

"Yeah, I have a four-power Weaver."

"Good choice."

"I'm an .06 man, too," Freddy said with conviction. "I have a Remington with a four-power scope. We hunt everything from elk to deer and antelope with them."

"Antelope? That takes good shooting. I've never hunted antelope. I hunt other small targets at long ranges though," he said without a note of pride in his voice.

I changed the subject. I didn't like thinking about the human kind of target. We each do what we have to do, I thought. But that kind of work wasn't for me. Shooting game for the table was one thing or defending yourself, but to look through a rifle's scope at a man you've never met, then squeezing the trigger, putting a bullet through him, was something else.

That evening we were allowed to return to our quarters with an MP (military police) to pick up our gear, even though technically we were under quarantine. We now wore our handguns in their holsters.

"I see you guys pack shoulder holsters," Sergeant Macron commented.

"Yeah, but we'd probably blow our foot off in the excitement if we ever had to draw them," Freddy answered.

This brought chuckles from Hanson, Macron, and Hamlin. I didn't really see the humor in it because it was too close to the truth. It was hard to kill a man at that close of a distance.

The major came in and began our briefing on what was called "Operation Quick Silver." He covered the technical aspects of the job, along with what was expected of each man, then wound up with a question and answer segment. Some of the questions we already knew the answers to, but wanted to make sure everyone else was in agreement. Some were hypothetical and not pleasant, but had to be addressed.

"If we get hit and someone can't be moved and we can't stay? What?" Hanson wanted to know.

"You don't leave anyone for the gooks to torture, period," Hamlin said. "I would want a bullet in the head. Gooks hate our guts so bad they'll skin us alive like the Apaches did. I found three men hanging upside down with their cocks cut off and stuffed in their mouths. All of them had been skinned alive. A bullet in the head eliminates that."

I thought about what we were getting into. We had dodged more bullets than could be counted when we were flying, but hand-to-hand combat for our lives was something that had just been an ever so slight possibility. I always thought if my death came, it would be by a 50 caliber from ground fire or crashing the helicopter. Now we were expected to put a bullet in each other's head if we were on the ground and couldn't be moved. I couldn't see Freddy or I having to shoot one another. I wanted to go home.

"The bad part about being where you aren't supposed to be is there won't be anyone around to pick you up. Bottom line, you're on your own when you cross the border. You do what you have to do to survive. If that means leaving someone behind, you know what is expected," the major said, looking serious as he searched our faces. "The NVA are massing, and they know their business when it comes to warfare. Chances are they'll suspect you're CIDG (Civilian Irregular Defense Group, CIA sponsored.) If they do, they'll really get tough on you. It would be better to take a bullet then be taken by them. That brings up another unpleasant subject. I have to issue each of you a sealed pill; it's a last ditcher. Sometimes it's a little easier to take a pill than have to shoot each other."

The major opened a small oddly striped envelope and spilled the contents out in the palm of his hand. Five small envelopes with black and red stripes on them lay like tiny vipers in a little pile. He handed each of us a packet.

"There's one pill per envelope. The pill's hard and you don't have to worry about getting the envelope wet; they're waterproof. When put in the mouth, it takes effect in less than fifteen seconds, and for what it's worth, it's not painful. Full effect in less than thirty seconds. You'll notice a small notch on each of the four corners of the packet. Any of these will allow you access to the contents. You can swallow it or put it under your tongue; either way is fatal. Now to something more pleasant."

"Your helicopter is stripped for more than identification purposes, it's lighter and will allow you more maneuverability. The turbine has an extra nine yards, and I'm sure you're wondering why we don't employ these modifications on our standard Hueys. This improved turbine has a much shorter life. It'll do a faster more efficient job, but it puts it's power or heart, if you will, into getting a job done, therefore it has a shortened life span. Modifications have been made throughout the craft, and I highly suggest you play with it a little while en-route to your assignment. Going in you'll have an M-60 on a bungie. At point Dearborn, break it down and kick it into the river. We don't want it to fall into the wrong hands. Secondly, we don't want you identified with the military. This is strictly a defensive weapon and not intended for aggressive use, remember that, gentlemen. If you encounter anything unusual, make mental notes, but remember what your main objective is. Your return will hopefully be under cover of darkness. You will have a handset for making contact with Fox 1, which will be on Hill 883. Mission name for Quick Silver is Viper. Identify yourself with the handset. The tower will then expect you. Any questions? No? Good luck and good hunting, gentlemen."

The briefing was concluded and we turned in for a couple hours of rest. I laid awake thinking about Annie back home and how for the first time I had some doubts about making it back. I got up and finding writing material on a small desk in the corner of the room, sat down and wrote Annie a letter.

Dear Annie,

We fly out in the morning from here on a mission that I would not have taken if it wasn't for the lives of a lot of good men hanging in the balance.

Annie, I know you love me with all of your heart and I also know that you know I love you with all of mine.

I don't want to make this mushy in any way, because it will be hard enough just knowing that I won't be coming home, if you get this letter.

I don't want you to mourn for me any longer than normal. I know it will be hard on you at first. Annie, my wish is that you will, in a reasonable time, find someone that will love you as much, if possible, as I do.

Don't waste your life on something that isn't anymore. I'm referring to us. It hurts me to write like this, Annie, but this letter will only be mailed to you if things don't go well. If you get it, they didn't.

Remember one thing, Annie, death is not painful and for what it's worth, a lot of men are safer because of what we've done.

Know that I'll love you forever, my Love.

Cole

I put the letter in an envelope and addressed it to Annie. Then I placed the envelope in a second larger envelope with a note attached to it, to be delivered to the major, with instructions to mail the letter only if after a reasonable time we weren't back.

I was sure he'd had letters of this nature before, and I looked forward to his returning it to me as soon as I got back.

I lay on my back listening to the others snoring and thought about home and what it would be like to be sitting across the breakfast table from Annie. I'd be pouring a large bowl of corn flakes and then some fresh milk that was half cream over the cereal. I'd take the honey and pour it all over the top of the flakes. Then with a spoon almost as big as a mixing spoon, I'd take a big bite. The milk would probably run down my chin. I could imagine Annie watching with a smile on her beautiful face. I wondered if it was possible to hold her in my lap while I ate. Hell, I'd never finish the cereal. With Annie on my mind, I drifted off into a deep sleep.

Chapter 24

"Sir, it's time."

I opened my eyes to see Sergeant Hamlin standing at the side of my bunk. He was fully dressed, and I could see that he had been up for quite awhile and had assembled his gear in a neat pile by the door. Sergeant Macron sat in a chair smoking a cigarette and looking at a magazine.

I lay there watching the two men, trying to imagine Macron looking at the latest hunting magazine while holed up in the wet jungle foliage. The magazine would have to be waterproof. I smiled at the thought of him looking intently at the book while pages fell to the ground in a soggy pile. This must be a real treat sleeping in a dry bed, I thought as I got up from my bunk.

"Hey. Rise and shine, Gray. You too, Hanson," I said loudly. "She's daylight in the swamp."

Freddy gave me the finger and continued laying in his bunk. "Bring me my coffee first or I'm not getting up. Better yet, have a good looking woman bring it to me, then wait outside."

Hanson got up and smiled. "I think they've cut us some new orders. They've had all night to figure something else out for Cambodia. The big bomb maybe. Then they're sending us to Da Nang for some women. You know, try all of them out and bring back the best." Hanson looked around to see if we bought any of it. "I take it I just dreamed all that?"

We laughed. Hanson was a great kidder. I just hoped he wasn't kidding about the maverick chopper.

We had been issued different clothes to make us look less like GIs. Pulling on my clothes and jungle boots, I ran a hand through my hair. Hopefully if we did get caught by the NVA, they would consider us soldiers of fortune. That would be our only cover, that and as a last ditch, maybe drug runners.

Either way, round-eyes were hated with a vengeance. At least if we were caught, they would probably kill us outright. Not bad compared to the torturing they would do to the military or the fucking CIA.

We were served breakfast in our quarters, and the food was exceptionally good this morning. I figured it was partially because of the shit we were going to be eating for the next couple of days. Cold, canned, boned chicken would be a real treat, if we were lucky and lived long enough to eat it. Good old C rations. We stocked up on coffee packets though. I could go without food for several days if need be, or eat bugs and reluctantly snakes and other crawlies, but I needed my coffee.

An hour before daylight, we were walking out to the apron where the ugliest helicopter I have ever seen had been moved out for us. Looking at it I knew why they wanted us to leave in the dark.

Without much talking, we each went about checking our gear and equipment. I squatted down then crawled under the slick, feeling for the fuel drain valve and let a few ounces of fuel out onto the apron to make sure there was no condensation. I reached in back of the console for the green book that was the crew chief's log for pre-flight and post-flight checks. I already knew the chopper had been checked out, but it was habit and old habits die hard. I found no green book then remembered our status, we were social outcasts, renegades.

The chief had plugged our helmet radio cords in and hung them on the overhead hooks. As we climbed in, Hanson buckled us up, then gave me a two circle wave to crank it up. Wheeling, he jumped in the back with Hamlin and Macron.

Flipping a switch and releasing the lock-down on the collective, I twisted the throttle to the indent starting position and squeezed the starter trigger. The electric starter motor began its high pitched whining as the rotors commenced rotation. The Viper, our call name, came to life as the turbine ignited.

Gauges moved into harmony, all except one. The EGT gauge moved to the red zone and stayed for a few seconds. This was normal and I waited until it moved back to green. Running my hand down the consoles once more to make sure everything was in order, I keyed my microphone.

"The door pins in, chief?" I asked. The pins had to be in place to keep the doors open and secure, otherwise we could lose them.

"That's a roger, Sir."

Slowly I pulled the collective up and the ship's nose and toes of the skids came off the apron, then the rest of her. I corrected for drift inclination, then pushing the cyclic slightly forward, felt the power of the ship for the first time. It felt like I was flying a balloon of helium. The helicopter shot into the air at what seemed like twice the speed of a normal Huey. Out of my peripheral vision I could see Freddy's grin. This was right up his alley. I had faith in my crew, with Hanson as crew chief and Hamlin and Macron knowing their business, the Army was finally doing something right.

I played with the ship, taking it into a steep dive, then flaring. I could feel the power of the craft giving me everything she had. I turned the controls over to Freddy, who was flying left seat and watched him grin at the feel of it.

"Would you believe this shit?" he said. "Think we can roll her?" Of course we weren't supposed to play games but by talking over the intercom, we were heard in the back by all three men. Hanson knew better, but Hamlin and Macron took the bait.

"What the fuck you talking about, sir? We're not out here to play around like this," Hamlin said with concern in his voice. "We heard it's impossible to roll a helicopter. If you're going to try that shit, put us down."

Freddy and I looked at each other, grinning ear to ear. Usually only Hanson would have an intercom in the back, but we had been rigged all around with headsets. Having fun with the two tough guys was entertaining. Right now we were the tough guys and they were the ones hanging on for dear life.

As the sun came up, we crossed the border into Cambodia. I had taken back the controls and without any warning to the three in the back, suddenly dove down into the river mist. The VSI (vertical speed indicator) showed almost a free fall for the first part of our descent. This drew shouts of alarm and then anger from Hamlin and Macron as they figured out that it had been deliberate. As we got closer to the river, we eased up to normal descent, and at three feet off the water, leveled, flying at 80 miles per hour. The trees became a blur as the craft increased speed.

A small boat with fisherman sat in the middle of the river as we rounded a bend. Both the fishermen and boat were in jeopardy as we climbed a few feet and skimmed over them. One of the men fell overboard because of panic and the rotor wash. I felt bad but couldn't help chuckling, then glancing over at Freddy, saw him grin.

"Probably collaborators anyway," I said as I flared for the quick hop over the boat, bringing a curse from both Macron and Hamlin.

"Everyone okay, chief?" Freddy asked.

"Everyone is smiling, sir."

"Bullshit," Macron said into his microphone. "Fucking near dumped me. Let us know when you're going to pull that shit next time," then he added gruffly, "sir."

This was turning out to be more fun than I thought it would be. Freddy was enjoying the ride and was on the controls lightly himself which was standard procedure when we flew contour because there wouldn't be time at this altitude and speed for the other pilot to take control if one of us took a bullet.

Within minutes we would be at the forks in the river and would be taking the left fork. There would be a swinging bridge just about half a mile up the waterway and about thirty feet off the water, according to our intelligence report. We were going to go under it, and I hoped there weren't any fuckups on the height or surprises such as danglers that we could hit. Sometimes the bridges would have weights dangling to help control swaying.

Freddy read my mind.

"You tell Hanson to sharpen the rotors?" he asked.

"I thought you did. Damn it, Gray, do I have to do everything?"

The intercoms in the back began to crackle with excitement.

"What the fuck are those two talking about? What did they mean by sharpening the rotors, chief?" Macron asked.

"Nothing to get upset about. We may have to fly under a bridge with danglers and we might need the rotor edges a little sharper than usual, that's all," Hanson said into the intercom. I looked over at Freddy and winked. Over the intercom we listened to the conversation between the two sergeants and the chief.

"What the fuck you talking about, Hanson?" Macron asked the chief.

"Nothing important. We'll be fine," he said. "I hope."

"Fuck!" Macron replied, "I'd rather walk than fly in one of these things."

As we closed on the fork in the river, I came up to fifty feet above the river and got ready to bank the craft so we could make the sharp left turn in the river fork without dropping the tail rotor into the water. "Everyone buckled up, chief?" I asked on the intercom.

"We're tight," he came back.

Within thirty seconds the fork loomed up around a bend in the river. I was still at fifty feet and flared hard, banking to the left.

"Son of a bitch," came the shout from both Macron and Hamlin, almost in unison. Then came the bridge and we dove to go under. The men had been looking out the open sides of the ship.

"I'll be fucking glad when we either crash or land this son of a bitch! I'm tired of sitting in my own shit," Macron said to anyone who'd listen.

I couldn't help but chuckle.

"Who the fuck is laughing? Just let me out of this deathtrap! I'd just as soon be in a fucking snake pit." Macron was definitely losing it. I was almost afraid he might shoot us once we were on the ground.

In a few minutes we banked left again and began our flight up a stream bed. If Macron and Hamlin were going to jump ship, this would be the time to do it. All they'd have to do was watch for a soft spot and bail out, we were flying so low we were clipping shrubbery on this leg of the trip.

No matter how many hours of skidding practice I had under my belt, I always got a little damp. Our rotors were 21 inches wide and would chop anything up to a couple of inches, but the NVA had started stringing cable across some of the well traveled routes in hopes of us catching one.

"Ssshhiit," came Macron's voice over the intercom, "let me out of this thing. Slow this son of a bitch down and I'll jump."

"Hey! Is this necessary? We aren't going to help the war effort if—shit, slow this motherfucker down!" came the voice of Hamlin. "They're going to smell us coming a mile away. That is if we live long enough to set this motherfucker down."

A hard bank to the right as we flew up the stream and we entered the deep canyon on the chart. Freddy double checked to make sure.

"We got another swinging bridge coming up in about half a mile, Cole. Looks like we can go under. Don't see any danglers. Looks like maybe thirty feet clearance." Then to the chief and the other two passengers Freddy said, "Everybody hang on back there, chief. Make sure your equipment is secure."

"Shit," Macron replied to the last part of Freddy's message, "these guys are definitely out of their fucking minds flying like this. I'm walking out of this fucking country. You'd have to be suicidal to voluntarily ride in one of these. Shit!" he yelled as we skipped on some river rock with the left skid.

Hearing Macron cussing and screaming made me feel good. Every once in awhile it was good to be appreciated, even if they screamed and cussed at us. When we could make the tough ones yell, we knew we were earning our money. Freddy knew what I was doing.

As we cleared the underside of the bridge, I asked the ship for a three-foot raise, and it responded so fast that Freddy and I exchanged glances. Never had we flown a faster responding craft than this derelict. The regular horsepower of a T53-L-13 turbine engine is 1300 horsepower. This craft had at least 1600 horses, coupled with being stripped down to lighten it from 5000 pounds to 4500 plus pounds, gave it the quickness of a cat. I would never cuss ugly again. In less than ten minutes after leaving the main channel, we neared our LZ.

After making a quick assessment of the area, we sat down in a small clearing. Macron and Hamlin unloaded and moved into the jungle. They would make a ground search of the area as we remained light on our skids. If they gave us the all clear coupled with the code name "Viper", over the hand held radio, we'd shut down. If it wasn't coupled with Viper, we were out of there in a flash.

If all was safe, after shutting down, we'd secure the LZ by setting out trip flares along with other early warning systems and prepare for a wonderful time sitting in the craft swatting blood sucking mosquitoes, while waiting for Macron and Hamlin to do their job. Then lift out and get the hell back to Vietnam before we were detected. I checked my watch and found it was still early.

Figuring one hour to target for the sergeants, then no telling how long they would have to lay waiting and watching for their shot, another possible forty-five minutes to return. Damn, it could mean an all-day and possibly a second day's wait. If they knew for sure which hooch the target was in, they could have taken it out with a rocket, but they didn't know where the target would be until they had a visual.

Freddy stood outside the ship waiting for Macron and Hamlin to return from scouting the area, while Hanson busied himself with the pre-flight check, making certain of procedures and settings for a quick crankup.

"How's it coming, Chief?" Freddy asked.

"Looking good, Sir," Hanson replied. "I think she's ready to crawl up a cloud."

Looking up I saw the sergeants coming across an opening about a hundred yards away. They looked like they were walking strangely close. Then I noticed Hamlin leaning on Macron's shoulder. I tapped on the canopy of the Huey, and Freddy turned toward where I was looking. Frowning and holding a hand up to shade his eyes, he took a long look.

"Something's wrong with Hamlin," he said. "He's limping or something."

"I don't like the looks of this," I said as Hanson walked around to where Freddy was standing.

"What do you make of it, chief?" I asked.

"Looks like Sergeant Hamlin's hurt. He's walking, which tells me it isn't real bad, but it could fuck up the mission."

Freddy got in the ship, and after releasing the lock down, I pressed the starter switch on the collective. The starter whined as the rotors began slowly spinning, picking up rotation speed to the point that I could start the fire in a heartbeat, ready to get under way if anything suspicious occurred. Within a moment's notice the turbine would kick in and we'd be out of here. There was always a possibility they had been captured and were being forced by the enemy to walk toward us to throw us off guard. We wouldn't be taken off guard if I had anything to do with it.

The chief walked cautiously towards the two men. My finger tightened on the collective's throttle as I watched for any telltale sign of something wrong. As the chief approached the men within about thirty or forty yards, I could see they were talking, then the chief turned and drew his hand across his throat, motioning for me to cut the power. They had given the code word, everything was in order. I cut the power, relieved, yet still concerned about the support that Macron was giving Hamlin. The chief turned back to the men, and taking the gear Hamlin was carrying, started back toward the ship.

Freddy and I climbed out of the cockpit and waited for them to reach us. Our training said never leave your helicopter unmanned and for one pilot to stay within ten feet of the ship with a door open at all times. This was one time it sounded like good advice.

As the three of them approached, I noticed Hamlin dragging one foot, then I saw why. His left leg was red with blood from the mid-calf down.

"What happened, Sergeant?" Freddy asked, looking concerned.

"Fucking bamboo swing stick," was all he said.

The swing sticks are a favorite of the VC and not usually used by the NVA. Being in Cambodia, they hadn't been expecting anything like this. Swing sticks are also used by tribesmen. These were probably set for small animals that frequented the trails. The VC however, used all kinds of debilitating devices for the round-eyes, much like the American Indians had in the early years in Montana. Grandfather had told Freddy and me how the white man had suffered from all kinds of booby traps.

"White men don't watch anything but the birds in the sky," Grandfather said and pretended to walk with his head held so he was unable to see the ground.

Now I knew what the old man was trying to teach us. His words lasted even though death had long ago claimed him. I was thinking of Grandfather's wisdom more and more as we met the enemy on his own ground.

Hanson cut the pants off Hamlin's hurt leg with his knife, while I went to get the first-aid kit in the ship.

"Sergeant, you're not going to be able to do your work in this condition. Can Macron do it?" Freddy asked, as Hamlin grimaced.

"I don't have any choice," he said, looking grim. "A lot of men are going to die if I don't do it. You'll have to patch me up the best you can."

"I can't work miracles, Sergeant. Your leg isn't critical, but you won't be able to hobble on it, let alone run," Hanson said, then turned to me, "What do we do, sir?"

I thought for a minute. "I don't know what we can do," I said looking at the men. "We came here to do a job, and now the one person that's qualified to do it is disabled. Anyone have any suggestions?"

The quiet was deafening, until Hamlin broke the silence. "There are three ways to go on this. One, make for home base and miss a chance to save lives. Two, I try and make the objective and you guys head for home. I can make the objective and do the job, but chances are, I won't make it back. Three, one of you, the best one for the job, as far as marksmanship, will go with Macron, leaving everything up to him. He can talk you through it, if you can get close enough. There's no way Macron can do the job by himself. You can't effectively be both shooter and spotter. That's a proven fact."

We all stood there trying to absorb what he'd said. Sergeant Hamlin made sense, but I couldn't see sending a man to his death. That left out option two. Heading for home without completing our objective was not much of an option either.

That left option number three. It only took one pilot to fly the helicopter out. That left Freddy or me as the logical trigger. Freddy reached that conclusion about the same time that I did.

"I can do it," I said.

"Hell, I can outshoot you any day of the week," Freddy came back.

"In a pig's ass. Besides, I'm the commander. I'll make the decisions, and I say I go. That's an order."

Freddy was on the verge of exploding but held his temper, knowing that I was in command and there was nothing he could do about it.

"Okay, it's settled then," I said, turning to Sergeant Hamlin. "You better brief me on procedures."

"Okay. You've used a 30-06. Right?" Hamlin asked.

"Many times."

"You've been used to a four-power scope, right?"

"Yeah."

"This is nine power. That means it's zeroed in for a lot farther than you're used to. Looking at a man through nine power is deceiving, not like looking at an antelope on the prairies. It's imperative to know your ranges. You zero in your scope for how far?"

"About 225 yards," I said. "That way my mid range trajectory is about as flat as I can get it and still be able to reach out and hit an elk at three hundred yards without the bullet being too high at mid range."

"You know your guns and scopes, good. My rifle is zeroed in for four hundred yards. The usual for antelope at three hundred yards is about nine inches mid range with the 180-grain bullet, right?"

I nodded.

"This is where the spotter comes in. He and he alone will determine the distance and time of the hit. He will tell you the range and conditions, wind, temperature, etc. On the scope are some marks; each slash is fifty yards. You must know the yards and the slashes. It's imperative, you must know the slashes on the scope. You ever shoot four hundred meters?"

I shook my head.

"You've shot ground squirrels, right?"

"Yeah."

"It's the same thing; hit your target before he ducks back into his hole. It's important to hit him the first time, not just scare him. You have to hit him square and do it with the first shot. You usually don't get a second chance. You shoot a second round and they'll have you spotted. Never shoot a second round, unless you're ready to die. You shoot, then scoot. You got that?" he asked.

"I got it, Sergeant."

"You will probably have trouble shooting a person the first time, but you can't let that stop you. It's normal to look into your target's eyes if you're up close. Don't. You will want to resist shooting, if only for a moment. You must recognize these symptoms and head them off at the pass, as you say in the West. You'll have only one chance at the target, don't fuck it up. Your instincts will screw it up, don't let them get in the way. It's not natural for anyone to shoot someone else. But you're not shooting a person, you're shooting a walking, talking target to save lives. Lots of men's lives depend on what I'm telling you. One enemy's life for perhaps hundreds or thousands of American lives. Do you understand what I'm saying?"

"Yeah, I think I do." Then, with conviction, I said, "I understand what you're saying."

"Good," he said, staring hard at me for a moment. "As soon as the shot is made, pull the bolt from that rifle, it'll only slow you down. Carry the bolt with you for at least half a mile then throw it as far as you can into the brush. The fucking Army can buy me another one."

"You sure you don't want me to go?" Freddy asked. "I don't have a wife."

That was the first time Freddy had ever admitted to the fact that Annie and I were husband and wife.

"Thanks, brother," I said, looking at him. He knew what I was feeling and smiled.

"What's this all about?" Hanson asked.

"Family thing," Freddy said, then picked up the rifle and handed it to me.

The Winchester had been painted camouflage colors and felt heavier than normal. The scope had been wrapped in a shock absorbent type of material that would take a small amount of bumping without knocking it off its zero. I hefted it to my shoulder and looked through the scope, seeing what Hamlin meant by slashes. There were marks up and down from the cross hairs.

"Shit," I muttered.

"What's the matter?" Hamlin asked.

"Nothing. I've never looked through such a complicated scope before."

"Let me look," Freddy said, reaching for the rifle.

He lifted it and looked through the scope, "Shit," he said, then he handed it back to me. "Good luck!"

I looked down the barrel again, keeping both eyes open as I sighted.

"Good, you're the first two guys I've seen that look into a scope and still keep both eyes open. I guess it pays to be country boys," Hamlin said. "Most shooters close one eye and squint the other. No fucking wonder they have trouble finding their targets. That extra split second cost a lot of sure shots. It takes a lot of time to take that out of a shooter. Sometimes you never can. They don't make the grade or end up dead."

Macron nodded his head in agreement.

"Do you know how to find the target?" Hamlin asked.

"Yeah, no, I'm not sure what you mean," I answered.

"That's where I come in," said Macron.

"He's the spotter, the brains of the team," said Hamlin, "You listen to Bob and you'll do fine. Pull rank and you could both be dead meat. I don't mean to sound disrespectful of rank Sir, but out here in this territory each man has his job. Yours is to fly us in and out without anyone getting hurt. Ours is to get the ground work done any way we see fit. Do I make myself clear, Sir?"

"You're coming in loud and clear, Sergeant. I have no problem with that."

"Thank you, sir," Sergeant Hamlin said and grinned. "We'll all do fine."

"You fly a mean ship, Sir. Now it's my turn to get even," said Sergeant Macron, smiling.

I liked both of these men.

"We've got some work to do. Let's get started," Hamlin said, looking at each of us.

"You're the boss on the ground, as long as we're in an area that is foreign knowledge, Sergeant. If it comes to a decision that I don't agree with, I'll have to pull rank. Understood and agreed?" I asked.

"Yes sir," they both said in unison, nodding their heads.

"I've always looked forward to telling an officer what to do," Macron said. "Now's my chance. Would you stand at attention if I tell you to?"

"Don't push your luck."

That brought a good laugh and helped to break the tension.

"Okay, let's get to work," said Hamlin.

We turned to the charts first.

"Question," I said, "Why do I have to know the charts as well as Sergeant Macron?"

"If he gets killed, you're on your own. Plain and simple. You're a team but you have to know the game plan," Hamlin said.

"I could get snake bit and be dead in less than thirty seconds. Then you will have to proceed to the objective and get the job done on your own, or at least try. Your probability is cut to a thirty percent effectiveness. Not too good, but on this type of job, it's better than nothing. You'll have to work into a close range. The closer the better. Chest shot range. Your hide will have to be good. You could end up spending several days in one place. The only time you'll be able to move from your hide is in cover of darkness. Always try to look for better ones, closer or better angles. Never find a hide that'll put the sun in your face morning or evening. You can't see worth a shit in a glaring scope. Never find a hide that will heat from direct sun. It's bad enough to have to lay for hours or sometimes days in wait for the right target, but you'll go out of your fucking mind waiting in the direct heat. Never drink over a swallow of water. If you have to piss, it can cause problems. You'll sweat off a swallow. But if you do have to piss, turn on your side, piss down hill or you'll have to lay in it, no fun. Carry only what you can leave behind in unusable condition, always. Don't carry any food that has an odor. No exceptions. Don't carry any containers that will clank or make any sounds whatsoever. Those fucking biscuits they give us will give you something to do with your time. You might even get to eat a whole one on a long day. Always bury your leftovers. Don't swat bugs and don't use repellent. Repellents smell. We're used to the smell, the gooks aren't. The fucking bugs don't eat much and help with your camouflage," he grinned. "One man panicked when a bamboo viper crawled across his arm. He almost got them both killed. Luckily the other man was able to hold a hand across his mouth while he died. It hurts like hell when you get bit. You're dead out here without a medic. You'll die quietly, making a big deal out of it doesn't help anyone. You're dead anyway. Better to bite n a stick; it's rough on your teeth, but what the hell, you're through with them."

The team went on and on about the do's and don'ts of how they did their work. A lot of what they were saying went along with what Grandfather had already taught us, but I listened quietly, occasionally nodding my head that I understood. We went through breathing techniques, trigger pressure, the scope, the proper rest for the rifle and shooter.

He wanted to know if I was prone for charley horses or other forms of cramps if I had to lie still over long periods. How were my toilet habits? Did I get blurred vision or shakes when watching at a particular angle for a long time?

"Some people get to twitching from prolonged periods of lying in the same position," he explained.

I seemed to have all the right answers. Freddy sat in on the entire program in case I failed to make the grade.

We moved to the field for the finals. I practiced dry firing at given targets for a couple of hours. Macron watched my every move. The trigger pull, eyes for flinching, the end of my barrel for wobble. He would describe different targets that I was supposed to pick out, then have me describe an object at one side of the target. This would tell him if I was on the target he was directing me to. In turn, I would talk him back onto it. At first it was difficult, and I didn't think I would ever make the grade. Then everything began to come into focus, almost like we were on the same mind wave. Finally returning to the ship, Macron looked at the others and grinned broadly. "We got ourselves a trigger.

Hell, Howard, I might just trade you off for this man."

Hamlin grinned, "You can when you pay up the money you owe me, Bob, but until you do, you're stuck with me."

"We've got two hours before it gets dark. That should be about right. We'll try for our target at sunrise," Macron said looking at the rest of the men.

"How we going to know when to crank up?" Freddy asked, looking at Macron for the answers.

"These fucking radios aren't worth a shit in the jungle. If they don't short out from the moisture, they'll drag you down with the weight. Their range isn't worth a damn either. We'll do our best to let you know before we break out into the open. Don't want Howard shooting our asses off. Don't give him anything for pain that'll knock him out. We might need all hands on deck. You keep this bird ready to get us the fuck out of here as soon as we break cover. If you sleep, make it in shifts. Remember chief, keep this mother ready, okay?" Macron said.

He turned to me. "Let's kick some ass."

We covered the first mile without any problems, crossing a creek in a steep canyon. I realized how hard it would have been on Hamlin had he tried this with his injured leg. Going down the side of the canyon incline reminded me of my boyhood in some of the canyons back home. Freddy and I would put our fishing poles in our teeth while we'd carefully climb down the steep crumbling banks to get to the creek. Now here I was having to shoulder a rifle and rucksack and climb down a crumbling steep bank for a bigger fish. Scrambling down the steep slope, I could hear dirt falling into the water below. According to the map, there was a bridge about half a mile further up the canyon. Macron knew what he was doing, so I didn't say anything.

Once we reached the water, I turned to him and asked, "We coming back this way?"

"We might, or if things look bad, we might have to pick a different way back," he said giving me a grin.

"Shit," I grumbled.

"I remember a pilot that scared the shit out of me one time," he said as his eyes twinkled. "It's get even time."

"Did I ever tell you about my heart condition?"

"No, I don't believe I've heard that one." He turned and started across the creek, "Don't forget to take care of Junior," he added.

Junior was what he called the Winchester. If you fell, you held your rifle up over your head. If you knocked the scope off, you were just wasting time and risking your life for nothing. It was for sure you didn't zero it back in while on the job.

Twice I almost fell on Junior but caught myself in time. As we scrambled up the creek, I learned to walk in the water without falling. It was like my boyhood, hugging the sides of the larger boulders so that I had some footing sideways. Move out from the boulders and the moss could put you on your ass. I chose the boulders, and wedging my footing against them, proceeded upstream behind Macron.

We came to a place that made the climb out a lot easier than the place we had hiked down. Without looking back, Macron started climbing and I followed. The rifle still secured on my shoulder.

I hadn't really had time for a breather, but refused to call for a break. Macron, on the other hand, was used to putting miles between jobs and didn't seem to mind the bugs or limbs that hit him in the face. I began to think I'd gone soft, but when Macron finally turned and looked back his face told me he was about done in too. I felt better watching him labor for breath.

"You ever been here before, Macron?" I asked.

"Nope, first time," he answered.

"You seem to know where you're going."

"On the chart," he answered, "All part of learning to read them. You'll learn. You probably read city maps, right?"

"Hell no, I get lost in cities."

"Yeah, I forgot, you're a country boy. Okay, you understand mountains and creeks, right?" he said as we stood catching our breath.

"Yeah, I can read those."

"Same thing as these jungle charts, except these have to be updated periodically. The jungle closes in or gets cleared sometimes, but it's the same. You guys look at maps and charts when you fly, the only thing is some of us are in our right minds and stay on the ground. You look at things as if you're looking from heaven; we're looking as if we're in hell. I'd get lost for sure if I had to read them as air charts, probably end up in Cambodia," he said and laughed.

"That happened to me recently."

"Come on, daylight's a burning."

I put the Winchester back on my shoulder and flinched as the sling snuggled into the groove it had worn into my muscle. I thought again of what Hamlin said about leaving this monster behind. I looked forward to this job being over and done with. It would seem good to fly my normal bullet dodging missions.

We made our way across a clearing and then through a bunch of bamboo. I made the mistake of trying to move some of the leaves out of the way with my hand and ended up with a cut between the middle and index finger of my left hand. I'm left handed and I couldn't afford to have a bad trigger finger. Clenching my hand didn't seem to stop the flow of blood, and when I looked at it a few minutes later, it looked like I'd cut myself a lot worse than it was. As we cleared the bamboo thicket, Macron looked down at my hand, blood dripping from the fist I was making.

"What the hell happened?"

"I cut my hand," I said and held it up.

"Let it bleed as much as you can. How bad is it anyway?"

"I've had worse on my pecker."

Macron grinned and began looking around. Spotting what he was looking for on the ground, he walked over and picked the small plant. From what I could see it was something like moss.

Reaching over he opened my hand and examined the cut. "You ever think of wearing gloves?" he asked and took the handful of herbs, rubbing it vigorously between his palms crushing it, then stuck it on the cut.

"Hold this on it for a few minutes and it'll stop bleeding. It'll make your hand numb for awhile. Next creek we come to we'll wash the blood off and you'll be as good as new. Better get a move on, it'll be getting dark before long. We need to be in a good hide before then." He turned, and without saying anything more, started off again.

Within a few minutes I couldn't feel any discomfort from the cut. When we came across a creek again, Macron pointed to the water. I washed my hands and looked at the cut. The gash was a lot deeper than I'd thought it was.

Macron looked at my hand, turning it over and examining it from the backside "It looks like a saw-grass cut. It'll be all right until a medic can look at it. I had a guy that was gut shot once. We stuffed him full of Willie weed and he stopped hurting within a few minutes. Stuff really works. We always wondered how long the effects last."

"How long did it last the guy with the gut shot?"

"Till he died, maybe forty-five minutes," Macron answered. "Come on."

As we started through another bamboo thicket, I asked Macron why we hadn't brought machetes.

"We don't leave any trail for them to follow. If they have to spread out and look for signs, they travel much slower. The farther we go the less chance of them taking us. The ripple effect."

"Yeah, that makes sense," I said and picked up a stick to push the leaves out of my way.

Another quarter mile and Macron stopped to check his compass. I pulled mine out and checked it each time he did, wanting to keep my bearings. Macron watched me approvingly. I wasn't going to take any chances of getting lost in this God forsaken land. If something happened to Macron, I wanted to be prepared.

At both creeks I had set up a duck (three stones stacked on top of each other) as an indication of where we had crossed the stream. I don't know if Macron had noticed them, but I wanted to know how far I was from the rest of the gang and how in the hell I could find them. Twice I placed markers on trails that we encountered. The markers were arrows fashioned by placing sticks on the ground. Macron caught me doing this.

"What the fuck you doing?" he said, looking irritated.

"I want to know how to get out of this damned jungle if something happens to your ass," I said defensively.

"Shit, you're not even pointing the right way."

"I am for me."

"We came from that way, your arrow is pointing the wrong way. You're lost before you even start with that kind of trail marking," he said shaking his head.

"Sergeant, if you were the enemy and came across this sign, what direction would you think it was indicating?"

"I'd follow the fucking arrow," he said looking back at me. "Shit, I get it, you're marking 90 degrees off. Right?"

"Only you and I know that. It helps us, but it throws them off the track at the same time. If we reach the arrow first, we just give it a kick and they become sticks again," I said, "Always go to the right of the arrow."

"Well, I guess we all can learn new tricks. Where the hell you learn that?"

"My grandfather." I said, "Old Indian trick."

"Can't wait to show Howard," Macron said, turning he bent over as we stepped into an open area of elephant grass that was up to our shoulders. The section we were in was about a thousand feet from one edge of the jungle to the other and appeared to be about the same in width.

"Just across the clearing is our target area. I don't like a hide in this shit. Over there is a raise that'll give us some elevation. We'll work around to the right and see what that looks like. Watch for snakes in here. They're feeding on crawlies, but they'll bite you if you step on one."

There it was again, the fucking snake thing. I shuddered involuntarily. My eyes went to the ground as we advanced slowly toward our small hill.

Something jumped and ran as we worked our way through the grass. As it made a rustling sound the sweat popped out on my forehead. Whatever it was, it was as afraid of us as I was of it.

Macron turned to me and wiped his eyebrows. "You bring any toilet paper?"

I grinned weakly. "What the hell was that?" I whispered.

He shrugged that he didn't know. "Wasn't human though, come on."

We started moving again, with every nerve straining at the slightest movement in the grass.

As we reached our objective, Macron slowed our stalk. Twice he gave me the closed fist sign, which meant to freeze in step. I froze. The first time was a false alarm, but the second time wasn't. It was our first sighting of humans. As we eased forward and began our climb we saw a soldier standing near the hill. He appeared to be taking a leak and had his back toward us. After what seemed like an eternity, he finished his job, and looking in our general direction for a moment, turned and walked back toward the compound.

"This is going to be a good range if we can work our way up to the top of that hill. It'll give us a good advantage," Macron whispered and eased forward again.

We came to a dirt road that ran between the hill and the grass where we were hidden.

"Wait here. I'll take a look," Macron said.

I eased down on one knee while he darted across the road and disappeared into the grass on the other side again. After what seemed like an hour, but was probably only ten minutes, he reappeared and gave me the thumbs up.

Rising to my feet and looking both ways, I sprinted across the road and joined him in the grass.

"This is almost too good to believe," Macron whispered. "The hill is perfect for viewing the whole compound. They don't even have a guard on duty. Shit, your longest distance is only maybe three hundred yards and if we're lucky, two hundred. Fish in a barrel."

We worked our way up the hill, which was about a hundred yards to the top and had bushes and trees growing thick on all sides.

Looking at the sky, I knew we wouldn't have much time for a good hide before dark, but that was Macron's specialty, I was just a follower.

Macron seemed right at home.

We crawled up and looked over the top of the hill where I could see the layout below. A line of small hooch's bordered the main compound, which housed what appeared to be headquarters. The building was painted green which made it harder to spot from the air, but they weren't worried about any air or ground invasion. Cambodia was off limits to the allied forces, and they knew it.

As we settled in, Macron took charge as if we were on a Boy Scout camp-out.

"If you need to take a leak, now is the time to do it. No water other than a sip, if necessary. Better eat a biscuit to keep your belly from cramping, but take your time with it. It'll give you something to do." He was watching my reactions as he spoke.

"Yes, Sergeant," I said as if I were a private.

Macron grinned. He reached into his rucksack and began laying out our equipment. A spotting scope on a short tripod was the first to come out. Next an M-14 bipod (collapsible two-legged rifle rest), which he handed to me.

"Hook that baby up; it'll help steady you. I stole it from a marine," he said, a glint in his eye. "Here are some wonder bullets," he held out four 30-06 shells.

I took them and looking closer, discovered they were different than the usual GI armor piercing bullets.

"I wouldn't use these on anything but gophers back home. That soft point is going to make a mess out of anything it hits," I said as I held one up for closer inspection.

"Over here there aren't any rules except win or die. We're here to win."

"How many grains is the bullet?"

"150-grain soft point but with a special twist. They expand deeper than most soft points, titanium core in case there's some shoulder bone. In the core is a poison that will make a poisonous snake seem like a toy. These bullets get the job done. Never lost a gopher with one."

"I thought we were supposed to use full metal jacketed bullets. You know, the convention agreement?"

"We never signed that agreement. Everyone just thinks we did, and this isn't really declared a war. We're in Cambodia illegally, so what the fuck's the difference? I'll tell you something, no one knows what the fuck is going on here in southeast Asia. We take real estate then give it back. You ever wonder why? Think about it."

"I already have several times. I don't have an answer either. Why you giving me four shells if we're only supposed to fire once and get out?" I asked looking over at him.

"This is the Army. You waste all you can. And just if, and I repeat, if you fuck up and we still have a chance, you'll have to take a second or third whack. We don't quit until we do our work or have no other choice. Each shot however triples our chances of not getting out in one piece. Just don't fuck up the first time around and we're in deep clover, as you cowboys say."

We prepared to spend the night. Darkness came over us, and we lay awake talking in whispers about our lives, knowing it was going to be a long, stressful night.

"You ever kill anyone before?" Macron asked.

"Nope, I've shot people but I hope it wasn't fatal," I said. "You?"

"Yeah, I've killed before," Macron said. "You have to look at it in a realistic way. If you don't, it'll take its toll on you. You show signs of denial."

"What do you mean by realistic and denial?"

"This is war and we all have a job to do. For instance, you fly, but in flying you're part of the big war machine. You dodge bullets like the rest of us. You fly us in and pick us up along with the dead and wounded, then fly everyone out. Without you, we wouldn't have much of a war. Not here anyway. They figure that's why the French lost their fucking war here, no helicopters. You're as much a part of this war as any of us, maybe more. This is a helicopter war and you're the pilot. We can't wait to get off your fucking clay pigeon. They're always after your asses. Hell, you even have a bounty, you know that?"

I nodded.

"Our job is a shitty one. We sneak around and kill people taking a crap, screwing a woman, or telling a joke. Nothing is sacred."

I watched the outline of his face as he looked down at his lap.

A full minute passed then he took a deep breath. "You got to think of this job as a teeter-totter. One side of the board is American soldiers and the other side is the enemy. You have to pick which one you're going to save. For each gook you shoot, you've potentially saved an American soldier. In the case of our target tomorrow, we take out the side of the teeter-totter that will save hundreds or maybe thousands of American lives. It's that simple. We fuck up and it will cost a lot more than a wasted bullet. It'll cost a lot of good men. That's why it's important to keep your psyche. You let yourself go soft and you're less than worthless. I think you're going to do a good job, but if you let yourself think about the deed rather than the effect, we're fucked. All that man is, is a deadly virus that's infecting lots of GIs. You and I are the doctors who can remove it. You follow?"

"Yeah, I hear what you're saying. I'm not going to let you down, Sergeant. I don't think I'd want to make this my profession though."

The mosquitoes were driving me crazy. I continued to swat at them, but they just came back in force.

"Here," Macron said and handed me a piece of netting, "put this over your hat and tuck it into your shirt loosely. That won't allow them too many opportunities. Some will get through where it touches your skin though. That's why you want it loose around your neckline. Stick your hands in your pockets. That buzzing is just them tuning up their violins for tonight's concert and banquet. Just keep your mind off the little motherfuckers and try for some shuteye. Morning comes early."

Lying there on the damp ground, my thoughts turned to Annie and home. I wondered what she had been up to for the last couple of days. I closed my eyes and saw her standing nude in front of me. Damn, she was beautiful. I couldn't believe it, here I was, letting the mosquitoes chew on me while I waited to kill a human, when I could be reaching out and touching her. What the fuck was wrong with the picture. I hadn't been drafted; I enlisted! I felt the frustration building. The most beautiful woman in the world was mine, and I had volunteered to fly a fucking helicopter. "Warrant Officer Stupid reporting for duty, Sir!" It fit me to a tee.

I lay awake thinking about what I had left behind. Women had to be the smarter sex. How many of them did you see over here crawling around in the jungles? They were content to raise babies and shop. Right now that made more sense than going across the world to fight for some obscure reason that didn't make jack-shit sense.

Annie was the practical one. I liked going shopping with her. Especially when she was trying on dresses. She'd come twirling out of the dressing room with that bewitching smile of hers. She could have worn a feed sack and looked great.

"Well? What do you think?" she'd ask.

She looked good in anything. When I'd tell her that, she would shake her head and tell me I wasn't being any help. With Annie, I spoke the truth. She looked good in anything. The way she filled a dress was always magic.

The hours passed without sleep because of the mosquitoes buzzing, trying to penetrate the netting, and thinking about Annie. The thought of having to kill someone tomorrow didn't help either. I kept having doubts about pulling the trigger on a human being. Yet I knew I was going to have to do it regardless of my feelings and without hesitation. If I hesitated, I would be lost. The reality of it made me sick to my stomach.

I don't know what time it was when I finally drifted off, but the next thing I knew I was being shaken lightly. My eyes popped open and I lay trying to get my bearings. Macron was watching me closely from a half-sitting position.

"Thought maybe you'd died on me last night," he said in a low voice.

"How long you been awake?"

"Long enough to want a hot cup of coffee. Ten minutes maybe. Here, coffee beans. Better than nothing." He held out his hand.

I took them and stuck one in my mouth. It was black and bitter. Damn, it was good though. Macron had given me a half dozen of them.

"You stingy or something?" I said and grinned. "A half dozen beans to kill someone. What's this Army coming to?"

"All you get until the fun's over. Don't want any shakes," he said flatly then handed me one more. "You look tough enough for maybe seven, but eat a biscuit with it. They can make you sick eating them without water."

"I usually have raw bear steak for breakfast back home. Wash it down with coffee strong enough to make this shit taste like puffed wheat."

"You sure you ain't from Texas?" he asked, smiling. "Come on, it's getting light enough to start looking for our gopher. If it's that building, it's 250 yards. You use the first slash up from the cross hairs. That will put you dead on. Got that?"

"I got it, Sergeant," I said. Removing the piece of waterproof cloth from the gun, I looked through the scope at the closed door. Hell, I'd killed a lot of gophers from almost this far. I snuggled down and put the cross hairs on the doorknob. "Piece of cake," I mumbled to myself, keeping my mind off what I was going to be shooting at in a few minutes. I was deliberately preparing myself for a moment that was going to come whether I liked it or not.

Men started going in and out of the doorway, and I pretended to pick them off. It helped me to get adjusted to the real thing or at least that was the way I figured it. I hadn't pointed a gun at a human being without cause since I was a kid pretending to shoot bad guys, then it had been a play gun. This was real. All I had to do was close the bolt on this rifle and it was ready to kill anything I squeezed the trigger on. I shuddered at the thought, then got hold of myself, remembering what we had talked about last night. The teeter totter thing. One end was going to be one human enemy and on the other there would be hundreds of American GIs. That helped me keep everything in perspective, at least I hoped it did. I had practiced shooting all my life; this time it would really count.

Yeah, keep thinking that way, Morgan. Beat the war drums. This is for all the marbles, and I can shoot marbles with the best. I wanted to save American lives. Come on, you bastard, no mercy. I'll shoot your nuts off. I was really psyching myself. Any more pep talk, and I would charge the compound with my knife.

Macron looked at me puzzled, then grinned. "That's the spirit. I've seen Hamlin look the same way. Kind of like working up the courage to ask a good-looking woman to dance. Keep that attitude and we'll kick ass, Sir. Nothing like a hungry trigger."

"I wish the son of a bitch would show his face. I'd show you how to change his expression," I said, looking at Macron. I could see where war drums could be effective. I was ready to draw blood.

"We're as ready as we'll ever be. I knew I had a killer as a partner."

I didn't mind him calling me a killer at the moment; I felt like killing. It was a feeling, I can't explain it, but it was there.

Time passed and it grew hot. When I checked my watch it was 0942 hours, and still nothing. I was losing my edge again.

"Don't quit me, Sir, our time is near," Macron said, looking at me closely.

"I wish the bastard would show. How the hell do you guys stand all this waiting?"

"Part of the job."

Children began playing in the compound, running after a small pup or pig, I couldn't make it out for sure. One of the kids threw a ball towards the doorway of the building. Another ran to retrieve it. The child looked like a girl about five or six years old. At the same time the door came open, and a man in uniform stepped out, holding the door open for an older uniformed man.

I slid the bolt of the Winchester closed, making sure it closed on a shell.

Macron stiffened. "That's the target," he said in a flat professional voice, the kind of voice that demanded attention. "Man two. Not wearing a hat, old. Got him?" he asked.

"Got him," I answered, putting my scope on his chest, checking the right slash on the scope. My finger began to feel funny.

"Slash one, you on him, Sir?" Macron asked again as I waited.

I didn't answer as I watched the man bend over and pick up the child.

"He's holding that little girl."

"It's a shoot, Sir. You can go through the package. You gotta shoot."

"He's got a little girl in his arms, Sergeant. I can't get a clear shot." Sweat began to run down my forehead.

"You gotta shoot, Sir. You gotta shoot now," he said, as he looked through his spotter's scope.

"What the fuck you talking about. I can't shoot through a child. I can't get a clear shot," I said, feeling panic setting in.

"You have to shoot through the kid. Take your shot, Sir. Do it now."

I reached up and wiped the sweat from my eyes, my mind racing wildly.

Put the fucking kid down. Please. Damn it, please, I thought desperately as I returned to the scope.

The target remained with the child in his arms as he spoke to a couple of men. He was obviously enjoying the children. My mind went blank as I looked through the rifle's scope again. I held on the middle of the man's chest, but the scope refused to go around the child's back. Dear God, what was I doing with the cross hairs on a child's body.

The rifle gave a loud crack and the target disappeared. I had squeezed the trigger and the rifle had responded.

"The target is down, Sir. Let's go!" He reached over and shook my shoulder. "Sir, come on, we gotta get out of here."

Somehow I pulled the bolt on the Winchester. Taking hold of the end of it, I smashed the scope glass. Then without looking at what I had just done, I staggered to my feet. We began to run back down the other side of the hill toward the road and elephant grass.

I felt numb. I couldn't quit thinking about what was in the cross hairs of the rifle as I pulled the trigger. I knew I had shot the child along with the target, which was all I had called the man. He didn't have a name as far as I wanted to know. The child had no face, but somehow I knew it was a little girl. Dear God, what had I done to a perfectly innocent little child?

Several times I wanted to turn and run to the compound and see if I could have missed, but I knew I hadn't. I stumbled and ran with Macron in the lead, and I guess I was fortunate he was in charge.

Dropping down the first canyon to the stream below, I stopped and reached down, splashing cold water on my face, then over my head, running my hands through my hair.

"Come on, Sir. We're halfway. You'll feel better in a day or two. It's not easy to do what had to be done."

This was one of the cocksuckers that had got me into this. I wanted to kill again for a moment, only this time by hand.

"Get fucked!" I said, glaring at him.

"Yes Sir, not a bad idea," he knew what I was going through and said later that he was glad to see some fight left in me.

My heart was numb and rage consumed me. I was desperate to get my hands on something and vent the pain I felt. I wanted to hurt something, anything. I wished we'd run into a bunch of gooks. I needed to wash the memory of what I had just done out of my mind. I would have welcomed the diversion and at this point I didn't care if I lived. Death would be better than the guilt.

After what seemed like an eternity, we broke out of the jungle into the clearing we used for a base camp. The helicopter sat with a camouflage net over it. The rotors weren't secured which would have been procedure at the base.

Just before we stepped out of the foliage and into the clearing, Macron stopped and gave a whistle. Hamlin was on guard duty and immediately answered with a counter whistle.

"Like fucking Indians," I mumbled to no one in particular, then added, "Sorry, Grandfather."

By now I was starting to feel a little better. I'd had time to think about what happened, and the exercise of running for our lives had helped. I kept turning the events over in my mind, attempting to justify what I had been a part of. I tried to convince myself that it had been partially an accident. I blamed the rifle for having a hair trigger. The accident had taken care of the teeter totter condition. I had done what had to be done. That the child was in the way was an unfortunate side effect, but I knew down deep that I was responsible for the death of an innocent child.

"Let's get the hell out of here," Freddy said as the chief ripped the netting off the ship. Leaping into the cockpit, Freddy cranked her up. Hanson ran around to my side of the ship. As I slipped into the web seat of the pilot's station, he helped me with my shoulder harness. Looking at me, he gave the thumbs up, and wheeling, jumped into the back.

As Hanson jumped for the deck, the front of the skids came off the ground. After two clicks on the intercom confirmed everyone was buckled in, I pulled the collective back, at the same time giving it a twist of throttle. Leaning back on the heel of the skids, the ship jumped into the air like a turpentined cat.

As soon as she had enough air, I eased the cyclic forward. She came to the nose down and all business position, and we shot forward and up. Given the significance of the situation, we appreciated the extra power.

Freddy gave a yee-haw cowboy yell as we sprinted forward and banked to the northeast toward the river. We climbed to five thousand feet and turned for home.

"You take it," I said to Freddy.

"Got it."

No enemy fire met us as we made for the Vietnam border. We had been a total surprise to the enemy.

"Don't fuck with the Army!" I yelled out my window. I had to let off a little built up aggression.

Freddy looked over at me in surprise. Then a broad smile ran across his face and I felt like everything was going to be all right. It would just take time. Maybe a trip into a bar and bump heads with a GI looking for some diversion from this fucking war. I didn't even care if he won. I shook my head and changed my mind. Bullshit! I felt like kicking ass.

"You nervous?" Freddy asked.

"No, why?"

"You keep tapping the floor mic switch."

The Huey has a microphone foot switch that is used when you don't want to touch the switch on the cyclic, which is extremely sensitive to touch. When the left seat pilot is at the controls and you have to use the microphone, you activate the switch on the floor a lot like a dimmer-switch on a car. On the cyclic you have the switch at your fingertips while your feet are on the tail rotor pedals.

I'd be relieved when we reached the base. We'd be there for evening chow and for once that sounded good. It would be brown, hot and taste like shit, but I was looking forward to eating at home.

We crossed the border back into Vietnam, and as we got close to the base we dropped to two thousand feet. Approaching our checkpoint, I got on the radio.

"Fox One, this is Viper. Repeat, Fox One, Viper coming home, you copy?" I asked.

"That's a roger, Viper. This is Fox One. We read you loud and clear. Welcome home. Fox One out."

It seemed good to hear friendly voices again. I felt like we'd been gone a long, long time. By the time we touched down, I had lost my desire to go to chow. What I wanted was a fifth of whiskey and to feel my bunk and pillow.

As we sat down on the apron, I looked over at Freddy.

"Three weeks out of this shit hole. I'm going to lay everything in sight," he said, slapping me on the shoulder.

It was great to see good old dependable Freddy still thinking about the most important thing in his life, getting laid.

Climbing out of the ship, we saw two Chinook sky hooks just down from us. These helicopters were the giant wreckers that went out and retrieved the downed Hueys. I wondered what they had been up to since we left, how long ago? I thought about it and shook my head. It seemed like a lot longer than two days.

"After debriefing, I'm going to go write Annie, then turn in. If you go to chow, bring me a goodie," I said to Freddy.

"You going to be okay, Cole?"

"Yeah, it's just going to take some time," I said and patted him on the shoulder as we walked toward operations and the debriefing.

We poured ourselves a well deserved cup of hot coffee and waited for the major to enter. There were five of us sitting in the office, and we all stood as he entered. Then sat back down as he motioned and spoke, "As you were."

We sipped on our coffees, waiting for the meeting to start. The major scanned the room.

"All here, I'm pleased to see. Any problems?" he asked, looking around from face to face.

"I hurt my lower leg on recon, Sir. We had to run a sub trigger," Sergeant Hamlin said, then waited for Sergeant Macron or me to take over.

I spoke next. "I went trigger, Sir, Sergeant Macron took charge of the operation. He is to be commended. Sergeant's Macron and Hamlin were on top of it all the way. It was an honor to serve under them," I said, looking over at the two men.

They both nodded ever so slight, and you could tell they were pleased with the recognition.

We went over the operation from start to finish. With reluctance I told about the child. The major remained silent as he listened to the details. I kept a poker face, not revealing my feelings. Freddy was the only one that could see through my facade. Then Sergeant Macron recounted his part of the operation.

As the briefing wound down, the major handed me the envelope containing my letter to Annie, and I thanked him.

After the debriefing, the others headed for the chow hall while I started for my quarters and a bottle of good whiskey, but first I borrowed a lighter and burned the letter, hoping I'd never have to write another. As I lay on my bunk all I could think about was the little girl. She had no face, perhaps it was just as well. Back home they were referring to us as baby killers. I would never be able to deny that accusation. The words came back again to haunt me, "Send your conscience home, if you don't you'll die here." I thought about what the grunts had to live with as they were forced to take part in the brutality of this war and felt deep sorrow for them. I tried to get my mind off of her little body by thinking about Annie and home, but no matter how hard I tried with eyes open or closed, over and over again I saw her small body jerk as the bullet struck her. How much had I actually seen or how much was being shut out. At times I denied seeing anything after the shot was fired. Then I would see her body arch with the impact of the bullet. Sweat soaked my uniform and stung my eyes. I rationalized that in taking that life I had saved perhaps hundreds of American soldiers and began to relax a little until I closed my eyes and again saw that small body jerk. How would God ever be able to forgive me when I knew I would never be able to forgive myself? I lay on my bunk until Freddy came in and seeing me staring at the ceiling, walked over.

"Hey, come on, I'm buying the beer and salties," he said.

"You sure? I'm damned thirsty," I said without much conviction. I swung my feet off the bunk. "Some of the shit we won't do for a beer," I said, trying to lighten up.

"Come on, you earned it." He gently laid his hand on my shoulder, and squeezed.

We got hammered that evening.

Chapter 25

The next day our three weeks of R & R started. Freddy decided he was going to go to Taiwan for his leave. He called it the land of lays.

"What I hear is they can't get enough of GIs there. You have to fight them off. Not me, I'll start my own race. How does this sound? Graywanese, kinda sings, doesn't it?" He grinned at the thought of all the women waiting for him. "You sure you don't want to come along Cole? The women are hot and the beer is cold. Hanson is going. We can have a contest to see which one of us is the last man left standing."

"No, I don't think so, Freddy. I think I'll hang out in Da Nang. Maybe visit LeeAnn. I like the cooking. More like home."

Freddy gave me a knowing grin, "Uh huh."

"Now there you go, giving me that look again. I'm not going to fool around on Annie, you asshole. Besides, when we go home, you'll have the clap and I'll be as clean as a daisy," I smiled at him, "and my dick won't be falling off like yours will."

"I plan on wearing it out before that happens," Freddy said.

We left together that morning, taking a Huey to Da Nang for a major overhaul. Hanson flew along with us. From Da Nang he and Freddy planned to catch a hop to Taiwan. Freddy referred to the flight as his "ticket to heaven." I shook my head listening to him talk about his fantasies, but he wouldn't be Freddy without them.

At Qui Nhon we stopped to refuel and picked up a couple GIs that were also due for R & R. One of them sneaked a case of Budwieser on board, and even warm it tasted good. Within fifteen minutes none of us were feeling any pain. I dropped down from five thousand feet to about five hundred feet off the beach. Rounding a point of rocks we came upon some women and kids sunbathing and playing. They went wild for a minute, not knowing what was happening. Women gathered children and began running for the shelter of the trees.

I pulled into a hover as we stared at the group to see if there were any good looking women. Two of the younger women waved at us.

"Put us down," one of the grunts yelled out jokingly, "they want us. Put us down, we'll stay here, sir."

With all the excitement, I knew better than to hover at anything less than a hundred feet with these hornies to contend with. Freddy would probably jump at seventy-five if there was any water to break his fall. I wasn't sure about the others, but I couldn't help laughing at these pecker heads.

As the ship flew along the coastline, our passengers fell silent, each lost in his own thoughts. Looking at my watch, I saw it was 1215 hours. At home it would be around midnight. Annie no doubt would be asleep or reading. She often curled up in the easy chair, feet tucked under her, with cup of hot chocolate on the end table, and read late into the night. Damn, I wished I were there to tickle her bare feet or just pester her any way I could. "I sure miss you," I whispered.

"I miss you too, Sweety," Freddy said over the intercom.

"Fuck you," I said. I had squeezed the button on the cyclic without thinking.

We landed for refueling and everyone got out to stretch his legs.

"Want me to get us another case of Bud, Sir?" one grunt asked, looking hopeful.

"No, we better not go in smashed. We can wait a little longer," Freddy said. "Now if you want to do something for me, find me a woman that'll sit on my lap until we get to Da Nang. Naw, best not do that either, that'd just embarrass Cole."

I gave Freddy the finger but didn't say anything. I was looking forward to my visit with LeeAnn. Not that I was interested in her, at least not in a serious way. Although, I knew if I were to sleep with a woman other than Annie, it would be LeeAnn.

"I've been here too long," I thought. "Gotta get home soon."

As they finished refueling, I watched Hanson climbing up the concealed foot ladder to finish his preflight check. He was very thorough and bent close to the rotor hub and mast doing a microscopic inspection to make sure nothing was fractured or out of line. The Huey has a flat roof deck, and it had to be hotter than hell up there, but that never stopped Hanson. I could tell all was well the way he suddenly stood up and placed his hands on his hips. Climbing back down, he gave us the thumbs up. I cranked up and could smell the sweet odor of exhaust from the turbine.

"Let's get the fuck out of here," Freddy yelled at me. "The heat is melting the patch tape." He was referring to the pieces of tape they put over the bullet holes in the ship to keep the rain from coming through.

Nearing Da Nang, I radioed for permission to land. We were cleared for approach and Freddy began singing one of his little ditties, as usual it had a woman in it. After putting down, we headed for operations to turn in our flight report, then walked to the officer's quarters where we cleaned up.

"I'm going out on tomorrow's flight. It's not too late to change your mind, Cole," Freddy said, looking at me.

"Thanks, pal, but I'm going to stay here, at least for awhile. Let me know where you'll be staying and maybe I'll drop in later."

That evening we caught the base bus to Da Nang and headed for LeeAnn's. As we walked in, she spotted us and headed our way. "Cole, Freddy, how delightful," LeeAnn said and gave us both a hug. "I've been thinking about you, Cole. Where are you staying and for how long?" she asked.

"We're at the base. Freddy is flying out for Taiwan in the morning. I'll be staying in Da Nang for awhile."

"You'll stay here then. I have a small sleeping apartment next to mine. You'll be my guest. Freddy, you're more than welcome to stay, too. I'm sure you can find enjoyment here as well," LeeAnn said, turning to him. "There are a lot of very eligible young ladies that would enjoy your company." She put her arm through mine, and we walked to a table marked with a reserved sign, which she removed. The table was on a small raised area with plush carpeting, next to a spectacular window view. A waiter came over and gave us a wine list. I could feel the tension leaving. Once again I was enjoying the company of the most beautiful restaurant owner in all of Vietnam. Hell, all of Asia!

"Look, there are several eligible young ladies here already," LeeAnn said to Freddy.

"LeeAnn, I have a friend who's wanting me to go to Taiwan with him. He wants to show me the sights, but thanks just the same, maybe next time," Freddy said.

"You don't have to be apologetic, Freddy, I understand," LeeAnn said, placing her hand on the back of his, then patting it as if he were a child.

Freddy grinned at her and then looked at me.

"I'm starving. Don't suppose you have any Montana beef here?" he asked.

"Not Montana, but how does a steak and seafood sound to you boys?"

"Just bring in the hind quarter and a sharp knife. We'll cut our own steaks," I said, rubbing my hands together with anticipation. LeeAnn stood, and excusing herself from the table, went to the kitchen.

Freddy, as usual, started giving all the women the once over, trying to figure out which one to hit on. Watching the pro at work, I marveled. This was a Friday night or Freddy night, as I jokingly called it, and some of the nurses were off duty. If I had been single, I would have gone nuts over the selection of women waiting to have fun.

Freddy read my thoughts and grinned. "If there's two, you gonna help me out, old buddy?" he said, lifting his eyebrows a couple times.

"Get screwed, and this time I mean it," I said.

"Which one of the little lonelies looks like she needs me the most?" His eyes ran around the tables hungrily. "I've got a hell of an appetite. All those yummies and only one of me to go around. Oh well, they'll just have to settle for me one at a time. I need a dance book, only I think I'd have to turn it into a screw book. It's the only fair way to spread myself around," he sighed longingly at the mass of females to choose from, "Don't be bashful, my beauties," he said in a low voice.

Our drinks came and the waiter refused our money. I looked around and saw LeeAnn standing across the dining room watching us as she talked to a couple of nurses. She caught my eye and walked back to our table.

"Those two young ladies are all alone, Freddy. I told them you were looking for companionship for the evening. They both seemed anxious to meet a real Army helicopter pilot." She batted her eyelashes a couple times to emphasize their interest. This and the news of the young women built a fire in Freddy.

"Well, it's wartime. I shouldn't disappoint the troops," he said, sliding out of his seat. I'd seen him in action enough to know that at least one of them would be spending the night with the horny bastard.

"Did I do it right?" LeeAnn asked.

"Oh yeah, that's all he needed," I said, watching him move into action.

Both nurses were smiling warmly as they introduced themselves. They were sitting at a booth, and as one of them made room for him, he slid in beside her. If I was a betting man, and I was, I would lay odds that he'd have his hand at least on her knee within ten minutes.

"Freddy seems right at home," LeeAnn commented, watching him. "I'm glad you're not like that, Cole. It fits Freddy, but you're different."

I looked at her, then down at my drink. A few moments went by and I glanced back at her. She still hadn't taken her eyes off me. As usual, she had her chin resting lightly on the palm of her left hand. Her eyes were captivatingly beautiful like Annie's. I looked away again.

LeeAnn kept watching me, and I could feel her eyes burn into my head and heart.

"You ever dance with your customers?" I asked, trying to make conversation.

LeeAnn's business was not only a dining room, but a lounge with a dance floor. It was small, and a band played there on Friday and Saturday nights. It was mainly American GIs in the band and they were paid well for this part of the world.

"No," she answered after a moment, "but I'll dance with you."

I squirmed inwardly. Standing, I excused myself under the pretext that I had to use the men's room. Freddy saw me leave the table and followed.

In the men's room, I told him my dilemma. "Freddy, she's coming on to me, and I don't know how to react. I'm married. I don't want to cheat on Annie."

"Why the hell does this happen to a shithead like you, instead of me? I work my ass off to get laid, and you work yours off trying not to. LeeAnn is the best looking woman I've ever seen, and I might add, I've seen a lot of beautiful women in my time. I'd trade places with you in a heartbeat, Cole. But she seems to have this sickness for you. I don't understand it, but she does." He held his hand up in the air in frustration, then dropped it suddenly.

"Cole, it'll be six months more before we end our tour in this hell hole. Six months, brother! You're going to drive yourself into an early grave, and then you're going to look back, and say, 'Old Freddy was right, I should have screwed my head off when I was alive. Now it's too late!'"

I smiled at him. "I'm so glad I got to talk to you. I feel a hundred percent worse," I slapped him on the back. "Freddy, I say this with brotherly love and I don't want you to take it the wrong way, okay?"

"Okay."

"I hope your cock falls off. Really, I do, but I hope the skin is all worn off before it does," I said and gave him a big warm grin. "As usual, you've been a hundred percent worthless to me in this conversation."

"Thanks, Cole, you don't realize what that means to me, coming from you. Really. Thank you. If I can be worthless to you again, don't hesitate."

"You've done less than I ever expected already, but I won't forget your offer," I said turning to leave.

"Cole?"

"Yeah?" I stopped and turned around to hear the bit of wisdom that I knew was coming.

"I'm a good judge of horseflesh, you know that, right?" he said with conviction.

"Yeah, so?"

"You'll be passing up the greatest piece you've ever experienced, or are you still a virgin?" he asked, looking mischievously at me. "We're like brothers, don't be afraid to admit it."

"You dumb fuck," I said and gave him the finger as I shook my head, then turned and left the men's room. Good old Freddy, was he ever going to change? I hoped not.

As I approached the table, LeeAnn looked up at me. My eyes took all of her in as I stood for a moment above her. She wore very little make up, perhaps just a touch of lipstick. She had beautiful features, and her hair framed her face and neck perfectly. Her face was the face of a goddess. She wore a light yellow dress with a low rounded neckline. Just below her neckline I could see the gentle swelling of her breasts. As I stared at her, she sat motionless. LeeAnn's waist was small, and her hips were beautifully proportioned to the rest of her. I wondered what she looked like without clothes.

Damn, this was a mistake in the making. I should go with Freddy and Hanson to Taiwan. There, at least, I wouldn't get involved. This was going to get complicated if I wasn't careful. But it was like taking a drug you knew wasn't good for you. I wanted the high and thought I could handle it. I sat back down. LeeAnn must have sensed my uneasiness.

"Tell me about your wife." she said, trying to ease my discomfort. "What's she like?"

"Annie? Well, she's a lot like you. I mean you're a lot like her. You know."

LeeAnn laughed at my fumbling. "Which?" she asked, not helping me out.

"Well, for one thing, you're both alike in the fact that you're not helping me out of this hole I've dug. Instead, you both seem to enjoy watching me squirm."

"What does she look like?"

I began describing Annie as LeeAnn watched, her eyes never leaving my face. I produced a picture of her from my wallet.

"I envy her very much," she said, still holding her chin with the palm of her hand as she looked at the picture. "It's a once in a lifetime thing to get a man who loves like you do. She's very beautiful, Cole."

"You'd have to know her," I said, looking into LeeAnn's eyes. Her stare was hypnotic.

"Someday maybe," LeeAnn said, "I'd like to meet this Annie of yours. She sounds like quite a wonderful woman."

Our dinner came and LeeAnn sat quietly watching me eat.

"Tomorrow we'll go to the marketplace and look for a present that you can send your Annie."

What a wonderful lady to think of Annie that way, I thought.

After dinner we walked into the lounge and took a small table that was reserved.

As the waitress brought our coffee, LeeAnn leaned toward me, and giving me a radiant smile, asked, "Cole, would you dance with me?"

Taking her hand, I led her to the dance floor and put my arm around her waist. At first we danced at a distance. But like magnets, our bodies moved closer, and I could feel her breasts against my chest. Moving in time to the music, I caught the light scent of her perfume, and could feel her thigh as it brushed against mine. It felt good to hold a woman in my arms again, too good. My heart beat wildly, and I could feel the longing in my loins.

"Aaah," I said and stopped dancing, holding my back.

"What is the matter, Cole?"

"My back has been giving me fits," I lied. "Those seats we sit in are a bitch."

"Come, let's sit down," she said, a worried look on her face.

I was relieved. I couldn't think of any other way of getting away from her body without hurting her feelings, but I was beginning to get a hard-on from dancing so close. I put my hand in my pocket to hide the evidence as we walked back to our table.

As we sat down, LeeAnn still looked concerned, and who was sitting at a table across the room watching me? Yep, good old Freddy.

Our eyes met and Freddy gave me the old, you-gotta-be-kidding! look.

"Screw you, Freddy," I mumbled, looking at him.

He grinned, knowing exactly what I'd said.

"What are you thinking, Cole?" LeeAnn asked, a half smile on her face.

"Kick that guy out of the place and I'll tell you," I said, nodding toward Freddy.

"You two are close like brothers, aren't you?"

"Yeah, we know each other pretty well, I guess. Can't help but love the son of a bitch, excuse my language."

"He's very lucky to have a friend like you, and you're fortunate to have him also," she said, holding her coffee cup close to her lips while watching me. "I'm lucky to have a friend like you too." A small wrinkle appeared on her brow. "I realize this isn't the time or place for this kind of confession, Cole. But I feel I need to be honest with you. I find you very attractive and stimulating both mentally and physically. To be honest with you I have never felt like this before. I envy your Annie. She must be a wonderful woman to have your love. I won't try to come between you. I give you my word."

I could feel her struggling to choose the right words.

"Your friendship is very special to me, Cole. I promise to keep it in its proper perspective, but I feel better laying my feelings out in the open. There, I feel better now," she said again and tried to laugh.

I sat turning her words over and over. I knew that LeeAnn cared for me, and part of me felt like maybe I was getting in over my head while the other half was denying it. I enjoyed being with her, perhaps more than I was willing to admit to myself. I sipped my beer, then suddenly realized I wanted something stronger and motioned for a waiter. A couple of whiskeys and I started feeling much better.

LeeAnn suggested we go to a different nightclub, saying she felt we could have more fun in another establishment. "Let's ask Freddy and his ladies if they would like to join us. It will make it more festive, don't you think?"

"Anytime he's around it gets pretty lively, all right," I said. "I'll ask him."

I got up and walked over to where he was entertaining both nurses. "LeeAnn wants to go somewhere else. She was wondering if you good people would care to join us?"

"It's party time," he said, then smiled. "Lead on, brother."

Lead on I did. We hit the better places and then some of the not so nice ones. Those were Freddy's idea. But LeeAnn said nothing. On the contrary, she made the party wherever we went. At one of Freddy's choices, the bar had a strip show. I felt uncomfortable during the performance in the presence of three women, but they made the best of it and kept the party going. I was even more impressed with my companion, she was a real trooper.

"Where you staying tonight, Freddy? LeeAnn offered us an apartment at her place if we want it," I said around one o'clock in the morning. I hadn't recovered from our mission and was still feeling the aches and pains. During the evening, weariness that was bone deep and mentally oppressive had crept over me, as I fought to keep the image of the child out of my mind.

LeeAnn sensing my fatigue, suggested we call it a night, then left to call a cab.

"You guys go on and turn in, we're just getting started." Freddy said. "I've got a lot of steam to blow off, and my little beauties are going to do the blowing if I have anything to do with it."

Both nurses laughed, each clinging to an arm. I wasn't sure how he was going to work it with two women, but knowing Freddy I was sure he would find a way to keep both of them happy.

When the cab arrived, the driver came in to let us know he was there, then waited patiently while we said our goodnights. As we left the bar, LeeAnn slipped her arm through mine and we walked out the door.

"Good evening," the driver said to her, bowing respectfully. He appeared to know LeeAnn and respect her.

"Good evening. We'd like to go home, please," LeeAnn said, and the cab driver bowed again then hurried to open the door. The downtown streets of Da Nang were still crowded with soldiers and ladies of the night. When we arrived at LeeAnn's home, the cab driver hopped out and opened the door for us. I reached into my pocket for money to pay him, but she pushed my hand aside.

"No Cole, you are my guest," she said in a matter of fact manner. "Some day when I visit Montana, I will be your guest."

"You'll get the pleasure of riding in my old pickup truck," I said in a low voice.

She smiled, then taking my arm, we walked to her door. I stepped back as she rang a bell. Within seconds a small window opened in the door, and the housekeeper looked through at us. The door swung open and she stepped aside, bowing as we entered. I bowed in return then followed LeeAnn.

As my eyes roamed the room, I could see nothing had changed. LeeAnn had very good taste and was an art collector. Paintings hung on the walls and carved ivory statues lined one shelf. The room was definitely French in décor, with elegant furniture and ornate tables supporting luxurious lamps

The first time I visited LeeAnn's home, I was impressed with the way she lived, and commented on it, " Wow, I sure didn't expect anything like this," I'd said.

"My father gave me most of this, when I decided to live in Da Nang. It's nice, but it's not necessary, it just makes living more pleasing," she had said.

She was right, it was a very pleasant room, and we had spent many hours talking and playing cards here, while I was stationed in Da Nang.

"This is your sleeping chamber, Cole." LeeAnn opened the door. The bedroom was as elegant as the living room. Among other things, it contained two full-sized beds.

"My room is just down the hall from you, if you need anything. The cook will be on staff at six o'clock. Until then you'll have to fend for yourself, or if you like, I would be pleased to prepare something for you. I'm a very good cook, Cole," she said, looking up into my face.

I felt a stirring as she searched my face. "No thanks, I'm kind of tired, LeeAnn. I didn't intend to spend the night here. I left all my duffel back at the base. I should have caught the bus back," I said, feeling a little uncomfortable.

LeeAnn took my hand, and gave it a squeeze.

"You're at home here, Cole. I'll send a boy to get your things in the morning. What time do they let them on the base?"

I felt the knot in my stomach. Lee Ann was a beautiful sensuous woman, and I knew I was tempting fate. She was making every effort to make me feel at home. I knew that if anything was going to happen now, it would be my own doing, not hers. Now all I had to do was trust myself. That should be easy, I'd just think of Annie when I felt weak.

"I'll be fine, LeeAnn. I'm just not sure how to respond to this kind of situation. It's a little awkward for me to be staying with you. Maybe we could have a cup of hot chocolate."

"I'd be pleased to make you some. In fact I think I'll have a cup also. I haven't drank chocolate at this time of morning before." She laughed and her eyes danced. "We might start something new. I can just see one of us knocking on the other's door, 'It's three o'clock, time for hot chocolate!"

We both laughed.

This had to be as awkward for her as it was for me. Yet she was doing her best to make me feel at ease and it was working.

We sat around the table and drank a cup of what in Vietnam would be considered hot chocolate. It wasn't anything like we had back home, it had neither milk or sugar, but the company was pleasing so the drinks were good.

LeeAnn and I talked more about our different cultures, and I found the French to be a lot like we are. Warm and sometimes a little over confident in their ways.

We discussed the war and I began to understand that there were more than two sides to the conflict. It started with a simple question from LeeAnn.

"Why are the Americans over here? I know they're trying to stop communism from taking over, but why Vietnam? What is there here that matters to the world that much? There are only peasants trying to raise enough rice to feed their families. I don't understand," she said.

"I'm not sure I do either. There doesn't appear to be any threat to the free world that I can see. I joined the Army to fly helicopters and to defend the United States, not to fly over rice paddies, being shot at as I delivered troops to their deaths. If I just knew we were doing something right, gaining over the communist or something, I would feel more like risking my neck. The one thing that keeps me in the air and willing to be shot at, is our men on the ground. They deserve the best I've got to give. Helicopters are their hope out of this hell. We had an older pilot talk about a military industrial complex or something like that. It makes me wonder if it isn't all politics and money."

LeeAnn reached over and took my hand. "I didn't mean to get you talking about the war. I'm sure you're getting enough of that. You're here to get away from it, forgive me," she added, squeezing my hand. Then LeeAnn brightened. "My sister and nephew are coming to visit me for a few days. They are due tomorrow morning. You'll like them, Cole. My sister is a widow. Her husband was killed almost two years ago near Qui Nhon. They have a plantation near there. My nephew is almost eight years old. He's a very bright young man. I'm sure you two will get along splendidly. He is a great admirer of the Americans. Meeting a helicopter pilot will be a great honor for him," she said with enthusiasm.

"I didn't know you were having company. I can stay at the hotel down the street."

"No. Please. I have plenty of room. These are my quarters, I have another guest apartment that I'll put them in. I would be hurt if you stayed anywhere other than here," she said and again took my hand.

I was beginning to enjoy her touch. No, that would be an understatement, I thoroughly enjoyed it. Her touch excited me, and made me feel guilty at the same time.

LeeAnn suddenly put her hand to her face. "Do you know what time it is?"

The way she held her hand and her expression made me think of Annie. That was the way Annie did when she was surprised, embarrassed, or her emotions were stirred in some way. Annie's was followed sometimes with a giggle. I almost felt like taking LeeAnn in my arms, just to hold the memory of my wife.

"What are you thinking about, Cole?" LeeAnn asked. "You look lost."

Evidently I had been staring at her with a bewildered look. "Huh? I'm sorry, I was just watching you."

"It's been a long evening, or should I say night? We should get some rest. I'm looking forward to another breakfast like the one we had when you first came here. Remember?"

"At the open market? Yeah, I remember. Probably be lunch instead of breakfast though, if we don't get to bed," I said, checking my watch.

"We have three weeks, Cole. I want them to be the best three weeks we can make them."

Getting up from her chair, LeeAnn walked me to my sleeping quarters. As I reached for the door handle, she looked at me and without hesitation tiptoed and kissed my cheek. "Good night, Cole."

"Goodnight," I said as I watched her walk away. I didn't sleep very well that night. The bed was too soft, and I kept thinking about LeeAnn, just down the hallway. Damn, she was beautiful. I could still feel the way her breasts felt against my chest as we danced. The smell of her perfume, the touch of her hand on mine. "Annie, what I wouldn't give to be with you tonight," I thought, trying to get LeeAnn off my mind. Finally after tossing and turning until almost dawn, I drifted off to sleep and sleep I did, awakening about eleven that morning. I showered quickly, even though it felt good to have real hot-and-cold running water. I found a razor on the stand beside the bathroom sink. After using it, I dressed and left my room, closing the door quietly. I thought I was being silent, but felt like I had beat a brass drum with the immediate appearance of the housekeeper. I couldn't remember her name so I ended up calling her Hazel. At first I'd gotten a curious look, but then when she realized that was my name for her, a smile of acceptance and perhaps approval had come over her old face.

Hazel bowed to me this morning and said something in her native tongue while indicating I was to follow her. Shrugging, I bowed and obeyed. As we entered the dining area she motioned me to a chair, then poured a cup of coffee. A peeled grapefruit and sliced fruits were served in such an artistic arrangement, I hated to disturb them. A bread basket with a white towel filled with what looked and smelled like fresh hot dinner rolls was set in front of me. Orange marmalade and some sort of crushed grape, cranberry mixture, accompanied the basket. I hadn't realized how hungry I was until the smell of all this hit my nostrils.

Hazel returned with a small envelope with "Cole" written on it. Handing me this, she bowed politely and left the room. I opened the envelope, it was from LeeAnn.

> *Cole,*
> *Forgive me for not being here when you awake. I didn't feel I should wake you. I went to pick up my sister and nephew and will return by early afternoon. It is almost eleven. I hope you slept well. I left instructions with my housekeeper concerning your breakfast. I hope everything is to your liking. If you need anything more, you had better speak Vietnamese or go up to the restaurant and get an interpreter. The entire staff is at your command, just find the ones that speak some English and they will see that your wishes are carried out.*
> *I look forward to this afternoon as I am most anxious for my family to meet you.*
> *LeeAnn.*

I re-folded the note and placed it in its envelope, pocketing it. Sipping a second cup of coffee, I made plans for the day. I didn't want to be late for LeeAnn's return, but I needed to get my things from the base. Calling out for Hazel, I motioned for her to bring me a piece of paper and pen. I was delighted with the results when she returned with everything I needed. I might add, the smile I got back indicated that she also was pleased.

I quickly scribbled a note.

> *LeeAnn,*
> *I slept very well, thank you. Thank you also for your kindness in furnishing my breakfast. It was great. Hazel is very accommodating.*
> *I am going to the base to get my things. I will see you as soon as I return. I am looking forward to meeting everyone.*
> *Cole*

Handing Hazel the envelope with LeeAnn's name on it, I made sure she would give it to her as soon as possible. Hazel understood from the start I suppose, but I wanted to make sure. The old woman gave me a gentle pat on the shoulder that said she had everything under control.

Stepping out into the sunlight, I put on my sunglasses and waited for the cab. It arrived in a few minutes, and as I climbed in I gave the driver instructions to take me to the base bus stop. If I planned it right, I'd be on time to catch the noon bus.

Who was waiting at the bus stop but my best friend with the usual huge hangover.

Climbing out I paid the taxi driver then turned and clapped my hands as loud as I could, shouting a greeting to Freddy who was sitting on the bench, looking like death warmed over.

He made a grab for his ears. "You son of a bitch!" He flinched as he spoke, even his own voice was too loud. "You get laid?"

"You know better than that. I drank hot chocolate and enjoyed the company. From the looks of it, you must have had lots of fun too. You're just not able to remember it, that's all."

"Fuck you," he said, grinning sickly at me.

The bus pulled up and we got on. As usual, Freddy sat next to the heavily screened window trying to get a breath of fresh air. As our bus pulled through the gate, Freddy glanced at his watch.

"Shit," he shook his head, "I missed my fucking flight."

I chuckled at him. "There's always tomorrow, Freddy." We walked slowly toward the officer's quarters.

"What're you going to do today?" he asked.

"I'm going to go back downtown for a few days. How about you?"

"Beats the shit out of me. I sure as fuck don't want to hang around here that's for sure. Maybe I'll grab my stuff and go with you."

"Come on along. I'll introduce you to the cleaner side of life."

"Too much clean living is bad for you," he mumbled, turning toward the latrine. "I gotta go throw up. Be ready as soon as I take a shower and change, might even shave," he added, shrugging his shoulders with indifference.

We hung around and caught the 1:30 bus back into town.

"Where we staying?" he asked.

"At LeeAnn's. She's got lots of room. She'd be hurt if we didn't stay with her."

"I don't feel comfortable just popping in like this, Cole. Maybe I'll get a room downtown, besides, I gotta catch the flight out tomorrow morning. What do you say we get together this evening, could be I'll behave myself for once and see if I like it. I doubt it though. But what the hell, everybody should try something new once in awhile, right?"

"The bedroom has two double beds. I'm sure she won't mind your staying. After all, she invited you to stay last night. There's a private bath with a real modern shower and everything." I knew this would get his attention.

We arrived at LeeAnn's a little before three in the afternoon. She and her company were sitting in the living room. When we were announced LeeAnn came hurriedly to where we stood then hooking me through the arm gave it a squeeze.

"Freddy, I'm so glad to see you. I have a young man that's looking forward to seeing what real Montana cowboys look like," she said.

Freddy and I both wore cowboy boots and jeans when we were casual. Today was no exception. As we came into the living room, LeeAnn introduced us. "Everyone, these are my American friends."

A very attractive woman rose from her seat, and with her hand outstretched, advanced towards us.

"Hello. My name is Jeanette. I have heard so much about both of you," she said in a warm French accent; shaking my hand, then turned to Freddy and extended her hand to him.

I noticed that Freddy's handshake was a little longer than mine. "What have we here?" I thought. Freddy seemed taken by the woman and was in no hurry to let go of her hand. She finally looked a bit embarrassed, and withdrawing her hand she turned to a small boy hanging back.

"This is my son, Andre. Andre, these are the real cowboys that your Aunt LeeAnn was telling us about. They fly the American army helicopters."

I liked them immediately and evidently so did Freddy. He kept looking from the boy to his mother.

"You will be staying with us, won't you, Freddy?" LeeAnn asked.

"Yeah, my trip to Taiwan didn't materialize," he lied, not taking his eyes off Jeanette.

LeeAnn still had her arm through mine. As we watched Freddy and Jeanette, she squeezed my arm.

I had never seen my friend this interested before. He couldn't keep his eyes off Jeanette. Each time their eyes met I thought I could see the sparks jump between them. Hell, you could practically hear the hum of the electricity.

The boy came over to his mother's side and leaned against her leg as Freddy and she stared at each other. Finally Jeanette looked down at the boy and LeeAnn knew it was time to break the spell.

"Why don't we all go into the dining room for tea and become better acquainted, shall we?" she said, smiling warmly. "But first you and Freddy put your baggage in your room. Cole, will you show Freddy, please?"

With Jeanette leading the way, LeeAnn took Andre by his small shoulders and ushered him into the dining room. Looking back, she gave me a surprised but pleased look; which told me she also understood the situation.

We picked up our bags, and Freddy followed me to the bedroom.

"Can you believe it? Did you see how she looked at me? That has to be the most magnificently gorgeous, classy woman in the world, Cole. The little boy, he's a fine looking lad. You said she's a widow, right? They'd play hell trying to kill me if I were married to someone like that. Think she'd go out with me?" he asked, sounding like a schoolboy again.

"You lied about Taiwan, you lying bastard. You're stuck here now."

"No reason to leave, I'd be nuts to go. Do you believe in love at first sight, Cole?" Freddy began whistling as he used the bathroom. "You know," he said through the partially closed door, "we need to take them out for supper tonight. Someplace other than LeeAnn's, so we can pay the bill."

I couldn't believe my ears, Freddy wanting to go out for dinner. No mention of getting drunk.

"You mean go out and not drink?" I asked through the door.

"Yeah, can't drink with the boy along. Be rude to leave him home. There should be a lot of things to do around town without getting drunk, right?"

I looked at Freddy, amazed, wondering if he really meant it. Had he been struck by love's lightning bolt?

"Hey, you got any identification? I'm not sure who I'm talking to. This doesn't sound like 'Jack Daniel's Man of the Year,' speaking."

"I'm in love, Cole. I think I'm really in love this time. Did you see her eyes?"

"Yeah, she had two, I think."

"You gotta help me out. You know, tell her how great I am," he said, and grinned, "The truth according to Freddy. Okay?"

"Come on, Don Juan," I opened the door.

The women were seated at the table talking, and Andre was looking at a bird in a cage in one corner of the room.

As we entered Freddy and Jeanette's eyes locked again, and I thought I'd have to take Freddy by the arm and lead him to a chair.

LeeAnn looked delighted. Kind of like the cat that swallowed the canary. I looked at her and winked. She returned the wink and I felt my pulse quicken. I swiftly looked away.

"You like animals?" I asked Andre.

"Oui, yes," he said, correcting himself. He was a little bashful.

"I do too. You have a lot of animals and birds here. All kinds that we don't have back home," I said.

"Do you have tigers?"

"No, we have mountain lions, but nothing like tigers. We have bears though," I said, making a ferocious face, "grizzlies."

He drew back a little but smiled.

"I saw a picture of a grizzly bear once. It had big teeth," he said, "I'm going to shoot one someday."

LeeAnn stood off to the side listening to us talk.

"Andre is quite a boy. He's a lot like his father was," then she caught herself and quickly changed the subject. "Andre is going to be a great man someday."

"We have lots of animals in the highlands. Mother says we can go there after the war is over. I want to go see the mountains. Have you ever seen the mountains?" he asked.

"Yes, I, we," I corrected myself, motioning to Freddy and then back to myself, "Freddy and I are stationed just west of where you live. We are near Pleiku. Do you know where that is?"

"I've never been to Pleiku. Mother says it's near the mountains. Isn't that correct Mama?" he asked, looking towards Jeanette.

The boy was very intelligent for an eight year old. I was impressed with his English.

"That's correct, Andre," his mother answered. "Someday we'll go to the mountains."

"When the war is over maybe I'll take you, Andre," said Freddy. "Maybe we'll search for treasure. Wouldn't that be fun?"

"I'd like to search for treasure. Wouldn't that be fun to search for treasure, Mama?" he asked, again turning to her.

"Yes, Andre, that would be great fun. You will be bigger then," she said.

Freddy looked at Andre and winked.

Andre winked back.

LeeAnn watched us and smiled. Only one other woman in the universe was as lovely.

LeeAnn's gorgeous blue-green eyes looked into mine, and for a moment I sat mesmerized. Was she an enchantress? I wondered if it ran in the family, perhaps something that was passed on in the women's bloodlines?

She lowered her eyes and I breathed again. The only thing that kept me from throwing myself at her was my wife. I would never be able to look Annie in the eye if I betrayed her trust, nor would I be able to look at myself in the mirror. I stood up.

Freddy came over and began talking to Andre. "Your aunt LeeAnn tells us that you like helicopters."

"Yes, very much," he answered with a sparkle of interest in his eyes. "I get to watch them when mother and I go to Qui Nhon. They are big ones. Sometimes they have smaller ones that they carry below. Do you fly the big ones?"

"No, Andre, those are Chinooks that you are seeing. They go out and get the crippled helicopters. We fly Hueys. They aren't as big as the Chinooks," Freddy said.

Andre looked thoughtful for a moment, then asked, "Do they have guns?"

"Some do, but Cole and I fly the ones that only have two in the back. They're called Slicks. We fly men and equipment."

I was glad Freddy wasn't being graphic about what else we flew out. Adults would have a hard time trying to understand our job, but a child? That would be cruel.

"Do you ever see tigers when you fly?" he asked.

"No, I don't think they like to hear the noise of our helicopters. We don't see very many animals, just birds, and sometimes water buffalo or elephants," he said.

I thought about all the wildlife we killed with our bombs, napalm and air assaults. But this is war. Looking at Andre my mind flashed back. For a moment I am haunted by a pair of sad lonely little eyes as I see the small girl. I cringe inwardly. I had never seen her eyes, except in my nightmares, when she turns, and looks at me, her arms outstretched, waiting to be picked up. As I reach down to pick her up the vision changes. Once again I am on that hill in Cambodia getting ready to pull the trigger. The little girl turns to look at me, but has no face. I turn and run. Tripping, I start to fall. That's when I wake up in a cold sweat. Will these nightmares ever stop? "Dear God, please let me find peace from what I have done," I prayed silently, feeling sick to my stomach. LeeAnn noticed the expression of pain on my face, and it was too late to hide my feelings.

"Cole, would you like to take a walk? I feel like some exercise," she said, rising from her chair. "You don't mind, do you, Freddy? Jeanette and Andre are enjoying your company so much."

I stood up, not saying anything. Lost in my pain I followed LeeAnn like a small boy obeying his mother.

Stepping out in the late afternoon sunshine, I automatically reached for my flight sunglasses, then remembered I'd left them on the table.

"Cole, do you want me to go back for them?" LeeAnn asked, noticing.

"No, I'm fine, it's just a habit anyway. We have to have them to fly sometimes. Where would you like to go?" I asked.

"It doesn't matter to me. You looked like you could use some air," she said and gave me her enchanting smile.

"You're good medicine, LeeAnn," I said and reaching over, caressed her cheek with the back of my hand.

She looked at me for a moment, then broke the spell. "Come, now I need the air also." She smiled and taking my arm in hers, began pulling me down the street.

As we strolled along, I stopped to look at something as an excuse to break her hold on my arm. LeeAnn continued to stroll ahead at a slow pace, lost, I guess in her own thoughts. Damn she was cute and her French accent was driving me nuts. I walked a little behind her for a few feet, viewing her figure from the back.

She turned to see what was holding me back. Smiling, she began walking back to me, reaching out to take my arm. "Come on, you big kid," she said looking pleased with my obvious admiration. "Your Annie would not appreciate this."

I grinned like a little boy who had been caught with his hand in the cookie jar. "Right," I said, "I'll never look again."

She jabbed me with her elbow. "Never?" she asked, pretending to be hurt.

"Maybe on rare occasions," I said.

We looked at each other and again I felt excitement coursing through my veins. I could see that Lee Ann felt it to. My heart started pounding so hard I thought I was going to hyperventilate. I panicked and broke the spell.

"It's too hot to walk very far," I stammered. "You want a cup of tea or coffee?"

"Tea would be nice," She answered, taking my hand and pulling me across the street to a small tea shop. "It will be cooling soon."

The weather in Vietnam was either hot and dry or hot and very wet. Both are uncomfortable.

As we sat in the shade of the building waiting for our tea, LeeAnn watched me silently, then finally broke the silence.

"Cole? Something was bothering you awhile ago. Would you care to talk about it? Can I help?" She asked, reaching across the table, and taking my hand. "I've never seen you look like that before. It worries me."

"It's nothing I can talk about, LeeAnn. It's something I'll just have to work out for myself," I said and patted her hand.

Our tea came and I watched in fascination as LeeAnn drank hers without adding anything. I was raised to put sugar in my tea. Because there wasn't any on the table, I sat watching her drink hers.

"Cole, you're not having your tea?" she said.

"I'm just enjoying your company," I said and smiled at her.

The thoughts of drinking tea without sugar was repulsive, but I sure wasn't going to ask for any. I thought about back home and how spoiled we were. Every eating establishment had salt, pepper and sugar on all tables. Here, if you wanted salt in a restaurant, it was served in a small dish, and looked a lot like brown sugar. You reached into the dish with your fingers and sprinkled it on. Maybe that was why it wasn't white.

"Pourquoi riez-vous?" she said in French.

"What did you say?"

"I am sorry, Cole. I just asked why you were laughing. Please forgive me."

I shook my head. "I was just thinking of how people differ in other parts of the world."

"Why do you say this?" she asked with that French accent. I was fascinated with her voice. Her sister had even more of an accent than LeeAnn, and little Andre spoke with such an accent that I had to listen closely or I couldn't understand him. Although after awhile, it got easier. They must speak French when they're alone. I chuckled again. What a dummy I was. Of course, they spoke French, they are French.

LeeAnn noticed my amusement and looked confused. This time she said nothing, but cocked her head sideways, studying me. Damn, she's lovely to look at. Who would have thought that here in a God forsaken part of the world like Vietnam, a woman so lovely could be found.

LeeAnn broke the spell. "Cole, since you're not drinking your tea, would you like to walk some more?" I had been staring at her for quite awhile, I suppose, lost deep in thought.

"Yeah," I said, snapping out of my day dreaming. "Sorry."

"That's okay. As long as you're thinking pleasant thoughts."

"You'd slap my face if you only knew," I said, laughingly.

"You might be surprised. Come, let's walk."

"Where to, boss?"

"Let's just walk. We'll know when we've had enough," she said and smiled. Her smile was intriguing. It seemed to say everything and nothing at the same time. I have always had a certain self-satisfaction in being able to see through the cloak most women put on trying to impress people. This woman impressed me, without doing anything to provoke that feeling.

As darkness fell, we found ourselves back at her place. LeeAnn rang the doorbell, and it was immediately answered by Hazel looking through the small window.

As we entered the room we were greeted by Freddy, Jeanette and Andre, looking very content.

Freddy looked up and smiled broadly. "About time," he said, "we'd begun to worry about you two."

"We were just out walking off some pent-up energy." I said, "How are you getting along with intelligent people for a change?"

"It's a real switch from the army," Freddy answered, looking at Jeanette.

LeeAnn turned to me and asked, "Do we want to go out this evening or stay in and Jeanette and I will cook for you?"

Andre smiled, "J'ai faim, Mama."

Jeanette reached down and patted Andre's head lovingly and said, "Parlez-vous Anglais, Andre?"

"Oui, yes Mama," Andre said to his mother, then turned to Freddy, "I am sorry because I did not speak English, Monsieur Gray." Turning to me, "I am sorry, Monsieur Morgan."

He looked up to see if his mother approved of his apology. The way she smiled at her young son spoke more than any amount of words could have. It wasn't hard to understand Freddy's fascination with this fine lady and her son. I sensed a refinement and grace in Jeanette and LeeAnn that was of the same depth as Annie's. I was happy for him.

"You have quite a family," I said to LeeAnn.

"Thank you, Cole," she smiled and bowed her head slightly.

A shock wave ran through my body. She reminded me so much of another woman. I felt a pain in my heart as I stood there. I longed to be home holding my wife. But at the same time I felt the urge to take this woman into my arms and hold her tightly against me. Never had I felt confusion like this before.

Freddy noticed my look, "Hey, let's go wash up for dinner. We'll take these lovely ladies and this young man out for an evening of fun," he said, touching me on the shoulder and then turning to our hostess, asked to be excused.

LeeAnn noticed the change in me. I gave her a smile and turned to follow Freddy to our room.

"You okay?" Freddy asked. "You looked lost a moment ago."

"I'm fine. I was just reminded of Annie. That's all. Damn, I miss her sometimes. What the hell am I talking about, I miss her all the time," I said, shaking my head. "LeeAnn, looking the way she does, makes me homesick. I'm fine. Hey, how are you and Jeanette coming along? I mean, do you still wish you'd gone to Taiwan?"

"Nope. Hey, that's a pretty sharp boy. Did you see how he apologized. Man, that was class and he's only eight. That's the kind of kid that can really get to you. I mean, he's a charmer just like yours truly," Freddy said and pointed his thumb at his chest. "I'm telling you the truth, Cole. I'm in love. I'm not talking through my dick now. I'm coming from the heart. I'm going to marry Jeanette, if I can work it. You got my word on it. I know this is really sudden, but I feel like I've been struck by lightning."

I saw Freddy from a new side. He meant every word, and I felt good about the turn-around. The folks back home weren't going to believe it.

Mrs. Gray always said that when the right girl came along, he would fall like a ton of bricks. He was falling. I sure wished I could be there to watch their expressions when they heard the news. Annie would be the last to believe it.

"How am I going to handle this, Cole?" Freddy asked. "I've never been serious about a woman before."

"Hey, buddy, you're just going to have to work at letting Jeanette know how you feel, but these things can't be rushed. You could scare her off. She's only been a widow for a short time, but if it will help any, I think she's interested in you."

"You really think so?"

"Yeah, I know the signs. The way she looks at you when you're not looking at her."

"Really?"

"Yeah, really, LeeAnn and I talked a little about how things have been with Jeanette, when we went for our walk. She hasn't been interested in a man since her husband died. I'm sure she's had other chances, going back to France and all. Besides, where else would she find a man of your caliber, right?" I said, giving him a big grin.

"Damned right. Hey, I'm a real catch!" As usual, he was very confident in everything he threw his heart into. Somehow the bastard always won by the skin of his teeth. I admired him, not because I loved him like a brother, but for his tenacity. A man to be reckoned with.

"What are you thinking?" Freddy asked, looking at me suspiciously.

"Oh, nothing."

"What?" he persisted.

"Just at how a dick-head like you always manages to come out on top of things."

"Yeah, I guess I have been a dick-head. You know, you were right all the time. This screwing around isn't worth it. I mean with all the clap and stuff. You don't think I have the clap do you?"

"I don't know. I hope not."

Freddy got up from his chair. "Come on, time's a wasting."

"Okay, let's dazzle them," I said as we walked to the door.

"Cole? Do you think she really likes me? I mean I know she likes us, you and me, but do you think I have a chance with her? You know," he made a back and forth gesture between himself and an imaginary person with his hand, "you know what I mean. I mean, oh shit! You gotta help me out here. I'm used to just jumping their bones. I'm not used to telling them the truth, only what they want to hear." He threw both hands in the air with frustration.

"Quit worrying. I think if you're just you, everything will go fine. Be yourself," then as an afterthought, "better yet, be like me."

"Right, like you, got it." he said and faked vomiting. Then he looked serious again. "I don't know how to talk to a real lady. Jeanette is the type of woman we all look for and seldom find. You don't have that trouble. You have too many, but for a bastard like me?"

"Hey, just be yourself, Freddy. I know what I'm talking about. Jeanette likes you and Andre thinks you're great. Shit, if the truth were known, LeeAnn and I think you're great. Well, at least LeeAnn. I know better."

"Smartass, come on, they're waiting," Freddy said and put a hand on my shoulder. "There's a place uptown that has a buffet. It's a French place. I've eaten there a couple of times. Maybe we could take them there. You ever wonder about French words?"

"Like what?" I asked.

"'Buffet', for instance. What the hell does it mean?" Freddy asked, looking puzzled.

"It means, get up and get it yourself," I said.

We were both chuckling as we entered the living room area.

"Hey, we know this French place uptown that has a buffet. How does that sound to everyone?" Freddy asked.

"The Flamingo? I do not think so. This place only allows adults," LeeAnn said, shaking her head.

"Bullsh—, nonsense! I've eaten there several times. The food there is great. Come on," Freddy said.

As we closed the door behind us, Freddy turned to me. "Cole, you think I handled that right? I almost slipped and cussed," he said.

"Hey, I couldn't have handled it better, and I noticed your language has changed. You're becoming civilized again."

"Yeah?" He looked pleased with himself.

"Yeah," I answered, as we climbed into the cab.

"You boys telling secrets again?" LeeAnn asked.

"Yeah."

"This word 'Yeah,' you use it often? What does it mean?" Jeanette asked.

"Oh, it's just a slang word for 'ya betcha,'" I said and Freddy and I laughed.

"I do not understand what this means also," she said and shook her beautiful head. I could tell LeeAnn knew I was pulling one of my jokes on her sister and she was going with along it.

LeeAnn spoke in French to her sister, and they both turned and laughed at us. It was their turn.

As we rode in the cab, I noticed the smog from the day's hustle and bustle. I shook my head in amazement at the amount of pollution.

"Damn, the air pollution here is bad. We don't have anything like this back home unless we have a forest fire. This can't be good for your lungs," I said.

"In Montana, you never have smoke from the motorcars?" LeeAnn asked.

"Yeah, we have smoke, but not like this. I mean, we don't have this kind of traffic. Ah hell, one day I'll have to bring you to Montana. Then you can see the difference yourself. How would that be?"

"I would like that, Cole. Will this be soon?" she asked.

I looked over at Freddy. My look said, "Help!"

Freddy grinned. "We'll bring everyone to Montana. How would you like to see my home, Andre? I think you'd like it, riding horses and roping cows?"

"I would be a cowboy? I do not want to shoot Indians though," the boy said with a serious look on his face.

Freddy and I laughed.

"We don't shoot at each other anymore, Andre. We're friends," Freddy said, reaching over and ruffling his hair. "Cole's grandfather is half Cheyenne Indian."

Someday Annie and I would have a son like this, I thought and smiled to myself.

LeeAnn was watching me. As I looked at her, I couldn't help but wonder what it would be like if things were different. A guilty feeling quickly overcame me, and I dropped my eyes. I felt like I had just cheated on Annie. "Forgive me, Annie," I thought. "It's just that this wonderful lady has been a God-send for my loneliness. I know you'd approve of her."

Our cab stopped in front of the Flamingo and we got out. I paid the fare and tipped the driver well. After counting the tip he gave me a look that seemed to sincerely say he wouldn't shoot at me for the next few days.

Walking into the restaurant, we were greeted by a man with menus. As his eyes drifted to Andre, he spoke in French to Jeanette. "Les enfants de moins de seize ans ne sont pas admis," he said in a low tone.

"What'd he say?" I ask LeeAnn.

"He said that Andre isn't allowed here."

Freddy stepped forward and I followed.

Freddy reached up and placing his hand on the man's shoulder, backed him up a few feet before speaking to him in a low voice.

"You understand English?" Freddy asked.

"Oui. Yes," he whispered.

"Then listen closely, my friend. We're here to have a nice evening with our ladies. The boy is my pride and joy. I would kill if I had to for him. I," then looked at me, " my fellow officer here and I, will personally tear this fine establishment to pieces if we aren't welcome with our guests. If for some reason, above and beyond our control, we can't do you and this fine establishment a lot of damage tonight, plan on the entire United States Army coming back very soon. One fine night we will come back and drag you out in the street, then beat the hell out of you. Following that beating, we'll drag your bleeding body back in here and burn this fucking place down. You understand what I'm saying?"

I noticed his hand digging into the man's shoulder muscle as he spoke quietly to him. Freddy had his undivided attention, and the man's eyes did not leave Freddy's for a moment. Freddy released him then reached over and smoothed his lapel as if they were old friends.

"Now partner, where would you like to seat us?" he asked.

The Frenchman regained enough composure to lead us to the best table in his fine establishment. "Our finest table, Monsieur. If I can be of any further service," he said, glancing nervously first at Freddy then at me. He snapped his fingers, and we were handed menus and a wine list by a waiter. He then turned and hurried away.

"What did you say to him? He seems so polite. You are good friends?" Jeanette asked.

"The best of friends," Freddy said, glancing at me.

"Oh yeah, Freddy has a way with people. It's that Montana charm we're known for."

"It is very impressive, Freddy. You must teach me some day, yes?" Jeanette said, looking at him with admiration.

Freddy and I exchanged grins. That would be interesting, I thought. It would be like teaching a kitten to be a tiger.

We took our time over dinner, as is the custom of Europeans, one of the customs that I wished we as Americans would adopt.

Returning to LeeAnn's, Jeanette put Andre to bed. Freddy followed her.

"Freddy seems to be very interested in Jeanette." I said. "I wonder if she's as interested in him?"

"Jeanette has been alone for too long. I think this is a good thing for her. I would like to see Jeanette enjoy the company of Freddy more. Will Freddy stay awhile longer?" LeeAnn asked.

"Yes, I think he will. He's very attracted to Jeanette and Andre. They've totally captivated him," I said, looking into those beautiful hypnotic eyes. I turned away trying to re-group my thoughts.

"I know this is going to sound a little premature, but I think Freddy is more than just interested in Jeanette. I think he is falling in love for the first time. Freddy and I grew up together. I know him. His heart is changing. I've never seen him like this before."

She was looking at me with a faint smile on her lips. "I have noticed this also with my sister. I have seen the special way they look at each other. When she lost her husband and went to live in Strasbourg, which is where his family is from, she refused to do anything but be with Andre. She stayed for six months, then returned to our parent's plantation. She has seen no one until now. If this is true, I am happy for her and Andre. I am glad for you and Freddy's stay with us. It means a lot to all of us, Cole."

"Do you think there could ever be anything more than just friendship between Jeanette and Freddy? I know that Freddy hopes there will be," I said, going for broke.

"I would think so, with time. My sister is a very beautiful and intelligent woman. She is not as you say, superficial? I can not speak for her, but I see possibilities. I will be very interested to see how this comes out. She is like me, when we love someone, we love them with all our hearts."

As LeeAnn said this she looked at me. I felt a tingle of both excitement and regret flow through my body.

"You are very special to me also, LeeAnn, but I love my wife. If this were another time..." I reached out and touched her cheek.

She closed her eyes as my hand lingered on her soft skin. Slowly I withdrew my hand, feeling both emotionally and physically stirred.

"I know it's wrong and I don't expect you to love me, Cole, but I do love you. I did not want this to happen. I respect the marriage of you and Annie. I meant what I said before, I won't do anything to come between you and your wife. She is so special to you," she said, tears welling up in her eyes. LeeAnn forced herself to laugh a little, "I hate myself for being this way. I promised myself many times it would never happen. Can you ever forgive me?"

I was speechless. I could feel her heartache, and my heart was breaking for the both of us. I loved her, but I loved Annie and she was my wife.

I wanted to take her in my arms, hold her and feel her against me. With that, I could stop both of our suffering, at least for now, but I also knew that this was not the answer. When my tour of duty was up, I was going back to Annie. By giving into my feelings and pursuing a short relationship with LeeAnn, it would hurt her even worse, not to mention what it would do to me.

I looked away at a painting hanging on the wall of an old man in a straw hat. The painting was old, but I felt older, much older. I would have gladly traded places with the old man in the painting at this moment if I could, just to have gotten out of this situation. In my desire to be with a person who was considerate, kind and caring, I had been playing with fire. Now it had gotten out of hand. All this time, LeeAnn had been watching me. Each time my eyes met hers, my body ached to take her in my arms and never let her go. I became more tortured with each passing moment. I was so very tempted and damn the consequences, but Annie deserved more from me and LeeAnn deserved more from life than to be loved then left. Why had life dealt a hand like this? Damn it all! I felt like getting drunk.

Freddy and Jeanette came back from putting Andre to bed and stopped as they entered the living quarters.

"Are we interrupting anything?" Freddy asked, seeing LeeAnn wiping her eyes.

"No, please," she said apologetically, motioning for them to stay. "I was just being emotional. You caught me." She made an effort to laugh and took my arm to show there was nothing wrong between us.

Jeanette smiled and came over. "Let's freshen up, shall we?" she asked and the two women excused themselves.

I turned to Freddy. "Hey Pal, I think I've got problems. LeeAnn's in love with me. I don't think I did anything to encourage it," I said, looking at Freddy for help. "Now it's your turn to help me. I don't know how to handle this. I'd rather die than hurt her."

"Want to go have a drink? We can take the girls?" Freddy said grinning, then sobered. "Sorry, Cole. Bad timing, huh?"

I couldn't help but grin at the bastard, even though I could feel my world caving in. How was I going to handle this? I realized now it had been a mistake to see LeeAnn again. I didn't want to hurt her. All I wanted now was to get back into the air. Dodging bullets was preferable to this dilemma. At least I knew how to handle that. Live or die, simple and basic. Here, it was watch a beautiful friend suffer. I'd take dodging the bullets.

"Freddy, I think I'd like to go back to the base. Any ideas on how I could work it without hurting LeeAnn? Heaven only knows I've done enough to her already."

"I'm sorry I made a joke of the situation, Cole. I'll do what ever I can to help. You serious about going back to the base?"

"Yeah, I think I've done enough damage here."

"How long will it take to get your things together?"

"Two or three minutes." I turned to go into the bedroom, "Thanks, pal."

Entering the bedroom, I grabbed my bag and began throwing clothes into it. I hadn't brought much, and it took only a minute to cram the duffel full. Closing the bag, I looked around to see if I was forgetting anything. Nothing was visible, but if I did, Freddy would bring it with him. I picked up my bag and walked back into the living room. The girls still hadn't returned.

Freddy had called a cab. "Sorry Cole. I want to stay but I'll go with you if you really need me to," he said.

"No, I'm fine. I just think it would be better if I got this over with. I know this sounds funny, but I love her. It's crazy, but I do. I just love Annie more. She's my whole life, and there's no room for two women. LeeAnn is in love with me, and there's nowhere for it to go. She's hurt enough. I won't add to it by staying around. I best get going before she comes out. Make something up. Tell her I had to report back and I forgot until just now. Shit. That sounds phony. Tell her the truth, Freddy. She deserves that much. Tell her I care about her too much to hurt her any more than I have. I'll write her and explain everything."

I opened the door. My heart was heavy as I looked back. I was saying good-bye to a friend whom I had caused a great deal of pain. Life sometimes isn't fair. If people have a counterpart, LeeAnn was Annie's. That was scary to think about. My heart was breaking for this wonderful woman who I had fallen in love with.

As the cab drove up to the main gate of the base, an MP came out to see who was in the cab. I showed him my identification. With a salute, he stepped back and we passed the guard station. The cab driver stopped at the officer's quarters and I got out. Walking up to the desk, I checked in and was given sleeping quarters. After putting my bag away, I went to the officer's club to get a drink.

We had been in Da Nang for such a short while and here I was ready to go back to work. It's strange how the twists and turns of life change your best-laid plans. At first I denied what I had let happen. But little by little the truth came. I had deliberately brought this on myself and had hurt LeeAnn. I was not the honorable person I thought I was. If I had been, I wouldn't have allowed this to happen. With that thought, I got drunk.

At two in the morning I stumbled back to my quarters and passed out. I was awake by six. I headed for the shower. After shaving, I went for the nearest coffee, then the flight office to book my return to base. The sooner I could put distance between LeeAnn and me, the better. They booked me on a fixed wing to Qui Nhon, then from there on to An Khe. It would be good to let someone else do the flying for once. I checked my watch. It was 0940 hours. My flight wasn't until 1345 hours. Four hours to kill. I went to the lounge and selected a hunting magazine, then turned to find a seat by a window. As I looked up, there stood Freddy.

"Cole? I have someone here to see you buddy. I know you don't want to see her right now. It wasn't my idea. If you don't want to see her, I'll make up a story that I couldn't find you. But I think it would be better for the both of you to talk. She's taking this pretty hard, Cole. We talked all night. Her heart is broken. LeeAnn blames herself for what's happened. The ball is in your court, buddy."

Freddy waited for his words to settle. For once I was at a loss for words, even with Freddy.

"Where is she?" I whispered.

"She's in the visitor's room with Jeanette and Andre." Freddy motioned with his head. "There's nobody in here but you. Why don't I go get her. Jeanette, Andre and I'll have something to drink. I'll show them around, take your time. We're in no hurry," he said and smiled sympathetically.

"Thanks, Freddy. Yeah, I'd like to see her."

In a couple of minutes, LeeAnn appeared in the doorway, hands clasped in front of her. She held her head low, as if she were about to get scolded for something. I wanted to run to her and take her into my arms, but I dared not show this because it would only make matters worse.

"Do you want something to drink?" I asked, fumbling for words.

She shook her head. "No, thank you,"

"Please, let's talk over here," I said, motioning to a couch by the window.

LeeAnn followed me.

"Cole? I'm so sorry. I have spoiled everything. I have caused you to feel bad. I never meant to do that. What I said of loving you, this I can never take back, nor do I want to, but I should not have said this to you. Will you forgive me? Please?" LeeAnn said, looking at me without blinking, tears welling up in her eyes. "If you will come back, I will never again mention this. Freddy and Jeanette understand the situation. I have apologized to them both for my behavior."

"Wait," I said, holding my hand in the air, "LeeAnn, you are not at fault. It's something that just happened. I love you, LeeAnn. I don't know whether Freddy told you that, but I do. I never thought it possible for a man to love two women at the same time. I love you, but I also love Annie and she's my wife. The one I've chosen to live with for the rest of my life. This sounds contradictory. I know that, but it's true just the same. I'm at as much of a loss as you." I held my hands up in confusion. "I think, in all honesty, LeeAnn, that it would be better at this time for me to return to my base and think this thing out. I don't want to hurt you anymore than I have. You don't deserve it. If I stay, I'll hurt not only you, but Annie. The two people I love. I couldn't bear that either. Do you understand what I'm saying?"

"I always knew one day you would come along. You did." She slowly shrugged her shoulders and shook her head, trying to make sense of her thoughts. A tear ran down her cheek. She reached up and wiped it with the back of her hand. "I thought perhaps just being near you would be enough. I could have you in my heart."

Her eyes bright with tears stare at me unflinching, her dark brown hair shining in the sunlight. Damn, she was lovely. She was mine for the taking. All I had to do was take her in my arms. Only a fool would do what I was doing.

"LeeAnn, I never meant this to happen. I..." I didn't know what to say.

LeeAnn nodded. Then slowly she stood and without looking at me, turned and started to walk away.

Stopping, she turned back to me and brushing a tear from her cheek, said, "I love you, Cole. I loved you from the moment I saw you in my restaurant. I knew you were the man I had been waiting for all my life. You still are. You will always be. I want you to know that. I respect you very much and I envy Annie. Au revoir mon amor. Good-bye Cole." Then she turned back towards the door and walked out of my life.

Feeling despondent, I went back to my quarters and picked up my bag for the trip back to the base.

As the plane lifted off and circled over Da Nang, I stared down at the city, trying to see LeeAnn's place, but from up here it all looked the same. I settled back and closed my eyes trying to erase the last few days from my mind. I thought about how I had gotten the three week pass. The child's faceless form plagued me. What had she looked like from the front? Did I really want to know? All Asian children looked the same, big sad eyes and lonely little faces. Damn it! My teeth gritted with tension. I knew I had to keep control of my thoughts. This was war and I didn't have a choice in the matter. I did what I had to do.

Chapter 26

The trip to Qui Nhon was a restless one. As we set down at the airfield, my mind began to get back into the swing of work. Anything was better than sitting around thinking of all the mistakes I had made. I had seen this happen to other people. They were consumed little by little. I would not let that happen to me if I could help it. I was a fighter and that would be the way I would go down.

I still had plenty of time before reporting back for duty, and I decided to spend some of it just kicking back and relaxing. After all, I still had two and a half weeks of leave to play with, that is if they didn't catch up with me. We were short on pilots.

I caught a bus into Qui Nhon, then headed for the nearest bar for a drink. Sitting in the dive, I thought about what I would do with the rest of my leave. First I'd go back to the base and check my mail. I knew Annie would have written at least one letter. Maybe there would be one from the folks, too. It was also time for my outdoor magazines to start showing up. After I read my mail, maybe I'd get a hop to Saigon. Some of the guys had told me about cameras that could be purchased at about a third of what they would cost us in the states. I had saved up some money, even though I sent most home to put in the savings account Annie and I had opened in Kalispell.

Finishing my drink, I caught a bus back to the base where I booked a fixed wing for Pleiku. The next morning at 0800 hours I boarded a C130. I knew two other soldiers on board, and we chatted about everything and anything.

"I've still got seventeen days left of R & R," I said.

"How do you rate? You one of Westmoreland's nephews?" Hendricks jabbed at me.

"You just have to know whose ass to kiss," I said, grinning. "I think I'll go to Saigon for a week or ten days, after I get my mail."

"Shit, Morgan, tell me you're kidding," Bryson said.

Bryson flew a gunship.

"Nope. That's just the way it is when you kiss ass," I said, shaking my head.

"How do you do that?" Hendricks asked, wanting to know the secret.

"Promise not to let this out to anyone else?" I asked, looking around to make sure no one could hear me. "Go to the old man and tell him you're bored. Tell him you want extra duty. Night flying is something they all notice."

"You're shitting us, right?" Hendricks asked in a low voice, "I mean, nobody wants to fly nights."

"That's the point. Nobody wants it. You volunteer. Word gets out that you're looking for action and they'll notice it."

"Sounds like a way to get grounded," the other pilot said.

I turned away and pretended to read a magazine.

"I think he's out of his fucking mind," Bryson said in a low voice.

"I don't know, look at his R & R time. Three weeks? He's done something right," I overheard Hendricks say. "I think he's kissing ass or something."

"Yeah, brown nosing," Bryson came back.

"Come on, guys, there's a difference between kissing ass and brown nosing. It's called depth perception. My depth perception is perfect; it was ass kissing."

I grinned to myself as the C130 began its decent. If these two listened to me, I would have to avoid them in the future. I wasn't going to be very popular.

I headed to get the mail, my excitement building with each step. I felt like I'd been away for a long time. My big stack consisted of four letters. Two from Annie and one from her parents and one from mine. I checked the address carefully again because Freddy's parents usually sent their love in Freddy's letters.

I looked at the letters from Annie. One was a large envelope that I guessed contained pictures. I opened it first. Then stared in wonder and disbelief, not understanding what I was looking at. Annie was in a hospital bed smiling and holding a baby. My heart pounded so hard I thought it would break out of my shirt. A second picture showed Mr. and Mrs. Gray standing on either side of the bed, both looking as happy as when Freddy and I had graduated from high school.. The third picture was my mom and dad standing the same way, one on each side of Annie and the baby. In the last picture, Annie was holding the baby so I could see it from the front. The baby had its eyes open a bit, hands held at shoulder height and fist clenched for a good fight. I grinned. Then I realized I didn't know if this was a boy or a girl.

In all of the pictures Annie looked radiant. That beautiful smile of hers twisted my heart. I missed her so much. I began to read Annie's letter, stopping every few words to look at the pictures again.

> *My Dearest Husband;*
> *I know by now you have seen the pictures of our beautiful daughter, Ann Coleen. I didn't want to tell you I was pregnant as I knew how hard it would be for you to be away and keep your mind on your job. I worry about your safety all the time.*
>
> *Our daughter is beautiful and perfectly formed. I have counted her fingers and toes three times now. When I hold her in my arms, it's like holding a part of you. Cole, I miss you so very much, each day I mark off another day on the calendar. I can't wait until we're a family again. How I wish you could have been here to share this wonderful event with me. When I first looked at Ann Coleen, it was like I reached up and touched God. The wonder of this beautiful child conceived in our love is more than I can fathom.*
>
> *The grandparents are so excited. When I first told Daddy, he was really angry and I was glad you weren't here. When he finally calmed down and I told him we were married by Indian customs, he settled down and said he wouldn't make a steer of you as long as we get married legally as soon as you come back. After he saw our baby, he said as far as he was concerned we were just about as married as we could be. Your folks couldn't be prouder or happier for us.*
>
> *Mom is ecstatic, she can't wait for Ann Coleen to call her grandma.*
>
> *My love, I miss you terribly. It seems everywhere I look brings back happy memories of our life together. When I think of the few nights we had together, my body aches to feel you beside me and hear the beat of your heart as my head rests upon your chest. Thinking about how much longer you will be away and the danger you're in, I want to run to your side so I might be there to protect you, as if I could.*
>
> *Just know my love that each day we are apart is like an eternity. The only consolation is knowing when your time in Vietnam is finished, we will have our lifetime together.*
>
> *Please, please, I beg you, don't take chances and don't try to be a hero. Just take care of yourself, Morgan, and come home to us.*
>
> *Tell Freddy "hello" from all of us. I'll write to him and send "Uncle Freddy" some pictures tomorrow. Tell him to write to Mom,*

she looks for a letter everyday and is always very quiet when she doesn't hear from him. Although she doesn't say anything I know she is worried for both of you.

Well, my love, I will close for now as it is quite late and caring for a baby is hard work. Know that our daughter and I love and need you so very much, so please, please, please be careful. We love you.

Forever my love, Annie and your daughter, Ann Coleen

It was a girl! She was a girl. I looked at the pictures again and again. This was my daughter. I was her dad. This made three of us. I stared at the pictures amazed at what we had done. Now I could see what Annie had meant about leaving part of me with her. This was what we had made together, a beautiful little baby girl. I was astonished by Annie's wisdom; she was an extraordinary woman.

Ann Coleen. She had named her Ann Coleen. I turned the name over and over in my mind, looking for flaws but could find none. Ann Coleen, it was perfect and beautiful, just like her mother.

My eyes clouded up with tears, and I glanced around to make sure no one was watching then pretending to yawn, I reached up and wiped my eyes. This was almost too much for me to handle at one sitting.

I re-read Annie's letter, glancing every few seconds at the pictures of my daughter and her lovely mother. Damn, life was beautiful.

I read Mom and Dad's letter next. They were so proud of their granddaughter. They couldn't wait to share her with me when I got back home.

Then I read the Gray's letter. Mrs. Gray said my wife and daughter were doing fine and would come home Friday. This meant she had been home for several days.

I hated this miserable son of a bitching hot country, but never realized how much until this moment. I ached to go home and see my family, and I had another three and a half months in this shit hole, dodging bullets while flying live soldiers in and dead and wounded out, three and a half months of hell on earth. I couldn't believe how stupid I had been. I should have gone to Canada with Annie. Instead, I was ducking doom every moment I was away from the base, and that was most of the time. I had been lucky so far, but now that I was a father I began to get scared. I couldn't afford fear. Fear was a deadly disease in this business. The gooks got a reward for every chopper they shot down. I felt like a duck in a carnival shooting gallery. Knock down the Huey and win a prize. I'd picked up a piece or two of Plexiglas fragments in my legs when we were hit with light rounds, but so far the fifties had eluded anything more than metal. And by damn, if it was up to me, I was going to keep it that way. I had no fear of death, that is until now. It was almost normal to feel you were eventually going to buy the farm and it was just a matter of avoiding the event as long as possible. Here, after a while, death was just another part of the equation. I had become indifferent to the extent that I didn't let it interfere with my flying. Death was only a silent tick away. Silent because you bought it before you heard the tick of the bullet passing through the craft. Shit, I'd gotten as bad as the bastards that say, "When your time is up, it's up."

The realization that I might not live long enough to see my wife and daughter scared me. A small shudder ran down my back. I stood up trying to shake off the feeling that had settled in my mind.

I was a father now; I could handle anything. I just had to use my head for more than a place to hang my hat. I grinned. Pop had used that expression when he wanted Freddy and me to think.

Now I was a dad. I still couldn't get over it. I walked back to my quarters and lay down on my bunk, but couldn't seem to settle down. The damned heat was unbearable. I began to sweat profusely. Clutching my pictures, I went back outside. Two more weeks of leave. I guess I could go to Saigon for a few days. I'd enjoy the change and a new camera would be just the thing to send home to Annie and my daughter. Ann Coleen, I couldn't say that name enough.

I hopped a flight to Saigon, which lies about 250 miles south of Qui Nhon. As we flew, all I could think about was what my daughter must look like? What she would look like as she grew? Would she be as fortunate as her mother? Annie was a beautiful woman. I sure hoped Ann Coleen took after her instead of me.

Boys! They were in for trouble. I'd kick their asses but good. Now I was wide awake. I could see some little bastard wanting to take my daughter out on a date. He'd probably be like I was, sneaky around the parents, pretending to be a nice kid. But when he got the chance, he'd be looking down her neckline. My blood pressure hit an all time high. I'd kill the sneaky little piece of shit. Then I chuckled to myself. I had the secret weapon. I knew enough to spot the little sneaks; I'd been one.

The plane began its decent over the tin shanties of Saigon. I wondered how many VC were looking up, imagining they had a fifty caliber zeroed on us.

With a squeal of tires we touched down. I stepped out of the plane and almost fell on my face with the heat coming up to meet me from the hot pavement. The temperature had to be at least a 130 degrees bouncing off the tarmac.

Taking a bus from the air base into the main part of the city, I could feel the heat pouring through the top of the vehicle; sweat ran down my neck. A young Army private sat down next to me. He was all bright eyed and excited about being in Vietnam. As we rode the bus, he asked questions about this and that.

"Why do they have the windows covered with screen? Afraid we'll change our mind and jump out?" he asked, grinning at his wit.

"That's to keep the VC from throwing a grenade through a window," I explained. This gave him something to think about. He seemed like a nice kid, probably a couple of years younger than me. But for each month spent here, you aged two or three years and I felt I was old enough to be his father.

"What do you do?" he asked.

"I fly Army helicopters."

"What kind, Sir?"

"Huey." I said, not wanting to talk about it. "Slick."

"Wow, that must be exciting. You must see lots of action."

I just stared at him. If only he knew. I finally answered him. "Yeah, lots."

"I sure wish I could have got into flying helicopters."

"No you don't." I said, and frowned.

The kid flinched, and looked away for a moment. "The air's sure polluted, kind of reminds me of back home. I'm from California. Where you from, Sir?" he asked.

"Western Montana, up by Glacier park."

"How long you been in Vietnam?"

"Too long, lad, too long. I'm looking forward to seeing my family. I just got promoted to dad. We have a little girl. Here, I've got some pictures," I said, taking my pictures out of the envelope. The young private was polite, and looked at them as if we were related. I couldn't have been more pleased until he took out his billfold and started showing me his family. That's when I began looking forward to getting off the bus.

As we entered the main part of town, the smoke and fumes began burning my eyes. I thought Da Nang was polluted, but this was something else. The bus was so hot we hadn't dared to close the windows, but it was a toss up whether it was better to burn up with the windows closed or choke with the windows down.

Pulling up to a main street, I yelled at the driver that this was as far as I wanted to go. He pulled the bus over to the curb, and I climbed out with sweat trickling down my back. Grasping my bag, I stood a few moments looking up and down the street trying to get my bearings. I squinted, my eyes burning from all the exhaust. Looking at all the people, I shook my head. Where the hell were they all going?

An American soldier came walking down the street and I stopped him. "Hey, fella? Where would a man find a good affordable room around here?" I asked.

"You kidding? There ain't any good affordable rooms here. Your best bet is two blocks that way, other side of the street," he said, pointing down the street. "If you can afford it."

"Thanks," I said and started down the sidewalk. Women with babies strapped to their backs walked past me with vacant expressions on their faces. Good-looking women wearing white dresses brushed by on their way to who knows where. People riding bicycles rode with trance-like expressions on their faces.

A group of five young Vietnamese men walked by, looking as if they'd like to meet me in a dark alley. I felt my stomach tighten as they looked me over.

"Come on, you little fuckers. I'll rip your heads off," I whispered. They seemed to sense what I was saying. One glared at me, but the rest turned their stares straight ahead. I gave him a look which said I would welcome anything he wanted to throw at me. Giving me a last hateful look, he walked on by. I stopped, watching my back until I was sure they weren't coming back to grab my bag or stick me with a knife. I almost wished he'd try me. I had a double-edged short bladed dagger in my boot that would have loved to cut his heart out. Finally satisfied that I was out of danger, I continued my walk toward the hotel.

Crossing the street was a real challenge. I chose the middle of the block to cross. I didn't feel like walking clear to the end. The young VC punk had put me in an obstinate mood.

Entering a hotel, I found the prices a little out of my range and settled for a dive a couple blocks away. But what the hell, all I needed was a place to sleep.

Cleaning up, I set out to find an officer's club, and a good old American drink of whiskey. Going downstairs I asked the desk clerk where to find a club. He gave me directions, then offered to call a cab.

No doubt they had a split for the fares from rich American GIs. I went outside and stopped the first GI I came across. He said there was a club only two blocks east.

As I walked along the street, I stopped at various shops. Annie would have enjoyed looking in these places, with all the different colors and the hustle and bustle of people shopping. Annie loved to shop. But more than that, I think she would have liked watching the people, seeing the difference between our culture and the Vietnamese's.

Vietnam is quite primitive compared to the United States. The people don't seem to mind walking or riding bikes, or using primitive equipment to farm with. If people would leave them alone, I think they would be content to just live and let live. I don't think they really cared who ruled this country, as long as they were allowed to work and take care of their families.

The club was upstairs turned out to be nice, some of the waitress were round-eyes. Who they were I don't know, but they were as noisy as the Vietnamese women with all the laughter and chatter. I stared at them for a while out of curiosity, until a blonde came over. At first it seemed good to see a round-eyed woman, and I made the mistake of buying her a friendly drink which was kind of like feeding a stray dog. Feed them a morsel and they would follow you home. I figured I'd never get rid of her.

"What do you do for the Army?" she asked.

I wasn't in the mood for a lot of chitchat. My mind was still on Annie and the baby. I decided to lie to her.

"Medics, I work on corpses. You know, cut open their chests and see if they've had heart problems. Check their lungs to see if they smoke and how it effected them. Exam the inside of their bodies for any signs of venereal diseases or drug abuse," I said, looking like I was really going to go on and on.

The blonde tried to conceal her revulsion and began to fidget, wanting to change the subject. I closed in for the kill. "Hey, you haven't heard the interesting part about my job," I said. "When you cut a chest open, it's like looking into a window and seeing how they lived. If you ever want to see what I'm talking about, come on out to the hospital. I can get you in."

She'd had enough. She stood up, pretending to see someone across the club.

"Excuse me," she said, walking away quickly.

I grinned and wondered if Annie would have been proud of what I had just done? Probably not; but she'd understand. I didn't have any more women bothering me after that. I guess the word got around.

The first couple of days in Saigon were fun, but by the third, things began to get a little boring. I needed some excitement. I had seen all of Saigon I really wanted to. Getting back to work was starting to sound better than being here.

I was standing at a busy crosswalk, debating which way to go, when a young Vietnamese man approached me. The gook looked around carefully to make sure no one was watching. He seemed nervous as he held something small in his cupped hands. I watched him with suspicion as he approached.

"Captain. I have good thing to show you. You like jewelry? I have something to show."

I knew at a glance that here was a desperate man. It was written all over him. He was almost in a sweat as he looked tensely around.

"What the hell you talking about?"

"Come," he said, looking around anxiously, " I show."

He had aroused my curiosity and I followed him to a shop entrance, where after looking cautiously around once more, he held a Keepsake ring box out for me to examine.

I opened the box and saw the most beautiful set of diamond rings that would ever grace a woman's finger. The engagement ring alone knocked me right out of the saddle. I looked up at him suspiciously.

"I sell you, five hundred American dollar, Captain. But must buy quickly. I get caught, go to jail." he said, still looking alarmed.

The little son of a bitch was trying to sell me hot jewelry. As nervous as he was, I could tell he was in the wrong business. I glared at him.

"I take from VC. Him have store in city," the man said, looking worriedly at me.

"VC? You telling me this belonged to a VC?"

"Yes, Captain. Him VC."

The VC son of a bitch deserved everything he got. I only wished I could see his face when he discovered he had been burglarized. Served the bastard right.

"I'll give you fifty American dollars," I said.

"No, Captain, three hundred all I can sell for. Very pretty. For the Captain, three hundred American dollar. Okay, Captain?" He said, still looking around nervously.

The little bastard was scared and I knew I had him in a bind. Any time the cops would be showing up, and he would be arrested.

"One hundred American dollars. That's all I have," I said, lying.

"Okay, one hundred American dollar. You hurry, Captain. I must go fast."

I smiled to myself. The dumb son of a bitch could have held out for the five hundred. I'd have gone that for these beauties.

I reached into my pocket and peeled off five, twenty-dollar bills.

He was sweating now as he reached for the money. I held it back, indicating that I wanted the rings in my hands first.

He opened the box and removed the rings, casting the box in a trash barrel that was in the street.

"You put in pocket, Captain," he said, handing them to me.

The man was obviously street smart, putting the box in my pocket could arouse suspicion. I handed him the hundred, and he motioned for me to leave.

Putting the rings in my pocket, I left before he changed his mind about the price. I turned to see him reach into the trash and pick the box up. With a shrug I walked away. If he wanted to get caught with the damned box that was his business, I had the rings.

Between the camera I had bought the day before and the rings, my trip to Saigon was a successful one. I caught a flight back to Qui Nhon, where I spent the rest of my leave. Every once in awhile I took the rings out and admired their beauty, putting them carefully back into a piece of silk I had bought to wrap them in, then replacing the rings in my shirt pocket, patting them to make sure they were in the right place.

The next couple of days went by fast, and all too soon it was time to return to duty. I reported back on Friday at 0600 hours, just in time to see my brother-in-law show up bright eyed and bushy tailed. This was a real change for Freddy. Usually he was hung over and looked like something the dogs had drug in, and the cats were trying to cover up.

"Hey, good to see you, buddy," Freddy greeted me.

"Hi, Freddy, how was your leave?"

"I'm going to ask Jeanette to marry me. This is the big one, Cole. The love I've been waiting for, but I guess we already discussed that," he said, grinning from ear to ear. "Where did you end up?"

"I went to Saigon. Had a good time," I said in a matter of fact tone. "Bought a camera. Got a good deal on things."

We looked at the duty roster, running down the list to see what our assignments were. I was assigned along with six other pilots to fly some rockets and other munitions to an artillery position north of An khe.

We went our different ways, promising to catch each other up on the happenings over a beer real soon. I knew my mission would involve a couple days and it was all I could do to refrain from telling him about my daughter, but this was very special and deserved a special occasion. I couldn't wait to show him my pictures.

Our cargo had to be sling loaded, a little tricky if you'd never made a sling haul. As the helicopters hovered low, the ground crew gave their hand signals to guide us over our cargo lines, which had been readied for the belly hooks on the Hueys.

The crew chief would stick his head out and talk us into position for the hookups. This was not necessary if the ground crew was on the ball, but it did make it easier. A good crew chief was always looking for ways to make it easier on the pilot. We were a team and it showed.

As the ships were hooked up, the pilots took up the tension on the lines and waited for the rest of the Hueys to complete their hook ups. Then on a given signal from the flight leader, we began our climb. The weight of our loads caused the ships to respond erratically. Sling load hauling is tricky at first and dangerous if the pilot over-corrects, which is a natural thing to do. I'd seen a new pilot crash on take-off a couple months back, killing all on board. Too much throttle and your craft got too far ahead of the load and you started the pendulum. New pilots over-correct, compounding the problem. The lessons were learned early or you died.

Two gunships were assigned to go with us. For the first part of our mission, we didn't need them, then things took a change for the worst. We came to a pass, and the ground got a little closer than I felt comfortable with. We were flying the staggered V formation when the tracers from the fifties started passing us. With the cargo we had, we were spaced further apart than usual in formation. My craft was designated Orange three, and I flew the right wing of the formation. Red four was on my left and approximately at 150 yards off. Red One was flight leader.

Trying to control a heavily loaded helicopter is a full time job because the chopper wants to continually lose altitude. I felt like I was always pulling on it to keep the ship in the air, and in a way, I was. The aerodynamics of a helicopter are the same as a rock, neither want to fly. Airplanes were just the opposite. At times like this I envied the fixed wing pilots.

When the fifties started, the gunships dove to cover us. The fifties raced by in a steady stream, visible only by the tracers. As they arched across the sky in front of us, I watched the other wing of our formation.

Red three took a direct hit and exploded into a ball of fire. As the explosion flashed out our window, I looked to where the fireball had came from. Striker and Severs had been flying Red Three. Both were seasoned pilots and had families. I wasn't sure who the chief or gunner were, but in the blink of an eye, they were all a part of war history and just as dead as if they'd lived a hundred years ago. My heart went out to the families they had just left behind. Severs, I'd only known for a short time because he came in from another Air Cav. Striker, however, had been a friend and my dart partner. He still owed me sixty-three dollars in IOUs. We were always joking that when we found the golden Buddha, he would square up with me out of his share. Of course we never expected to pay up except for an occasional beer. But we still kept track of the wins and losses. I was going to miss him. Striker was a lousy dart thrower, but he had been a real kick-in-the-ass sort of friend.

"So long, buddy," I whispered, then forced myself to concentrate on business. Now was not the time for missing anyone. My ship was in the throws of the shock wave from the explosion and our sling load was not helping matters any. The concussion hit, and felt like it would roll us, which for a helicopter was sudden death.

"Arming the sling, chief," I said as I depressed the cyclic intercom switch.

"Roger that." The procedure was to disarm the electric switch after hooking up to the belly hook on the underside of the craft. The release switch could and sometimes did automatically release if left on, so it was disarmed while in flight as standard operating procedure. If all else failed and I couldn't get the ship back in control, by having it armed we could dump our load. Not a recommended procedure, but fuck the army. If I felt we were out of control, this shit was out of here. My crew came first. Once armed it would be up to me to push the release button on my cyclic.

"Break formation, repeat, break formation," came the command over the radio from the flight leader.

"Break formation, my ass," I thought. The explosion had all but broke it for us. We were flying the staggered daytime formation. Getting the craft under control was my first concern, maneuvering it back into a formation wasn't a priority. After regaining control, I keyed the microphone again. "Everyone okay?"

"Affirmative, Sir," the chief informed me.

"Damage report, chief."

"We look in good shape, Sir."

"Roger that, chief."

"This is flight leader. Status report," came the call.

"Red Two here," came the first report.

"Red Three here," came the second.

There was a hush as Red Four remained silent.

"Flight Leader." I said. "This is Orange Three. Red Three is lost. Repeat, visual on Red Three. Red Three took a direct hit, Orange Three, out."

"Orange One here," came Orange One's status report. "Orange Two here. Possible hit in tail rotor. Getting vibration. Repeat, possible hit in tail rotor. Orange Two standing by."

"Orange Three here. Orange Two, looks like you're losing one of you're webs. I see no visual on your rotor. You want to shut down for a minute?" I said and grinned at my wit.

"That's a big fuck you, Orange Three. Thanks for the advice though," Orange Two said and we chuckled.

I had closed on Orange Two so close I could hear the buzzing of the tail rotor and looked it over closely. We couldn't make out any damage other than a hook up line being cut. He was probably flying on automatic rough. Roughly translated, when other crafts are getting hit, your imagination starts playing tricks on you. We dropped back to a safe distance again, and I thought about the men we had just lost. This type of work didn't allow a pilot the luxury of dwelling too long however. It could have just as easily been me as Striker and Severs. Now that I was a father, I felt the need to take better care of myself. Suddenly reality hit me, for the first time in a long while, I felt fear. Fear was different than scared. Scared is slow to creep in. Fear came on with an unexpected rush of adrenaline that hit so hard and fast, I thought for a moment I was going to vomit. They say fear gets you killed if you let it get a grip on you. That scared me even more. How many dead guys had felt this way before they had bought it? I had sent my fear packing after seeing so much death. It was either that or live in terror for a year. Now it was back. It wasn't that I thought more of my daughter than Annie, but somehow it was different. I was a dad. Annie was my wife and mother of my daughter. I couldn't get used to the new word, daughter. I hadn't had time to tell Freddy the good news yet. I wanted to live long enough to at least do that.

As we approached Deboto Khe, north and a little west of An Khe, we saw our troops had rolled out the red carpet of enthusiasm for us. Loosely translated, three or four grunts glanced our way as we landed.

The others didn't bother even looking up. All were haggard and dirty. Would this fucking war ever end and let us all go home.

We landed at the LZ and armed the belly hook then off loaded our supplies. I stretched my cramped legs as the crew chief went about his business of post-flighting us. Looking at the grunts I could see they had all been here a long time. Their faces were haggard and hardened. As I walked among them I tried to imagine how and what they had been before coming here and what they were going to be if and when they went home. They were changed forever, that was for sure.

This had been a village not too long ago, and some of the men had a couple big pots boiling at one end of the hooches. I could smell meat cooking, though it didn't really smell good. I walked that direction, having nothing better to do.

"I wouldn't go down there, Sir," came the voice of a private sitting on his haunches smoking a cigarette. "You won't like what they're cooking."

"I'm not hungry. What're they cooking?" I asked.

"They're boiling the meat off some gook skulls. I think they're fucking nuts," he said with some indifference, "If you ask me, ears are the way to go, that is if you have salt, otherwise the flies will blow them before they get dry."

I was hard pressed to believe what I was hearing. I looked into the young grunt's eyes as he stared vacantly. Shit, what was this war doing to us? I had always thought of headhunters as savages, but here we were, civilized men doing the same thing. I returned to my helicopter with one more hideous depravity to add to my growing list of things to forget. The list was growing daily. A Cessna 01 Bird Dog flew over and waved his wings as I sat on my heals under what little shade I could find. I joined the Army to fly helicopters and defend my country against all invaders. Instead I had become the invader. We were given orders to kill the Vietnamese resistance, whether NVA or VC. They were all the same, young, old, man or woman. Who were they? The answer was simple and honest: They were the enemy. Why? Because they were defending their country against us, the invaders!

The frustration and futility of senseless killing was exacting a terrible toll. Helicopter pilots weren't immune and we began to show fractures in our psychological makeups. Irrational thinking had become the norm. A couple times I had been tempted to kill one of our own. One had been a gung-ho green first lieutenant who had taken over a squad of men, ordered me to set his men down on a suicide mission. A sergeant had tried to make him listen, to no avail. As it turned out, none of them came back. If I had put a bullet in the lieutenant's head none of this would have happened. If I'd have had the balls to do it, I could have saved a squad of good men. As an officer, I owed it to them, but now I had to carry this with me for the rest of my life.

I eventually realized that you sometimes had to take the worst situation, reduce it to its simplest form. Then learn to live with it.

Damn, what I wouldn't give for a good bottle of whiskey.

Lifting off a few minutes later to return to base, I was apprehensive. The trip back was high, and when we came to the pass, we skirted a couple of miles further south. The gunships came in ready for anything louder than a heartbeat. The fifties seemed to know what was good for them and remained silent. After clearing the pass, I started thinking about Striker again. Who and how were they going to tell his wife and kid about how he had died. Would they just say he was killed in action? Or would they elaborate? Striker had given his all. I didn't know the crew chief or gunner, but I was sure they were good men.

The war was making me crazy. It wasn't that I was losing my nerve, but I felt we were over here dying for nothing. Every time we managed to take a little ground, we ended up giving it back. Killing gooks was like stamping on an anthill; they continued to swarm until eventually they succeeded. The casualties and equipment losses were high. What the hell were we trying to do? Keep people free by disrupting their lives, killing them, and shooting their sons and daughters. I had to quit thinking like this.

Was it the taking of an innocent child's life? I hadn't learned how to deal with that one yet, and I was beginning to think I never would. My mind always skirted around the first body, blurring it in the scope. Not admitting to anything more than a package in the target's arms. The little bundle had arms and legs, there was no way of denying that. The body refused to come into focus though. I knew it had a body, but I couldn't see it. Damn, why couldn't I see it? In my nightmares it was always a little girl. I had to quit rehashing this. Flying with this guilt was no good. It could cost me, and my crew dearly. Should I ask to be grounded? That was a laugh, we were always short on pilots.

I tried thinking about Annie and the baby, but that haunting memory was lodged in the back of my mind.

The base and the landing field came into view, and I felt relief. The air traffic control officer gave us our landing instructions. I landed and headed for debriefing. I knew I was in for a lot of paperwork because of witnessing the loss of Red Four. I dreaded this twice as much. One, I hated paperwork, and secondly, I knew Striker and Severs. It was never easy to re-live a friend's death. I had been lucky in most of the reports that I had made out. I had seen a lot of ships blow or shot down, but only once before had it been a close friend. Rule one was never get friendly with anyone. Rule two: When rule one was broken, you get drunk.

After the debriefing I finished up my report and turned it in. Then needing a drink, I headed for the club knowing that if Freddy were on base, he'd be there. Looking around the smoky bar, I spotted him sitting with his back to the door and walking up, slapped him on the back.

"Hey, Morgan," he greeted me. Then scooting his chair over, he looked around for a chair for me. There were no chairs available around his table. Looking over at the table next to him, he tapped a fellow pilot on the shoulder. "Hey, Kemp. There's someone trying to get your attention back there by the door."

The man came to his feet and turned toward the door. Freddy reached over and took his chair. "Here Cole, sit down and tell me how things are hanging," he said, grinning at his shenanigan. I sat down before Kemp caught on. Kemp turned back and seeing he'd been tricked, gave Freddy and me the finger, and walked over to another table, and stole his own chair.

As we sat drinking a beer, Freddy filled me in on his day, the special letter he had received from an old flame who had moved to Spokane, Washington.

"How do you tell your fan club that you're no longer available?" he asked, looking serious.

"Don't know. When you fall in love, things get complicated," I said, watching for my opportunity to break the news. Freddy could tell something was on my mind.

"Okay, Cole, what's happening in your little world?" he asked, setting his beer down and looking at me.

"There's bad news and good news," I said. "Striker caught a direct hit. I was there and saw it."

"Damn," he whispered. It was bad enough when we hauled out men we didn't know. I let Freddy take in the loss.

"Now for the good news. You're not going to believe what I am or you are for that matter," I said and reached into my envelope. "You ready for this one, Uncle Freddy?"

"Uncle? What's this uncle shit?"

I shoved my pictures toward him. Freddy looked down at the one of Annie holding our daughter.

"You're shitting me!" he said, looking as surprised as I had. "You son of a bitch. You did it. You made me an uncle. The old man is going to cut your nuts off for sure." A big grin ran across his face. "I'm an uncle." He shook his head in disbelief. Freddy looked at the pictures over and over, still shaking his head.

"I'll be darned. I have a niece," he muttered, not cussing for the first time. "What did Annie name her?"

"Ann Coleen."

"I like that. She put both of your names into it. That's neat. I get to be called uncle to boot."

We talked about Annie and the baby and kept drinking to them. After a while, we both started to feel our beers.

"So, what did you buy in Saigon? You did say you went to Saigon, didn't you?" Freddy asked.

"Yep. I got the deal of a life time on a camera and a set of diamond rings that'd blow your socks off."

"What kind of rings?"

"Keepsake wedding rings. You ought to see the rock in the engagement ring." I reached into my shirt pocket. I laid them out on the table. Freddy reached over and picked them up, whistling as he looked at the engagement ring.

"That's quite a chunk of coal," he said, turning it back and forth. Then held it up to the light and whistled again.

"Nothing like diamonds to get the girls," he said and picked up the wedding ring.

"Nothing cheap about this either."

"It was stolen out of a VC's jewelry store. It serves the cocksucker right," I said.

"My brother-in-law deals in hot jewelry. Cole, you never cease to amaze me. Hot jewelry," he said, teasingly. He kept turning the engagement ring over. "How much?" he asked, looking at me in a sly manner.

"How much what?"

"What will you take for the rings?"

"Who said I wanted to sell them?"

"Come on, Cole, you already have a wedding ring for Annie, your grandmother's. She wouldn't want anything else. What are you going to do with these other than sell them, and besides, I'm family. Now come on, make me a good deal. I'm going to need rings for Jeanette when we get married. So, how much?"

I had his interest and I knew I wouldn't need the rings. "Tell you what. You know, Freddy, we go back a long ways. How would a hundred dollars, the IOUs I owe you and a couple sports coats you have that I like and maybe some free beers now and then sound?" I asked, knowing I had him over the barrel. Where else would he ever find another deal like this?

"Shit, Cole, what did you say you paid for them? A hundred bucks? I'll give you your hundred bucks back and all the beer you can drink for a week. How's that sound?"

"Naw, I don't want to sell them. They'll be worth a lot when we get back to the states."

"Come on, man. You know that sports coat you like to borrow? The one with the emblem on the pocket?" he said.

"Yeah."

"I'll throw that and that tiger skin cardigan in on the deal. How does that sound?"

He had a cardigan that I was always trying to borrow back home. It was too hot over here for it, but when we got home that would be a different story.

"I'll tell you what, you throw in that new fishing pole you got, and it's a deal. How about that?"

"My new pole? You son of a bitch, I never even got to use it. No deal," he said, looking indignant.

"Okay. I kind of wanted to keep the rings anyway," I said, starting to wrap them back up.

"Okay, the sweater and pole, I keep the sports coat. Deal?"

"Huh uh. The sports jacket, too. These rings are worth a fortune back home. No one else would get them from me. Think what they'd cost back in the states," I said. "When you going to see Jeanette again?"

"In a couple weeks, I hope. She'll be back in Qui Nhon by then. I need those rings, Cole. Okay, you got a deal. Here's the money. You'll have to wait until we get back to the states for the rest." He reached into his pocket and counted out one hundred dollars. Handing me the money, he scooped up the rings and looked at them again.

"Jeanette is going to like these. Don't tell anyone where I got them," he said and grinned at me. "You said they were new, didn't you?"

"Yep, brand new," I said, still thinking about that fishing pole. He had paid close to thirty dollars for it. Hell, maybe I could get back to

Saigon and find that guy again. This could be a good racket. Not the most honest, but what the hell, the stuff came from stores that belonged to the VC. It would be my way of fighting my own little war.

"A member of my own family is a fence for stolen jewelry. Who'd ever have thought it?" Freddy said, pocketing the rings, "Someday I'll see your picture in the post office, and I'll be so proud. Ten most wanted. Its got a ring to it, doesn't it?" he said. "A ring, get it?"

"Fuck you. Besides, I'm thinking about going into business. I thought about making you a partner, but you're a pussy. I can't afford to get mixed up with weaklings," I said, grinning at the smart-ass.

"Hey, you produce ice like these beauties and you can count me in."

"Want to see my wife and kid again?" I asked, looking back at my pictures.

"Sure, let's drink to them."

"You sure about getting married?"

"Absolutely, I love them both," he said. "I always figured that the phrase, love at first sight, was horse-shit. It isn't," he shook his head slowly. "Cole, I couldn't love her more if I had been dating Jeanette for ten years."

"I can see why. Jeanette is what you've been needing, and Andre is a nice boy. He'll make you a fine son. You going to screw around any more?" I asked.

"No way. I'm hanging up my spurs. This is for real and forever." Reaching up, he patted his pocket with the rings in it.

"Freddy, how's LeeAnn doing?"

"I think she's hurting pretty bad. She's been keeping herself busy. But she sure is a trooper. Couldn't be happier for Jeanette and me. I don't know if she will ever get over her feelings for you, Cole. Jeanette said she's never cared about another man the way she cares about you."

Chapter 27

The next two weeks seemed to drag. Every night I'd go over to the officer's club and down a couple of beers, hoping to pass the time until it cooled enough to sleep.

As I sat sipping a beer three pilots walked in. One was Freddy.

"Hey," I yelled over the noise of the rain hitting on the tin roof of the building. "Hey, Gray. Over here," I held up my beer. When I shouted everyone turned and stared at the three watersoaked guys standing at the door.

Freddy smiled and held up his hand. The rain let up for a moment and it was quiet. Johnson and Revetti stood on his left side, and using the silence Freddy called back, "Got to go slow, Cole. Revetti is wet and has a boner. He's beat it so much in the shower that every time it rains he gets a hard on." That brought a howl from everyone. Even Revetti seemed to enjoy the ribbing.

The rains were in full bloom, and we looked forward to the dust again, so we could look forward to the damned rain again. Red mud was everywhere, and we tracked it wherever we went.

One of the pilots found a snake that was trying to come in out of the rain. It turned out to be a bamboo viper. After that several of the pilots bought mongooses for pets from the local village kids. I thought about it, because I'm real partial to pets that kill snakes, but decided against it because they smelled. However, one of the pilots had a little female he had named Lola. She had taken a liking to me, and in the mornings I'd find her curled up behind my head. I guess it was the tidbits of food I brought back from chow that had won her over.

On the fourth of September, Freddy got a weekend pass and flew to Qui Nhon.

The next thing I knew he was walking on air. Jeanette had said she would marry him. Monday evening as we got together for our ritual beer, he was so excited I knew before he broke the news that she had said yes.

"Well, guess what?" he said, sitting down, not touching his beer.

"What did she say?" I asked, letting him tell me.

"I gave her the ring and she cried. Then she told Andre and he gave me a hug. I tell you, Cole, that was the happiest day of my life."

"I'm really happy for all of you, Freddy. I mean it, this is the greatest thing that is ever going to happen to you. That is until you have your first baby. Having Andre for a son is going to be great. Wait until your folks meet Jeanette and the boy. I'm glad for you. Let's drink to all our health. I mean, let's get drunk, what the hell, we've got reason to."

"Don't want to get drunk. I told her I'm a changed man and I mean it." Taking another swallow of his brew.

"So when do you figure on tying the knot?"

"We got a little over two months to go here. I figured we'd get married in Da Nang. Her parents will come up. You're my best man and LeeAnn will be maid of honor. I need to get permission from the brass. That shouldn't be any problem. We talked it over, and she's willing to marry me just before we ship out. I checked and we can have all the paper work done so Andre and she can come back to the states with me. This is going to be the longest couple months of my life."

"Yeah, but it'll go fast enough," I said and took another drink of my beer.

Two months, it wouldn't be all that much longer before I'd be home and could see my daughter, take her in my arms and feel the little bundle of silken joy. Her skin was going to be smooth like her mother's, and she would be moving around. I couldn't wait to see and feel her and my Annie. I thought about how fantastic it was going to be making love to the one I had chosen to go through life with. Afterward we'd take our daughter and put her between us and play with her. What more could a man ask out of life?

"Hey, Cole, where you at?" Freddy asked. "I've been talking my head off and you just stare at me. You're giving me the willies."

"Thinking about my family," I said.

"Yeah, hopefully it won't be long before we'll both have that to think about. Won't it be great to take our families camping together? Damn, we've come a long ways since we were kids. Kind of full circle almost. Let's have another beer; I'm buying."

"I'm going to turn in. Gotta write a letter. Thanks anyway."

"I don't know why you don't bring your writing material here."

"You gotta be kidding. All of this racket and interruptions. Come on, this dive isn't for my family. Besides, everyone wants to look over your shoulder." I grinned at him. "Although I doubt if any of these bastards can read."

"Got a point there." Chuckling, he took another swallow of beer. "You ever feel like deserting?"

"What the hell brought that on?" I asked, half-smiling at the question. "Yeah, I guess I've thought about it."

"The other day I came close to flying my bird as far as I could out to one of the islands. I just wanted to disappear from this bullshit. The only thing is, you have to surface someday. At least with Jeanette and Andre, it gives me something to look forward to."

"I know how you feel. Sometimes I think about what it would be like. I think we all do. Part of it is the situations we're subjected to. You see so much death and destruction that you want to turn and run. You're not by yourself, trust me on this one," I said, remembering all the carnage we were constantly bombarded with. We were the most hated part of the American Army. Without helicopters the NVA and VC could easily deal with us. Helicopters made the difference, allowing us to go anywhere and move anything without building roads or bridges. Subsequently, when there was a chance to put a helicopter out of commission, they went for it with all their heart. Quite a few had been blown up by the VC infiltrating the ARVN (South Vietnamese Army,) as they off-loaded from a helicopter drop. They had been known to wheel around and try to kill the pilots or throw a grenade back into the ship. We found it almost impossible to deal with suicide troops. When you flew them anywhere, you laid your pistol in your lap and used it when in doubt. You didn't have time to think if it was moral or not. The law of the land was kill or be killed, and by now I had reluctantly learned the skill.

On the way back to my quarters, I stopped to check the duty roster. I had been assigned special duty along with two other choppers. I shrugged. At this point, I just wanted to make it through the next few weeks without any bad incidents and go home.

The next morning I reported to operations and was told I was flying a field advisor and his men to Hill 1338. Things had heated up just out of Dak To, which lies north of Pleiku and KonTum.

Several platoons of paratroopers had been separated and pinned down. The radios were buzzing between Charlie Company, Alpha Company, and Bravo. Alpha was really taking it in the shorts. The NVA had put pressure on them, and they had called in the heavy artillery. All hell was breaking lose, and I was going to fly right into it.

Because of the rain the previous night, a heavy fog hung thick enough to cut with a knife over all the valleys and in patches on the mountains. The jungle below was double and triple canopy, not allowing any visibility. With some of the tree canopy well over two hundred feet above the floor of the jungle, it made heavy artillery almost useless, causing the shells to explode in the treetops instead of on the ground.

It seemed that everything had gone wrong. The Army had scattered CS crystals (tear gas in crystal form) across the foliage to stop the enemy. The reinforcements had come in with gas masks, but the mask filters had gotten wet and were useless. That had a disastrous effect on the whole company, putting them to their knees retching and vomiting. The area was so thoroughly contaminated that no one was able to get through.

The A-1E Skyraiders were called, in and began dropping five hundred pound bombs and napalm. The NVA, figuring this was going to happen, moved closer to Alpha, knowing they'd be safe from the bombardments if they hugged their perimeters close enough.

As we searched for our troops by radio, I also looked for a place to set down. The NVA was not much of a threat to us as long as we stayed over the cover of the canopy, but finding an area to set down was a different story. We became vulnerable every time we got near a clearing.

The radio helped us find our GIs as we flew a grid over the jungle floor.

"You're over us now," came the voice of the RTO, (radio telephone operator) "Watch yourself, Charlie is all over the place. We'll keep watch and try to give you cover."

"Affirmative. I see a possible LZ at one six zero degrees, two hundred meters, give me cover."

At about ten feet or so from the ground, I felt the tail rotor shudder and my craft began going out of control as I lost tail rotor authority. Quickly I cut power, and pulling pitch, put the Huey's skids on the ground. Brush flew everywhere as the rotors tore through the undergrowth. It was not a graceful landing. As we hit I called for everyone to abandon and keep low, forgetting we had a high ranking officer with us. As we jumped from the crippled helicopter, AK-47 rounds ripped through the ship, shattering the Plexiglas and sending fiberglass shrapnel everywhere. I looked around in time to see the crew chief, who had turned back for something in the chopper, get hit; spraying a steady stream of blood onto the side of the craft from a throat wound. The chief had a confused look on his face as he stood for a second or two looking at the blood, then collapsed. He had bled to death in a matter of moments.

Drawing my pistol, I ran with the others toward a direction we figured our troops were covering us from. Instead, we found we were heading right into the NVA.

I yelled out as I saw the first gook stand up at the edge of the clearing. Without thinking, my pistol fired and his head snapped backwards. We wheeled and ran around the ship to what we hoped would be our cover fire. The elephant grass was ass deep and I felt it tug at my boots as I ran. Twice I looked over my shoulder at the gooks running toward us, intent on not letting us make it to the tree line thirty feet on the other side of the helicopter.

I turned and fired three more rounds at a gook sighting in on us. My second or third round must have hit his rifle, because it flew out of his hands, leaving him standing for a second looking shocked. Then the sound of an M-16 cut him in half.

I turned and started to run, then discovered after the second or third step that my legs didn't want to work as well as they should have. There was no pain, just sluggishness in my left leg. There wasn't time to figure out what was wrong, with bullets flying all around us. I made for the cover of the trees in time to hear our M-60 machine guns open up and start clearing the problem up.

"How you feeling, sir?" came the voice of a medic as he looked down at me. What the hell kind of question was that to ask? I felt fine, kind of funny, but fine.

"We got the saw from your helicopter. They're clearing a larger LZ."

"When in the hell did you do that, we just landed?" I asked.

The medic chuckled. "Won't be long before we'll get you out of here. Jolly Green is on its way. You're lucky. It looked bad at first, but you're going to live. You just won't sit down too much for a while. You ever fly standing up, Sir?" The medic asked.

"No. How come I feel funny?"

"I gave you some morphine; it helps the pain."

"I don't feel any pain. Fact is, I feel pretty fucking good."

"Great, that means I done it right," he answered, patting my shoulder.

"Where'd I get hit?"

"You don't want to know," he said, and chuckled again, "Let's put it this way, your pants will cover the scar."

"Fuck! I won't have to squat to pee, will I?"

"No sir, you're all intact. You took one in your tailbone that's all. I don't think it's too deep, but I'm not taking any chances," he said, patting me again. "No exhaust pipe damage."

Great, but Freddy would probably call me his half-assed buddy now. "Where exactly?" I asked the medic.

"It looks like it caught you about three or four inches below your belt. Not as bad as it could have been. Your legs still work. That's a good sign. It was low enough that it missed your spine and doesn't look like it went all the way through. I probed and if I had to make a guess, I'd say it was probably a spent bullet. Possibly hit your helicopter or something before it struck you. Maybe just bad enough to send you home," he said, then asked me to move my feet a little.

I moved my left then my right leg.

"Good, I think you're going to be okay. Probably be going home though," he repeated.

"Home?" Damn, home sounded great. Annie and my baby daughter. I drifted off, and when I woke, I was in a bed. A medic was standing over me with a chart in his hands.

"How you feeling?" he asked.

"Where am I?"

"Base hospital, you should be feeling better soon. You got smacked pretty hard on the tail bone. Between that and the morphine you went to sleep for awhile. We just spent some taxpayer money on you. You'll have a nice scar on your backside. Got someone outside that wants to say hello. You feel up to it?"

"I feel fine. Who?"

The medic turned and motioned for someone to enter.

"Hey buddy. How you doing?" Freddy asked as he approached.

"Hi, pal. I feel fine. This hospital thing is a pain in the ass though," I said, grinning at him.

"Yeah, I heard you were the pain in the ass. I guess I'll have to start calling you Ol' Buttshot," he said and grinned back at me. "They going to medevac you out?"

"I guess. I'm ready if they are," I said, feeling like I was fixing to desert him. "I don't think I'll be sitting down for awhile, not much demand for a lamed-up pilot. Maybe trade places with my gunner."

We both laughed at the thought of me doing that. I'd be spending all my time just staying in the craft.

"This should get you a discharge," Freddy said, raising his eyebrows a couple times.

"I'll go for that. I mean, I hate to leave this paradise, but gotta make room for the cherry's, right?"

"Right," Freddy answered. "Maybe I'll do what Flagger said that time, remember? Shoot my toes off."

"You'd probably miss and shoot your fucking leg off instead," I said and we both laughed.

"How we ever going to dig up that Buddha now?" Freddy asked, grinning at me.

"It can wait until after the war. We'll come back and not have to worry about dodging bullets. Too bad Striker isn't still alive. Maybe we could send his share to his wife. She could probably use it. Shall we plan on treasure hunting when the war is over?"

"Yeah, it ain't going anywhere. You know that Buddha is probably made out of brass anyway. I was poking around. There was a lot of those left in the temples."

I remained at the medical facility in Pleiku for five days. Each evening Freddy would drop by and spend an hour or two visiting me. On the third day, he snuck me a beer, and when that went over great, he brought two for me and another couple for him the next visit. We had a blast keeping the beer a secret from the medics, although I think they knew. The next morning they medevaced several of us out of this little piece of heaven, and I didn't get a chance to say good-bye to Freddy.

The army flew us to Saigon where we were detained for three days at the military hospital. On the second day three officers and three enlisted came by my ward. I couldn't believe it. One was a general and two colonels. They were there to give me medals.

"Sir, permission to speak frankly," I said.

"What's on your mind, Mr. Morgan?" the general asked.

"Sir, with all due respect to my country and the United States Army, I don't want any medals for what I've been through. Sir, I respectfully request that my name be struck from all military records. That's all I ask, Sir. I mean no disrespect for the United States Army or my country," I repeated. "I just want to forget the things I've done and seen. I would like my life to be private, Sir."

"I'm sorry you feel that you have to be stricken from the records, Mr. Morgan. I wish I could grant you your request but your records can't be removed, son," the general said.

One of the colonels spoke quietly. "There is a provision for this. Records can be scrambled."

The general looked down at me. "I only wish we had a lot more like you, Mr. Morgan." Then he shook my hand and stepping back one pace, saluted me, "Have a good life, Mr. Morgan."

The other officers each shook my hand and saluted me then turned and left.

As the colonel started out he turned. "Don't worry Mr. Morgan, the Army takes care of its own. We throw smoke and keep secrets." Then he gave me a wink and left.

Chapter 28

I arrived in the states and was hospitalized for only a week at Walter Reed Hospital before they had me walking with a cane. I improved to the point that I was released from the hospital and received a discharge. They explained that if I needed anything from the military, all I had to do was give them a number, which would call up my military records, and allow me medical access. I wouldn't need anything; what I wanted was just to be left alone.

I decided to not say anything to Annie or the folks about my return. I wanted to surprise them.

The next day I was on a plane headed for good old Montana and the Flathead Valley. With some discomfort, I managed to sit for the trip home. The stewardesses couldn't seem to do enough for me. Old Freddy would have eaten this right up. If it weren't for looking forward to getting home, I would have enjoyed their attention a lot more myself.

My mind drifted back to the ideals I once had. A lot of water had flowed under the bridge since then. I began to sweat thinking about the little girl. Lord, I'm so sorry. I need forgiveness. I need to forgive myself first though, and I can't.

In Spokane I couldn't wait; I gave Annie a call. I couldn't keep back the news any longer. I first called the Grays and found Annie was at my parent's house. Mr. Gray didn't recognize my voice. I guess he wasn't expecting me. I hung up and called home.

"Hello?" came the beautiful voice.

"May I speak to Mrs. Morgan?" I asked.

"Which Mrs. Morgan would you like to speak with?" she asked, not recognizing my voice.

"The cute one."

A scream nearly broke my eardrums, "Cole! Cole, where are you?" she stammered. "Tell me!"

"I'm in Spokane. I'm waiting for my flight out of here. I should be home around one."

"Spokane? Oh Cole, Spokane! I can't believe this," she said, starting to cry.

Even her crying sounded good to me. "How's my daughter?" I asked.

"She's sleeping. Want me to get her?" she asked. "Oh Cole, I can't wait. Hurry, please hurry!"

"I don't have time to talk right now, that is, if I'm going to catch my flight," I said, checking my watch.

"I don't want to hang up. Oh, Cole, hurry. I can't wait to tell everybody."

"I called because I didn't want to have to walk home from the airport," I said. "Got to go kid or I'll miss my flight."

"Okay, I'll be there waiting. We all will be. Oh, Cole, I can't wait."

"Like the flower needs the rain, I need you my love," I whispered and hung up.

As I boarded the plane, I had to laugh at her asking me to hurry. My heart pounded at the thought of seeing her and my daughter. I was excited about seeing my parents too, but nothing compared to the excitement of seeing Annie and my baby.

After what seemed like an eternity, the plane began its approach to our airport and the excitement began to really run my adrenaline to a peak. The wheels touched the runway, and I knew my prayers had been answered. As we began to taxi up to the terminal, I grabbed my flight bag and cane. My heart pounded as I began walking toward the exit door of the aircraft. Searching the terminal I saw a small crowd of familiar faces with one jumping up and down like an excited child. My lovely Annie.

With a shriek that could probably be heard clear to the parking lot, she pushed through the crowd at the gate and come racing up to me. With tears of joy she threw herself into my arms. I dropped my cane and grabbed her with both arms.

"Cole," she sobbed, "I can't believe it. You're home. You're home, my love! Oh, thank you God, thank you!" She leaned back to look at me then once again I hugged her tightly to me and kissed her eyes her nose and her lips.

The rest of the family held back for a moment, finally rushing forward to greet me.

Pop reached down and picked up my cane. Standing for a moment in silence, he handed it to me without saying anything.

Mrs. Gray stepped forward with a bundle of baby blankets, and a little hand waved just above the upper end of the covers. Annie, in the meantime, began dragging me toward our baby, beaming all the while.

I approached the baby with both caution and anxiety. This was the moment I had waited for, dreamed about. I had lain awake many a night imagining this. Now the moment was here. My heart pounded as Annie took our daughter and handed her to me, glowing with pride. I reached out and took the little bundle, afraid I was going to hold her too tight, and afraid if I didn't I'd drop her through the blankets. I stared at the little baby. My baby, our baby! Tears ran down my cheeks as I looked upon God's gift to us.

Annie clung to me desperately. Then she took the baby and clinging to my arm, waited for everyone else to greet me. They had held back and let me see my family first.

Mom came forward first and between tears and kisses, welcomed me. I told her how much I loved and had missed her. She in turn promised me all the pies I could eat. I had missed her baking for a long time. If I decided to hold her to her promise, she was going to be busy.

Pop had that twinkle in his eye, the one that said if you pushed it he was going to get a little misty eyed. I held his stare for a long moment or two, then reached for him. "I love you, Pop," I said and hugged him.

He patted me on the back as we embraced. "Welcome home, boy," he said in a low voice, "welcome home."

"Good to be home, Pop."

I hugged Mrs. Gray and she kissed me on the cheek. Mr. Gray stared at me for a moment, then gave me a hug too. "Welcome home, son."

Annie was hanging on to me as if she were afraid I might sneak off. Taking my daughter I cradled her in my other arm as we all began walking back toward the terminal, everyone talking all at once. I found it difficult holding onto Annie and my daughter. Pop noticed my difficulty and suggested that I free one hand. Annie immediately took little Ann so I could walk with my cane.

"Cole? What happened?" Annie asked, looking at the cane.

Everyone was silent as they waited for me to answer. "I'll explain when we're driving home, right now let's just enjoy being together."

"Okay," Annie answered as she hugged me.

I stopped more than once to look at my daughter, who was sleeping as if the world around her was non-existent. Between using my cane with one hand and holding my wife with the other arm, I felt awkward, but we took it slow. Annie looked first at me, then at Ann, a smile of contentment on her beautiful face.

"You did it," I said quietly to her.

"Yep, we sure did," she said, looking at me, her eyes holding mine. "Welcome home, Morgan."

As I looked into those beautiful eyes I knew I was home at last. I had been through a lot since I had last gazed into those gorgeous pools of blue. I had changed from a ranch boy to a man, who had been hardened by the stark realities of war. I had done my duty, and I hoped I would never again have to face what I had gone through.

"Let's go home," I said to Annie and kissed her lightly on her lips. With a smile, she hugged me, and we stepped into the world we had dreamed of all our lives, our world.

We drove home in the Gray's van, with Annie, the baby and I choosing to ride in the back seat. We couldn't keep our hands off each other and the baby. As we were driving toward home, Annie chattered about all the things she had done or was going to do, stopping every once in awhile to lean over and kiss my cheek.

I loved these moments, and while in Vietnam, had lain awake many a night and dreamed of this. Don't ever change Annie, I thought as I listened to her and tried to answer everyone else's questions. How I wished we were alone. I enjoyed our parents company but that could come later. Right now, I just wanted to be with my wife and child. I wondered what kind of arrangements were in the makings at home. Would they let us stay in the same bedroom? Could they or would they expect each of us stay in our own parent's homes? This was something Annie and I were going to have to face. What the hell! We had a baby daughter. That should prove we weren't virgins; we were man and wife.

Annie lay her hand on my knee. "I can't wait to show you how things have changed. I put in a flower garden. I guess I wrote you about that though. Come to think about it, I wrote you about everything I did," she said looking at me, a faint smile on her lips.

Damn, I couldn't wait to get Annie alone. I felt my stomach knot up. She seemed to sense this and patted me gently on the leg. That didn't help.

After what seemed like a year of riding, we finally came in view of our ranch, or I guess I should say Mom and Dad's. I was a man now and it was time to find my own place and provide for my wife and child. Wife and child, it seemed so strange to say that. I had left home a big kid and came home almost a year later a battle seasoned man. I shook my head. I had taken many a human life since I had left here. It felt strange when I thought of it like that. Particularly the life of the little girl. Would I ever get over the guilt? Or would it leave me permanently scarred? Would it fade away with time? I had a lot of questions that needed answering. I began to sweat.

"Cole? What's wrong?" Annie was looking at me with concern. Damn, I'd let my guard down. I would have to do better than that. Nothing worse than a nut to contend with!

"Huh?" I said. "Nothing, I was just thinking about something. I'm okay now, I was just remembering things. Boy, it's good being back home again. Can't wait to see the old homestead."

"We're here. You're home, sweetie," Annie said, patting my knee again. Then she reached up and put her arm around my neck and kissed me on the lips.

Little Ann was sleeping in the seat next to Annie. I looked over at her little face and the tears came to my eyes.

We pulled through the main gate and drove up to the house. Mr. Gray parked the van in front of the house about ten feet from the gate. I remembered Mom making Pop put the fence up because of the cows getting out of the field fences and raiding her flowers. It only took once and the yard fence went up. Women in the Morgan family packed a lot of authority.

Our dog, Turk, short for turkey, came out and began to bark. As we climbed out of the van, Turk started smelling everyone, making sure nobody was sneaking in. He went nuts as he came to me. I dropped to one knee and gave him an ear rub with both hands, he squirmed and twisted trying to climb all over me. It was good to see the old dog. I wondered if Turk was still as good as he had been at gathering cows. Old Turk was starting to show his age, but then, who wasn't?

As we entered the house, our mothers went to work on something to eat, first putting on a pot of coffee.

Pop, Mr. Gray and I with Annie on my arm and the baby cradled in her other arm, went into the living room. Annie wasn't about to turn loose for a second.

"I'm stuck to you like glue, Morgan. If you go to the bathroom, I'm going in with you," Annie said and laughed, her eyes twinkling.

The two men laughed, understanding how she felt, because they had lived around her the year I was gone. Both had been through a war themselves and knew we wouldn't willingly leave each other's side for quite awhile. The Grays had accepted me as Annie's husband, partially I'm sure because of our daughter. Mrs. Gray had accepted me before I had gone into the army, and I think she even had suspected our relationship. But Mr. Gray was something else to contend with. He always had left me with the impression that he'd throw me, tie a leg up, and castrate me if he ever found out I was messing with Annie. Sometimes I felt that maybe he was just waiting until he got me off where no one could save me, then he'd raise the octave of my voice a couple notches. I grinned to myself. Even though things seemed different now, Mr. Gray might still be worth watching for a while. I pitied the son of a bitch that ever tried messing around with my daughter.

"What are you grinning for, Morgan?" Annie asked.

"Nothing. I was just thinking about our daughter."

Annie, the baby and I sat on the couch, while Pop and Mr. Gray sat in easy chairs facing me. Annie leaned on my leg, her feet curled under her. Our baby lay in her lap. I felt my life was complete with my family so close to me.

Old Freddy was still flying and sleeping in bug hell. I'd make a point to write him in a couple of days, explaining the difference between the warm horse piss that we drank for beer over there, and this good old invention called refrigeration. I'd be sure and describe each sip of the suds and how good it was with chips and peanuts and his favorite, those little hot sausages in the pickle juice.

"Freddy," I'd write, "cold beer isn't all it's cracked up to be, but when combined with good roasted peanuts, these little hot weenies and fresh potato chips, I think it beats hell out of what you're probably holding in your hand while you read this."

"What are you looking so smug about, Morgan?" Annie asked, cocking her head to watch me.

"Just thinking about writing that brother of yours."

"How long do you have to use that cane?" Pop asked.

"They said I could try walking without it in a couple more weeks. I walk short distances without it now, it just feels more comfortable having it to hang onto. I didn't get hit too bad. The bullet just took my tailbone off. They figure it was almost spent before it got me. The way the damned medics were acting, I thought I had been cut in half. The morphine didn't help my thinking any, although after a shot of that I didn't care whether I was half or whole. I asked for my pistol because we were still shooting at the gooks who were all around us. They refused to give me my gun. They said I might decide one of them was a gook. That morphine is powerful shi ..., powerful stuff," I said, grinning.

Annie lovingly patted my leg. I liked to feel her touch. It held a lot of comfort and I felt I needed her contact. Before I had left the hospital, they told me I might need some counseling and that if I felt like I did, I could get it at the Army's expense. Screw the army. I didn't want anymore to do with them. I had my family and we'd make it just fine.

Mom and Mrs. Gray came into the living room and pulled up chairs. I really would have rather talked about something other than Vietnam, but that was all there was to talk about, I guess. So we talked, and I felt like it was more of a question-and-answer session. Almost like a debriefing. The questions got a little braver as time went by and finally Mr. Gray asked the big one.

"Did you or Freddy ever have to kill anyone, Cole?"

"Yes."

I looked at Annie. Her eyes were wide with amazement.

"You said you were flying mail. You weren't doing that, were you? You said you had a safe job. You lied to me."

"I flew with your mail," I said in defense. "Annie, there wasn't any sense in worrying you or Mom. Over there it's a lot different than you read about in the magazines. That's all a bunch of bullshit. We're going to lose this war. They say we're making the NVA and VC back down. That isn't true. We're just wasting good men. It's like fighting a ghost. One minute you're shooting gooks and the next minute they're gone."

I was starting to get that fighting panic feeling. I guess if I had to use a term that would be the one I'd use. I felt both panic and like fighting gooks all over again. Everyone watched me with expressions ranging from bewilderment to complete surprise. I'd played enough poker to know the looks.

"It was pretty bad over there, wasn't it, Son?" Pop finally asked.

"Yeah, Pop, it isn't what they say it is. We don't have anyone on the run. They kick the shit out of us whenever they want to. I'm sorry for saying it that way, but that's the way it is. I don't know how else to put it."

"That's okay, Son. A spade is a spade. Don't apologize for honesty," Mr. Gray said.

"You want a drink? I think John and I are ready for one," Pop said, rising from his chair.

"We have coffee ready in the kitchen," Mom said, starting to get up. She didn't approve of Pop offering me a drink.

"He's a man now, Mother. Let us have our drink or two."

Mom shook her head. She knew what Pop was saying was true. I had become a man in the year I had been gone. What she didn't realize was that I could drink with the best of them, maybe even Pop, although the time wasn't right to prove it.

Pop returned with a bottle of good whiskey and three glasses. Setting them down on the coffee table, he poured three healthy drinks and handed one to Mr. Gray and one to me. The women looked on as we toasted my homecoming. I drained mine without the shudder, which usually followed the first drink of whiskey. I wished I could've had a large water glass of the liquor; it felt good going down.

Pop left the bottle on the table, and in a few minutes, he motioned for me to pour another drink if I wanted to. Annie looked a little concerned, then I thought about what Freddy had said. He had said, women will try to run your life if you aren't careful. I poured another drink.

Pop and Mr. Gray followed suit, then we let the whiskey set. It was our way of saying we were in control of the situation. The whiskey was having an effect, and I felt a little more comfortable talking about how it was over there. Hell, a couple more shots and I'd be willing to show them my wound. Yep, that whiskey was doing a fine job.

"Dinner will be ready in a few minutes. Don't you men spoil your appetites," Mom said, rising to check on supper.

Mrs. Gray and Annie followed her. Before leaving, Annie put a pillow by Ann to make sure she wouldn't roll off the couch. As she straightened up, she patted me once more on the leg.

"Oh, by the way, you've got a letter from Freddy on the refrigerator," Mom said from the kitchen entrance. "I must admit the letter addressed to you was a surprise to all of us. We thought maybe you boys had lost track of each other over there and this was his way of contacting you through us."

"I'll get it for you," Annie said and went into the kitchen. Returning, she handed it to me, then stood waiting for it to be opened. It was short and sweet.

"Cole, you son of a bitch. Don't touch my sweater or sports jacket. I had the rings appraised, and they said they were a nice set, and I could pick up another set just like them from the dime store for about two bucks. I'm going to kill you when I get home.

Love, Fred the Fearless."

I cracked up. So the little gook had pulled a fast one on me. Me, the sly and crafty dog that I was.

"What's so funny?" Annie asked.

I related the whole story to the family and watched them split their sides laughing. Annie leaned over and kissed me on the cheek. Looking down her neckline, my stomach did a flip, and I started wondering what kind of sleeping arrangements had been made. Annie gave my shoulder a final pat and went into the kitchen to help with dinner preparations.

I felt the whiskey giving me the extra courage I needed to approach Mr. Gray about Annie. "While the women are in the kitchen, I want to know how you feel about me and Annie, Mr. Gray. Annie is my wife by my grandfather's customs. I know they aren't the white man's ways, but she is my wife now and forever. Ann Coleen is our daughter just as much as Annie is yours. I know you want us to be married by a minister, and we're ready to get married any way that it will satisfy you. But she is my wife and the mother of my daughter," I repeated. "I want to be with her tonight and forever."

Mr. Gray sat for a moment staring at me. I began to feel uncomfortable and almost wished I hadn't spouted off like I did. Damn the whiskey. Pop waited to see what was going to happen.

Mr. Gray spoke at last, "Son, I'm an old fool. I should have let you kids get married when you asked me. I didn't because I'm hard headed. I thought I was doing the right thing by making you kids wait until Annie was out of school and you were back from Vietnam. I was wrong and I'm sorry. You and Annie are husband and wife as far as her mother and I are concerned. It took that little girl to make me realize it, but I wouldn't change anything even if I could. You'll need to get married again, according to the state law, so you kids will have the benefits you should have. But it doesn't mean any more than just that. It'll give you kids the legal loopholes that the law says married people have. You three can live with us or live here until you get a place of your own. I was going to act like a hard head just for fun, but Helen said she'd hit me with a skillet if I did," he said and laughed. Pop and I laughed with him and I felt a great deal of relief. Annie came in from the kitchen.

"What's so funny?"

"Nothing, honey," Pop said, holding up his hand, still chuckling, "man talk."

"At our expense, I suppose?" Annie crossed her arms and smiled.

"Yep." I said.

"Supper is ready," Annie said. Giving us the brush off with her hand, she returned to the kitchen.

We sat around the big dining room table and talked about everything that had gone on around the valley for the past year. One of our old work horses had twisted a gut while rolling and had to be put down. Old man Gilbert's stud horse had got its tallywhacker broke when a mare kicked him while he was trying to breed her. That brought a laugh from us guys, while the women shook their head at what we found amusing. Their reactions made it even funnier. We howled hysterically, our sides about to split, tears running down our cheeks. As the laughter began to fall off, I took my arm and bent it down, imitating what the stud must have looked like. That did it. All three of us about fell out of our chairs. By now the women knew we had lost our minds, and shaking their heads, started passing the food around, filling our plates. To tell the truth, I think by now we would have rather taken the bottle and gone back in the living room, but we ate instead. Damn, it sure was good to be home again.

After dinner Mrs. Gray spoke, "Annie, you kids can have our house for the night. Dad and I talked it over and decided to stay over here to give you kids some time together."

I looked a little shocked at the announcement. Annie gave me a knowing look. My heart raced.

"We can leave the baby here with the grandparents if you want, Cole," Annie said.

"No, I want my daughter with us. I've dreamed about having her sleeping between us. I want to take her with us," I repeated with conviction.

"All right, Cole, I'm glad. I wanted to take her with us too, but I didn't know how you'd feel about being woke up several times. Besides, I didn't bring a breast pump."

I felt my face flush.

"You were raised on a ranch Morgan, you know about milking, don't you?" Annie asked, laughing at me.

I looked at my watch. "I'm getting a little tired," I said pretending to stifling a yawn.

"It's only five o'clock," Annie said and laughed. "I think you can stay awake another fifteen minutes."

"Granddad, I think we need to run over to the house and get a few things for the night. One of us can bring Annie's car back," Mrs. Gray said.

Mr. Gray stood up, reaching for his hat. "Okay, Grandma, still sounds funny being called Granddad. Which brings up another matter, Cole. I can understand your calling Helen and me Mr. and Mrs. Gray. Hell, you've always done that and that was fine, but now you're a part of the family. I don't expect you to call us Mom and Dad, but at least call us by our first names."

"Okay. It's going to be kind of hard at first, but I'll do it."

Ann squirmed a little and Annie turned to tend her. She beamed as Mr. and Mrs. Gray came over and looked down at their grandchild lying asleep with her little hands held up to the sides of her head.

I felt a sudden rush of pride and love as I looked at my wife and daughter. Little Ann Colleen was dreaming about nursing and her little lips were making a sucking motion. She was a beauty and someday would be a heart breaker.

After the Grays left, we all sat around in the living room and visited. It seemed good just to settle down for a short while and talk about the future instead of the war.

"What do you kids plan on doing? If you want, the old Benson place is up for sale. You might think about that. I don't think they want too much for it," Pop said. "I don't want to talk you kids into anything though. It's just a thought."

"I think we need to discuss it. We haven't had much of a chance to talk about our future yet," I said, "but we'll sure keep it in mind."

"Son, the other day when I was over at Johnson's garage. We were discussing what you actually did in the Army. I mean with you being a special task pilot. Who did you work for mainly?" he asked.

"When we weren't on special use assignment, we flew for the 173rd Airborne Brigade mainly."

"Are you going to stick to flying?" Pop asked.

"No. If I never see another helicopter it'll be too soon. The fun is gone. After I got hurt I had a lot of time to think about it. The Army transferred me to the hospital in Da Nang. The brass from Saigon were in Da Nang at the time, and visited with me while I was in the hospital. They said they wanted to give me commendations for my service to the Army. I refused them, Pop. I felt like they were giving me medals for doing something I'm not very proud of. I can't talk about it for another thirty years. I was sworn to secrecy and signed a document stating I couldn't discuss anything about it."

Pop gave a nod.

"I asked for my name to be removed from the Army's records. They scrambled my records and filed them away. My files have been smoked. If they're dug up, they show I was in another branch back in the fifties."

"You were still in school then," Pop said.

"That's the Army's smoke. I have a number I had to memorize. My file's can't be opened unless I authorize it. Only the false one to let me have medical access."

"What do you mean, son? What happens if you forget your number and need medical help?"

"I won't. I told them I just wanted be left alone, but they said if that ever happens I could still get help. They'd make sure." (In 1974 the Right to Privacy Act was brought into force to protect the GIs.)

"They had a reporter and photographer from the Stars and Stripes come to the hospital to interview me. They were nice guys, but I told them I didn't have anything to say. Pop, I don't want anything more from the Army. I just want to disappear and my records with me. Medals don't erase anything or make things right. They'd only remind me of what I want to forget. I just want to erase the damned war from my memory. I can take care of myself."

Pop gave me that slight nod again. "What do you want to do with your life?"

"I think I want to write. Maybe I won't make a living out of it, but that's what I want to do."

"Someday Cole is going to write a love story about us. He promised me a long time ago, didn't you?"

"The only love story I'm writing is how I love to hunt and fish," I said, teasing her. Everyone laughed at my joking, and Annie punched me lightly on the shoulder.

"You promised," she said, pretending to be hurt.

"Maybe someday."

"Promise me right here in front of your mom and dad, that you're going to write a book about you and me and our families. There aren't very many people like us, you know. You and me, Grandfather said we're the Loon People."

"You're loony all right, Grandfather didn't know just how accurate he was when he named you that."

"He would have really loved to see his great granddaughter, wouldn't he? He seemed to know so many things. Perhaps he was able to see into the future and did see her," Annie said. A tear ran down her cheek. "How I miss him."

Mom and Dad both nodded. "We all miss him, honey," Mom said.

I looked out the window at the sound of Turk's barking and saw Annie's folks returning with the van and Annie's car.

"You kids can go any time you want to, however we're sure enjoying your company. It's just so good having you home again, Cole," Mom said, "and I know I'm not the only one that feels that way." She looked over at Annie and smiled.

The Grays walked in. John removed his cowboy hat and hung it on the deer-horn coat hanger next to the doorway.

"Well, what did we miss?" he wanted to know.

"Nothing, I'm trying to get this big lug to promise he will write a book about us. He promised me he would a long time ago. Daddy, you make him promise, okay?" she said, looking like a little girl again. We laughed at her.

"How was Freddy doing the last time you saw him, Cole?" John asked. "I didn't want to hit you with a lot of questions on your first day back, but his mother put me up to it."

"John, I was just asking you if Cole had mentioned anything about him. I didn't tell you to ask about him."

"It's okay, Mrs. Gray ... Helen. I don't mind talking about anything," I lied. "Freddy is doing fine. He's got a French girlfriend in Qui Nhon. That's by the coast in South Vietnam. Her folks own a tea plantation near there, kind of inland from there actually. You folks will love her. I was going to let Freddy tell you all about her and her little boy."

"We got a letter from him, and it was filled with her and her little son, Andre. He sounds pretty interested in the two of them," Helen said.

"He is. The boy is one of the smartest kids I've ever known and good looking, too. Kind of like I was when I was his age," I said, and grinned at Annie. She rolled her eyes in disbelief. "He's going to make a super grandson if Freddy plays his cards right."

"How old is she? If he's eight, she has to be older than you boys?" Mr. Gray said.

"I'm guessing around twenty-five. She was married at sixteen. She's a great person and a real lady. Freddy couldn't do better if he looked a hundred years."

"I'd like to meet her," Annie said. "I've read Freddy's letters and he sounds so different this time. You know how he's always been woman crazy. Now he sounds so settled on one woman. She must be something to do that to him."

"Trust me on this. Freddy's bringing home a French wife and son. You're going to love them both. I'll guarantee it," I said in a matter of fact voice. "You best pick up a pony for Andre, Mr. Gray ... sorry, John."

"A granddaughter and a grandson. My, how our family is growing, Granddad," Helen said and reached over and patted her husband's knee.

"Freddy should be about finished with his tour of duty. Four more weeks, he's a short timer now," I said.

"I'll be glad when he's back in the states," said Helen. "I worry every day with him being over there. Cole, I know you wouldn't lie to me. Is he as safe as he says he is?"

"I'm sure he's okay."

"It won't be long now, Mother," John said.

The baby began to stir. "I think somebody is getting hungry." Mom looked over at the bundle of blankets starting to move.

"Us guys can go into the kitchen while you feed her," Pop said and got to his feet. Mr. Gray stood and I did the same.

"I breastfeed," Annie said, at my confused expression, "You don't have to go. None of you have to go. I can put a blanket over my shoulder or go into the bedroom."

"We'll go into the kitchen," Pop said. "It'll give us a chance to tell a few lies without you women catching us."

"I'll go into the kitchen, too," I said, following Pop and Mr. Gray, "maybe get another drink of that good whiskey."

"There's coffee on the stove, Morgan," Annie said, as I went through the archway.

"Whiskey's more fun," I called back over my shoulder.

We sat around the table and had a good time swapping tales about the service. Pop and John had both been in the army, and we talked about how things had changed.

I tried to hide my feelings, but they could tell that certain subjects bothered me. It especially got to me when the conversation got around to the torturing of prisoners.

I had been told by a counselor while I was in the hospital that talking about the way I felt and the things I saw was good up to a point, as long as I didn't dwell on them. I felt differently. I didn't really want to talk about Vietnam. I just wanted to put it behind me.

John related a story about how the Germans had tried to torture a confession out of a soldier by pushing his head underwater while making the other prisoners watch. It had backfired though; and the soldier had drowned rather than confess.

It seemed like one gruesome tale led to another and pretty soon I was sucked into relating one of my worst experiences.

"I took a search team into where one of our helicopters had gone down," I said, and took the last sip of my whiskey. "It was early morning when we received the distress call. We went in as soon as possible. Two gunships escorted us as we sat down on the crash sight. The five-man search team checked the helicopter over and found the gunner dead. The crew chief was in a sitting position with his hands tied behind him to a tree. He wasn't wearing any clothes. His belly had been cut open, and I'm sure he had watched his own guts spill out. The two pilot's bodies were found about a hundred feet away. Both of them with their eyes scooped out. They had been castrated. One had been shot in the back of the head, probably trying to run for it. The other's cock had been cut off and stuck in his mouth; they say he choked to death on it. I gave them a hand with the bodies. The worst part is that after a while, you get used to death and accept it as part of life. You wake up one day and a certain part of you is dead. You don't feel anything any more."

Pop and John sat silently. Then Pop poured me another drink.

Mom spoke in a quiet voice from the kitchen door, "How you boys doing?"

I don't think she heard any of our conversation, but I was glad she showed up. It made us quit talking about war.

"Annie wants to see you, honey," Mom said.

I stood up, relieved to be doing something else. Walking into the living room, I saw Annie with the baby still nursing under the blanket. I had seen Vietnamese women nurse their babies, but this was a real thrill to see my own baby nursing. A feeling of pride came over me. My wife nursing our child. Annie took the blanket down, and I got my first look at what she looked like with our baby at her breast. Walking over, I stared down at the two of them. The baby would suck a couple of times, then stop, why I don't know. But she would wait for a couple of seconds, starting once again with vigor. Annie watched me with the gentleness of a loving mate. This is what was worth fighting for, not politics and money. I felt a lump in my throat.

"I've been sitting here thinking, Cole. I'd like to go up to the lake. Just you and me and Ann. Maybe stay for a month or whatever time it takes to put our lives together. You can hunt when you feel up to it and I'll just be the loving wife and mother. Kind of like playing house."

Helen had walked into the living room and heard what Annie said. "I think that would be wonderful for you kids. Get away for a few days. Enjoy yourselves. I don't know if I like the thought of you being away for a month, but maybe a week. Any longer than that and we'd have to walk in to see our baby."

"What do you think about my idea, Cole?" Annie asked.

How could I ever say no to this beautiful woman, not that I wanted to. "Sure, we'll talk more about it tonight."

"I don't think we'll do much talking tonight," Annie said, a twinkle in her eye.

"Annie, you're embarrassing Cole," Helen scolded, looking at my face.

"Maybe a little," I admitted.

"Want me to really embarrass you?" Annie asked, as she looked mischievously at me, that slight smile on her face.

"No, I don't. If you do, I'll talk like we did in Vietnam, and you can trust me on this, you won't like it."

"I've probably heard worse. I used to hear you and Freddy when you didn't think anyone was around."

"We were still good kids then. Believe me, this would curl your hair."

"Okay, no mushy talk," she said. The baby had quit nursing and Annie lifted her to her shoulder and began patting her back. Her breast was still partially exposed.

I looked at her with a little lust. Hell, more like a lot of lust. Annie caught my look, and reaching over with her free hand covered her breast, giving me a sexy coy look.

Annie laid the baby down and rearranged her bra and blouse. Then stood, "I think we'll run along." She smiled devilishly at me. "Cole is looking tired."

"There it is again. You and your little embarrassments. You enjoy making me look like a dirty old man." I said grinning. "This is war."

The women laughed at my expense, and I was forced to laugh a little at it myself.

"I'll get my coat," Annie said, starting for the closet.

Mom picked little Ann up and patted her back as she walked her around in circles. It felt good to see how much everyone loved our baby. Annie had certainly done something very special for everyone. The greatest gift God gives to man is a good woman and children.

Annie waited for Mom to hand her the baby. She never seemed to be in a hurry. That was a quality everyone admired in her. Like Grandfather, she was not only a peacemaker, but had a calming influence.

Mom handed the baby to her, and Annie wrapped Ann in a blanket, pulling it up so it covered her little head, and we started toward the door. Pop and John walked up. Each took a turn looking at their grandchild one more time before we left. You could see the love and pride in both men.

I had wondered many times how John would to take my coming home and confronting him with getting his little girl pregnant. I had known him all of my life and knew you didn't mess with him anymore than you did with Pop. I was uneasy to say the least, about our first meeting. Now both sets of grandparents followed us out to the car.

My eyes met John's straight on. Ever so slightly he gave me his nod of approval, then smiled a fatherly smile at me. "I wouldn't have it any other way, Son," he said.

I opened Annie's door, and she and the baby got in. As we drove to the Gray's ranch, Annie put her hand on my knee and patted it like old times.

"Just think, Cole. You're mine forever now. No more army making you go anywhere. Just thinking about it gives me a thrill."

"Yeah, it does sound good. So, how many kids we going to have?" I said, looking over at her, raising my eyebrows in anticipation.

"We'll just practice for awhile. Then we'll decide," she said, kissing my cheek.

As we drove up to the house, Cricket, the Gray's shepherd cow dog ran up barking her greetings. I started chuckling.

"Okay, Morgan, what's so funny?"

"I was just reminded of old Rocket. If he had barked like he was supposed to, I wouldn't have got to see that cute bottom of yours."

"Oh, you mean the one you shared with all your friends?" she said and laughed.

"Not all. There are guys in town that didn't get to see it. Only the guys in the north valley."

"How many did you say there were? Although I don't think I really want to know who they were. It would be a little awkward meeting them in a store, don't you think?" she asked, giving me a look of disapproval.

"Hey, we'd never seen breasts the size of a lemon before. What we expected was cantaloupes," I said, poking fun at her.

"Keep talking like that and you'll be sleeping on the couch, Morgan," she said and elbowed me. "Besides, what did you expect from a fourteen-year-old?"

We got out of the car and I looked around, remembering the wonderful memories the old ranch held. It was sure good to be back. I looked over where we had first met, and in my mind, saw a little girl holding a stuffed animal that had one good eye and one black button eye. She was leaning against her mother's leg. Then I heard the little voice say, "Do you want to see my swing?"

"What are you thinking, Morgan?" Annie asked.

"About a small girl that stood right about here," I said, pointing at a spot just in front of us. "I can feel her presence here now. Any idea who?"

"There was a very handsome boy standing here, too. He followed her to the swing and was hooked; he just didn't know it at the time," Annie whispered as she looked up at me.

As we entered the house, the wonderfully familiar smell of the interior filled my nostrils. This had been my second home. We entered through the living room door, something us boys hadn't thought about when we were growing up. The kitchen was always our target area for quick snacks, our doorway to pies, cakes, and cookies.

Annie crossed over and laid our daughter down on the couch while she took off her coat. I stood in the living room and looked around. The house hadn't changed any with the exception of pictures of Annie and the baby. There was a large hinged picture frame. On one side was a picture of Annie and me that had been taken before I'd gone into the Army, on the other side a picture of Annie and Ann Coleen. I looked at them; we were a great looking family.

Annie came up behind me and put her warm arms around my chest. I could feel her breasts pressing against my back. My blood came to a boil. Turning, I put my arms around Annie and drew her into me tightly.

Her eyes searched mine. Reaching up with both hands, she drew my head down to hers, kissing my lips tenderly.

"Let me get Ann put down and we'll go to bed," Annie said her voice husky as she pulled away.

My heart raced wildly. Thinking about her lying next to me with her smooth soft skin pressed against mine was almost more than I could stand. I wanted to rush into the bedroom, lift her off her feet and lay her on the bed, not giving her a chance to protest. I felt almost as barbaric as a savage. I grinned; I could live with that feeling, I thought.

It seemed like an hour before Annie came back into the living room. My heart gave a jump as I viewed the most beautiful, sensuous woman that had ever walked this earth. Annie stood in a nightgown of blue and white. The material was translucent. My hungry eyes took in her figure just beyond the fabric that graced her body. My breath became labored and my legs turned to rubber. I knew it could never get any better than this.

Crossing the room, I took her in my arms, feeling her softness. Ignoring my injury, I lifted her into my arms and carried her into the bedroom, where I lay her down on the bed, then stepped back for a moment while my eyes devoured every inch of her. She lay there, quietly staring up at me, her eyes soft with desire. She had turned off all the lamps but one, giving the room softness. The bedroom was all Annie, with the frills of femininity right down to the curtains and bedspread. On a high shelf was a row of stuffed animals I had won over the years at the county fair. Jaju the old stuffed animal sat silently at the end, staring at us.

Getting undressed, I dropped my clothes onto a chair and lay down beside her, feeling like I wanted to take her without even a kiss. Reaching over, she drew my lips to hers. Immediately I became erect and began pushing against Annie's leg. With a moan, she reached down and grasped my penis, then began to stroke me. With a loud groan I reached down to stop her. A year's pent-up emotion was about to explode. Our hunger for the touch of each other was insatiable, turning voracious as we clung to one another. My hand went to between her legs, and she moaned loudly, digging her nails into my back. We were in a hurry, yet wanting to savor every moment. But the moment was now. I rolled over onto Annie, and without hesitation I entered the warmth of her body.

Morning came all too soon. Neither of us got much sleep other than a catnap. Twice through the night I had watched as Annie nursed our little daughter. We had left the lamp on through the night, not wanting to miss being able to look at one another at any time. Now lying next to her, watching the peaceful way she cuddled our child to her breast, I couldn't think of anything I could ever want more than this.

Annie's eyes were on me most of the time, watching with pleasure, sensing my feelings. At around six o'clock I finally drifted off to sleep with little Ann lying beside me. Annie had gotten up to make coffee. She had the rancher attitude that if you weren't up before the sun, you'd missed the best part of the day.

Lying there in semi-sleep, being aware of my daughter lying beside me, was fantastic. I couldn't let myself go into a deep sleep, fearing I would roll over on her. Feelings of contentment and deep love for my child flooded my being as I felt the warmth of her little body. How many dads had given their lives for that worthless cause overseas, never to lie like I was doing this morning? Damn the warmongers who had reaped the blood money. I began to sweat, and had to force myself to quit thinking about Vietnam, before finally drifting off.

Around six-thirty Ann woke me by wiggling. It was her breakfast time and with a little cry she brought Annie on the run.

"Sorry, Cole. She's hungry and probably needs changing. We'll go into the living room and you can get some more sleep. You're tired," she said, apologetically.

That was Annie, always thinking of others. "No, I'm awake. You got coffee on, don't you?"

"Want me to bring you a cup?"

"No. You've got plenty to do with Ann. I'll jump in the shower, then we'll both have a cup," I said, rising and giving her a kiss.

"Another one of those and I'll jump in the shower with you."

I came out of the bathroom with just my shorts and pants on, although I'd shaved and combed my hair.

Annie whistled as I walked into the kitchen and sat at the table. Pouring a cup of coffee, she walked over and sat it down in front of me. "I've been thinking. Let's go to the cabin today. We'll run into Kalispell and get what we'll need for a couple of weeks. You can get whatever you need for fishing and hunting. We can spend all our time together. How does that sound?"

"Hunting season isn't here yet, but the rest of it sounds pretty good. Has Pop or anyone been into the cabin this year?"

"I don't think so. We can ask. Why?"

"Oh, I was thinking of downed trees across the road was all. I don't want to spend my first day sawing trees to reach the road's end. I got better things to do. What about Ann? Will she need anything?"

"Just some diapers. I've got everything else right here," Annie said and lightly touched her breast.

My blood began to heat up. She knew how to do it to me.

"I just want the three of us to be alone for a few days. Does that sound selfish? I don't want to share you. I've dreamed about this for too long."

"Okay, we'll go to the cabin. I think I'd like to get away with my wife and child for a few days, too. Maybe catch a fish or two."

Annie lit up with a big smile. "Oh, Cole. It'll be so much fun. You just wait. I'll make you some pies and cakes. You'll have fresh bread and biscuits." She danced around like a little girl. I watched the happiness that had come over her with a delight I hadn't felt in a long time.

"Come into my office and we'll talk about it," I said, nodding in the direction of our bedroom.

"Breakfast is a good time to talk. What would you like to eat?"

I looked at her sensuous body and raised my eyebrows.

"Food, Morgan, food," she said and backed away.

"Man does not live by bread alone."

"Down, boy, we've got all day and the rest of our lives, although I must admit you're tempting me."

After breakfast we returned to the bedroom, where we made love. I looked at the clock it was almost nine. We dressed for the day ahead of us.

Annie set about doing the dishes and making the bed while I played with our daughter. After she finished tidying up, she changed and dressed Ann for going out in the cool morning air.

I carried our little bundle out to the car with Annie at my side. Opening the door, Annie got in and I handed her the baby.

As we pulled into the folk's yard, Turk announced our arrival to everyone within a half mile. Mom and Helen came to the door and stood waiting to take Ann, giving both Annie and me a kiss on the cheek.

"Where's Pop?" I asked as we entered the kitchen.

"Your dad and John are up at the barn. One of the milk cows is having trouble calving. If you're hungry I'll fix you kids some breakfast," Mom said.

"We've eaten, but I can use a cup of coffee," I said.

Pop and John came in, both hanging their cowboy hats on the deerhorn rack.

We raised black baldies which are a cross of black Angus bulls and Hereford cows. But we also had a few head of milk stock.

"How are things going?" Mom asked.

"We got another bull calf. Just what we need," Pop said, shaking his head.

Bull calves from milk stock are virtually worthless unless you're raising breeding stock. They're too bony and not good weight gainers, compared to beef stock.

"We're going up to the lake for a couple of weeks," I said.

"You'll have to restock the food. Dad and I haven't been up there since you left, Cole," Mom said.

"We're going into Kalispell first and get some supplies," Annie said.

"You kids coming back here before you go to the cabin?" Mom asked.

"Yeah, we have to get some of my fishing equipment. I gotta have something to do up there," I said, grinning.

Annie punched me in the stomach. "I'll find something for you to do. Changing diapers should satisfy your creative urge."

Everyone chuckled.

"Your mother and I have been talking about giving you kids something to pass on to your children. Now seems like as good a time as any," Pop said, glancing over at Mom. "You kids can have the Whisper Lake cabin and property. It isn't much good for anything other than a getaway, but we never use it anymore."

Annie put her hand over her mouth and looked at me. Then she let out a little cry of happiness and threw her arms around my neck.

"Thank you. That's my favorite place in the whole world. I want to spend my whole life there," she said, turning loose of my neck and grabbing Pop around the shoulders, she hugged him tightly. Then she turned to my mom and hugged her. She was as excited as I've ever seen her.

"Thanks Pop. And thank you, Mom," I said, giving her a big hug and a kiss. Then turning to Pop, I hugged him. "I couldn't think of anything better than this for a wedding present."

"Well, now I have to try and match it, I suppose?" John said. "Helen and I've talked it over kids, and if you're interested in the Benson ranch, we'll look it over. If it's what you want, I'll make the down payment and pick up the first two year's payments.

"Oh, Momma, Daddy! Thank you. You guys are the best parents in the world," Annie said, giving each of them a hug.

"John, Helen, I don't know what to say, except thank you," I said, reaching over to shake John's hand and giving Helen a hug.

"Well, it's money better spent than on a ceremonial wedding," John said. "Annie already has the ring and everything she wants."

Annie blew her breath on the ring then rubbed it lightly against her blouse. She was very proud of it and should have been. It had been in our family for five generations.

"This is all any girl could want. Well, almost all," she said, looking at me.

I kissed her in front of everyone. "Yeah, almost," I said, then kissed little Ann on the forehead. "Well, if we're going to go to the lake, we probably should get a move on. By the time we get our supplies from town and everything we need from here packed up, we'll be pressed for time."

We drove to town and bought our groceries, white gas for our lanterns, and of course, more fishing tackle, as if I didn't already have enough.

We had lunch at Sykes and the waitress made over our little daughter. Annie beamed with delight and I guess I did, too. She got a good tip. When people recognize beautiful babies, they deserve a good tip.

Chapter 29

Anxious to get to the cabin, we hurried home and loaded everything we could think of. I was going to have one hell of a time getting it all packed in to the lake, which is a little over a quarter-mile walk from the end of the road.

I was pleasantly surprised to find the road hadn't been covered with blowdowns. Only twice did I have to stop and take the chain saw to a tree lying across our road. We finally pulled up to where we had to park. As we finished unloading the truck, I looked at all the junk we had felt was necessary. I decided to leave part of our supplies till morning. We walked in with what we figured we'd need for the night. As far as I was concerned, Annie and the baby were all I needed.

I chopped wood and built a fire in the stove while Annie straightened and dusted. With little Ann put down on our bed, we walked out on the porch, leaving the door open so we could hear her if she started crying.

I went back in and brought out the old double rocker that we had stored in the corner of the cabin. Sitting down, my arm around Annie, we looked out on the lake, like we had so many times before.

"Just think, Cole. This is ours now. I'll never give it up. I want to be buried here like your grandparents."

"Hey, let's talk about living, not dying."

She smiled at me. "Sorry."

Around seven we went back into the cabin, had a bite to eat, then sat around the stove with the oven door open. As usual, I propped my feet on the door.

We talked of all the good times we had had growing up.

"You were always popular with all the girls. They liked going out on dates with you," Annie said as she stood up and walked behind me, placing her hands on my shoulders.

"I just treated them like they were you," I said as I reached up and caressed her hand on my shoulder. I confessed that I had lain in bed and thought of her many a night. Annie reached over and kissed me with all the desire of a woman in love.

I stood up and gently took her up in my arms. She tiptoed as she kissed me, never once taking her eyes from mine. With as much passion as life will allow, I undressed Annie and lay her on the bed beside our baby.

We made love until after midnight. After exhausting our energy, we lay in each other's arms and talked late into the night.

I told Annie about Vietnam and the terrible suffering I had seen. How I felt about what was happening over there, of how we hadn't been allowed to pursue the Vietcong once they crossed the Cambodian border, and of the frustration of fighting in the jungle, the bugs, snakes and the awful heat and humidity. As we talked I could feel the tears of frustration at what I had been helpless to stop. Of what I was forced to do because of my commitment to the other men. I hoped the people that cause these wars for profit would rot in hell. My hands opened and clenched involuntarily as I thought of all the atrocities I had witnessed.

I also told her about LeeAnn and the friendship that had developed between us and of how I had hurt her. I wanted no secrets between my wife and me. Annie listened intently, not saying anything until I finished.

"Cole, I feel so sorry for LeeAnn. I know what it's like to love you and to think that love will never be returned," Annie said with sympathy in her voice. "I hope someday she meets another man who she can love, and that he will love her as she deserves. She's Jeanette's sister, isn't she? Maybe I'll get to meet her if Freddy marries Jeanette and they move back here.

"Annie do you know what a very special person you are? You are beautiful both inside and out. I'm a very lucky man. I love you and thank God for you every moment of every day." I kissed her tenderly at first, then as our desire heightened, our passion once again ran its course. Exhausted we fell asleep, my arm around her as she lay with her head upon my chest. I was completely content with my lot in this world.

Morning came with the little cry of a very special young lady. I checked my watch, it was five-thirty. She was going to be a rancher all right. I'd get even someday, maybe when she was old enough to do the chores. Five-thirty was about the right time for milking, mornings and evenings.

"Sorry. When she's hungry, nobody sleeps. Daddy says he can set his watch by her."

"Don't apologize. It's time to milk anyway," I thought of how that had sounded, "I mean," I stammered, "milking cows, not you."

Annie smiled at me. "I love you, Morgan," she said then kissed me. I grabbed her and was attempting to pull her to the bed, but she resisted.
"I have to be milked, remember?"
I watched the two of them as Annie showed her breast to little Ann. The baby attacked the nipple as if she was starving. This was by far the most beautiful thing I had ever witnessed. I could see Annie's breasts were full, and she switched so Ann could take them both down. I was absolutely fascinated. God had done things just right.
"You enjoy watching me nurse the baby, don't you?"
"Yeah, I guess I do. I think you're the most beautiful creature on earth, Annie. I used to dream of how you would look nursing our baby. You're even more lovely than I ever imagined, and trust me when I say, I've always thought of you as beautiful beyond belief.
Annie's eyes welled up with tears.
"Oh, Cole, you're so precious," she said in a quiet voice. "I'm so lucky." A tear ran down her lovely cheek.
I knelt down in front of her and laid my head on her lap. "Now and forever, you're my lady." I would have considered it an honor at any time to give my life for her. I would slay dragons with a club for this wonderful creature.
After Ann had been fed and changed, Annie set about making breakfast. At the table we made plans for the day. As soon as it warmed up enough for the baby, we'd hike back to the pickup and retrieve the rest of our supplies. The air was always so fresh here in the mountains. There were still huckleberries on the bushes in some of the patches on the hillsides. Nothing is more fun than turning your fingers and mouths blue with the sweet juice they held. That afternoon after the work of packing supplies into the cabin had been completed, we decided to pick some for one of Annie's great pies.
Getting a large coffee can and a paper bag for the berries, I strapped on my pistol and carrying the baby in a backpack, we climbed the mountain on the north side of the lake. The tradition of huckleberry picking has been in our family for three generations and I hoped it would continue for many more. The berries were thick on the bushes, and in no time we had our containers filled to the brim with berries almost the size of small marbles.
Picking a berry, I crushed it then touched my fingertips to Ann's little lips. Annie looked over at me a little concerned.
"She isn't used to anything other than breastmilk, Cole," she cautioned, "Anything more than that and she might get an upset stomach."

I withdrew my finger from Ann's lips, while she continued to make a face and twitch her little mouth, "I think she liked it."

"Babies are very sensitive to foods, even the ones the mother eats. Remember when our cows got out and ate some snowberries?"

Snowberries are white and about the size of a pea. They grow on low bushes, and oftentimes can be found along the ditches. Cows seemed to like them, but when they ate snowberries it made the milk bitter and undrinkable for days.

I began to learn the do's and don'ts of being a father, as Annie instructed me with love and patience. I enjoyed every moment of it, and with a little practice, I could change a diaper as well as she could, or so I believed.

We played house in our own little world of the cabin and lake. Each day a thrill for both of us. I'd sit and hold our daughter while watching Annie gather rocks for bordering the flower garden she was planning to plant next spring. She worked with gloves so her hands wouldn't become rough on Ann. I helped with the bigger rocks, but mostly I just sat and played with our daughter.

Next on her project list was a bird feeder, and with this I helped. We hadn't brought any bird food along, so we used oatmeal and corn meal. Annie hung the feeder in a tree a few feet away from the kitchen window, so when she was working, she could watch the birds.

She had made me promise not to peek at what she had in a large package she brought from home. "You go fishing for awhile and when you get back, we girls will have a surprise for you," she said, handing me my pole and wicker fishing Creel.

I walked over and took the canoe paddle out of the corner of the cabin, which was reserved for sporting equipment. We always left the paddles inside the cabin. A porcupine had showed us the error of our ways one time long time ago by chewing the paddle in half when we had left them with the canoe. We'd been forced to nail a pie pan on a stick for a paddle that trip. It still hung in a tree as a reminder.

Launching the canoe, I stepped in and taking my seat, quietly dipped the paddle into the water. The craft cut silently through the clear waters of the lake. Watching the bottom, I drifted over to an old raft that had once been my dad's when he was a boy. Someday I wanted to dive down and hook a rope to it. It would be fun to see it up close, and see the small boy attempts at make it a mighty ship.

I caught enough trout for our supper while I drifted from one old memory to another. Each part of the lake held a special story. As I completed a slow circle of the lake, a voice called from the porch.

"Morgan, come see our surprise."

I beached the canoe and after taking my fish out and putting them in the water to keep, walked toward the cabin.

Annie met me at the door, making me shut my eyes. "No peeking." Her voice sounding excited, which wasn't unusual for Annie. This girl was always high on life.

"Okay, you can open them now."

Looking around, I saw curtains on all the windows, along with bows tying them open. On the bed was a bedspread that was perhaps a little feminine for hunters, but this was her cabin now. The room looked more domestic than I had ever seen it. I smiled.

Since my grandmother had died, the cabin had been kept more masculine, mainly because my mother hadn't come up here very often. Now it had a feminine touch again. I knew my grandmother would have been pleased. Looking closer, I saw pictures on the wall of the three of us. One of Annie and the baby was recent, another was of Annie and me before I went in the Army. Annie had hung one on the wall above the bed, another stood on a cabinet in the kitchen. There were a couple framed and hung on the wall beside the door. One was of Freddy and me standing in front of a helicopter with our crew chief sitting on the deck giving the camera the finger.

Annie stood with her hands on her hips, smiling broadly. "Well? What do you think?"

"It's home," I said, turning around, looking at the four walls. "I think it's great, Annie." I took her around the waist and pulling her into me, kissed her passionately.

"I've got a great idea, let's go swimming. We can put Ann in her bassinet and stay close to shore. What do you think?"

"Skinny dipping?" I asked, slowly looking her up and down.

"You're not thinking of swimming, Morgan."

Chapter 30

Our time at the cabin was the happiest either of us had spent in a long while. Time flew and before we knew it, it was time to go. We had spent ten glorious days together as a family, now it was time to get serious about our future.

Returning to the valley, we drove by the Benson ranch. First slowly, then turning around, we drove back, stopping periodically to view it from different angles. The more we looked, the more convinced we were that it was perfect.

In one end of the south pasture, the river flowed through it making a slow bend that was reminiscent of Miller's bend. That made my mind up.

I could tell Annie liked the ranch from the way she looked at the house, which sat a couple hundred feet off the road.

"Cole, can we drive in? I'm sure they wouldn't mind us doing that."

"I guess we could take a closer look," I said and pulled into the driveway. As we neared the house, my eyes fell on the shop that had been hidden from the road. "Damn," I whispered, "look at that."

"What?"

"The shop." The workshop was fantastic, with large double doors that were open, giving me a view of the work area.

"Look at the backyard, Cole. Look, it has a garden too and over there crab apples. You like crab apples. That is, after you outgrew shooting them with your slingshot."

I grinned. I'd found crab apples just right for shooting with my slingshots. Annie had gotten madder than hell at Freddy and me for splattering them against the barn. That was great, because she had had to pay attention to me. I guess I loved her even then.

"Let's go talk to your dad. We both like this old place. You think you want to spend the rest of your life out here?"

"I'd spend the rest of my life on a desert island with you, Morgan. But I think I'd be just as happy here. I think this place would be fun to fix up. It's homey. Just think, our own ranch. We could raise special breeds. Oh, Cole, let's buy it!"

"Let's go tell the folks. I hope your dad still remembers what he said about the down and helping with the payments for awhile."

"Don't worry about Daddy; he meant every word. Besides, he'll do anything to keep his granddaughter close."

"Suppose he'd spring for a new pickup, too?"

"You're pushing your luck now, Morgan."

"Just a thought."

We drove home with both of us jabbering, not really listening to each other. We were excited to say the least. Our own ranch. It only had eighty acres, but what the heck, it was not how much you had, it was what you did with it.

Annie's parents were the first to know because of the offer John had made. They were excited about the prospect of us living within a few miles. John said he'd be glad to talk to the Bensons and make all the arrangements for us to look the place over closer. He wanted to do the final check on the technical things like the well and septic system. I was glad of that, because I was still a beginner.

Things moved along quickly once he got involved, and the next thing I knew, Annie and I were the proud new owners of the new Morgan ranch.

Mom and Dad gave us a start on some cattle from their breeding stock, a dozen laying hens and a noisy rooster Pop couldn't stand because it crowed all night. Mom told us to put him in the stew pot and get another one.

One day John and Helen got a letter from Freddy. He had married Jeanette just before his tour of duty in Vietnam was up. Freddy said he was being stationed back at Fort Rucker, Alabama, as a flight instructor. He and his new family would be coming home to visit over Thanksgiving. That got all the women in a tizzy. Annie worked night and day painting and cleaning our home. She wanted the house to be just right when she met her new sister-in-law.

I took a job with Pop, logging. Painting was not for this boy. I'd rather shovel cow manure than use one of those damned paint brushes. When Annie looked like she was fixing to ask me to help with the painting, I told a little lie to cut her off at the pass.

"You know, I think I'm allergic to that paint. I hope you can hurry up and finish that room, so I can go in there. I think it affects my breathing."

Annie got a serious look on her face. "Cole, you stay away from that room until it's completely dry. I'll open a window and maybe that'll speed the drying time."

I felt guilty for not helping her and shortly afterwards miraculously was healed, and started painting. One night I confessed, and took a small jab in the ribs for worrying her.

Annie and our moms went to work on the interior of the house making new curtains and arranging furniture. In no time at all they made it homey.

We moved into the house, and I started fixing up the shop with Pop and John's help.

One evening in early November, as Annie and I sat at the dinner table, she came up with an idea to break up the work.

"Cole, let's go to Spokane. We can go before Freddy and Jeanette get here. There's some things I'd like to get for the house, and we could have a honeymoon, too. Come on, big guy, just you, me and Ann. We'll get a motel with a indoor swimming pool, maybe go to the show and have some fun. Daddy can watch the place. What do you say?"

"We can go by that big sporting goods store." My mind turned to the fishing tackle. "Maybe get together with old Sparky. He's working in a sporting goods store in Spokane, maybe I could get a discount on a few things."

Annie's eyes danced with excitement. "We'll go?"

"Yeah, let's do it."

Annie called her folks and arranged for them to watch the place for a few days.

"I told Mom we were going to get a minister to marry us in Idaho. That did it for her. Daddy didn't have a chance to say no," Annie said, and laughed. "It isn't that Momma doesn't think we're married, Cole, but for Ann's sake, they wants us to be legal with the state."

"Hey, that's okay with me. I think it's a good idea anyway. You'll have to obey me then. Right?"

"Creep."

I kissed her forcefully and she pretended to struggle.

"I'm going to shop for a new outfit to wear when we meet Freddy and Jeanette's plane," Annie announced, head held high as she batted her blue eyes.

Annie made me promise to look closely at the clothes she was going to model. I was to take it seriously this time or she said I couldn't go with her and Ann again. Of course I was terribly worried about that.

We left early the next morning acting like a couple of big kids.

Our first stop was in Idaho as scheduled. After going through our wedding vows in front of a justice of the peace, we were finally on record as husband and wife. It looked comical with Annie standing beside me holding a baby. But I guess they'd probably seen it all before. We had a good chuckle though. Then it was off to the big city. We got a motel with an indoor swimming pool. It was always a treat for me to see Annie in a bathing suit, however I wasn't the only one staring at her. The pool had three young boys, probably around fourteen or fifteen, who couldn't keep their eyes off her when they thought no one was watching. I grinned, remembering when I was a kid, and had felt the same way about good-looking women a few years ago.

Annie smiled and shook her head. "You boys never change, do you?"

"You never change, woman. You're still a banquet to starving eyes," I said. "You have any plans for tonight?"

"Are you asking me for a date?"

"Yeah, I thought maybe we could take in a movie. Then we could go back to my room and just talk. I'm new in town and lonely."

"Your line isn't new. I suppose you're a lonesome soldier?" she asked, looking at me with suspicion, "Are you sure all you want to do is talk?"

"Absolutely," I said, raising my right hand.

"I still charge the same. My time is money."

"How much?"

"Is a hundred dollars an hour too steep for you?" she asked, looking at me in a sensuous way.

"Are you worth it? I'm looking for a really good time and you come highly recommended, but a hundred dollars, I don't know ..." My eyes slowly traveled down her body.

"When I'm bad, I'm very good," she said in a sultry voice, eyeing me up and down. "For you I'll be very bad."

"Good," I said, still eyeing her, "I'll think about it. A hundred bucks, huh?"

Annie puckered her lips, and half closing her eyes, rose and walked back to the diving board, standing on her tip toes she threw me a kiss, and with a light spring dove smoothly into the water. Surfacing, she smiled. Her hair flowed back away from her lovely shoulders. Having a baby certainly hadn't hurt Annie's figure any. If anything it had made her even more sensual than she was before.

The afternoon passed with Annie and I taking turns swimming and watching our offspring resting peacefully in her infant seat. Annie watched me dive, giving me helpful hints. I would never be as graceful as she was, but neither would anyone else.

Evening came and we dressed for our big date. At the show we got our popcorn and pop. While Annie carried the refreshments, I carried Ann. Sitting in the balcony, I felt like a kid again and threatened to throw some popcorn over the railing.

"I'll have to make you sit downstairs if you don't behave," Annie said with authority. I grinned. It was the same as when we were kids. Annie, Freddy, and I would sit in the balcony, and Freddy or I would start tossing things like popcorn and candy wrappers down on our friends. We were caught occasionally and taken down to the ground floor, once or twice even put out in the street. They were good memories. Annie snuggled up to me as the show started, and it was like old times. After the movie we went to a restaurant up on Division Street for supper, then looked in a few stores before returning to our room.

The next day we stopped at the sporting goods store where Annie found the fishing pole she had to have. "You're going to be sorry you bought this for me, Morgan. With this pole I'm going to catch every big fish in Whisper Lake. You'll be consumed with envy when you see them. This pole is going to be magic."

My heart danced with happiness at Annie's excitement. I bought new sleeping bags that zipped together, and two new lanterns for the cabin.

We went to several more stores where Annie made more purchases. One was a picture of an old man and a boy sitting on a bank fishing. She said this was my grandfather and me. Annie bought a few girl things, which included a new nightgown. We went to an import store where she bought two large wooden bowls with lids.

"They'll be good for nuts and candy at Christmas, besides, they go with our cabin."

I shook my head in disbelief.

"Have a little faith, Morgan. Everything has a use," she said and smiled.

All too soon our trip to the big city came to an end.

"I had a great time, Cole. Thank you."

Driving home, Annie and I made all kinds of plans for our future. We decided we'd raise cattle like our parents, maybe even eventually get into some registered stock. The cow market fluctuated, but all in all, it was a fair income. I'd have to supplement it with outside work to make ends meet, but that was all right with me. I had never been afraid of honest work.

We talked about my writing career. Annie suggested I take a few classes locally. Maybe later on, I could go on to the university in Bozeman. She would get a job to help support us until I graduated.

She could really talk when she was excited, which was almost all the time. Annie never babbled, but she did like to talk when we were alone.

"I'd like to arrange my garden like Mom and Dad's, beside the backyard. That way I can keep an eye on Ann and her little brother while I'm working," she said, watching my reactions.

"Little brother?" I said in shock.

"I was just wondering if you've been listening or just saying, 'uh huh', every once in a while. Mom warned me that husbands do that," she said, leaning over and kissing my cheek.

By the time we got to the Idaho border, Annie had planned out her garden, even deciding where she was going to plant roses. We rebuilt the ranch from one end to the other as we drove back toward Montana and the Flathead Valley.

Pulling in the yard, I made a discovery. "Hey, you know what we forgot? You have any idea what we forgot?" I repeated as I sat there holding the steering wheel.

"What?"

"I don't have a cow dog. Every ranch needs a cow dog. I don't have one."

"You nut, I thought it was something serious," she said, slapping me on the shoulder. "I was really worried for a minute."

"Well, I need a cow dog. Tomorrow we'll go into the feed store and look at the bulletin board. Besides, Ann needs a puppy to play with."

"Don't you think she's a little young for a puppy?"

"Hell, I had a dog when I was her age. I remember it well. Running through the fields with my dog."

"Wait a minute, Morgan, you had a dog and ran through the fields at Ann's age?"

"I was very advanced for my age." I said and grinned. "If she's going to be my right hand man, she needs one too." I affectionately looked down at my daughter sleeping quietly between us. She was my pride and joy.

Again came the pain of Cambodia. That child had been loved by her family, too.

"I'll be glad when Freddy and Jeanette get here," I said, trying to get the child off my mind.

"Me too. I'd like to take Jeanette shopping with me. I can't wait to meet her. Just think Cole, I have a sister."

The day finally arrived to pick up Freddy, and his family at the airport. The women had been busy cleaning and baking pastries for the last couple of days. You'd have sworn they had invented a new holiday.

"We should be leaving in a few minutes," Helen said.

We all checked our watches, and agreed, being anxious to see them.

We arrived at the airport a few minutes early so we waited at the pickup area. Helen and John had a hundred questions about Jeanette and Andre. Most of them I couldn't answer but I did my best.

"What will Andre call us? I hope Grandma and Grandpa," Helen said, smiling happily. "After all, that's what we are," she said with conviction, looking around at all of us. "Oh, I hope he likes us."

"Stop worrying, Helen," John said, patting her hand. "You act like you're meeting the president of the United States. Andre is eight years old."

At last the plane's arrival was announced and we moved toward the gate to wait as it taxied up and stopped. Annie gripped my arm tightly as I held Ann.

"I think I see them," she whispered as she dug her nails into my arm.

Then Freddy and Jeanette, with Andre clutching his mom and dad's hands, walked through the plane's doorway and peered out into the waiting crowd. Freddy was still in uniform. They made a great picture of an American family as they descended the airplane's loading ramp.

Helen broke through the gate, not waiting for it to be opened all the way and rushed toward them. Freddy stepped forward and hugged his mother and dad, then stepping back he stood for a moment looking at Annie and me. Grabbing both of us, the three of us hugged as if we'd never let go. Annie cried as she kissed him over and over.

"Freddy, you've grown. You're bigger," Annie said, still grasping him about the waist. "You're not taller, but you're more muscular."

"Army cooking, sis. Those great C rations," he said and chuckled. Freddy stepped to one side and put his arm around Jeanette. "Everyone, this is my beautiful wife and son," then jokingly got their names mixed up, making Andre grin broadly. Jeanette smiled and playfully slapped Freddy's shoulder. You could tell they were already a close knit family. I am so glad to meet all of you at last," Jeanette said, with a warm smile. "Freddy has spoke so much about all of you. This is very exciting to Andre also. Is that not right, Andre?" she asked, turning toward her son.

Andre stood holding her hand as he nodded his head. "Yes, Mama." Helen knelt and hugged Andre to her. John followed suit. "We are so glad to have you for our grandson, Andre. You are going to like Montana," Helen spoke as she held the boy a short distance from her and looked him in the face.

"You ride bicycles, Andre?" John asked. "We have several at the ranch. Maybe you can go riding with your mother and dad. Maybe you and I will go riding. Would you like that?"

"Can I ride a horse? Papa said you have real horses." Andre said, smiling hopefully.

"You sure can. If you'll come visit us often, Granddad will buy you a horse of your own. How would you like that?" John asked.

"I would like a horse of my very own. Wouldn't I, Mama?"

"That would be very wonderful, Andre."

Then Annie and my parents were introduced and Jeanette hugged Annie as if they had known each other all their lives. Never had I ever heard so much excited talking.

After all the greetings were over, we drove back to John and Helen's. I couldn't wait to get old Freddy over to the side and find out how everything was in our old outfit.

Annie and I talked all the way home about how good it was to have the old gang back together again. The next few days were a whirlwind of visits. Uncle Freddy and Aunt Jeanette were a real hit with Ann. Andre played with her on the floor like a big brother, and seemed to really enjoy every minute. These two would be the best of friends as they grew up.

Hunting season was in full swing so Freddy and I decided it was time for Andre to learn a little about the ways of our people. Putting the camp tent and other equipment into the back of the pickup, we were ready. Andre was excited, but Jeanette was a little nervous about her little boy becoming one of the guys. However, Annie and Helen calmed her anxiety with the reassurance that we knew what we were doing.

The three of us headed a few miles east, going up into the Hungry Horse area, where you could usually depend on seeing a few bear. We pitched our tent at the end of an old logging road. After making sure everything was ready for the evening, we decided to take a short hike and do some hunting. Freddy handed Andre the little 410 shotgun, and he and I shouldered our rifles.

Less than two hundred yards from camp a grouse sat in the trail. With excitement, Freddy gave the boy instructions on how to shoot the bird. "Hold the gun tight against your shoulder, son," he instructed Andre. "Now look down the barrel and put the front sight in the middle of the bird. Don't worry about missing, this is why they make shotguns. There are lots of small round lead shot that will come from the barrel."

Before Freddy could finish his instructions there was a loud report as the old single shot fired and the feathers flew.

"I got him, Papa! I got him!" Andre shouted. "I did well?"

"You sure did, Andre. You got dinner for us. I'm very proud of you, son." Freddy said, rumpling the boy's hair, and smiling with pride. "Uncle Cole will show you how to clean the bird, won't you Uncle?"

"Yeah, Uncle Cole will teach you," I said and gave Freddy a look. Darned if he hadn't conned me again, like he had to many times down through our lives. I set about cleaning the bird with my nephew watching every move. Hell, I was enjoying this.

Andre had taken his first grouse and would get three more before our hike was over. That evening after supper of fried grouse with bread and butter, we sat around the campfire, and the boy listened to Freddy and I as we told him about some of the hunts we had done as boys. Of course we embellished a bit, but to Andre, it made the tales very exciting as he listened to the bull session.

"Tomorrow morning we'll kill a big buck to take home and show your mother," Freddy told Andre. "But we had better get some sleep if we're going to get up early.
What do you think?"

"Will I shoot a deer tomorrow, also?" the boy asked.

"No, son. Your shotgun isn't big enough for that, and you're too young to shoot our big rifles. Your day will come, be patient," Freddy said as he looked at the boy tenderly, sounding just like grandfather used to.

The next morning we were up early, and by daylight we had hiked a couple miles up the trail from camp. At the edge of an open area, Andre got real excited when his dad showed him a nice buck. It seemed strange to think of Freddy being a father, but fatherhood seemed to come to him as natural as swimming to duck.

"You see him? Right next to that big tree?" Freddy pointed from our concealed position. "We'll wait for him to turn a little bit more. We don't want to ruin any meat by taking him through a shoulder. He's going to make fine eating."

I watched as the two of them talked about stalking game and was so amazed at how Andre took to it. He would one day be a good hunter. I could tell by the grasp he had on everything Freddy and I showed him. He already had caught the biggest fish a few days earlier and hadn't hesitated to let everyone know. Freddy would look at me and wink as the fish kept getting a little longer with each telling. He was one of us all right.

Finally the buck turned sideways, and with a smooth motion, Freddy brought the rifle up and fired a perfect shot. The kill was clean. Slowly we picked our way across the opening and up to where the deer lay. Both Freddy and I noticed the boy hanging back.

"Are you okay, son?" I asked.

"Mother says we shouldn't kill," he answered.

Freddy and I exchanged looks, and Freddy looked like he was at a loss for words.

"Son," I said, "It's wrong to kill without a good reason. To pick a flower is wrong if it is only to kill it, or to step on a little ant or harm anything. If we were to kill an animal and walk away, that would be wrong. The deer we took this morning has a purpose. To hunt it like we did, then take it home to eat, that is what God meant for us to do. That's part of the reason he put the game here, to feed his people. If we know in our hearts that we have not done wrong in God's eyes, then we have not done wrong, and no one has any right to judge us. God would sit at our table, and enjoy our meat with us. Do you understand?" I asked.

The boy seemed to brighten after that and even wanted to help dress the deer out, asking what different parts were. We explained to the best of our knowledge what each organ did.

"I want to clean my deer someday when I get bigger. I know how to do this now," he exclaimed with pride.

We dragged the deer down the mountain, finally reaching camp about noon.

"Andre, you gather the wood, and build a fire," Freddy said.

"I will build a large fire," the boy said with glee in his voice. "I am a mountain man now, isn't that right?"

"That's right. You are a true hunter now," I said.

"I'm very proud of you, son," Freddy looked lovingly down at the boy.

"How do hot dogs and marshmallows sound to everyone for supper tonight?" I asked.

"I want to put one on a stick like you showed me. Can I Papa? I can cook it on my fire."

"Well, you'd best get that fire going if we're going to roast hot dogs," Freddy said and rumpled his hair.

Freddy and I walked down to the creek with soap and towels to wash our hands. I turned to make sure the boy was out of hearing range.

"How's LeeAnn? I feel funny asking, but you know me," I waited for Freddy to speak, feeling awkward.

"She's selling the restaurant, Cole. She has a job in France, teaching school, a college, I think. You'd have to ask Jeanette. I know it's difficult for you to ask about her, but come on Buddy, it's me. If you can't trust me, then who?"

"Thanks, Pal. I just wanted to know ...."

"I know, don't ever worry about how I might take it. You know me better than that. You're my brother, Cole."

"Thanks, Freddy." I put my arms around him, and held him tight for a moment, then patted him on the back before releasing him. "I love you, brother."

"I love you too." He said, and gave me a big squeeze.

After a lunch of hot dogs and burnt marshmallows, we set about breaking camp, and loading the gear, and buck into the pickup.

"Who's driving?" I asked, looking first at Freddy then Andre.

"Not me, I'm tired." Freddy said. "What about you, Andre."

"I do not know how to drive," the boy said, looking panicked.

Freddy and I chuckled. The boy caught on that I was joking and laughed also. He was learning fast, and tumbled to almost everything Freddy and I tried to pull on him. One day he would be as full of bull as we were, and that was saying a lot.

Arriving home that evening, Freddy and I were tired, and all we wanted after hanging the buck in the shed was a hot bath, and a cold beer. Freddy and I managed to get off alone and had a beer in town. The two grandpas were busy showing Andre how to be a rancher.

As we sat in our old haunt drinking a beer, I asked Freddy how things were in An Khe.

"It's getting tougher than shit all the time. After you left, half of our bunch bought it. We're going to lose this war sure as hell. It seems like they don't give a shit what happens to the men, as long as we use all the equipment, and they have to build more. Just like we were told, remember?"

"Yeah, I remember," I whispered, staring at my drink. We got mildly drunk.

Thanksgiving Day dawned cold and cloudy. We hadn't had snow yet but the feel of it was in the air. Andre was disappointed, and asked almost everyday if it was going to snow. Thanksgiving dinner was going to be at the Gray's place, and Annie had stayed up late into the night making pies. Early that morning we went over to the Grays so Annie could finish helping her mother get things ready.

The table was so laden with food, I think we could have fed half of Kalispell. Helen had baked a couple of the grouse Andre had shot. Mom brought the turkey and dressing along with fresh rolls.

This was the first Thanksgiving for Andre and Jeanette so Annie told Andre the story of the first Thanksgiving with the pilgrims and Indians. We grew silent, finding ourselves captivated by her storytelling ability. Afterwards we sat down to our meal. As we sat around the table, Andre once more told everyone about our camp-out, and related the story of the hunt. It kept growing as he polished his tale. Andre was so proud that he had supplied the grouse for our table that he insisted his mother taste the bird. Occasionally one of us guys would ask Andre how a particular part of the hunt went, then sit back, and listen to the tales all over again. The women smiled, and shook their heads with amazement at the boy's enthusiasm.

As usual we guys overate and while the women folk cleared the table and did the dishes, each of us found an easy chair in the living room and went to sleep. Later that evening we played games just like old times. What a feeling of peace to have all of us together again.

The days flew by and all too soon it was time for Freddy to report to Fort Rucker. As the day rolled around for them to catch their flight out, you could tell how Jeanette had accepted the family. There was a closeness that had grown with each passing day until Jeanette felt we were her family, and we were. Annie had immediately fallen in love with both her and Andre.

Pop had made Andre a slingshot out of a fork in a tree limb and some good rubber. Between John and Pop, they had taught the boy to shoot it. It was just like the hands of time had been turned back to our childhood. The boy thought the sun rose and set with these two men. When Andre wasn't with Freddy and me, he was with one of his grandpapas, as he called both of them. I could see that Jeanette was both impressed, and pleased with the way the boy had taken to his new family. Aunt Annie glowed with her new title, and I have to admit Uncle Cole wasn't half-bad. Damn we were going to miss them.

Chapter 31

The rest of that winter was spent getting the farm equipment ready for spring planting. The Bensons had thrown in the tractor and implements with the ranch, thanks to John's ability to bargain. In the spring I planned on sowing a couple of new fields of pasture grasses and a big alfalfa field.

The months flew by and before I knew it, it was time to start working my fields. I was like a little kid. It wasn't like I hadn't done this many times in my youth. But the feeling of doing it for myself was exhilarating.

Annie would come out to the fields, holding little Ann in her arms, and watch me proudly as I worked the ground.

Little Ann started trying to walk that spring. We were so proud of her. Every day or two, we'd go down to Annie's folk's place, then on to mine to show them how Ann was progressing. Ann would smile broadly at everyone as she tried to go from the coffee table to the couch. Then one day she made it on her own. The way everyone made over her, it was like she had danced a ballet. Ann caught our merriment and began laughing. That really did it for all of us, the frosting on the cake, so to speak. Within a month she was walking all over, and Annie really had her hands full. Pots and pans were all over the kitchen floor, and everything that wasn't put out of her reach was soon pulled down for closer inspection.

In July, we went to the cabin and stayed for a week. One evening we were out on the lake paddling the canoe when Annie suddenly held up her hand for me to stop the canoe. She was sitting in the front of the craft, wearing Grandfather's old fishing hat. He would have got a kick out of how cute she looked in the floppy old thing.

"Here's where the big one is," she announced with excitement, continuing to hold her hand in the air.

"How do you know?"

"Because I do. That's how," she said, giving me a matter of fact look.

"For your information, mister smarty, I've been reading your fishing and hunting magazines. I know a lot about catching fish, thank you very much!"

I laughed at her, mainly because of her way of telling me off. Now we were in the canoe and the world of reality was fixing to set in. She picked up her pole and started to cast.

"You're doing it all wrong," I said, "watch." Then grabbing my pole, I cast my line, maybe not the best cast I'd ever made. But she was a girl; she would never notice.

"You mean like this?" Annie said and laid a perfect cast near the half sunk log.

"Yeah, kind of," I said and grinned. "Lucky cast."

Annie's line had no more than hit the surface than a boil in the water indicated a strike.

She squealed, her pole bending double. "Cole, I caught it! It's a big fish." She wasn't the only one excited. I almost dumped us in the process of coaching her. "Don't horse it," I called out as I grabbed for her pole.

"My fish, Morgan," she said as she put her hand out to stop me. In the excitement, I had forgotten the rules. As she played the fish in close to the boat, I netted it for her. I have to admit, it was the biggest fish I'd ever seen in Whisper Lake.

That evening Annie talked on and on about how she had read everything she could find on how to fish. "Tomorrow I'll teach you how to fish," she said, flashing me that beautiful smile.

"You couldn't have caught that fish without Grandfather's help," I said jokingly, pointing at her hat.

"Thank you, Grandfather," Annie said, turning to the water. A raven called from the other end of the lake. "Cole?"

"I don't know, Annie. I was joking," I said without taking my eyes from the direction of the call. We didn't hear anything more from the lake except the frogs until after supper.

Annie fed Ann, changed her and put her down for the evening in the little bed which had been mine long ago and my dad's before me. We moved our little one just inside the screened door and sat on the porch in the double rocker Grandfather had built for my grandmother so long ago.

As we sat rocking slowly and enjoying a cup of coffee, the evening serenade started with coyotes on the side of the mountain. Within moments the loons started their evening songs, perhaps prompted by the howling. The frogs joined in, and we had a full symphony. Annie snuggled up to me, laying her head on my shoulder. She patted my knee lightly. "I love you, Morgan."

"And I love you, fisherman."

She patted me again, not saying anything more as she rocked us contentedly, listening to the night sounds. Finally she broke the silence. "We have to go home tomorrow, don't we?"

"Yeah, you know we do."

"I was just hoping we could stay another day or two. You still going to Spokane?"

"I have to. I have to have that pump back as soon as possible. The fields will be getting dry. I've put too much work into the land to see it dry up and die."

I had sent my water pump into Spokane for repairs, and now I had to get it back. Shipping was going to take too long with the weekend almost upon us. They said they'd have it finished by Friday; that was tomorrow. I figured I could save a couple days by getting it myself.

"I want to go with you. Ann wants to shop," Annie said, giggling.

"Um hum, just Ann? I suppose you're going with her to make sure she doesn't buy anything too sexy for a girl her age. Right?"

"Right."

We left the cabin early the next morning, and stopped off at the ranch for a quick bath before leaving for Spokane. Little Ann rode between us with her doll grasped tightly as she bit on its hand. Annie and I grinned at her constant chewing.

"She's cutting teeth. If we had that puppy you've been talking about, she'd have his ears chewed off," Annie said and laughed. Ann seemed to know we were talking about her. Looking up at us, she laughed.

Arriving in Spokane, I dropped Annie and the baby off at a department store, then went to the repair shop and picked up my irrigation pump.

Returning to the store, I searched and finally found the two of them busy trying on girl things. Me, I'd just go in and pick out a pair of jeans, pay for them and walk out, but I don't think Annie ever bought anything without going over it with a fine-toothed comb.

"I hate to rush you girls, but we've got a long ways to go."

"Lunch first, okay?" Annie asked.

Ann was getting to the age where she enjoyed some of the foods that we ate, although I think she preferred to wear most of her food in her hair.

After lunch we stopped for gas. By three o'clock we were finally on our way back home. Little Ann fell asleep with her head on her mother's lap, her stomach filled with all the things Annie didn't approve of me feeding her. But what the heck, wait until I started taking her to ball games, then she could complain.

Annie and I had lapsed into daydreaming as we rode along, the radio playing softly, she sang along with all her favorite songs, reaching over every so often to tickle my ear. The sun was setting behind us as we headed east toward the Montana border. Where the truck came from I don't know. The only thing I remember was a light, possibly from a headlight. Then the horrible sound of metal crushing as it ground into the passenger's side of our pickup. An eternity of grinding, then silence. Deafening silence. We had been shoved across the highway, and into the ditch.

"Annie! Annie! Annie, are you all right? Please, Annie!" I cried out in panic.

I heard her moving, and reaching for our baby. I panicked, and began looking desperately for our little daughter.

"Please, God! Please!" I cried out, panic-stricken. "Oh, please God!" Blood began running in my eyes and I couldn't see. I wiped at them desperately, trying to clear my eyes enough to see while frantically feeling around for Ann with my other hand. I felt something familiar. Gripping the little bundle, I pulled our baby from under the dash. I knew as soon as I touched Ann that she was dead. The normally joyous baby lay still. With a cry, I clutched the little form to my chest, and holding her little body against me, turned to Annie.

She lay in a twisted position, but conscious. "Cole? You have Ann. Is she all right? Cole, my baby. Let me have my baby, Cole. Please let me have my baby," she pleaded, blood coming from her stomach, just below where her right ribs were. I could see she was hurt badly.

I placed little Ann in her arms; not knowing whether she would know Ann was dead. Tears ran from my eyes, helping to clear the blood.

Annie clutched our child to her breast.

Dear God, why? Why? I listened to Annie soothing our baby as I eased my arm under her head, wanting desperately to hold her.

Annie closed her eyes and gasped in pain.

"Annie!" I yelled. "Annie!"

She turned her head ever so slightly, looking up at me. Her eyes clouded with pain.

"Cole? I'm cold." she whispered. "Hold us, please hold us. Don't turn loose."

"Hang on Annie, everything will be all right,"

Cole, our baby, she's gone. My baby is gone," she sobbed, looking up at me.

A cough racked her body as blood flowed from her wound. I could feel her body slowly relaxing, and knew she was leaving me.

"I love you so much Annie, you can't leave me, please don't leave me," I pleaded, starting to cry.

"I love you," she murmured as her voice grew faint. "Take us to our cabin Cole, take us home."

I begged Annie not to leave me. I felt so helpless. I wanted her to hold me, and tell me it was going to be all right. I wanted to grow old with her. I wanted to watch our kids playing. I wanted my Annie.

Annie slipped away while I held her. She kept looking at me as I held them both tightly in my arms, but the life slowly left those beautiful eyes. My Annie and our baby were gone.

Chapter 32

I'm not sure what transpired over the next few days; I have no memory, only shadows. I guess I don't really care what happened; my life died with my family.

I was released from the hospital a week after the accident. Following my instructions, Annie and Ann Coleen had been cremated. Their ashes were kept for me at my folk's ranch.

Freddy and Jeanette came home for the memorial, but I wasn't able to talk much with Freddy. Every time I looked at him, I saw my grief mirrored in his eyes. After the services, I went immediately to the cabin, taking Annie and little Ann's ashes. I couldn't be with the others. Their grief was more than I could bear.

The cabin had never seemed this dark and empty before. Annie's memories were everywhere I turned. As I sat one night by the fire, I finally broke.

"Grandfather!" I screamed as I ran out the door, "Grandfather, where are you?" I fell to the earth, beating my fist against the rocky ground in torment and anger until the skin split from my knuckles and the earth ran red with blood.

"Where is the Great Spirit now, Grandfather? Why has he taken Annie and our baby from me?" I threw my head against the rocky ground and screamed in anger and anguish so loudly that the canyon echoed with my voice. I ground my face into the earth and welcomed the pain.

"My son," a soft voice drifted on the warm breeze that touched my face as I looked up. "My son," I heard the voice again, "there is no peace for you now, your spirit is torn. We have both drank from the same bitter cup, and only time can heal your pain. Your path is long, my son. Remember, love never dies." The leaves stirred as the breeze past on.

Time passed. I don't know how long, a week maybe. I don't remember much except day drifting into night and night into day. Finally, I went home to my parent's ranch where I spent the next few weeks sleeping in my old bedroom. I would go home to our ranch and work around the place. Fencing allowed me to keep to myself and I welcomed the hard labor. I couldn't bear to enter the house, choosing to sleep in my shop on a cot. I just couldn't bring myself to face the memories.

Mom and Pop meant well, but they didn't help. On the contrary, Mom's face was always sad. I know she missed Annie and Ann, and I suppose she was feeling sorry for me, but it only made my grief harder.

I avoided the Grays mostly. The only time I saw them was when Helen and John came to see me. They understood, and I loved them for their understanding.

One of the folks would come by to check on me every couple of days. The women would bring baked goods and hot meals. I didn't have much of an appetite, and they scolded me for not eating. They would pick up my laundry, and bring fresh clothing out to the shop.

At last I decided to pack the car and travel for awhile. After talking with the families, we decided that I should lease out the ranch. Pop said he'd take care of everything and John agreed to help. Mom and Helen packed up the house, and moved everything up to one of Pop's good sheds.

For the first few months I traveled around the northwest. I found that whiskey worked well, as long as I kept plenty handy. I soon tired of Washington, and headed down the coast, working in different sawmills. It didn't matter what I did as long as it kept a roof over my head and whiskey in my glass. I often rented a small room in town, staying out of people's way, and avoiding contact.

Once in awhile a woman would come on to me, and I would wake up sleeping next to her. I never let any of them get close. It never took me very long to pack, and move on. I only had a couple suitcases and a cardboard box to fill.

I dropped Mom and Dad a card once in awhile as the months turned into a year and then two.

I found myself in Newport, Oregon. I'd prowl the waterfront on my time off, attracted to the sea.

I bought a crab trap and spent time catching crabs off the docks around the bay, just for something to do. Oftentimes I'd turn them loose. Almost every evening I'd sit in a bar down on the waterfront, trying to drown myself in whiskey. The nights were the roughest. There was time to think. I'd see Annie sitting across the table from me or feel her arm in mine as we walked. Damn, I hated the night! The bars were always noisy and crowded. One night I decided to buy a bottle, and go down on the dock where I could be alone. As I stood looking out on the water, I saw Annie as I had so often in the three and a half years she and Ann had been gone. I knew it was just my imagination. But the loneliness was like a knife in my heart. As she faded away, I bowed my head, agony and torment had been my constant companions since that awful night, and in my wretchedness I fell to my knees, tears flooded my cheeks. "Annie," I whispered, "why did you have to leave me?"

"Cole, my son," I heard a sigh on the wind.

I looked up. "Grandfather?"

"My son, what are you doing?"

I looked at him for a long moment while his eyes held mine. "I am killing myself, Grandfather. Have you seen Annie and my baby?"

"Cole, life is not easy. There are many hurts as our time passes upon this earth. Some of them cut more deeply than others, you can not heal the hurt if you wallow in its misery."

"Grandfather, Annie and little Ann are dead."

"Cole, your heart can be healed. You must help it."

"I don't want to. I want to die, and be with my wife and child. Why Grandfather, did God choose to punish me?" I asked. " Was it because of the child in Cambodia?"

"My son, why do you do this to yourself? There are many things that we don't understand. I cannot answer for the God. You will have to seek your answers yourself."

I hung my head.

"Cole," he said sharply, " would Annie be happy to see you as you are now? Do you think she would be proud?"

"Grandfather, I loved them so much. They were my life." The tears welled up again.

"Remember, Cole, life cannot defeat you. It is only you that defeat yourself. Do not flounder in your sorrow, meet life head on." I felt a breeze blow through my hair, and then heard a faint whisper. "Go home and put your sorrow to rest, my son."

I covered my eyes with my hand, rubbing the tears away. "Grandfather, I have been lonely for so long. I've even thought how I would have been better off to never have known Annie than to have loved her and Ann Collen then lose them. But I know in my heart that is not true. I know now how fragile life and love are." I said as I opened my eyes. He was no longer there. Perhaps he never had been.

I returned to my small room and began packing my clothes. Early the next morning I headed for Montana and home.

As I pulled into the yard, Mom ran out to greet me. "Cole! You're home! You're home!" She cried out, running with arms opened wide, crying.

Pop was up at the barn and came down at a fast walk, removing his gloves as he came. "Glad to have you back home, son," Pop said, giving me a hug, then slapping me on the back. This time the tears flowed freely from his eyes.

We went into the house and I felt good for the first time since the accident. It had been a long time.

Over the next few months, I worked hard at everything I could lay my hands on. I spent time with the Grays, helping out around their ranch, but I never could get over the sorrowful feeling that overwhelmed me while I was there. Everywhere I looked there was a beautiful, yet painful memory. Pictures were everywhere. Some of a little blue-eyed girl, and others of a laughing, lovely woman, my woman. At times I was choked with grief and had to leave.

I began to have a shot of whiskey whenever I came home from their ranch. Mom and Pop noticed, but didn't say anything. They just watched me out of the corner of their eye. I'm sure they didn't realize my vision had been honed to a fine edge.

Finally, I settled down to just helping Pop with the ranching. When I ran out of things to do, I'd write like Annie had encouraged me to do so many times.

Then the Grays came over for a visit one day and broke the news to us.

"Helen and I are selling the ranch. We've decided to move to Portland, Oregon," John said. "Cattle aren't doing very well, and I'm getting too old to bust my butt on a losing proposition. Freddy isn't interested in coming back to the Flathead."

He turned to me. "Son, you come on over and take anything you can use. The barn and sheds are full of good tools, and equipment that a young fellow can make use of. You might want to pick up that sports coat before Freddy finds where Helen hid it," he said, chuckling for the first time in a long while. It was good to hear him laugh.

"We didn't know what to do with all the stuffed animals and things," Helen said. "I hope you don't mind. I gave them to the Salvation Army. I didn't think you'd want any of those things to worry about. Everything else is packed away in boxes. Oh, I saved Jaju." She reached over and patted my arm lovingly.

"Thank you," was all I could say.

Shortly after that, the Grays moved away. The old house was boarded up and the land used for pasture by a neighboring rancher who had bought them out.

Chapter 33

The months turned slowly to a year, then several. I've started to get a little gray in the temples. Every once in a while I receive a letter from LeeAnn; she never married. She sold her restaurant shortly after I left Vietnam, and moved to France. She says she still wants to see Montana someday. I answer her letters. My replies are short. There's not much to write about. But she writes that she looks forward to getting them.

Freddy didn't stick out his twenty years with the Army. After the war was over, he and his family moved back to Vietnam, and they had two more kids. We write back and forth. I'm happy for them. Andre is a fine young man. I received a letter the other day with pictures of the whole family. Freddy invited me to visit them. He's probably trying to get his sports coat back. I'm not sure how I'll feel about going back. Old wounds heal, but the scars are always with me.

Three years ago I moved to the cabin on Whisper Lake. Come December, it'll be two years since Pop died in a logging accident, and Mom moved to California to be near her sisters. She says she sees more of me now than she did when she was living up here. I fly down every few months and seem to stay longer because of the flight. When Mom lived here, I would visit her, but couldn't wait to get back to the cabin and solitude.

I still own the ranch but lease it out. I doubt I'll ever go back to ranching, the spark went out a long time ago.

Sitting here at my old writing table, I talk to my love as I have ever since she left. I know she hears me, even though she has been silent for so long.

"I used your fishing pole, Annie. You know you were right, it does catch bigger fish than mine. I know you don't mind my keeping it; after all, we're partners. I pretend I hear you laugh every time I catch a nice fish. Silly isn't it? I am so in love with you, Annie. Even though you are no longer with me, you will always be in my heart. My love, I'm the last of the Loon People, and I'm so lonely."

They say time has a way of healing all wounds, but I wonder, will time ever be able to heal the lonely emptiness I have felt these many years since Annie and our little Ann Coleen left?

"Annie, people are moving into our country, and it will only get worse with time. I don't want them to intrude on our cabin, and yet, I can't always be here to watch over it. People will come and some will write or carve their names on our walls like I've seen them do to public property. Little by little they will trash and destroy all that you loved. I can't and won't let that happen. I bought a gallon of kerosene in Kalispell, Annie. At first light I'll put our cabin and you and little Ann out of these people's grasp."

"Looking over at the other side of the lake, high up on the mountain's side I can see in the moonlight where a road is being built. I have thought of every possibility and there is no other way, Annie. I have given the lake and the land to the state for a game preserve. I notified the Forest Service that I will be burning early in the morning.

"I will never forget our time together. I have written our story, finishing the book that I promised you so long ago. Maybe it won't be the great American novel that we dreamed I would write, but it's about the way we were."

Fall is here, and the evenings are turning cold, there is snow on the high mountains in Glacier Park.

Putting on another pot of coffee, I stoke the fire in the old cook stove. Waiting for the coffee to perk, I stand at the counter, and mix the sourdough for biscuits the way Annie taught me. My eyes travel around the cabin, stopping every once in awhile to remember something special.

On a shelf in the corner is that ugly old stuffed animal she named Jaju. Annie kept him all her life. I saw her holding it when we first met so long ago, a little girl with big blue eyes and light brown hair, clutching her beloved Jaju. How many times has he reminded me of her? I walk over and take Jaju down.

"She loved you a lot, old boy. I think she'd like for you to join me for breakfast," I said, smiling." Hell, I'd like that too."

Jaju looks back at me in silence, with his button and one good eye.

After breakfast, I clear the table, doing up the dishes, replacing them in their proper places, then put my manuscript into my briefcase, snapping the locks shut.

The two wooden bowls that Annie bought in Spokane, rest on the table where they have been since I moved to the cabin. The larger holds my beloved Annie's ashes and the smaller, little Ann Coleen's. Soon now it will be time to bid them farewell for a while. I will take my precious Annie and Ann Coleen to where my grandparents are resting and scatter their ashes near the apple trees. Annie would like that.

Placing Jaju on the table beside Annie's wedding ring and the old hunting knife, which had been a part of our marriage ceremony, I sit down once more at the stove and stare at the little gathering of my most precious treasures.

Then at last rising from my seat, I take the wooden containers of Annie and my little Ann's ashes to the canoe and place them in the front of the craft. Pushing the canoe out into the lake, I slowly paddle toward the other end, which is visible in the moonlight.

As I pass our wedding rock, a warm feeling comes over me, and I hold my paddle from the water as the craft silently slips past. A few feet farther and the canoe's bow quietly grinds to a stop on the shore.

Stepping out and taking my precious cargo from of the canoe, I walk slowly up to my grandparent's graves. The blood of my ancestors once more courses through my veins as I stand for a moment.

"Grandfather, I bring Annie and our little one to rest with you and Grandmother. I know you will watch over them now and forever and I thank you. If I could join them, I would gladly do so, but as you would say, my time has not yet come. I only hope that when it does, I will be laid to rest here also. But regardless, my spirit will return."

Turning, I sprinkle Annie and little Ann's ashes together as I know they would want me to.

"Grandfather, I am going to put our cabin into your world. If this is wrong, please forgive me. I can't bear to see it abused with the coming of civilization. I have seen what some people do. I can no longer stay here all the time to protect it. I have finished our book, and it is time to see what is left for me. Here, there is only heartache which is a slow, painful death. Out there, perhaps I can find a purpose for my life."

Turning to where my loved ones ashes are, I say my last good-bye. "I love you Annie, and my little Ann. You will be with me forever."

I turn and with a heavy heart, walk back to the canoe. Pushing off, I drifted slowly backward in the direction of the cabin. As the canoe silently passes our wedding rock, I remember my vows, and whisper them again. "Forever Annie, and that's a long time." Then picking up my paddle, I return to the other side of the lake.

As the canoe quietly comes to rest on the shore, I sit and look at the old place trying for one last memory to take with me, but none come. The cabin is still, waiting. Going back inside, I pour another cup of coffee, then walk outside and sit my cup down on a large rock in Annie's garden. I pick up the gallon of kerosene and pour it around the outer walls. Standing in the doorway one last time to make sure the interior is clean and everything is in its place for eternity, I check to make sure I have left Annie's and little Ann's fresh flowers on the table. Then going back outside, I strike the match.

Flames quickly encircle the outer walls of the old dwelling as I walk down to the lake's edge. Sitting down at the picnic table we'd used for so many years, I watch the flames grow in the dawn, and listen to the crackling of the old logs as the hungry fire consumes all that is precious to me.

It's strange how imagination, and the need to see loved ones again, play tricks on the mind. As I stare into the flames leaping and racing for the heavens, twice I could have sworn I saw Annie holding our little one, giving me that special smile I had seen so often when we were young.

Hours pass, or is it a lifetime? Finally all that is left of the cabin is burning embers. As the sun breaks over the mountaintop, spreading its cloak of warmth over the little valley, I know our time is over. As with my grandfather's people, the People of the Loon are now gone forever. Who is left to remember or care that we were once here?

I shoulder my pack and slowly start down the trail. At the far end of the lake I hear floating on the morning's mist, the lonely call of a Loon.

THE END

ABOUT THE AUTHOR

L FRANK HADLEY RESIDES IN WHITEFISH, MONTANA. HE HAS WRITTEN SHORT STORIES AND NEWSPAPER COLUMNS.

'SONG OF THE LOON'
IS HIS FIRST FULL LENGTH NOVEL.